GLASS CLOUDS

Suzanne Cass

S C

STORM CLOUD
PRESS

Glass Clouds

Storm Cloud Press, Perth Australia

Copyright © 2018 by Suzanne Cass

Cover by Germancreative

All rights reserved.

ISBN: 978-0648266822

In memory of my brother, Doug.

CHAPTER ONE

Plate held in one hand, Charlize gripped the iron railing with the other and took each stone step with careful deliberation. When both feet landed on the gravel pathway, she let out an unconscious sigh of relief. The smell of lavender filled her nostrils as she brushed past rows of bushes, limping toward the wrought-iron table and chairs set beneath a gnarled olive tree. She pulled out a chair, sat down in the dappled shade, and placed her food on the table.

Lifting her fork, she let it hover over the plate. What to eat first? All of the ingredients were bought at the local market this morning. There was fresh asparagus with a lightly poached egg and homemade hollandaise sauce, two slices of *jambon cru*, or prosciutto, half a baguette, some green olives marinated in garlic, and slices of melon. The heat of the day had finally left the garden and a light breeze wafted through the leaves of the fig tree stretched over her high stone wall.

A bumblebee buzzed, gathering the last bits of precious pollen before heading back to the hive for the night.

Summer in Provence was much like the baked heat of her hometown in Western Australia. But in Provence there was a softness, a greenness, even in the height of summer that was at odds with the desperate parching dryness that surrounded Perth.

Charlize popped a piece of melon wrapped in prosciutto into her mouth. The resident brown mouse poked her nose out of a hole in the wall, its whiskers twitched once, bright eyes searching for any fallen crumbs. Charlize broke off a tiny piece of baguette and dropped it on the ground. The mouse would come and get it the moment her attention was elsewhere.

Charlize leaned back in her chair and savoured the taste of her meal. In her small enclosed garden, ivy climbed the crumbling stones to her right, hiding the places where the mortar fell away. A row of pencil pines stood tall and straight to her left, protecting the side wall. Cicadas hummed and songbirds sang their goodnight to the setting sun. It was the closest thing to a refuge she'd found. Perhaps even a place where her healing could start.

The rusty corrugations of the iron table were cool beneath her fingertips. It was so calm here, but would she ever again be the woman she used to be? Could people see it in her face? The changes? Mottled shadows danced over her plate, her fork stalled half-way to her mouth. The damaged, missing parts inside of her might never return. She let her fork continue its journey.

Loud, raised voices broke her ruminations. Charlize went back to enjoying her meal and tried to ignore them. People often used the intersecting alleyways that ran behind her back wall as a shortcut through to the car park on the outskirts of town, or to the shopping mall in the next street. Tourists mainly, speaking English or German in their brash, penetrating tones. Charlize cut into the perfect globe of the poached egg and the bright yellow yolk ran freely over the green fronds. She took a mouthful, appreciating the crunch of the asparagus against the creaminess of the egg.

'Mmm.' Pure bliss.

The voices got louder, almost shouting now. Then pounding feet echoed down the alleyway. She cocked her head to the side.

Someone was running.

Nope, it was none of her business. She needed to quell that cop-instinct, which had her wanting to get up and poke her head over the wall to see what was going on. She'd relinquished her job on the force. Left it behind eighteen months ago back in Australia. For better or worse, she was a civilian now. And she needed to learn how to live like one.

Charlize picked up an olive and placed it in her mouth, carefully working her teeth around the pip, allowing the bitter saltiness to settle on her tongue, determined not to let the sound of the outside world break into her reverie.

But she couldn't ignore the scrabble of feet just outside her garden, followed by a loud grunt. The bulky shape of a man wriggled over the top of her wall and dropped to the ground not three feet away from her.

For a second, Charlize froze. Her mind whirled, as useless as a spinning top. Then half-remembered training kicked in, muscles moved and tightened of their own accord and she stood, balancing on the balls of her feet, unconsciously compensating for her crippled leg, facing the man. Ready to fight.

'What the—' The man raised a finger to his lips in a silent entreaty to be quiet. She stepped backwards, away from the stranger and his fierce hazel eyes. Hell no, she had a good set of lungs when she needed to use them. Opening her mouth, she got ready to scream.

'Please,' he whispered. 'Don't.'

The cry caught in the back of her throat.

She should scream. Now. The other voices were getting closer, almost level with her back wall. Help would come if she wanted it. But something stilled her vocal cords. Was it the appeal in his eyes? Or the way he hunched over to the left, making him seem somehow less of a threat?

'Please,' he entreated again, mouthing the words. 'I'll leave as soon as those men go.' He pointed a finger toward the wall. His English was perfect, but with the familiar French accent. A local? If he was, she hadn't spotted him in any of her daily treks around the small town. Just below his ribs on the left, a dark blotch stained his light blue t-shirt. Blood. It was definitely blood.

Charlize hesitated, fists raised, adrenaline fizzing through her veins. The man took a step away from her, palms out in a gesture of submission.

She drew in deep ragged breaths through her nose to calm her racing pulse. He was taller than her, which made him perhaps a couple of inches over six feet. Skin the colour of espresso coffee, dark, but not the deep ebony black of the African men she'd seen in the markets today. Close-cropped hair covered his head, a manicured dark goatee beard sheathed his chin. Broad shoulders stretched the t-shirt material across impressive pecs. A different kind of shiver twisted through her belly. Bloody hell. He was gorgeous. *Concentrate, Charli.* She blinked once, twice, not allowing her fists to lower.

Giving a sharp nod of acquiescence, she let him know she wouldn't call out. But she didn't let go of her guard either, muscles tensed and tight as a drum, heart as jittery as a bat. His features relaxed visibly at her nod, and he dropped his hands down by his sides. Then one hand came back up to press against the wound, a grimace flittering across his face. Silence slid between them as they studied each other like wary cats. A slither of sweat ran down between her shoulder blades. What was she doing? Why would she allow a stranger—a wounded stranger— to stand in her garden, while men were hunting him outside? The whole scenario was surreal. The tremble in her gut increased, quickly moving down her legs. She braced her thighs together to stop the shaking. Never let an offender see your fear.

Hazel eyes gave her a hurried once over. She hadn't bothered to put on a bra. Why should she, when she was supposed to be cocooned in her little Provencal garden? Her thin white t-shirt would hide nothing, and she had to resist the urge to cross her arms over her chest. His gaze slid quickly down her long legs, bare in short cut-offs, to the scars skulking over her left knee and down her shin. She ignored the impulse to move her leg out of his line of sight.

Voices sounded over the top of the high back wall, and she flinched. It was two men, both speaking French in quick static sentences. Her French had improved in the past six months, but not enough for her to understand everything they said. One man ordered the other to do something like to *look around the corner*. The man's voice was cold, shrewd and something about his icy tone made

Charlize want to shrink back from the venom in it. The tall visitor half-crouched and turned toward the wall as if expecting them to come over the top, his right hand reached around behind him.

That's when she saw it. Tucked into the waistband of his jeans. It was a Sig Sauer with some kind of tactical attachment. She'd seen this type of gun before. This changed everything.

She took a careful step backwards. She needed to get away from this dangerous man. He hadn't turned around yet, still focused on the voices on the other side of the wall. One man mentioned something about searching gardens, and Charlize was frightened they might try to scale her stone wall. Wary of the wounded stranger, she was perhaps more afraid of the men outside.

As she took another step backward, a sudden pain shot through her left knee. She had to stifle a cry as she half-stumbled, grabbing hold of a low branch on the olive tree just in time to save herself from falling. Bloody leg. Letting her down. Again. The man spun around and raked her with a calculated gaze.

She stared back at him, hoping like hell he didn't see the terrible weakness that trembled in her. Give no quarter, pretend she was strong, so he'd just go away and leave her alone. This man who stood bleeding in her courtyard with a gun in the back of his jeans. The men's voices faded into the background as they went around the corner toward the car park. Handsome Stranger glanced toward the wall.

'*Merci, Mademoiselle*,' he said, voice silken with French intonation. '*Au revoir*.' With that, he scaled her back wall, strong fingers finding the cracks in the mortar, and was over the top and gone. Leaving her open-mouthed and staring.

She had a sudden need to sit down. The after-effect of the adrenaline—which had kept her standing, defying him —now left her shaken and numb.

Then the tears started to fall.

* * *

Pain screamed through his side as he landed—a little more heavily than he'd intended—on the paved pathway of the alley. Jean-Luc Munulo crouched down and did his best to ignore the agony while he surveyed the crisscrossing alleyways for movement. Nothing. It was quiet, the cicadas already resuming their loud hum after their momentary lapse.

Merde. He should never have let them get that close. Stupid. It was time to get a move on. He stood up straight and took the left-hand pathway—the one that went in the opposite direction to the car park. He needed to get away from here. The quicker he disappeared, the better.

Why that woman hadn't given him away was a mystery, but she could change her mind at any second and scream her bloody lungs out. It wouldn't take long for Vincent's thugs to hear her if she did, and return, guns blazing.

Long strides soon had him around the corner of the alley and into a short pedestrian tunnel leading to the main street. Once there, he could blend in with the crowds of tourists who strolled through the myriad shops and cafes. They'd never catch him then, and even if they did, they wouldn't dare shoot with so many people about. Would they? *Merde*. He bloody well hoped not.

As he neared the end of the tunnel, he put a hand over the stain on his t-shirt, to try and cover as much of the bloody evidence as possible. At the same time, he defied the urge to put pressure on the wound to ease the pain. It wouldn't do to have some tourist—or worse, one of the gendarme wandering the streets—to notice he was bleeding. It was a stupid rookie mistake to let one of those thugs close enough to get a look at him, but even more stupid to get shot. At least it wasn't bad, the bullet had just grazed his side as he'd dodged and weaved away from the two gunmen. But it'd still need stitches. Where in hell he was going to find someone to do that was a question he'd answer later.

As he entered the street, Jean-Luc slowed his pace to match the rest of the crowd. No one took a second look at him. Nothing seemed out of place. The street was full of sleepy tourists who wandered down the sidewalks, eating gelato, stopping to admire a row of pretty postcards or a glass-front shop full of silver jewellery. A few locals dodged in between the tourists, some with bags of food bought at the market, intent on their errands. No one was running. No one was shouting. There were no men dressed in dark clothing skulking in shop doorways. It was all perfectly normal.

A little way down the street was a store that sold all kinds of handbags, along with other brightly coloured souvenirs. Jean-Luc ducked in behind a large man in a t-shirt emblazoned with the American flag, who was bent over a basket filled with bags of lavender and managed to grab a leather satchel from the stand next to him. With the satchel swung over his shoulder, he positioned it to hide the stain on his t-shirt and kept walking.

Now all he needed was to get to his motorbike, and he was out of there.

His mind flickered back to the woman in the garden,

and for the second time that day, he wondered why she hadn't screamed. He could tell she wanted to. She was definitely afraid. But there'd been something else as well. A courage. A determination to stand her ground. He knew he could've taken her down if he'd needed to, but the way she held herself, fists up, weight forward, balanced on her toes, told him she knew something about self-defence. She wouldn't have gone down without a fight. Even with those terrible scars running down her leg, she'd stood up against him. Defiant. Nearly as tall as him, with short blonde hair curling around her face. And those intense green eyes, taking his measure in mere seconds, had him intrigued. Light green, the colour of the water on a duck pond ruffled by a small breeze. Like nothing he'd encountered before.

And she wasn't wearing a bra beneath that little white t-shirt. When he'd caught sight of those pert breasts, nipples peeking through the fabric, he'd almost forgotten where he was, and who was chasing him.

Pah. He shook his head to rid it of the images of clear green eyes and long, lithe legs and focused on the cobbled street beneath his feet. Away from this little town and Vincent's gun-happy hoodlums, that's where he needed to be.

SIMPLE FARE

INGREDIENTS
Fresh asparagus
2 Free range eggs
1 tbsp White vinegar
Thinly sliced prosciutto
Thinly sliced rockmelon
Your favourite marinated olives
Fresh baguette
French butter

Hollandaise Sauce
2 Free range egg yolks
2 tbsp Water
170g Melted butter
¼ tsp Salt
Freshly squeezed lemon juice to taste

DIRECTIONS
Make hollandaise sauce. Keep warm while you prepare the rest.
To Make the Hollandaise Sauce:
In a pan over medium heat, whisk the egg yolks and water together
for two to three minutes until thick and fluffy. Do not boil, or it may
curdle. Remove from heat and whisk for an additional minute. Then
slowly whisk in the melted butter a little at a time. Add the salt and
lemon juice to taste.
Prepare the rest of your plate. Place rolled up slices of prosciutto
and slices of melon along with your chosen olives and the baguette,
which has been cut in half onto the plate. Add a generous dollop of
French butter.
Prepare two saucepans of boiling water. In the first, blanche the
asparagus for one minute until they go bright green. Drain and place
on your plate.
While the asparagus are cooking, turn the water down in the second
saucepan until it is lightly simmering. Add the vinegar. Break each
egg, one at a time, into a cup and then gently drop the eggs into the
water. Let them poach for a minute and a half to two minutes
depending on your taste and then drain and serve immediately.

Place eggs on top of the asparagus, then ladle the hollandaise sauce over them both.

Best enjoyed in the shade of a hundred-year-old olive tree in a walled Provencal garden in the south of France with a glass of chilled Rosé.

CHAPTER TWO

The afternoon was hot and redolent with the smell of jasmine. Perspiration ran between Charlize's breasts, dampening the front of her floral print dress. Straw hat pulled firmly down over her brow, she ducked into the shade of a spreading olive tree and stood for a minute, staring out over the expanse of bitumen carpark. She was nearly home, returning from a late afternoon stroll through the outskirts of town. The alleyway that ran behind her villa was off to the left, with the carpark spread out in front of her, a row of shops skirting the main street off to her right, their rear entries presented as a row of partly shadowed doorways blanketed in a layer of grime and rubbish. Everything was quiet in the heat of the afternoon, most people preferring to take cover indoors until the cool of the evening drew them out again. It seemed she was the only person silly enough to be out in the summer heat.

Her doctor had prescribed lots of walking to keep the muscles in her bad leg fit and strong. He'd also suggested many other remedies, such as a special oil, to rub over the scars every day, and exercises—very painful exercises—to keep the burn scars that swirled over her skin like melted ice-cream supple; to prevent her ankle from becoming tight and hampering her movement even more than it already did. She'd taken his advice to heart, and made sure she walked for at least an hour a day, come rain, hail or shine.

The walking was therapeutic in other ways as well. Spiritually, Charlize found release in being able to stride out in the sunshine, watching the world go by while she mulled over her day. Today, the stranger in her garden filled her thoughts. The questions that buzzed about in her head were nearly endless. She was still none-the-wiser as to what he was up to or why he'd chosen her garden two days ago. He'd just disappeared like a phantom, leaving her to wonder if those few frantic moments had actually been real and not just a figment of her imagination. But the footprints in the gravel proved it wasn't.

The thought of it still made her go weak at the knees. After a headlong flight into her house to lock the door, she'd spent the night in agitated wakefulness, getting out of bed often to prowl around the house, to double and triple check all the windows and doors were securely locked. Then she'd had to force herself to go back into the garden the next morning, to try and drive away the images of the sinister men who still lurked in the bushes in her subconscious. Logically, it was stupid. The man was a one-off occurrence, her garden was as safe as it'd ever been. Two years ago she would've shrugged the incident off as nothing to worry about. But now she couldn't stop the way her lungs squeezed tight as she descended the steps, slowly one at a time. Or the way her eyes darted of their own accord into all the shadowy corners of the garden, her palms slipping on the iron railing, slick with sweat. Damn the man to hell for ruining her peaceful haven. She would overcome this fear. She wouldn't let it become debilitating. Not like before.

She'd just started to re-discover herself after the crash, was finally able to crawl out from beneath the crushing weight of the shame and the sorrow and find her way back to life from the shadow of the person she'd become.

She drew in a large lungful of air and dug around in the calico bag slung over her shoulder to find a bottle of water. The liquid was lukewarm on her tongue as she took a couple of big swallows. Today was hotter than she'd expected and now she was tired, sweaty and needed to get home for a shower. Could she be bothered to go the extra distance across the carpark and into the little grocery shop at the end? The open expanse of concrete carpark was still emitting a smoky heat haze under the blazing heat of the sun. But her cup of tea just wouldn't be the same without that dash of milk.

Charlize gritted her teeth and stepped out of the shade. As she made her way between the parked cars, her thoughts returned unbidden to the tall man with the gun tucked into his jeans. Who was he? She'd worried at that thought as if it were a loose tooth. And was he alright? The wound in his side had most likely been a bullet hole. If he was carrying a gun, then the probability the other men also carried guns was extremely high. The bleeding hadn't looked too bad, but who was she to pass judgement on a bullet wound. He could be dead now, for all she knew. Should she try and find out who he was, perhaps make a few discreet enquiries with some of the locals? Pull in a few favours with the local gendarme? Nope. The last thing she needed was to get mixed up in anything even remotely outside the law. She needed to concentrate on herself right now. To get better. A tiny voice inside her head—one she'd become familiar with over the past two years—asked her who the hell she thought she was, anyway. She was no longer a cop; it told her, could no longer handle the stress of being a cop. Leave that stuff to people who were better equipped to deal with it.

An image of the stranger's face floated back to her memory. His eyes were a light hazel, almost the colour of beaten copper. An odd shade for a dark-skinned man. But the combination had been...nice. Better than nice. Amazing. She didn't think she'd ever met a ma—

Charlize stopped dead in her tracks. She'd heard something. No, it wasn't a noise, more like a...feeling or a...tugging, somewhere in the back of her brain. The pulling sensation was telling her to change direction, go toward the darkened corner of the shop at the opposite end of the street, instead of the small grocery shop which sold milk. Colours, like a bag of mixed emotions, swirled in her head, turning into a vortex of intense sensations, making her stomach contract with concern. Without a doubt, someone out there needed help. She got an impression of someone lost, alone, frightened.

Something indiscernible fluttered in her gut and she covered her face with her hands. It was happening again. She hadn't had an episode since the fiery wreck two years ago.

The crash. Images of the crash beat against the walls she'd built around the memory. Walls she'd spent months, years, erecting. Xeon. Her beautiful horse, Xeon. His screams filled her head. No. The word echoed inside her mind. No, she wasn't going there. Not today. Not any day. She redirected her thoughts back into the hot carpark and the pulling sensation that still buzzed around in her head.

Charlize had thought the accident may have cured her. Taken this strange ability and driven it from her body, along with all the rest of her self-esteem and courage. But now the gift was back.

Gratitude and dismay warred equally in her chest. Perhaps this was a sign the true Charlize was still in there somewhere, fighting to be remembered. But did she want her ability back? The ability to feel someone else in pain, to recognise unequivocally they needed help. A call to the compassionate side of her nature.

Her mother called it clairsentience, but Charlize didn't like to put a name to what she could do. She'd never wanted this gift, hadn't asked for it. In the early days she'd even ignored it completely, in the vain hope it'd go away. Both her mother and her grandmother had the gift. Charlize had never wanted to be seen to be…eccentric… kooky…weird, all the things her mother was accused of over the years. So she kept her talent well hidden, hardly anyone else knew about it.

Should she follow the undeniable tug in her head? What would she find if she did? Or more to the point, who would she find?

She let out a grumble of frustration and turned toward the darkened back of the corner shop, stepping around the car blocking her path. Why couldn't she just leave it alone? It'd just lead to trouble.

There was no sign of movement coming from the back of the shop. It had a low wall screening off two-thirds, forming a small courtyard shaded by a low-slung rickety lean-to. There were boxes stacked untidily in one corner and two large trash cans overflowing with rubbish. A large pile of what looked to be rags leant up against the wall, threatening to overflow into the carpark. The shop was possibly something to do with a seamstress or tailor by the looks of the empty boxes and the piles of rags.

Charlize stopped just outside the low wall and stared into the gloom. Nothing seemed out of place. She cocked her head on its side, listening. Nope. Aside from the far away cawing of the dratted crows who hunted through the rubbish bins for food, and the low hum of cars going in and out of the carpark, there were no sounds that might give away someone in distress. No whimpers or sobs. Nothing to indicate there was someone who needed help in there somewhere. But her senses were never wrong. And when that part of her brain she just couldn't ignore told her someone was in need of help, if she didn't act, the repercussions could be huge. She'd ignored it once—only once—and a baby had nearly died because of her lapse.

'Hello,' she called out quietly. How stupid must she look to be talking to an empty courtyard. 'Is anyone in there?'

Nothing. No answer. No sound at all. But the tug, like a fishhook caught in the flaps of her mind, was strong; convincing her someone was desperate and unhappy.

'Do you need some help? Don't be afraid, I won't hurt you.' Still nothing. But there was tension in the air. As if everything had become still, stopped to listen with her. No crows cawed, no cars hummed. The stifling air closed in around her and she had to swipe a hand across her brow to stop the perspiration that threatened to run into her eyes. That voice in her head was back again. She should just go. Leave. There was no one here, she was kidding herself. But the tug, tug, tug was impossible to ignore. She couldn't give up. Someone's life might depend on her being able to stick this out. She stepped into the murkiness of the lean-to, wondering what she might say if someone came out of the back door of the shop and asked her what the hell she thought she was doing.

'I'm here to help,' she said in a low voice. Ducking her head underneath the eave of the lean-to, she peered into the gloom. Did something just move? Over there, next to the pile of rags? Charlize caught the flash of dusky skin, and an oval face, dark eyes like black holes stared back at her from the depths of the shadow. A shadow within a shadow. A small child. She couldn't tell if it was a boy or a girl.

'Hi there,' she said in a soft voice, crouching down, her good knee against the hard ground to support her bad leg. 'My name's Charlize. I can help you if you're in trouble.' The little face flinched and drew further back into the gloom. It was a boy. Short, stubby curls stuck out at odd angles from his skull. And she could just make out a pair of legs poking out of ragged shorts, with bare feet tucked in underneath the pile of rags, the pink skin on the underside of his feet standing out against the blackness of his legs. It was as if he wanted to bury himself in the mountain of material. Something had scared him, and badly.

'It's very hot today, isn't it?' she said conversationally. 'Are you thirsty? Would you like a drink?' Holding up the bottle of water, she swished the contents around enticingly. His eyes blinked and one of his hands twitched, but he didn't come forward. If anything, he sunk back even deeper into the rags. She had to look away from his face. There was something in his eyes that scared her. A misery, a blank emptiness, as if his very soul was nothing but a dark, unoccupied void. It sent a shiver down her backbone, raising goosebumps on her arms, even in this scorching heat.

Rummaging around in her calico bag, she looked for food or anything else that might coax him out, but came up empty-handed. She blew out a sigh and tipped her head toward the sky. The emanations coming off the boy were some of the strongest she'd ever felt. Raw fear—hopefully it wasn't her making him so frightened—desperation and hunger. She could practically hear his stomach growl from here, as if he hadn't eaten in days. From what she could see of his clothes, they were practically rags themselves. Dirty, ripped, she couldn't even tell what colour his t-shirt might've been once upon a time. The boy was definitely of African descent, with that midnight black skin. A few African families worked at the Saturday markets, but they were all selling their wares and probably not locals, just moving from town to town with each new market day. So where did the boy belong?

Charlize tried a few more words of encouragement to get the boy to come out. But there wasn't even a flicker of recognition in those wary, black eyes. She knew better than to reach in and touch him. Never provoke a cornered animal—or human; you never know what they might do. Her police experience had taught her that much. And she could tell by his aura he wouldn't welcome her moving any closer.

What to do?

Much as she hated to admit defeat, this might be a job

for the local law enforcement. They'd know if the boy was lost, or missing, or if he had a family waiting for him somewhere. But what if he didn't have anyone waiting for him?

Reaching into her bag, she pulled out her phone. She didn't know what happened to kids who fell through the system here in France. But when she'd worked as a cop back in Australia, dealing with juvenile delinquents, foster kids gone wild, kids with no future, no backup, no family, no place to call home—she'd found out enough about how the system operated. And it often wasn't good. But what other choice was there?

* * *

The cool water sluiced over her shoulders and beat against her skull as Charlize stood under the shower, thinking. Two interminable, hot, sticky and frustrating hours. That's how long it'd taken to untangle herself from the clutch of people who'd gathered around the back of the shop and the poor, lost boy. She almost wished she'd never phoned the authorities, had just left the kid where she'd found him.

It hadn't taken long for the gendarmes to arrive in their dark blue sedan. The two uniformed men hadn't even bothered to go into the courtyard, instead peering over the wall to confirm there was indeed a tiny black child secreted away in the pile of rags. Then they'd made a few phone calls and stood around chatting and smoking. An unexpected resentment rose in Charlize's chest at their complete lack of empathy or interest in the child. But when she'd asked what was going to happen to him, one of them waved a dismissive arm and told her in passable English, 'Bloody refugees. OFII needs to come and get him.'

That had surprised her. It'd never even crossed her mind he might be a refugee. When she'd asked them how they knew he was a refugee, they just looked at her like she was completely mad. Then when she asked what OFII meant, one of them said, '*Office Francais de l'Immigration et de l'Integration*,' as if even a simpleton should know that.

Charlize decided to wait, to keep an eye on the boy. Not that she didn't trust the gendarmes, but their lack of compassion was galling, and a simmering anger fired up in her belly. In a strange, twisted way, the anger felt good. It awakened something within her, something that'd lain dormant for quite a while now. She was stunned at the depth of the emotion. She hadn't allowed herself to feel anger like this for such a long time, instead letting sadness and dishonour swallow all other emotions.

The little boy never moved or spoke, just stared at them with huge, vacant eyes. The fear and isolation still oozed off him, as strong as ever.

Two immigration people turned up forty-five minutes later, a plump lady and a tall, balding man. Charlize was gratified they both seemed more concerned than the gendarme and tried to lure the boy out with water and food and softly spoken words.

When he still wouldn't come out, the immigration people moved away to confer with the police officers, who stood in the shade of a large conifer, smoking. At that moment, as if he knew his freedom was about to be taken away, the boy took the chance and bolted, running straight out of the courtyard and dodging through the carpark. But he hadn't stood a chance. He was so little, being chased by four large adults.

Charlize turned off the taps and stepped out of the shower, grateful to be cool and clean once more. Leaning over to grab a towel from the railing, she caught sight of herself in the bathroom mirror and was shocked at how grey her face was, how large and full of misery her eyes looked. The little boy's plight had affected her more than she liked to admit. Goddamnit, she thought she left all this shit behind when she'd quit the force. When she left Australia. The last thing she needed was to be expending energy on kids with no home and no family. It was too depressing. And life-sucking. She needed to concentrate on getting herself better, not on other people's problems.

The immigration officers had bundled the boy into the back of their car. Then one of the gendarmes, the one with the baby face and a moustache, had told her how more and more refugees were being found in their little town. Most of them were coming across the border from Italy, where they'd landed illegally. Some slipped through unseen at night, others blatantly boarded trains bold as brass, while the Italian security turned a blind eye. But these ones turning up in Uzes, the gendarme thought perhaps they were coming from somewhere else. He even hinted there might be boats landing on the French coastline. Which Charlize doubted. Surely the French coastguard would never let that happen. The gendarme admitted it was unusual to see one so young on his own— he must only be six or seven—but they caught one or two people a week nowadays. And that was only the ones they knew about. Many, many more were slipping through the nets, to escape up to Paris, to be lost in the maze of the huge city and its millions of people.

'If I ever get my hands on one of those people

smugglers…' the gendarme said, while miming as if he were strangling someone.

'What will they do with the boy?' she asked.

'Put him in the detention centre in Nimes, or maybe Marseille, until his status for asylum can be documented. Then…' The gendarme gave an unconcerned shrug. 'Probably put him with his own people, he's most likely Sudanese by the look of him. Or in the accommodation centre for unaccompanied children.'

The hair on the back of her neck rose at his words. 'What does that mean?'

'It means exactly what I said. Lots of these kids are turning up, without parents, relatives or even siblings. They have to be put somewhere.' The gendarme gave another very French shrug between puffs of his cigarette.

'You mean to tell me there is a centre just filled with children, nothing more? Like a huge orphanage?'

'*Oui.*' He looked at her as if she'd gone slightly crazy, while she rolled the concept around in her head. Surely this kid must have parents somewhere.

'But what happened to his parents? Does anyone even try to find out where the rest of his family are?'

The gendarme was growing impatient. 'Do you know how many refugees arrived in France already this year?' She shook her head. 'Over sixty thousand so far.' He glared at her as if it were her fault. It was only June now. Charlize was shocked into silence. Some part of her knew the problem was a growing one, especially here in Europe, but most of the time she ignored the news and other media bemoaning the situation. Perhaps she should pay more attention.

She hung her head. What else could she have done for

the boy? She hadn't known at the time who or what he was. And even if she had, would she have handled it any differently?

She dragged a t-shirt over her head and finished getting dressed, not even bothering to run a comb through her short hair. The tiles were cool against her bare feet as she went through to the kitchen, where she stood and stared out the window. The view took her out over the terracotta rooftops of the village, leading her eye to the tall spire of the township's castle. So different from the view from her kitchen window back home. A view filled with paddocks of nodding yellow flowers stretching to each horizon, broken only by the occasional lone eucalyptus tree, standing tall and brooding. A sudden yearning to see those paddocks again raked through her chest, surprising her with its intensity. She did miss home, miss her family. But that wasn't enticement enough to make her go back. She wasn't ready to face them yet. The sun and the food and the peace she'd found here were definitely helping. But if she went back now, there was no guarantee the dreams wouldn't return with a vengeance as soon as she set foot on the familiar red soil. That the stares, so laden with pity and condemnation, wouldn't drive her back to the edge of that precipice she'd so nearly toppled over. The crash wasn't her fault, her logical brain knew that. The death of her beloved horse, and the near-death of her best friend, hadn't been her fault, either. But tell that to the little voice at the back of her brain not tied to logic, or reason. Or sanity.

Her mum, Sharon, was so proud when Charlize had come home that first night in her new police uniform. She'd fluttered her hands in that oh-so Italian way she took from Nonna, and gave such a smile, her eyes glistening with delight that Charlize had almost been embarrassed. Her mum had always supported her dream of joining the mounted police, and although she'd never said as much, Charlize got the distinct impression Sharon was glad at least one of her daughters had sense to get away from the farm. But even her mum couldn't hide the regret when she'd first come to see Charlize in hospital after the crash. Regret and dismay. And Charlize couldn't shrug off the fear that she'd let her mum down in some completely unfathomable way.

Letta, her younger sister, had always been the tomboy of the two. Even though they'd been close—they'd shared everything, even slept in the same bedroom right up until Charlize left at nineteen to get her own place in town—Charlize never quite understood Letta's deep attachment with the land; the way she followed their father around like a shadow, soaking in all the knowledge she could about the intricacies of growing canola. Charlize loved living in the country, felt a connection to the earth and a fierce pride that her family ran a successful farm. But that was as far as it went. Letta would be the one to inherit the farm when the time came. But after the accident, Charlize had caught Letta looking at her sideways, with a speculative, wondering gaze more than once. When Charlize had told her sister she was leaving after the accident, going to Europe for a *holiday*, she couldn't quite hide the gleam of relief obvious for the barest of instants before she covered it with a concerned frown.

No, Charlize was better off here in France. For a while longer, at least. And at least the compensation payment from the government allowed her to do that. The hard-fought payout hadn't been massive; the WA police force didn't make compo payments easily. But the money would keep her comfortable here in France for another twelve months, as long as she didn't spend extravagantly.

She ran a finger lightly over the cool granite bench top. For dinner, she'd planned on cooking a Provencal fish dish, served with a crunchy salad, but she found she didn't have the stomach for it anymore. Instead, she wrenched the door of the refrigerator open and snagged a bottle of white wine, opening it and slugging the cool liquid straight from the bottle. Throwing a few pieces of goat's cheese and half a fresh baguette on a plate, she stopped to look vacantly out the window again.

Much as she hated to admit it, her clairsentience had come in useful when she'd worked as a mounted police officer. There'd been a few times when she found a felon hiding out in a backyard shed or in the scrub along the edge of a freeway. And once, she'd warned a fireman at the scene of a burning apartment block that someone was still trapped in the ground-floor flat at the back of the building. It'd turned out to be a frail old lady, who'd passed out from smoke inhalation and was found lying on the floor only a meter from the door. When the fireman had asked her how she knew, Charlize fobbed him off by saying one of the other residents told her the woman was missing.

And then there was the time when a baby almost asphyxiated. Her gift had warned her someone was in need of help in the house. She felt it when their mounted unit first arrived, to back up another police unit and help round up some dirty drug dealers cooking meth in a local suburban house. But on that day she'd ignored the familiar, insistent tug inside her head as she squatted in the backyard, waiting for the go-ahead from the senior sergeant. She'd slowly honed her gift over her years in the force, kept it centred on the one target who mattered, and effectively drowned out any other emanations she might encounter. This was supposedly a hard thing to do; her mother informed her most clairsentients often found it impossible to filter through individual auras and pinpoint the one person most in need. But some days she still resented her talent, and how it defined her. So on that day she chose to ignore it, because in a flash of adrenaline-fuelled eagerness she'd taken off at a sprint to pull down one of the felons as he tried to clamber over the back fence. She'd caught the bastard, but found out later a baby nearly died in the house when toxic fumes from the meth gone wrong furled through the rooms. It'd taken her months to get over the guilt. The baby recovered, but that didn't make her feel any less reprehensible. And she'd made a grudging promise to herself, never to ignore her gift again.

Not many people knew what she could do. Her close family, of course. The sergeant, and her police partner and best friend, Patty. That was all. But both the sergeant and Patty agreed no one else needed to know. People often shunned what they didn't understand, and the last thing the sergeant wanted in his team was disharmony.

Charlize picked up her plate and wine bottle and took them down into the garden. It was still light; it didn't get dark here in summer until nearly ten o'clock. But even the appearance of the bright-eyed little brown mouse, hunting for a bit of baguette, didn't soothe her as it usually did.

Two disturbing events in three days had turned her quiet life upside down. First the stranger and now the boy.

What was next?

As she ate, her mind was absorbed by a pair of sad ebony eyes and she wondered how a little boy lost might ever find his way in this big world.

CHAPTER THREE

'Jesus, Munulo! What the fuck did you think you were up to?' Mathieu Pickard stood up behind his desk and glared at Jean-Luc while he closed the office door behind him.

'Good to see you too, boss,' Jean-Luc replied as he pulled over a battered vinyl chair and sat himself down gingerly on the other side of the desk.

'What the hell kind of stunt did you pull? You nearly blew the whole goddamned operation. Eighteen months down the drain.' Pickard ran a hand over his short-cropped, balding hair and jabbed his square glasses further up his nose before taking a seat in his equally battered leather chair. 'I had to pull Patrice and Nico out in case our whole team's cover was blown. They were on surveillance at Vincent's house. Your stupidity nearly compromised two missions.'

Jean-Luc flinched inwardly. His boss had every right to be hopping mad. Patrice and Nico, partners, and part of the three-man team assigned to this op, would probably have some choice words for him next time they saw him.

'Yeah, but I didn't get caught,' Jean-Luc replied, giving

his best devil-may-care grin. The small office was dim and stuffy, and Jean-Luc had to stop himself from flinging the grimy window open to let in some fresh air. He didn't like feeling contained. It gave him a sense of claustrophobia. He needed to know there was more than one escape route in any given room. But not here. He'd have to endure this meeting long enough to satisfy his boss, and then he was out of there.

'Lucky for you,' his supervisor growled, deep voice gravelly and expression hard. The dark circles beneath Pickard's eyes were larger than ever. This op was taking its toll on all of them. But as long as they caught the bastards; stopped them in their tracks, then it'd all be worth it. Pickard was ex-RPIMa, the French equivalent of the British SAS; one tough mother and he still looked solid and well-muscled, even though he was chasing sixty. He was the right man to lead this counter-terrorist unit. Hard-hitting, demanding the best of his team, unforgiving, a mean SOB, but also prepared to do just about anything to protect his men.

'They know what I look like, so I'll have to make sure I play it low key from now on. Stay out of sight,' Jean-Luc replied, sobering beneath Pickard's steely gaze.

'If I allow you back in the field.' His boss impaled him again with a baleful stare, his grey eyes unwavering. 'You know how risky it gets once they've seen your face. If they ever put a name to your face...' Pickard let his words trail off, not needing to say anymore. Jean-Luc knew exactly what'd happen if Vincent's men ever discovered his true identity. It'd mean everything and everyone he loved would be in jeopardy. All the team knew the risks, however, and they were still prepared to take them. To do whatever it took to bring this gang down.

But the people who wanted him dead would never find out who the true Jean-Luc Munulo was. His actual identity was hidden behind walls and walls of lies and paperwork. Even if they learnt his undercover name, Louis Bernard, they'd think he was an every day, underpaid security guard, working for some security and protection firm based in Paris. His alter-ego was backstopped to within an inch of his life, with layer upon layer of completely believable documentation. The bad guys would never be able to trace his name back to his real family. And if they did… well, the idea was unthinkable. He'd just have to trust in the system.

Pickard's earlier words suddenly registered, and Jean-Luc's heartbeat stuttered in his chest. *Merde*. He'd have to tread carefully. Pickard looked like he might actually mean that bit about not sending him out in the field again. The absolute last thing Jean-Luc needed right now was to be transferred to another op, or worse, chained to a desk, forced to watch from the sidelines. This was his op. He'd been working this angle for the past eighteen months. Spent unending nights staked out in cars, doing detailed follow-up on clue after clue, slowly edging closer to nailing the bastard. Vincent Dellucci. A member of the Italian Mafia, if any of the rumours were to be believed. But more to the point, the leader of a ring of people-smugglers. Smugglers who turned a profit by bringing in refugees fleeing Africa. An act, which even on its own was deplorable enough; to get rich off the desperation of others was sickening to Jean-Luc. But there was more money to be made from just smuggling refugees. Hidden within the hundreds of innocent migrants, specially trained extremists, were also being smuggled into the country. Terrorists. And terrorist groups paid extremely well. Vincent was making millions from bringing in people whose one aim was to wound and kill and cause as much disruption and fear as was humanly possible. Jean-Luc closed his fist and smacked it into the palm of his other hand. God, how he wanted to get hold of that bastard, what he'd do—

'You alright, Munulo?'

'Sure, boss.' He unclenched his fist. 'You wouldn't do that. There wouldn't be any op without me.' He went to cross one ankle over his knee and had to hide a wince as the wound in his side twinged. Keeping his face blank, he left his foot on the ground.

'Don't be so sure about that.' Silence filled the dank office as Pickard glared at Jean-Luc and he pretended nonchalance in return. Finally, Pickard said, 'At the very least, I'm assigning you a partner. You've spent far too long on your own.'

'I work better on my own, boss.'

'Well, not anymore. I've found a good guy, a sniper for the Republican Guard, but he's looking for a secondment to something with a little more bite to it. He knows the area, was born around here, so he'll be real helpful in that way. Good hand-to-hand defensive skills, trained in Savate, so I'm told.'

Like hell. There was no way Jean-Luc was taking on a partner. Not now, not at such a late stage in the game. Not when he was getting so close. So what if the man was trained in the French traditional form of street-fighting and martial arts? It probably made him bloody dangerous, but he didn't care if the man was Jason Lee himself. Jean-

Luc tuned out the rest of what his boss said about the new guy, staring out the window instead.

Once Pickard's tirade had ground to a halt, Jean-Luc jumped in with a quick change of subject. 'At least I got us a face,' he said, leaning forward in his chair, 'before they spotted me.' It'd taken weeks to find out where this particular meeting was going to take place. Weeks of grooming informants and greasing palms. One of the men at the meeting was well known to Jean-Luc. Vincent's lap dog and right-hand man, Enzo, always eager to do his dirty work. Jean-Luc recognised the second of Vincent's thugs as well. He'd seen him at one or two other meetings, but didn't know his name. The third man was a stranger and therefore of huge interest. It was imperative Jean-Luc find out who this new player was. What he might offer to Vincent.

So Jean-Luc had taken a chance and ghosted the meeting. While he leaned nonchalantly against a tree and smoked a cigarette, pretending to read the local newspaper, he got as near to the three men seated at the outdoor café table as he dared. It was just unfortunate Enzo had looked in his direction at exactly the wrong second, at the same time Jean-Luc chanced a quick glance over to get a better look at the unfamiliar man. The thug's eyes had narrowed, and even when Jean-Luc flicked his gaze away, acting casual, he could see the other man's shoulders tense from the corner of his eye.

Merde. They'd spotted him. Without looking back, Jean-Luc strode off through the Place de Herbes, dumping the newspaper in a nearby bin, but the sound of chairs scraping back over cobblestones told him he was being followed.

That's when he started running. And he thought he'd escaped them, too. After a sprint down a narrow alleyway, he'd dodged along the main street through the evening crowds and finally emerged right on the outskirts of the ancient town. He'd stopped with his back lent up against the stone wall of one of the many old churches scattered throughout Uzes, dragging in large gulps of air. It was quiet back here, the slope of the ground led away from the church toward a large unkempt park and then further down into the small valleys surrounding the town. No one was in sight, all the tourists and crowds left behind in the main streets. A grin of victory formed on his face. Then Enzo emerged around the far corner of the church, gun raised, and started firing.

It was a lucky escape; the bullet going through the fleshy part above his hip. A close thing. Too close.

'How's the injury, by the way?' It took a second for Jean-Luc to register Pickard's voice and come back from his musings.

'I'll live.' Jean-Luc touched his side in an unconscious reflex. 'Thanks for organising that doctor. But I'm not sure if the word *doctor* is completely accurate, though. Where the hell did you find that guy?'

'He was all I could get at such short notice. What do you expect, fucking miracles?' Was that a hint of embarrassment in his boss's grim mouth? He didn't blame Pickard. He was grateful to have someone, anyone, to patch him up. Whatever it took, so he didn't end up in a hospital. All that bloody paperwork was a pain in the proverbial arse. Not to mention the never-ending questions from over-officious gendarmes.

'Don't worry, you did good, boss. It was a straight

through and through. More of a graze, really.'

'Yeah, yeah.' Pickard would've already read the report from the doctor, making his own judgement on whether Jean-Luc was fit to go back into the field or not. So all of Jean-Luc's downplaying wasn't going to make a damn bit of difference one way or the other.

'So, now we have a face and a name, have we found the landing site yet?' Jean-Luc asked. Once he'd returned to HQ, he'd asked the sketch artist to draw up an identikit, a picture of the mystery guy at the meeting. Pickard recognised him straight away. It was Franco Piranjo, a very rich, powerful businessman, who owned a string of prestigious jewellery stores throughout Europe. This guy owned quite a few properties around France too, but one of them in particular was of great interest to them. A mansion down near Marseilles. This could be the vital clue.

'We might be onto something,' replied Pickard. 'Franco's estate near Marseilles overlooks a private beach. Actually, his property stretches for nearly two kilometres down the coast.' Jean-Luc pursed his lips at the news. This was good, really good. 'Obviously we can't get too close yet, or we'll spook the bastard, but our intel guys have put drones in the area, and there are a couple of spots that'd allow boats to land right up on the beach without being seen.'

'That's good news.' Jean-Luc didn't allow hope to flare. They knew the smugglers must've been landing their illegal immigrants on French soil, but up until now were unable to pinpoint the exact location. Of course, it'd have to be confirmed. Confirmed and reconfirmed, a solid, watertight case made before they could make a move. But it was a really good lead. The best they'd had yet. Perhaps this might even mean an end in sight to this damned investigation.

'Just as long as you haven't spooked them, so they cancel the whole operation,' growled Pickard. Jean-Luc tried to ignore the tight flicker in his gut. A stupid mistake. *Merde*. He hoped Pickard was wrong and Vincent didn't pull the plug on any future drops.

'Nah, Vincent's in too deep to stop now. He's too much of a greedy son-of-a-bitch to worry too long about us,' Jean-Luc replied, trusting what they knew of Vincent to be true. He was a violent, vicious felon who'd stop at nothing to make a buck. But he wasn't the brightest bulb in the lighthouse, and it was well known he often made his decisions based on mercenary concerns rather than on rational grounds.

'What about the woman?' Pickard asked.

'Who?' Jean-Luc narrowed his eyes at his boss, feigning innocence, but his stomach plummeted at Pickard's question.

'The one in the garden.'

'Oh. That woman.' He wished there was some way he could've omitted her from his report. She was blameless in his blundering mess of a mission and didn't deserve to be put under scrutiny. But Pickard would show no mercy. Any hint of a breach in protocol, a breach that could expose his team in any way, and the ex-RPIMa sergeant would pounce. Put her under *protective custody* until further notice.

Since he'd returned to HQ, Jean-Luc had only had enough time to give the cover page of her file a quick glance, to glean the barest of details about the woman in the garden. Of course, Pickard had compiled a file on her as soon as Jean-Luc reported the incident, so he'd definitely find more time soon to peruse the rest of that very interesting story. At least he now knew her name was Charlize Brewer, a twenty-eight-year-old Australian national, here on an extended holiday. Had once been in the police force—which explained a lot about her.

It wasn't these stark details he focussed on now. It was the pale hair haloed around her face, t-shirt stretched tight over pert breasts, a look of fragility and fear in her eyes. But with hands raised, ready to protect herself. A rush of blood heated his skin at the memory. So beguiling, obviously terrified, but resolute none-the-less. Something about her tugged at heartstrings he'd long thought broken beyond repair. He wasn't sure how to categorise the odd feeling in the pit of his stomach when he thought of her. Perhaps it was the fact he wanted to know why those scars covered her leg. Curiosity, is that all it was? No, it was more than that. Was it the vulnerability in her eyes? That vulnerability spoke to the protective side of his nature. Or was it that she'd agreed not to give him away? Why had she done that?

'Do we need to worry about her?' Pickard continued to push his point. 'How much does she know?' Damn, he needed to nip this line of questioning in the bud. Quell Pickard's fears. The last thing that woman needed was to have Pickard sniffing around in her life. She was an innocent bystander, nothing more.

'If you mean, is she a liability? Then the answer is no. I don't think she'll give me away.'

'Did she say as much? How do you know?' demanded Pickard.

'Well, she didn't give me away when she had every possible opportunity to do so.'

'And that's all you're going on?' Pickard was incredulous now.

'Call it gut-instinct then.' How was he going to explain to his boss there was something about this woman? The way she held herself. Ready for anything. With a sharp intelligence, she'd taken in the situation in a split second and made determined decisions.

'Gut instinct's not good enough for me. You need to go back and make sure once and for all.'

'Okay...' He hadn't thought about doing it that way, but now Pickard suggested it, the idea had merit. An excuse to go back to Uzes and check up on her. Not a bad idea at all.

'You're letting me go back then?'

'Yep,' his boss replied with a tight sigh. 'But keep your head down this time, Jean-Luc. Please don't blow this now we're so close. We know Vincent's men haven't been back to Uzes since they shot you. Probably think they've scared you off for good. The last thing they'll expect is for you to turn up there again. But stay out of sight, anyway.' Pickard tapped a pen on the desk, his gaze zeroed in on Jean-Luc. 'If you think this woman might be a liability, then you'll do something about it. Yes?'

'Yes.' Of course he would if the need arose. Nothing was allowed to get in the way of this op. Not even a woman with eyes the colour of spring grass.

Pickard started to talk again about this new man he wanted Jean-Luc to partner with, so Jean-Luc stood up and pushed the chair back impatiently. His boss stopped talking mid-sentence and glared at him.

'Sorry, boss, I need to get out of here.' He indicated the

door. 'Just tell me where I'm supposed to meet this Jason Lee bloke and I'll leave you to get on with your day.'

Pickard stood up slowly and his large frame filled the room as he leaned both hands on the desk.

'Don't go all fast and loose on me, Munulo. Or God help me, I will take you off this case.' He let the threat hang in the air between them. Jean-Luc just nodded, while Pickard told him when and where he was supposed to meet his new partner.

Closing the office door behind him, Jean-Luc strode down the long corridor. Not looking to either side, he concentrated on the light that shone through the cracked glass panels in the door at the end, drawing him outwards. With each step away from that dingy office, the feeling of claustrophobia diminished and by the time he laid a hand on the door and pushed, he could breathe normally again. What he wouldn't do for a calming glass of cognac right about now. Meetings with Pickard always did that to him. As soon as he got back to his small apartment, he'd open the new bottle he'd bought just the other day. The one treat he allowed himself. What was it about that office, and his boss, that made him so twitchy? Was it that Jean-Luc was never one hundred percent sure what Pickard was thinking?

Pah, he didn't have time to psychoanalyse himself today. He had more important things to do. Like slip back into Uzes and make sure the woman was really alright. Pickard had scared him, with his dire predictions and accusations. Jean-Luc should've been on top of that little problem, fixing it before Pickard even caught wind of her, but the bullet wound had put him off his game.

Ten minutes later, Jean-Luc sat aboard his motorbike. It

was slotted into the middle of a huddle of other motorbikes parked by the curb, leaning at an angle on their kickstands, like dominos all lined up. No better place to hide his machine than out in plain sight. Safety in numbers, and all that. He brought a brown paper bag up to his mouth and took a large bite out of the socca he'd just purchased at a nearby street vendor. His teeth broke through the crispy edges of the savoury pancake and sank into the chewy crust, almost burning his tongue on the salty deliciousness. The vista in front of him was enticing as he sat and ate.

Nice was a beautiful city, he'd give it that much. But even though he rented an apartment here, and his counter-terrorist unit had their office situated here, it never really felt like home. Sure, it had the Mediterranean right at its doorstep, was a member of the few elite cities strung along the Cote d'Azure that drew the young, beautiful and rich to their streets. But there was no soul to this city. Nothing spoke to that inner part of him. Give him a Provencal village, lined with cobblestones and rustic houses, and filled with people who called each other's names in greeting, over this flashy tourist haven any day.

A young couple strolled past him down the never-ending promenade. Jean-Luc took another bite and studied them. The man pushed a pram proudly, the woman with her arm tucked protectively into his. A light breeze lifted tendrils of the woman's long auburn hair and they curled around her face. She smiled at the man, brushing the hair out of her eyes and then, as if on cue, they both bent their gazes to the pram, cooing at the baby inside. A low coil of something dark tightened in his abdomen. They were so young, so in love. So filled with the possibilities life presented. That'd been him once, long ago. He'd had that same naivety, been taken in by that same weakness. Once, but not again. His fingers tightened, crushing the pancake into crumbs. The socca landed in a nearby bin. He was no longer hungry.

Images of soft baby fingers, wrapped tightly around his thumb, a downy cheek laid against his flittered at the back of his mind. Jean-Luc still remembered the weight of him as he lay on his chest, so trusting, so warm, so alive. Baby breaths gusting softly over his neck as he dreamed. Those memories speared him like knives of ice, hitting him in the solar plexus, the throat, his heart. He cleared his throat loudly and jammed the helmet down over his head. It'd do him no good living in the past. That was the pathway of no return.

Leo was dead now, and nothing would bring him back, certainly not any of these self-indulgent fantasies. Time to get back on the job.

SOCCA - CHICKPEA PANCAKE

INGREDIENTS
1 cup Chickpea flour
1 cup plus 2 tbsp Water
¾ tsp Sea salt
¼ tsp Ground cumin
2 ½ tbsp Olive oil
Freshly ground black pepper plus additional sea salt and olive oil
for serving

DIRECTIONS
Mix together the flour, water, salt, cumin, and 1 ½ tablespoons of
the olive oil. Let batter rest at least 2 hours, covered, at room
temperature.
To cook, heat your oven to 250°C. Oil a 23cm pan with the
remaining olive oil and heat the pan in the oven.
(You can use a cast-iron skillet or a non-stick tart pan.)
Once the pan and the oven are blazing-hot, pour enough batter into
the pan to cover the bottom, swirl it around, then pop it back in the
oven.
Bake until the socca is firm and beginning to blister and burn. The
exact time will depend on your oven.
Slide the socca out of the pan onto a cutting board, slice into pieces,
then shower it with coarse salt, pepper, and a drizzle of olive oil.
Cook the remaining socca batter the same way, adding a touch more
oil to the pan between each one.

This is best eaten with your fingers, standing up, staring out over
the Nice promenade, with the salty taste of the Mediterranean on
your lips.

CHAPTER FOUR

Charlize closed her eyes and savoured the liquid gold on her tongue. The syrupy sweetness was bright and filled with sunshine. And yes, she could taste the hint of lavender, as if it were a smudge of purple paint dropped into the golden hue of the honey.

'You like, Mademoiselle?' The old man, his small beard bristling with pride, stared at her with rapt attention.

'*Oui*,' she replied. 'It's *tres bon*.' Charlize made a smacking motion with her fingers against her lips. That was an understatement. This beekeeper's lavender honey was the best thing she tried all day. '*Je veux deux bocaux s'il vous pla"t*,' she said, holding up two fingers. Two jars of this wonderful honey probably wouldn't last long in her pantry, but she could always come back for more. Her salivary glands worked overtime at the thought of a fresh baguette, slathered with butter and this delectable honey for lunch today. The old man winked as he handed her the bag containing the jars, and she couldn't stop the smile forming on her face. These Frenchmen were such charmers. Paying the man, she eased her way back into the thronging crowds. Saturday morning was market day here in Uzes. Often touted as the best markets in Provence, they never failed to draw the people, tourists and locals alike.

Charlize drifted along with the multitudes, stopping to appreciate the soft slide of a silk scarf between her fingers, or draw in the wonderful scent of homemade jasmine soap. Her long, grey skirt swished coolly against her legs. At first, she'd made sure to cover her legs with long pants. But with the summer progressing, it'd become too hot. And it seemed no one paid the slightest heed to the scars climbing her leg, anyway. After a while, she almost forgot about them herself. They were starting to fade. No longer a deep angry red, now more of a light pink, the ridges of pain-filled skin sinking slowly back into the surface once more. At least she didn't have to wear the suffocating, hot, itchy and incredibly annoying pressure bandages now. In this slow-moving crowd, she hardly noticed her limp either.

A flash of bright red, the colour of a fire engine made her turn toward the centre of the Place de Herbes, to where the fresh fruit and vegetable stalls were lined up one after another, large awnings and umbrellas protecting their wares from the burning sunshine.

Tomatoes, larger than her fist, plump and round, sat in a layer of tissue paper. They'd be perfect for the ratatouille dish she was making tonight. She'd make chicken and tarragon with the fresh chicken she'd just bought to go with it and sit and eat it in the shade of her olive tree. She'd have to thank her teacher, Armand, for the tip on where to find the freshest chicken in Uzes. She'd discovered the little cooking school on her second day in Uzes. As she'd strolled down her street toward the main thoroughfare, there it was tucked in a small alley just behind the information centre, with a sign that advertised classes with the best chef in the south of France. And sure enough, when she'd ducked down the alley, there was a thriving cooking school set up in a four-hundred-year-old converted house. So inconspicuous from the outside, she might never have known it was there. French cooking had always intrigued her, inspired her. She'd never had the knowledge or the time to follow her desire to learn to cook back in Australia. But now, she had all the time in the world. Armand was opening doors for her she'd never even known existed. The rich, dark smell of a ripe cherry, the sound of her knife pounding a rhythm on the wooden chopping board, the feel of slippery fish scales beneath her fingers as she filleted it, was all so soothing. Her twice weekly cooking classes were a release, perhaps even a form of art, as Armand was so fond of saying.

Now all she needed for her ratatouille was some fresh zucchini, one of those baby egg plants and some basil. Her gaze roved over the stall-owner's wares and she pointed to a pile of plum-dark, glossy egg plants and held up four fingers. The petite old woman gave her a toothless smile and Charlize smiled back. Then she spied the basket of bright green basil leaves tucked in the front of the stall and started to pluck some of the best ones and put them in a bag. The smell was heavenly, this must be the freshest basil she'd ever—

'Bonjour, Mademoiselle. We meet again.' Charlize froze at the deep voice so near to her left earlobe. She spun around and there he was, standing right in front of her.

The handsome stranger from her garden, his mocha skin aglow in the midday sun.

Lost for words, she worked her mouth, like a fish out of water. He was the one person she'd never expected to see again. But here he was, a slightly quizzical smile on his face, waiting for an answer. Looking none the worse for wear from his gunshot wound—or whatever it was—he stretched his hand toward her.

'I was a little remiss the other day. Let me introduce myself. I am Louis Bernard.' What else could she do but take his hand and shake it.

'Hi,' she said, stumbling over her reply. For some reason, she was still lost for words.

After a few seconds of uncomfortable silence, he said, 'And your name, Mademoiselle?'

She hesitated. Should she tell him? He was dangerous, of that she had no doubt. But was he dangerous to her? Dressed in jeans and a button down black shirt, open at the neck, his short goatee beard neatly manicured and those fascinating tawny eyes bright and clear. He did indeed look dangerous, but not the kind of dangerous she'd originally thought. Perhaps dangerously handsome was closer to the mark. Shrugging her shoulders in studied nonchalance, she replied, 'Charlize. Charlize Brewer.'

'Interesting name,' he said.

'You seem… Better?' She looked pointedly at his left side.

'Ah, yes. That was just a little scratch, nothing more. I tripped and fell over.' God, his voice, that accent was making her weak at the knees every time he spoke.

To cover her reaction, she said a little more loudly than necessary, 'Oh really?' Sarcasm dripped from her tone. That was the biggest lie she'd heard today, and they both knew it.

'*Oui*,' he replied smoothly with a smile. But there was a tightness, a hint of warning in the creases around his eyes that told her he didn't want to pursue that particular topic. It was the first time he'd flashed her a full-on, genuine smile, and the effect was both energising and enlightening, hitting her like a punch to the stomach. He had possibly the best smile she'd ever seen on a man. Those wide, white teeth contrasted against his dark skin and full lips, showing the hint of a cheeky boy.

'Can I help you with your shopping bags?' Charlize was taken aback, the conversation galloping ahead way too fast for her liking. She'd only just learned his name, and now he wanted to carry her shopping. Why did the man who'd hidden in her garden to escape some kind of thugs want to spend time with her now? He was up to something.

'No thank you, I'm fine,' she replied, tone cool, guard back up. The old Charlize might've agreed. Out of plain curiosity, if nothing more. No normal person ran around in a sleepy little Provencal town being chased by men with guns. Two years ago she would've pinned him with her best penetrating glare and demanded he tell her what the hell he'd thought he was doing in her garden the other night. But she wasn't that woman anymore.

'Come on, I won't bite. Those bags look heavy.' Again he flashed her that brilliant smile and reached for her bags. 'I'll help you carry them home.' Before she knew exactly how he'd done it, the bags were in his hands and she was left standing, twisting her fingers together uncomfortably.

She should ask for her bags back. Send him on his way without a backward glance. That's what she should do.

What did he want? She stared at his hands that gripped

the calico handles. His fingers were long and lean, nails short and manicured, the nail-beds pink against the darker skin of his hands. Veins stood out on the backs of his hands and she traced the network of capillaries from his wrist over his knuckles with her eyes. Strong, supple, tantalising hands. They didn't look like the hands of a killer.

What was that old saying; keep your friends close, but your enemies closer. Was he friend or foe? It might be a good idea to find out what he wanted. A little of the old Charlize, the strong, tough, resilient Charlize, broke through her reserve, telling her to go with her gut. There was only one way to find out who or what he was.

'If you're sure,' she replied, still heavy on the cool tone. 'But only to the front door,' she warned. There was no way she was letting this man into her house. Not again. Not even a curious mystery such as him was enough to entice her now. Even if he was gorgeous enough to set her stomach jumping like a million butterflies were fluttering inside. Not when there could be danger involved in knowing him. That risk wasn't worth taking. She didn't need any complications in her life.

'It'll be a pleasure to accompany you,' he replied with smooth bravado.

'We'll see about that,' she quipped.

* * *

The calico bags surprised him with their weight. Filled with all sorts of garden-fresh produce, including some of the largest tomatoes he'd ever seen. A crusty baguette poked out from amongst bags of dried beans and green herbs. The bread was so fresh-baked he could smell the wonderful warm, yeasty aroma. She must be going to cook up some kind of gastronomic delight with all this fabulous food. Jean-Luc's stomach rumbled, reminding him he hadn't even had time to guzzle a coffee this morning, let alone have a proper breakfast. He'd been in such a hurry to get out the door of his cramped hotel room. And he couldn't remember the last time he'd had a home-cooked meal. An image came to him of a rustic table laid with dishes of vegetables, roast chicken, plates of cheese and bread, people laughing. Something inside his chest squeezed tight. His mother's table. How long since he'd sat with his family like that? So long he couldn't remember.

Where the hell had that thought come from? Perhaps Pickard was right after all. Maybe he was hanging on too tight. No time to think about that now. Back to the job at hand.

'Have you more shopping to do?' he enquired politely, wondering if she could possibly fit any more food into these bags. She gave him a considering look, as if weighing up her next answer. While she hesitated, he took the chance for a quick perusal. She was wearing a long skirt that flowed over her curvaceous hips, broadcasting their shape nicely. Sun kissed bare shoulders peeped out from a sleeveless pastel green top, a few freckles smattered her skin, matching the light ones running over her nose. The green colour of the top brought out the lustrous jade of her eyes. He couldn't remember ever seeing eyes quite the same colour before. Her scarred leg was barely noticeable beneath the folds of her skirt, but her limp was obvious, if not pronounced. She wore no makeup and looked casual and happy; at ease wandering around the markets, enjoying the French sunshine. His initial appraisal of her from the evening in her garden had been pretty accurate. She was just as lovely as he remembered.

'No, I've finished,' she replied.

He gave her a diverting smile, secretly relieved. If she'd wanted to tour around the markets for the next two hours, he wouldn't have had any other choice but to shadow her. But Pickard had told him to keep his head down, and he was doing his best to avoid the CCTV cameras, as well as keep a sharp eye out for any of Vincent's men. If he had to duck and weave his way around the market behind her, it might become obvious what he was doing. Especially to an ex-cop. He was here for one reason only; to make sure she hadn't leaked any information to Vincent or anyone connected with him. And to do that safely, he needed to get her somewhere quiet.

Plus, these heavy bags were weighing on his injured side. Not that he would ever allow it to show on his face.

She returned his smile, but it was tight, full of wary caution, her eyes brimming with inquiry and unspoken anxiety. She had every right to be suspicious of him. He disliked having to lie to her. Had she noticed that quick grimace he'd given as he gave his undercover name? It wasn't every day a stranger landed in your back garden and asked you to shelter them from armed madmen. She must be just about to burst with questions, but she was doing a good job of keeping up a mask of normality. At least she hadn't run screaming down the street when he'd approached her. Apart from her sarcastic comment about his health, she'd followed his lead, not mentioning the other evening while they were in such a public place. Respect for her quiet recognition of the situation bloomed in his chest. He was glad for her previous training as a police officer. It gave her an awareness a normal person wouldn't have. Most civilians wouldn't have been this circumspect when confronted with a potentially crazy man.

And most civilians probably wouldn't have let him follow them home either.

'Lead the way then, Mademoiselle,' he said, with a flourish and a deep bow. 'Your wish is my command.'

She gave him an odd look, but started to make her way out of the Place de Herbes toward the main street. He wanted to mentally kick himself. Why did he suddenly sound like an idiot? His only excuse was that he was severely out of practice. Hell, he hadn't done something as nice, or normal, as carrying shopping bags for a woman since… *Merde*. This was no time to think about Fleur. Their marriage had ended five years ago. What was she doing invading his thoughts now? *Get a grip*. Soon he'd start to stutter, like some out of practice teenage boy. He'd do better to just keep his mouth shut for a while. They wound their way up the crowded main street, threading their way through the many tourists, who stopped to admire a shop full of sweets, or haggle with a market stall owner over the price of a tea towel.

This was the same street he'd escaped down nearly a week ago. Rumour had it Vincent was expecting a *shipment* to come in tonight, meaning all of his hired guns would be busy. But that didn't make him any less vigilant. Vincent had only used Uzes as a meeting place once before in the whole eighteen months of the op, so it wasn't a regular haunt of theirs. Vincent was as canny as they came, always mixing things up, never meeting the same people in the same place twice. Never-the-less, Jean-Luc had scoped the area for a good few hours this morning before coming out to find Charlize. And even now was still hyper-aware of everything that was going on around him. Covertly, he studied every face that turned toward him, scanned the crowd for any unusual movement or anything out of place.

Charlize turned off the main thoroughfare and into a quiet alleyway. The sound of their feet on the cobblestones became loud in his ears.

'You don't really look like a typical Frenchman,' Charlize said, breaking the tense silence between them, referring to the colour of his skin. There was no beating around the bush with this woman. She drove straight to the point. He needed to make sure his story was solid as a rock. Because there was no doubt in his mind she was preparing to grill him mercilessly. And she probably had every right to do so.

'You are correct, Mademoiselle. I'm not wholly descended from pure French blood.'

'That's not what I meant,' she replied hurriedly. 'I didn't mean to say you weren't French, it's just that...'

'Don't worry.' He smiled to ease her embarrassment. 'You're right, of course. My father is from Africa. My mother's French, which is why I am neither truly black, nor truly white, just an impure mix of murky brown.' Keep as close to the truth as possible. That was Pickard's mantra. This part of his cover story was also true for him in real life.

'Oh, but you're not murky, your skin is gorgeous,' she blurted out, then immediately bit her lip.

She thought he was gorgeous? He'd encountered all manner of reactions to the colour of his skin when people found out his ancestry, ranging from the banal, to outright racism. Although people with African blood were tolerated in French society, they were rarely revered. Old wounds ran deep, as did the underlying prejudice a lot of people held beneath their façade of civilised politeness. Her words caused heat to rise at the base of his spine, and his hands clenched reflexively on the calico bags. He'd never been called gorgeous before. Not even by Fleur.

'Sorry. I... ' A tantalising flush started to creep up her collarbone. 'That's not what I meant either.'

'*Pah*, it's alright. I was teasing you. I'm actually quite fond of it as well. My skin, that is.' He kept his tone light. She muttered something under her breath, that could've been *what an idiot*.

'Are you cooking for an army?' He lifted one of the bags and pointed with his chin at the contents, tactfully changing the subject.

She gave a laugh. 'I love to cook.' The left-over flush from her embarrassment lent pink to her cheeks. It was the first time he'd seen her face light up in true pleasure, and it was breathtaking. Her laugh came from deep in her belly, full of joy. The sound jerked at something way down in his chest, an awareness of her presence beside him.

'Well, I love to eat,' he replied with a raised eyebrow.

'Hmm.' The wariness was suddenly back in her eyes. *Merde*. He'd overstepped the boundary again. He was making a complete mess of this. He was supposed to be getting her to let her guard down enough so he could ask the questions he needed answers to. Instead, he was still acting like an immature teenager. He daren't scare her away. Otherwise, Pickard would send in the rest of the unit to *take care of her*. His hackles rose at the mere idea of

Charlize being manhandled by the likes of Patrice and Nico. And while they probably wouldn't hurt her—not intentionally anyway—she'd end up terrified and alone and hating him.

They rounded another corner, and the alleyway meandered up a slight incline, well away from the main street now. The houses reared up on each side of the alley, hemming them in. The blonde sandstone bricks used to construct the villas reflected the bright sunlight, and Jean-Luc found himself having to squint against the intensity. Each house was three or four stories high, and all the wooden shutters and doors were closed against the heat of the day. There was no one else in sight, they were alone on the cobblestones.

'So, can we end this charade yet? Are you going to tell me what the other evening was all about?' Charlize kept walking, her eyes on the street ahead, but there was no doubt about the determination in her voice. He wasn't sure if he wanted to curse her or thank her for her forthrightness. She'd brought up the very subject he needed to discuss.

They must be close to her villa by now. He wasn't exactly sure which door was hers, probably because he'd scaled the back wall both times he'd been there, not used the front door like a normal person.

The time he'd clambered over her wall to escape Vincent's thugs wasn't the only time he'd been in her back garden. He'd returned yesterday evening, to plant listening devices and scope the place. Swept it to make sure no one else had done the same. Her villa had seemed comfortable, full of pastel colours and French Provencal rustic furniture. The main focus of the villa was the large kitchen, decked out with modern cooking appliances. The smell of fresh herbs and an array of cheeses on the sideboard had filled his nose. The memory stayed with him, and perhaps it was that thought that prompted him to make his suggestion.

'How about I tell you over dinner?'

'What? First you jump over my wall and scare the hell out of me, and now you're asking me out on a date? Who do you think you are?'

'No, not a date exactly. I was hoping you'd invite me to partake in the wonderful feast you've obviously got planned for tonight.' He dropped his eyes toward the bags, letting the cheeky smile most women found hard to resist curl up one side of his mouth.

She stopped walking and stared at him, incredulous. 'That's blackmail.' His charming smile hadn't worked on her after all. She obviously wasn't most women. 'And what makes you think anything would induce me to invite you, a complete stranger, into my house anyway?' Her voice held a demanding note.

Time to stop flirting with her and get down to the truth. 'I can tell you're the curious type.' He was learning she was the sort of person who appreciated candour more than manipulation. 'And besides, I want to tell you more—everything—but not here.' He indicated the street with a wave of his hand.

'Right,' she said. 'Just so you know, most women don't like to be bullied into asking a man over for dinner.' She narrowed her eyes at him. Was she going to turn him down? Her gaze flicked from his eyes, down to his shoes, back to his chest, and then returned to his face. A clinical evaluation, as if she were studying a crime scene.

'*Oui,*' he agreed. 'But I can already tell, you're not most women.' Her eyes widened at his remark.

His gaze locked onto her wary green eyes. He wanted to spend time with this woman. And it wasn't purely because he needed answers from her. She intrigued him.

'Charli. Yoo hoo, Charli.' A woman's voice drifted down the small alleyway. Charlize turned and squinted up the hill as the shape of a petite woman materialised out of the bright sunshine.

'Patty?' The word left Charlize's lips in a whisper. Then louder, she said, 'Patty, is that you?'

The small woman careened down the street, an oversized duffle bag flopping on her shoulder. Charlize ran to meet her, arms outstretched, her limp obvious. They embraced for a long time, not saying anything, and Jean-Luc began to feel an uncomfortable tingle, as if he were intruding on something deeply personal.

Finally, the smaller woman broke away. 'I've been wandering up and down this goddamned street for hours trying to find your house. I bloody well hope you've got a cold beer in the fridge, girl.' Then her eyes lit up as she spied Jean-Luc and she skipped over to him. 'Hi, I'm Patty LeVine.' She extended her hand. 'And you are?'

'Louis. Pleased to meet you, Mademoiselle.' He gave her his best winning smile.

'Mmm, listen to that gorgeous accent. Ooh, and I didn't realise how many French men were dark-skinned. Charlize, he's just…yummy.'

'Patty!' Charlize shook her head at her friend's bluntness. 'Sorry,' she apologised. 'This is Patty, my best friend, from Australia.' Then turning, she admonished, 'But you didn't even call me to tell me you were coming.

What if I'd decided to take off for a few days?'

'You know me, Charli, always the spontaneous one.' Patty was petite and dark, the complete opposite of Charlize. They seemed to be opposites in personality as well as physically. Not that he knew either woman at all, but Patty appeared impulsive and bubbly, compared to Charlize's measured, considering temperament.

Charlize turned that measured gaze back onto him, and his heart sank as realisation hit. His precious invitation to dinner tonight was going to be a no. *Merde*. And he'd been so close, too. She'd been about to say yes. Now he'd have to go to Plan B.

Putting down one of the bags, he dug his wallet out of his back pocket and handed her a business card. 'Seems like you're busy tonight after all.' He softened his comment with a grin. 'Here's my number. Give me a call. I really would love to finish our conversation.' More than that, it was compulsory to finish their conversation. Pickard would take great pleasure in pulling his entrails out inch by inch if he knew Jean-Luc was letting her get away tonight. 'Perhaps tomorrow night?' Now he sounded desperate.

She took the card from his hand, quickly tucking it into a pocket of her handbag. 'I'll think about it.'

'Did he just ask you out?' Patty stage-whispered into Charlize's ear. Charlize rolled her eyes and then turned back to him, an apologetic lift to her eyebrows. But before she could utter a word, Patty jumped in and said, 'Yes, she'll be there. Tomorrow night is it? I'll make sure she's there.'

'Patty.' Charlize's voice held a deep note of warning, but the little pocket-rocket smiled back at him, completely oblivious. Jean-Luc liked her already. Liked her more because she was a willing accessory to his plan. Albeit she didn't know the true reason for his request. But he'd take all the help he could get.

'I'll call you,' replied Charlize, taking control of the conversation once more. 'And thank you so much for carrying all these bags home for me.' She picked up the bags and headed toward an olive green door.

'Not a problem.' He turned back down the alleyway and started to whistle as he strolled away over the cobblestones. Chancing a quick glance back, he happened to see a pair of long legs take the single step up and disappear into the house.

Pah, now he had another day to fill in. Another day where he'd have to stay out of sight. And find an excuse to give Pickard for not being able to meet up with this new *partner*. So far he'd dodged Pickard's phone calls demanding he make an appointment to come back to Nice and meet him, by saying he was too busy following up a lead on Vincent as well as making sure that *the woman in the garden* wasn't being tailed or under any other form of surveillance. Which was all true. And tomorrow he'd have to do more of the same. Follow Charlize, to make sure she wasn't being followed. Ironic really.

CHAPTER FIVE

Charlize switched the weight from her left to right foot as she tried to ease the ache clawing its way up her leg. A few minutes more, that's all she needed, she pleaded silently to her crippled leg. She was so close to being able to serve, if she stopped stirring now, the cream would curdle. The delicate aroma of chicken sautéing in the creamy sauce drifted upwards, and she breathed in the heavenly steam. Her mouth watered at the thought of tasting her latest concoction.

'What's taking so long? I'm starving to death down here,' a voice floated up the outside stairs and through the kitchen door.

'Hold your horses, I'll be down in a sec,' she yelled back. It was so good to see her friend. Her heart swelled at the memory of Patty careening down the alley toward her this morning. Words couldn't explain how much she'd missed her gregarious, fun-loving nature. And her whip-sharp humour. They'd been so close. Back when they'd been partners in the force. Before the crash.

Damn, she'd forgotten to keep stirring. She took the pan

off the stove and checked its contents. Thankfully it looked perfect, no curdling. Chicken, tarragon and cream, mixed with the best dry Riesling she could find. All the ingredients bought at the local markets this morning. The seller assured her the chicken had been running around picking at millet seeds just yesterday. Charlize tried to put that part of the story out of her mind. If she allowed herself to dwell too much, the chicken would soon have a name, a personality, be the mother of ten adorable little fluffy yellow chickens, and she'd never be able to bring herself to eat possibly the freshest chicken she'd ever tasted.

Thoughts of the markets this morning inevitably brought Louis back to mind. She was still no closer to answering the myriad of questions she had about him. His presence had caused more questions than it'd solved. Patty had made sure she hadn't forgotten about him either, gently ribbing her all afternoon about the gorgeous man who'd asked her out to dinner. Wanting to know more about him, who he was, how she'd met him, and whether Charlize fancied him. Enthusiastically telling her she should take up his offer for dinner. Playing match-maker. Charlize had hedged as well as she was able. If Patty found out about Louis's little garden visit the other night, her generous thoughts about the man would change in an instant.

Something about the man bothered her, but she couldn't put a finger on exactly what it was. Her ex-cop senses were telling her something wasn't quite right about him. Was he lying to her? Chances were probably high if the gun in his jeans and the fact he was hiding from armed men were anything to go by.

Time to take the ratatouille out of the oven, where it'd been keeping warm. She laid it out with an artistic flourish. Almost restaurant quality.

Her mind was still abuzz with everything that'd happened to her over the past few days. Her life had gone from quiet and serene to a whirling vortex in only a few days. Apart from Louis destroying the sanctity of her garden, and Patty's arrival out of the blue, Charlize had also spent a fair bit of time making numerous phone calls. Phone calls that usually led to either her being left on hold for so long she finally hung up, or phone calls where her fledgling French left her confused and frustrated as to what had actually been said. But she was beginning to get a picture in her head of what'd happened to the little African boy she'd found in the carpark the other day.

She hadn't been able to get him out of her thoughts. Those lost, blank eyes haunted her dreams, and her waking moments as well. She had to find out what happened to him. To ease the guilt eating away at her insides, leaving a burning trail of shame behind it. She should've done something more to help the boy. That much had become blindingly clear to her over the past few days. But at least she'd made some progress. She might finally have tracked down the holding facility he was being kept in. It was a start.

It was time to serve the chicken. She shook away the memory of talking her way through layers of French bureaucracy. Government red tape was the same in every country. The chicken was served onto two plates next to the ratatouille made from those huge tomatoes she'd bought this morning. Then she balanced them both along her left arm, waitress-style, so she could hold on to the iron railing as she descended the steps.

'Oh, thank God! I was just about to start eating those raw olives straight off your tree, I was so hungry.' Patty half-rose out of her chair so she could waft her nose over the plate Charlize laid in front of her. 'Oh, that smells aaaamaaazing,' she cooed, not even waiting for the plate to settle fully on the tabletop before she dug her fork into the creamy mixture.

'You haven't changed a bit, Pat.' Still petite, with wild dark hair, left long to blow haphazardly in the wind. Charlize hadn't allowed herself to dwell on how much she'd missed her best friend's effervescent personality, along with that steel-lined core she kept hidden from most people. Had it really been nearly eighteen months since they'd last seen each other?

'Yeah, well, you have. You never cooked anything this good before,' replied Patty through a mouthful of food.

Charlize went around to the other side of the small table and hugged Patty from behind. 'It's so good to see you again.' She straightened up and swallowed hard, pretending to watch a bird flitting its way through the branches, waiting for the sudden lump that'd formed in her throat to dissipate.

'Have you got any more of this stuff? It's fantastic.'

'Wow, didn't they feed you on the plane?' Charlize laughed when she realised Patty had already wolfed down half of the food on her plate. She sat down and tasted her own meal. It was just as divine as she'd hoped. Delicate and creamy, the tarragon flavoured the chicken but didn't overpower it. The more robust, slightly acidic tomato and courgette flavours of the ratatouille melded nicely with the chicken. Delicious.

'Slow down, you'll give yourself indigestion. I've never seen you eat this much before,' she scolded Patty.

'Yeah, well, there's a reason for that.' As soon as the words were out of her mouth, Patty gave a small grimace, her fork stalled halfway to her mouth.

'Okay... ' A little voice started to nag at Charlize, telling her she wasn't going to like whatever it was Patty had to say, but she ignored it and kept her smile determinedly in place. An array of micro-emotions flittered across Patty's face, none of which Charlize could decipher. The cold lump in the pit of her stomach turned decidedly icy.

'So, what's the reason?' Charlize tried to keep her tone light. But instead of replying, Patty got out of her chair and came around to Charlize's side of the table. This was getting stranger by the second. Turning Charlize around in her chair, Patty knelt in front of her, hand resting on her knee.

'Hon, I've got something to tell you. It's part of the reason I came to visit. So I could tell you in person.'

Charlize wanted to ask what it was, but the words wouldn't come, as if she was suddenly paralysed in her chair.

'I'm so sorry, but you were going to find out sooner or later. I'm pregnant.' The words hung between them for seconds on end as Charlize digested their meaning. Blood pounded hot and heavy in her ears. She stood up and grabbed Patty by the shoulders, pulling her into a hug. But the motion was done on autopilot. A numbness invaded her muscles, and her own voice sounded like it was coming from a million miles away.

'That's great. Congratulations.' But even as she said the words, the pounding in her ears rose to a tremendous roar.

It threatened to drown out all other logical thoughts and actions. Patty was pregnant. *Oh Jesus, no.*

'I'm happy for you, really I am,' Charlize said, pushing them apart so she could stare down at her diminutive friend. But the tears forming in her eyes spoke of the lie in her words. She sat down before her knees gave out beneath her. Images swirled around her head, threatening to overwhelm her. Images of herself doubled over in pain, screaming. Of the doctor with that horrible solicitous look on his face as he told her.

'I know, Hon. It's okay. You go right ahead and cry. That's why I came out here, to be with you when you heard the news.' Patty knelt down in front of her again, sympathy brimming in her brown eyes.

'I'm fine, I'm not going to cry,' Charlize said, dragging in a large gulp of air. 'Well, if I do, it's only because I'm so happy for you.'

'You don't have to do the brave act in front of me, Charli. I know how much losing the baby in the crash meant to you.'

Patty had said it. The words were out in the open now, there was no avoiding them.

'It's okay, really. The baby. The whole thing between Shane and I. It was for the best in the long run. We're better off not together.' She and Shane would've been miserable together. They'd only been going out for five months, it was supposed to be a casual thing. He'd only said he'd marry her because she fell pregnant. Thank God they'd never actually gone through with the wedding. It'd made it so much easier for her to leave.

'You said that before you left Perth as well, Charli, but are you sure you meant it? Shane still asks about you.'

'I know, he still sends me texts sometimes, too,' Charlize admitted. Shane said he missed her, but she knew what he really missed was the life they could've had. Their fantasy life as a happy family together. He'd been looking forward to being a father, nearly as much as she had to being a mother. She'd only been fourteen weeks pregnant, hardly time to become attached to the thing growing inside her.

Swiping a hand across her eyes, Charlize drew in two deep lungfuls of air. She wouldn't break down in front of Patty. She wouldn't. She should be over this stupid crying thing by now. It'd been two whole years, goddamnit.

'I'm fine. Go back and finish your food, before it goes cold,' she told Patty, who was still kneeling on the hard gravel. Then Charlize gave a start.

'Hang on. If you're pregnant, then...'

A wide grin split Patty's face. 'I wondered how long it'd take you to figure that out,' she said self-consciously.

'So who is he? How come you didn't tell me before? Tell me all about him now.' Some of the numbness left Charlize's limbs as the notion finally wormed its way past all her own dark and sorrowful thoughts. Patty had a man in her life. Someone she was in love with if the goofy look on her face was anything to go by.

Patty got up and made her way back to her seat. She shovelled a couple more mouthfuls of food in before she started speaking.

'His name's Mike. Michael Marino, and he's a physio. He works at the QE2 hospital in Perth.'

Charlize processed this information, turning it over in her head. 'Did you meet him during your rehab?' It was a logical explanation. Patty had needed a lot of rehab after the accident.

'Yep. He helped me get my hip back into shape. Charli, he's sooooo gorgeous. He's Italian. You know, all dark hair and sexy eyes and beautifully hot-headed. We argue all the time. It's wonderful. I can't wait for you to meet him.' Patty actually dropped the fork so she could use both her hands to describe Mike. Charlize was genuinely delighted at how animated, how alive Patty became when she talked about her new man.

'So, it's serious then?'

'I love him, Charli. He asked me to marry him. We're going down that whole traditional *happy families with white picket fences* route.'

'Wow,' Charlize breathed.

'Don't look so shocked.' Patty screwed up her eyes indignantly. 'It had to happen sooner or later.' Patty had always been such a free spirit when they'd worked together in the mounted police. Leaping from one romance to another, never able to settle down, always seeing something better just over the horizon. Charlize had almost been a little jealous. Patty seemed to draw men to her like moths to a flame. They found her irresistible. But she also left a string of broken hearts.

'I just never found the right guy until now,' Patty said, as if reading her mind.

'That's great, Patty, I'm so glad for you.' Charlize wasn't just saying the words, she truly meant them. In a twisted way, she was glad something good had come out of the crash. If Patty had found the man of her dreams, it was a good thing. At least one of them was happy.

'We've only been going out for eight months, that's why I didn't tell you before now.'

'It's fine, Patty. You deserve to be happy.' Charlize

reached across the table and took her friend's hands in hers. 'I mean it.' Charlize held Patty's gaze, letting the honesty of her words sink in. Just because Charlize couldn't get her life sorted, didn't mean Patty had to put her own life on hold. They'd both had completely different reactions to the crash. Patty had taken it as a big wake up call to change her life for the better. Charlize had run away.

'So that's the other reason I came all the way over here to see you,' said Patty, her fingers entwining tightly over Charlize's. 'I was going to ask you to be my maid of honour.'

'Oh.'

Charlize knew she should say something else, but Patty's request took her completely by surprise. She should've been expecting it. Her friend's eyes were fixed on her face, anticipation showing in the tilted corners of her mouth.

'Um…' She tried to raise a smile, to allay the sudden dismay appearing in Patty's gaze as the silence stretched on. 'When's the happy day?' she asked instead.

'October the first,' Patty replied. It was mid-July now. Two and a half months away. 'We want to get married before the baby's born, and that was the earliest we could get everything sorted. But, Charli, if you don't—'

'Of course I want to, Patty, don't be silly.' Charlize shook her friend's hands, emphasising how wrong she was. 'I couldn't miss my best friend's wedding.'

'I wasn't sure when you were planning on coming back home.' Patty's eyes were still full of concern. 'But I hoped you'd be back by then. You've been gone for over a year, Charli. You are coming back, aren't you?' And there it was, the million-dollar question. How to answer Patty when she didn't even know her own mind on the matter. Again, the awkward silence hung between them.

'I am coming back, of course I am. I just needed time… you know, to sort things out in my head. But now you've given me the best excuse in the world. Thanks, Pat.' Charlize gave a bright smile, hoping to hide the fact that her heart was going a million miles an hour at the mere thought of having to face all those people back in Perth. That her chest was constricted as if a large boulder was sitting on top of it. Having to face all the unasked questions, all the pitying stares, the doubt and innuendo in the back of people's minds. Small towns were breeding grounds for gossip and allusion, for dissecting people's lives and finding them wanting and somehow inferior. And she'd have to face the gap in her heart where her horse, Xeon, had once been. The gap in her life where her career as a mounted police officer used to be. Because she knew she could never go back to that world again.

'Are you sure, Hon?' A look of muted hope had replaced the air of dismay in Patty's face. How could Charlize possibly let her friend down? She knew she'd been a bad friend up until now. Leaving Perth, for her own selfish reasons. Leaving Patty to cope with her injuries and nightmares on her own. Barely staying in touch with her friends and family. 'I mean, I know you're taking this time to yourself, to get better and all that. If you're not ready to come home, I'll be okay with that.'

'Yep, I'm sure. I'll be the best goddamned maid of honour you've ever seen. This wedding will be fantastic. I can't wait.' Charlize got up and came around the table to embrace her friend again.

'That's great. You've made my day, Charli.' Normally

Patty would've seen straight through Charlize's false bravado, but whether it was because she was so desperate for Charlize to be her bridesmaid, or because she was unpractised in reading the subtle nuances of her body language, Patty didn't seem to doubt the truth of Charlize's words.

Tiny stars popped out one at a time in the darkening sky as she held her friend in a determined embrace. Perhaps this was the kick in the butt she needed to get her out of this haze of ambivalence and delay. She had two and a half months to make a decision. To decide whether she could face going back home or not.

CHICKEN AND TARRAGON

INGREDIENTS
1 tbsp French butter
1 tbsp Olive oil
Whole chicken, cut into 8 pieces
3 Shallots, chopped
1 cup Chicken broth
1 cup favourite Riesling white wine
½ cup Fresh cream
4 tsp Fresh tarragon chopped
2 tsp Dijon mustard

DIRECTIONS
Melt the butter with oil in a heavy large pan over high heat.
Sprinkle chicken with salt and pepper. Cook, skin side down, until
browned and then turn over and brown on the other side. Transfer
browned chicken to plate.
Add shallots to same pan and reduce heat to medium-low. Sauté
until soft, then add the Riesling and simmer until liquid is reduced,
scraping up all the yummy browned bits. Whisk in the chicken
broth. Return the chicken to pan, skin side up and reduce heat to
low. Cover the pan and simmer until chicken is cooked (about 20
minutes). Transfer the chicken to platter while you finish off the
sauce. Whisk the cream, tarragon, and mustard into the same skillet.
Increase heat a little and continue to stir as it simmers until sauce is
thickened. Season with salt and pepper. Pour sauce over chicken.
Serve with homemade ratatouille or fresh pasta cooked al dente.

Best eaten surrounded by BFFs and/or family and slurped noisily as
you chat and eat.

CHAPTER SIX

The pleasant chatter of voices filled the air, along with the clink of cutlery against a plate, and the waft of cigarette smoke across Jean-Luc's table. Every now and then there was a raised shout from the group gathered around a television, set up outside the cafe on the other side of The Place, showing a European Premier League soccer game.

He'd chosen this little café because they served a divine locally brewed beer, as well as the best pizza he'd ever tasted. And because it was hidden from prying eyes. Set back in the corner of The Place de Herbes, it allowed Jean-Luc a good view over the rest of The Place, while he remained out of the line of sight of the CCTV cameras. It might be sacrilege to say it aloud near an Italian, but the pizza here was better than anything he'd tasted from any restaurant in Italy. The dough was light and crisp and melted in his mouth, with just the right amount of tomato and garlic smeared over the top, and a light dusting of basil and bocconcini, or maybe prosciutto and spinach. They also had the best salad nicoise in town, if Charlize decided she didn't feel like pizza.

The pretty waitress had given him the table on the furthest edge of the group arrayed outside on the cobblestones. He'd have his back to the wall, while facing outwards so he could see anyone or anything coming toward him. Being on the edge also allowed for easy escape if the need arose. *Merde*. He hoped the need wouldn't arise.

The pretty waitress had been more than obliging. She granted his request with an admiring smile and a lingering look as he took his seat, swishing her short skirt seductively as she walked back toward the kitchen. Perhaps he'd smiled a little too openly at her when he'd arrived, but he was a man, after all. And beautiful women were meant to be appreciated.

The water from the fountain at the centre of The Place splashed quietly, adding to the evening harmony of life going on in Uzes. It calmed him, this small-town normality, this buzz of humanity going about their everyday business, the warm summer evening lending a lethargy to the day. Reminding him of his own hometown.

He still only half believed she'd turn up tonight. When a text had appeared on his phone at lunchtime today asking where she should meet him for dinner, he'd jumped with guilty pleasure. The text had thrown him, not only because her name was the last person he'd expected to appear on his phone, but because he'd been watching her from around the corner at the same time. Watching her send a text. To him. It was vaguely voyeuristic. But then everything he'd done in regard to her today had been voyeuristic.

He'd monitored Charlize and her friend all morning. Latching onto them as soon as they left her villa, he'd ghosted behind them as Charlize showed Patty around the idyllic township.

Civilians were normally easy targets to tail, never remotely suspecting they were being followed. And why would they? Most civilians had nothing to hide and therefore weren't suspicious by nature. Charlize, however, was not so easy. She had a habit of checking her surroundings, casting her gaze up and down the street every couple of minutes and making eye contact with most people she passed. And now he'd read her file more closely, he knew why. She'd been a mounted police officer back in Australia. A damn good one if her file was anything to go by. So he tailed her as if she were one of Vincent's lap dogs. With great care. If she saw him, she'd never trust him again. Certainly not enough to reveal information about Vincent and his men. If she knew anything at all.

He'd listened in on some of her and Patty's conversations last night as well. The devices he'd planted in her garden, and in her living room and kitchen, had done their job exceedingly well. But while some of the information had given him increased insight into Charlize as a person—such as her hesitancy about going back to Australia—there hadn't been a hint of any knowledge on her part about Vincent or his thugs.

There'd been one bit of mitigating and perhaps disturbing information, though. When Patty had prompted her about how she'd first met him, Charlize hadn't told the truth. She'd said the first time they'd met, she'd literally run into him in the alleyway behind her house, dropping her backpack, with all its contents scattered, and he'd stopped to help her pick it all up. From then on she'd told the truth, that Louis had approached her at the markets today and offered to carry her bags home as a kind of penance for knocking her over the first time.

Jean-Luc wasn't sure why she hadn't revealed the truth. A large part of him was relieved—it meant one less person with any inkling he wasn't exactly who he said he was—but another part of him was worried. What reasons would she have to withhold that kind of information from her best friend? And another ex-cop. Her ex-partner, if Pickard's file could be believed. The info Pickard compiled on Charlize had been sketchy at best, his boss was sorely lacking in contacts when it came to the Australian Police Force, certainly not ones he could pressurise for intelligence, anyway. Surely Charlize would share something like that with Patty, though. Was she trying to protect him? And if so, why? Or was she trying to protect herself?

Jean-Luc shook his head to free it from all the numerous permutations. Women. The things that went on in their minds were nearly impossible to figure out, so why in hell was he trying with this one?

Speak of the devil. Or rather, should he say angel? Because that's what he was reminded of as he spotted her walking toward him. His gaze raked her from head to toe, taking in the way her golden curls jumbled in a riot around her face, and the way her long summer dress skimmed her hips on the way down to the ground, but left her shoulders bare to be bathed in the soft orange light of the summer evening. Something tightened way down deep in his gut. Appreciation. But it was more than that. He'd appreciated the pretty waitress tonight as well, but there hadn't been this feeling of relevance when he'd smiled at her.

He stood up, moving to pull out her chair and then smoothly push it in as she sat down. 'Good evening, Mademoiselle. You look beautiful tonight.'

'Oh…ah, thank you.' Her smile was a mix of embarrassment and sheer brilliance. Then she gave a small, ironic laugh. 'You Frenchmen, you're all so…well let's just say not many men in Australia would do or say what you just did.'

'Really?' he queried. 'Why not?' Resettling himself on the other side of the table, he cocked his head.

She shrugged. 'Perhaps it has something to do with being more laid back, but there's a severe lack of chivalry in most of the Aussie men I know. And they certainly don't throw many compliments around, whether they're warranted or not.'

'But my comment was sincere, Charlize. You are indeed a beautiful woman.' Her cheeks flushed a light pink at his comment, making her even more appealing in the evening glow. But she shot him a glance that might've said she wasn't as accepting of his compliment as she should've been. Did she really not know how stunning she was?

'Well, thank you again, I guess,' she replied. 'You look very nice yourself.' She couldn't hide the way her gaze flickered approvingly up his arms and over his chest, before coming to rest on his face. Her own cheeks still glowed pink. From her previous embarrassment or something else entirely now, he wasn't sure.

'Thank you,' he returned breezily. He knew without guile he did indeed look *nice*. He'd taken particular care tonight to dress with just the right mix of stylishness and casual abandon he knew most women found enticing. Beige linen trousers over brown Italian soft leather shoes, paired with a sky-blue button up chambray shirt, open at the neck and rolled up to the elbows, the colour a good contrast against his skin. He'd even taken the time to trim his goatee and splash on some cologne. Women loved men who looked good and smelled even better. Well, European women did. What Australian women liked was very much a mystery to Jean-Luc, but he hoped to find out a lot more about that topic tonight.

The waitress appeared, and he ordered them both an apéritif, a glass of Kir, to start their evening. Was it his imagination, or did the waitress cast a sharp glance at them both as she retreated? Charlize seemed to have recovered her composure by the time the waitress left and he dismissed the waitress out of his mind.

'Thank you for coming tonight. I wasn't sure you'd turn up.'

'Neither was I,' she replied. 'You should probably thank Patty, she was the one who nagged me out the door.'

Jean-Luc smiled at that. He could well imagine the diminutive woman hustling her much larger friend out the door, refusing to take no for an answer.

'But as they say, curiosity killed the cat. I came for one reason only. To get answers.' She turned that bottle-green gaze directly on him for the first time tonight, and the impact almost pushed him back in his chair. There it was again, that puzzling mixture of determined purpose and hesitancy, the same vulnerability he'd seen the other night in her garden. She was a paradox, a woman with a tough outer layer of hardened steel, concealing something that looked like fear or caution. Or perhaps a lack of faith in herself?

Then her eyes darkened to a deep ocean-green, and that glimpse of apprehension he'd seen just below the surface disappeared beneath the waves. She was once again a woman in charge of her own destiny. And that look told him she wasn't about to take no for an answer.

'Okay, ask away,' he said with a grimace. 'Let's get this over with.'

Her eyes widened at his statement. Obviously, she'd been prepared to face more resistance in getting the information she wanted, and it took her a few seconds to compose her thoughts. She'd applied a hint of pale pink lipstick, which made her lips shimmer in the lights above the restaurant. They were plump and almost too large for her face, but he was still mesmerised by the way they curled up at the very corners, as if she had a permanent smile hidden away, just waiting to be unleashed. She bit down on her bottom lip before she started to fire questions at him.

'Is Louis Bernard your real name?' Damn, she went straight for the jugular, this woman. He kept his expression cool and met her gaze.

'Yes.'

Her eyes narrowed in concentration. Then, as if accepting his answer, went on, 'Why do you carry a gun?' Ah, he hadn't expected that one. He hadn't realised she'd seen it while he was in her garden. His cover story had been concocted by Pickard's team to deceive much bigger fish than her; his story had to be iron clad to keep him safe. Admittedly, she was an ex-cop, but still, there was no way she'd have the power or knowledge to be able to peel back the layers and see through his veil of secrecy. This cover story had served him well previously, and it'd help to cover his arse with Charlize as well.

'It's part of my job.'

'Which is?'

'I run security detail for…clients.'

'What kind of clients?'

'I can't tell you that. They like to remain anonymous. Let's just say most of them are rich, powerful businessmen, who like to protect their interests.'

'I'm sure they are,' she muttered, half under her breath. 'So why were you in my garden?'

'I was leading those two men away, a decoy if you like, so my partner could get our client out of the area.'

'Can you tell me what those two men wanted from your *client*?'

'A competing faction didn't like the way he was carrying out his trade. They wanted to persuade him to change his mind about a commercial decision he'd made. Business can be murder out here.' Jean-Luc gave a lopsided smile, aimed at being disarming. Charlize didn't respond in the way he'd hoped. Instead, she continued to scowl at him. Damn, that smile certainly wasn't as strong a weapon in his charm armoury as he'd thought. At least not where one blonde, single-minded, stubborn woman was concerned.

'You mean someone put a hit out on him?'

'No, that's not what I said,' he hedged. 'It's not really that dramatic. These little…skirmishes, or differences of opinion, are more of a common occurrence than you might think.'

'You're saying you get shot every day?' Her eyebrows rose in disbelief. 'You certainly live in a very different world to me, Louis.'

'No, that *doesn't* happen every day,' he countered, wanting to say more, but knowing he couldn't. So he waited. But she sat there staring at him, a slight frown on her face, lips puckered in what he took for disappointment.

'What I do is completely legal, be assured of that.' For some reason, it was important she didn't think he was as dirty as those dogs who worked for Vincent. He could never tell her the truth of what he did for a living, it'd put himself and his whole team in jeopardy. But damn, he was suddenly desperate that she didn't think badly of him. 'I'm registered with a legit company, who only take jobs that are considered above board. Our company is audited yearly by the government, so we have to be squeaky clean.'

Seeming to ignore his last comment, she said, 'So I'm in no danger from these two men, then? They don't know you were in my garden? They won't be knocking on my door in the middle of the night?'

'Not at all. You're completely safe. Those men have absolutely no idea I was in your garden.' *Merde*, how he hoped that was true. 'We got our man to safety, and those two thugs took off. They missed their opportunity, end of story. They won't come back.'

'Hmm,' she murmured, unconvinced.

'But I want you to keep my number handy. Just in case anything...problematic happens.'

'Problematic?'

He couldn't let on he knew all about her past, about her being a cop, so he had to hedge around his answer. Being an ex-cop, she'd know what he was talking about.

'In case anyone starts asking you questions,' he replied.

She shot him a narrowed-gaze, pursed-lip look again, leaving him without a doubt she'd already come to the same conclusion. And she wasn't happy about it. Not one little bit. She knew there was a possibility those men could come back looking for her.

* * *

Shit. Shit. Shit. This man was trouble. She should've screamed when she'd had the chance back in her garden. Gotten him arrested and out of her life for good. Thrown in jail, where he probably belonged.

But that would've been no guarantee of her safety. If those men had heard her scream and come over her wall, she could well have been their next target. She'd done the right thing. But it didn't make her any less infuriated. With him, or with herself?

She wasn't sure how much of Louis' story to believe. Then again, what choice did she have? If it was a concocted story—and her instinct was telling her there was a high probability of that—then he wasn't about to turn around and tell her the truth just because she called him out on his bullshit.

Glowering at him from beneath lowered eyelashes, she tried to decide whether he was actually a bad man or not. Then he gave her one of his bloody disarming grins, with those straight white teeth, making the corners of his eyes crinkle with humour. It didn't help her decide what to do when he was so damn good-looking.

Just then, the waitress appeared. Talking in rapid French to them both so that Charlize was soon left behind and she had to ask Louis to repeat the question.

As soon as the waitress heard Charlize speak, she

switched to English, apologising profusely. 'So sorry, Mademoiselle, I did not realise you were a tourist.'

'Not a tourist, exactly,' said Charlize. 'I'm staying here in Uzes for a while.'

'Such a beautiful town, *oui*?' The girl gesticulated with her hands as she spoke. Her smile was friendly, but it didn't quite reach all the way to her eyes. 'Lots of the English, they come here for a week and end up staying forever.' Charlize forgave the girl for mistaking her as English. She was just trying to be friendly. Charlize couldn't fault her for that. 'Where are you staying? I have a friend who has a villa for rent, if you look for somewhere cheap,' the girl continued. Out of the corner of her eye, Charlize saw Jean-Luc shift in his seat.

'I'm fine, thank you. I have a wonderful villa up on Rue Xavier Sigalon. It's got everything I need.'

'*Oui*. I think I know the villa. Just behind the tourist information? That is a wonderful place to stay. I hope you are enjoying your time here.'

The girl had just opened her mouth to continue to wax lyrical when Louis cleared his throat. 'Would you like to order now? I can highly recommend the pizza.'

'Ah, *excusez-moi*, I get carried away by your beautiful lady.' The waitress bobbed her head in Charlize's direction. 'I will take your order now.'

'Pizza would be perfect, thank you,' Charlize replied with a laugh. 'You decide on the toppings, I'll eat just about anything. Surprise me.'

'Do you like anchovies?'

'I love them.'

Once the waitress had hurried back to the kitchen to convey their orders, Louis leant back in his chair and picked up his glass of Kir. 'She was very friendly. I think she likes you.' He gave her a suggestive wink.

'Yes, she is enthusiastic.' she said, also picking up her Kir. 'But I'm not the one she had her eye on.' Charlize couldn't condemn the girl. What woman wouldn't take a second—or third—glance at Louis.

'So, back to our conversation. Anything else you'd like to know about me?' He raised one eyebrow in a rakish question mark.

'Not at the moment. I'll let you know if I need more details,' she replied coolly, determined not to let his boyish charm take *her* in. She raised her glass toward him.

'*Salute,*' he replied. She took a sip. The cool slide of the sugary liquid ran over her tongue. It was good, and she took another large gulp. White wine and crème de cassis, a lusciously light drink to whet the palate. They sat, taking sips of the apéritif, not speaking.

'I haven't tried this restaurant yet,' she admitted, deciding the silence had stretched on long enough. 'I think the waitress must've scared me away.' She cast a mock-suspicious glance toward the café door. He let out a large laugh, and she had an absurd urge to make him laugh again. To hear the deep rumbling, rich sound that reminded her of molten lava pouring down a mountainside. His eyes also gained a wicked sparkle when he laughed, that teased at something cold and dark inside her, loosened the tight knots, easing them just a little.

'They do the best pizza in the whole of Europe,' he said expansively, downing the last of his Kir and signalling for the waitress. 'And the best beer, too. Would you care for one?'

'I'd love one,' she said with delight. She hadn't really

bothered with the beer here in France, assuming it wouldn't be as good as the Aussie version. Trying as many of the French wines as she possibly could instead. It'd be a nice change to go back to beer; a reminder of home. She watched as Louis ordered.

'Well, I tell a bit of a lie. It's the best beer apart from this one brewery back in my hometown,' he continued with a waggle of his eyebrows.

'Where's that?' she asked, curious now as to where this intriguing man with a gun and an attitude came from.

'Sault, up on the edge of the mountains, to the northeast of here.'

'Oh yes, I haven't been there yet, but I'd love to visit one day. I hear they grow the best lavender in the area,' she added wistfully. Lavender was one of her favourite things in the whole world. It was the embodiment of sunshine and luxury and divine bouquets. The purest essential oils valued more than gold in some ancient cultures. She'd often wondered if she'd ever be able to convince her father to switch from growing canola on his farm to lavender. It was an imprudent thought, one her father would never agree to, but Charlize liked to dream, nonetheless.

'Yes, we do,' he replied.

Charlize frowned at him, uncertain. What did he mean by *we*? He caught her confused look and grinned.

'My family owns a lavender farm.'

Oh. My. God. His family owned a lavender farm? Who was this man? He carried a gun for a living, had a father who'd escaped as a refugee from Sudan and was born and raised as a country boy in Provence. He couldn't be more of an enigma.

'It's been in our family for four generations now, on my

mother's side.'

'Wow,' was all she could manage. Just then, their beers arrived, and she was given an excuse to stop staring at him like he was some kind of apparition.

'So now we've finished the inquisition, do you mind if I start with the small talk instead?'

'Go right ahead.' A small, apologetic grin played over her lips. They'd done everything backwards tonight, dispensing with all the get-to-know-you small talk at the start. She'd come here to get answers, and that'd been her only objective. Now the Kir was giving her a gentle tingle of warmth low in her stomach, she found herself relaxing in Louis' presence, much to her surprise. But there was no way this was going to become a date. That's not what this meeting was about. Sure, she'd play the game, have a conversation with him, eat some nice food. But that's where it'd end. Patty might've convinced herself Charlize was going on a date, but she knew better.

'You have a wonderful accent. With your talk about Australian men, I'm assuming that's where you come from?' Those strange copper eyes gave her his full attention. It unnerved her just how completely and wholly he focussed on her. Taking a sip of her beer, she broke their eye-contact and looked down at the bottle. It *was* good beer. She'd have to remember this local brand and stock some in her fridge.

'Yep, you're right, I'm an Aussie,' she answered, clearing her throat a little after the frothy beverage.

'Ah, that's one place I've never been, but I hear it's nearly as beautiful as France.'

She laughed at his parochial statement. Nowhere was ever quite as good as France to a Frenchman.

'It's very different from France. But there are some places just as beautiful as here,' she challenged.

They carried on their banter, Louis asking questions about her life in Australia, how long she'd been in Uzes, how long she planned to stay. And she shot answers back at him, parrying with her own questions about where he lived now and the lavender farm in Sault that so fascinated her. He was surprisingly easy to talk to. It'd been a while since she'd talked to a man one-on-one like this. Even longer since she'd been on a date. Not that this was a date.

He never asked her if she was seeing anyone, and she never countered with her own query. He also never asked about the scars on her leg. Without a doubt, he'd seen them, but for some reason, he didn't bring it up.

Louis ordered them another beer each, and then their pizza arrived and they stopped talking to devour their food. It was as good as he'd predicted. She'd definitely come back to this restaurant again, if she could bear to face the waitress.

After they'd devoured two whole pizzas between them, she sat back in her chair and rested her hands over her distended stomach.

'Oh wow, I've eaten way too much.'

'Me too,' he agreed with a wolfish smile. 'But it was worth every mouthful.' He patted his stomach in imitation of her. 'Shall we finish with a cognac? It's a bit of a tradition for me after a wonderful meal.'

'Oh, yes, please.' There was nothing better than the smooth French brandy. They sipped their cognac and watched the comings and goings of other cafés and restaurants around The Place, listening to the vibrant hum of a summer evening unfold. Their corner of The Place was sheltered by the overhanging branches of a huge plane tree, which blocked out any view of the sky, but Charlize could imagine the stars as they started to come out above them in the darkening sky.

Without her conscious approval, her gaze was repeatedly drawn to Louis' forearms, her eyes roamed over the firm, brown skin, then traversed up to where the sky-blue shirt was rolled to the elbows, and then upwards again to where the fabric bulged with the breadth of his biceps. She remembered his hands from the day before, how strong and agile and attractive they were. Tonight, while his hands were still beautiful, it was the open shirt, with the muscles of his neck and upper chest that she couldn't tear her eyes away from. What lay beneath those few buttons? If she were to undo them one at a time, slowly revealing his pecs, his torso. There was no doubt in her mind his stomach would be awash with a set of killer abs.

These thoughts were taboo, but the alcohol in her system was blunting her judgement just enough that she no longer cared. Mellow and chilled, she glanced again at the hollow beneath his open shirt collar. In the dying light, his skin was darkening from a coffee colour to burnt toffee. The image of his dark skin suddenly pulled a memory from the recess of her mind. A little boy with skin the colour of liquorice.

'I found a little boy the other day,' she said before she could stop herself. A slight frown hovered on Louis' brows, but he had an expectant air that prompted her to go on. All of a sudden, she was pouring out the tale of the little African boy she'd discovered. The image still burned her memory, the pain in his sad eyes still seared into her own soul. She'd told Patty about her encounter, but the way she'd worded it had been more of a clinical re-telling, looking for Patty's take on what'd happened. A silent plea for Patty's professional agreement, she'd done the right thing, the only thing possible under the circumstances. To hand him over to the authorities. She hadn't admitted to Patty about all the phone calls she made, however. Trying to find out what'd happened to the boy afterward. Atone for her sins.

But with Louis, it was different. Perhaps it was the compassion in his furrowed brow and solemn mouth, loosening that tight rein she kept on her emotions. She found herself telling him how desperately alone the little boy had seemed, how her heart ached at the sight of him being loaded into the car like a bundle of discarded rags and driven away to an uncertain future. Perhaps it was the way Louis responded to her story. Those light hazel eyes growing serious, the twinkle replaced by a hard flat brown.

After she'd run out of words, he'd slid his hand across the table and let his fingers rest on top of hers.

'I still don't know if I did the right thing,' she admitted.

'What else could you have done?' he asked softly. 'It's so hard…this refugee problem. The government does its best to stop them from coming, to try and help them when they're here. But it's still not good enough.' His fingers stroked the skin on the back of her hand, his touch feather-light and electrifying at the same time. 'It's not the illegal immigrants' fault, they just want to find a better life. I feel so sad for them too. It's all such a mess,' he finished quietly.

Charlize was amazed by his empathy for the refugees. She could tell he wasn't putting on an act, saying these things just to mollify her. *Oh damn.* Of course, he knew exactly what that little boy had gone through. His own father was a refugee, fleeing from war-torn Sudan. What an imbecile she was. Bringing up this subject, admitting she'd just sent a poor innocent child off to be processed in some far away camp, perhaps even sent back to his own country. Shit, she hoped she hadn't insulted Louis in any way.

'Oh God.' She put her hand to her mouth. 'I'm so sorry, Louis. I wasn't even thinking.'

'Don't worry, Charlize, you haven't offended me.' That cheeky grin resettled on his lips. 'My father's experience was quite different from what's happening today. And besides, if he hadn't taken that dangerous journey, I wouldn't be here, talking to a beautiful woman under a Provencal night sky.'

Thank God he understood, she was only trying to do what was best for the boy. She'd love to hear the full story one day. How his mother and father met. It'd be an intriguing one, she'd bet on that. He still had hold of her hand. She reminded herself this man was dangerous, not to be taken at face value; not to be taken lightly. The last thing she should do was let him get under her skin. Like he was right now.

'Thank you for a nice evening,' she said, withdrawing her hand.

'Shall I walk you home?' It was a statement rather than a question. Why the hell shouldn't she let a gorgeous Frenchman walk her home? It was the last time she'd be seeing him, so there could be no harm in it.

'Sure,' she replied.

* * *

The urge to take her hand was strong. It swung mere centimetres away as they strolled up the main circular road through the town. She wouldn't appreciate it. And this was in no way a date. Even though it felt like one in every conceivable way. But he was rusty at this. Probably over-thinking things, over-estimating her allure, overrating his reaction to her proximity.

Her sandaled feet tapped lightly on the pavement as they walked and her skirt rippled around her ankles, the loose fabric brushed against his wrist now and then as it caught in the soft breeze.

They reached her door, the silence between them comfortable.

'Thanks again, Louis,' she said, turning to face him. He wanted to tell her that wasn't his real name. He wanted to ask her to have dinner with him again. The words caught in his throat, making him cough. What the hell was he thinking? He couldn't possibly ask her out again. Apart from the fact she'd definitely turn him down, there was the small complication of him being involved in an ongoing investigation. A very dangerous investigation; one that'd take up all his time and energy. Something he couldn't get her involved in. He couldn't afford to attract any more attention her way. He needed to leave her alone now, get as far away from her as possible, to remove any suspicion in Vincent's mind she was affiliated with him in any way.

'A very pleasant evening,' he replied as she took the first step up and inserted her key into the door latch. A half-moon had come out, hanging low in the sky to the east. It cast a pale glow over the cobblestone street, reflecting off her golden hair. Her lips were glistening in the moonlight. Another stupid urge overtook him. To kiss her. Just a quick brush of those luscious lips, nothing more. A swift goodbye.

'I guess I'll see you around.' He had to make a purposeful effort to refocus on what she was saying, dragging his concentration away from her full mouth and the way her lips parted as she drew in a breath. 'I've got your card, so if anything becomes *problematic*, I'll let you know,' she said.

'Ha, yes, problematic,' he replied. Let's hope that situation never eventuated. For her sake. 'I meant it in all honesty. Please don't hesitate to call if you think you might be in any...' he wanted to say danger, but it wouldn't do to scare her unnecessarily, so he said, 'need of assistance.' He caught her gaze and held it, trying to convey the seriousness of his words without having to say it out loud.

She nodded in reply. 'I can look after myself, Louis, but I'll keep that in mind.' He wasn't so sure, but he didn't say anything more. As an ex-cop she'd certainly have the skills to protect herself, he'd seen that first-hand the other evening in her garden. She'd been prepared to take him on if she had to. But then again, she'd probably never encountered anyone with Vincent's single-minded viciousness before.

'Goodnight, Charlize.' He let her name roll around on his tongue, savouring the word. Such a unique name, much like the woman it belonged to. He couldn't draw this farewell out any longer, he must go now and leave her to her safe life. So he gave a lopsided smile and stepped back. She gave a crooked smile in return, taking his retreat as the hint he'd intended, opened the door and disappeared inside.

Her smile played on his mind all the way back down the alleyway and around the corner into the main boulevard. The way only one corner of her mouth raised up made him think perhaps there'd also been an air of invitation as well. Had she wanted him to kiss her as much as he'd wanted it? It seemed to hold a hint of regret and maybe disappointment as well. Had he disappointed her in some way? Don't be stupid. He was reading way too much into that one small smile. And even if he had, there was nothing he could, or even should, do about it now.

Was he doing the right thing, leaving her to fend for herself? Was she truly safe here on her own in this little town? Pickard had tasked him with the job of finding out if she knew anything about Vincent, his gang, or his organisation. Told him to make sure she wasn't a threat to their op in any way.

He could go back to Pickard with good conscience and tell him she was in no way a threat. So why then was there an itch climbing along his spine which told him not to leave her alone? It was obvious she didn't know anything, but if Vincent ever happened to find out she'd helped him in any way, then she *would* be in danger.

He tried to shrug off the feeling of unease as he lengthened his stride and took off downhill toward where he'd parked his motorbike. There were still a few people left roaming the streets, emerging from the cafés and restaurants. It was a summer evening after all, and not really that late. Jean-Luc made sure to keep vigilant as he walked, avoiding all CCTV cameras, surreptitiously scoping the area, habit forcing him to plot all escape routes, catalogue every face, just in case.

Nothing out of the ordinary happened on the way to his motorbike, and a little of the weight that'd descended after leaving Charlize lifted from his shoulders. Shrugging on his riding jacket, he pulled his helmet down over his face and kicked the bike into life, never failing to delight at the deep, animalistic rumble of the engine as it purred to life. He'd chosen his Kawasaki Ninja because it blended in with the crowd. A common bike in France, plain black, it was completely unrecognisable. Just what he needed to make sure he stayed incognito. But he still loved riding it. It was powerful enough to get him out of any trouble if need be, fast as a hound from hell, and smooth and easy to ride. It was his ticket to freedom, as well as his mode of transport. He kept a little Peugeot 4WD garaged at his flat in Nice, but he hardly ever used the car. His preference was always the bike.

Knocking the bike into gear, he took off slowly down the circular ring-road, turning right onto the main concourse that'd lead him out of town. Uzes was beginning to grow on him. He could see why Charlize had chosen this place as her base. Although he'd love to show her Sault one day. Then she'd have to agree Uzes was not a patch on his hometown.

Mulling over the image of taking Charlize to see the attractions of Sault, he wound his way through the twists and turns of the road that led down through the valleys and out of town. It was dark down here, the infrequent street lights lending a flickering glow now and then.

Bright headlights came around a bend toward him, a low, sleek car hugged the road. He'd passed a few other cars on the road, and Jean-Luc was about to ignore this one as well, when something caught his attention. Something about the black car twigged in his memory and Jean-Luc tried to make out the face of the driver as they flashed by.

No. Surely not. It couldn't be.

Jean-Luc slowed his bike as he dissected the quick glimpse of the face he'd seen.

Merde. He couldn't be sure, but it might've been Enzo, Vincent's right-hand man, his main muscle. He hadn't caught a look at the face of the other man in the passenger seat, but it didn't really matter. If it was Enzo, then why was he heading up to Uzes at this time of night? Surely he couldn't be meeting a mark tonight.

Fuck. He didn't have time to stop and call Pickard if he was to turn around and tail the car. He'd have to make his own judgement call.

Braking hard, he swung the bike around and gunned it back up the road he'd just come down and followed in the wake of the disappearing headlights.

KIR

Is a popular French cocktail, served as a refreshing apéritif in most restaurants. Add about 3 tablespoons crème de cassis (a wonderful blackcurrant liqueur) to the bottom of the glass, then top up with your favourite sparkling wine. (French Champagne if you can afford it.)

BEST MARGHERITA PIZZA EVER

INGREDIENTS
3⅓ cups Strong bread or pizza flour
(It's important you use the right kind of flour)
1 sachet (7g) Dried yeast
1 tsp Caster sugar
300ml water
3tsp Olive oil, plus extra, for greasing
15 g Fine sea salt

Topping
Can of crushed tomatoes
Dried oregano
Mozzarella Cheese cubed
Fresh basil
Salt and Pepper

DIRECTIONS
Place your flour in a mound on your work surface and make a well in the centre. Add the yeast and sugar to the centre of the well, then pour in the water and oil and combine until the dough comes together in a ball. Add the salt, then knead on a lightly floured surface for about 10 minutes or until smooth and elastic. Place the dough in a lightly oiled bowl and cover with plastic wrap, then stand in a warm spot to prove for 1 hour or until doubled in size. If you want your pizza to taste even more amazing, let the dough mature by refrigerating overnight.

Take your dough, punch it down in the middle, then knead for 30 seconds or so.

Roll out to about 0.5 centimetres thick so that it fits your desired pan, then press the dough into the pan with your fingertips, which stops it rising in the centre.

Spread the crushed tomatoes over the dough, top with dried oregano and salt and pepper. Top with cubes of mozzarella cheese and lots of basil, plus more salt.

Cook in a 230°C oven for five minutes or until crispy and golden and gooey and delicious.

Serve with a chilled glass of Kir and sit in the shade on a balmy summer evening while enjoying the crisp simplicity of homemade pizza with the man of your dreams.

CHAPTER SEVEN

Charlize let the warm liquid slide down her throat and gave a soft sigh. She liked her tea well-brewed, dark, with a splash of milk. The hot beverage washed away some of the shadowy fatigue. Her bad leg ached like a bitch and she'd probably have to take some pain relief tonight, not something she liked to do. But the fatigue was the result of a great day out, and she didn't regret one minute of her over-exertion. She and Patty had spent the day exploring the nearby Pont du Gard, a two thousand year old aqueduct, a relic from the Roman era. It never failed to delight her, every time she set foot on those ancient stones, that something made by human hand could be so old and so beautiful. One of the many attractions of France, the wonderful history, steeped in myth and tradition that lay everywhere.

Patty was in the shower, washing off the sand and sunscreen after their swim in the Gardon River beneath the aqueduct. The water had been cold, but refreshing after the oppressive heat of the day. They'd lain on the sand while the other tourists and locals frolicked with their kids in the shallows. Afterwards, dinner had been a jolly affair at Charlize's favourite restaurant in town, and they'd only just arrived home, walking arm in arm up the alley beneath the starry velvet sky.

It was a good day. She enjoyed Patty's company, reminded of just how easy it was to be with her. But a few times during their adventurous day she'd found herself stopped, mid-step, staring but not seeing what was right in front of her, as a memory triggered. Having Patty so near, seeing her face, hearing her voice, was chipping away at the walls Charlize had built around her frozen memories. Memories of the crash.

She'd had a dream last night, too. Not the bad one, not the one where she relived the crash all over again in singular, minute detail. This one had been about home. About riding Xeon through a field of Canola. She'd floated on his back, the rhythm of his pounding hooves beneath her thighs, the smell of his earthy, damp hair as he galloped in pure pleasure. Her pillow had been wet when she woke.

Patty started to sing in the shower, her off-key voice muffled by the walls and the running water. Charlize smiled as she walked to the kitchen window, cup in hand, and stared out into the darkness. A few lights winked back at her from the main street as the sound of the water running in the shower rapped inside her head. It reminded her of rain.

Charlize remembered the smattering sound of rain on the windscreen the night of the crash. A vehicle pulled into the carpark at the end of her alleyway, the headlights flashing brightly into her eyes. A car flashing its headlights the same way reminded her of the dark country road two years ago. Against her will, Charlize was drawn into the memory.

The road unfurled in front of her, windscreen wipers ticking back and forth. Her headlights picked out tall stands of eucalyptus trees by the side of the road and the red reflectors on the guideposts, winking at her like demented wild animals crouched by the side of the road. The rest of the countryside was just a sea of blackness spreading all around them, as if they were in a bubble of light floating along the roadway. A car on the other side of the road flashed past, its headlights almost blinding her for a second, but then it was gone.

She took a quick look in the rear vision mirror and then both side mirrors. Checking the horse float being towed behind the Land Cruiser tracked smoothly and the horses weren't moving around too much. It all seemed calm and normal back there. The drive from Corrigin to Perth was only two and a half hours, probably less when the road was open and empty like it was now. Not many other people would be mad enough to drive in the country at two o'clock in the morning.

'I can't wait to crawl into my bed. I could sleep for a week. Thank God we don't have a shift tomorrow,' said Patty from the passenger seat.

'Me too,' Charlize replied.

'The crowd was well behaved today, I thought,' said Patty. 'Not a single arrest.'

'Yeah, it was good. Xeon got lots of pats, especially from the young kids.' Charlize smiled at the memory of how Xeon, her police horse, seemed to draw people to him. They all wanted to touch the huge, brown-eyed Percheron-cross. He was such a big softie and people seemed to sense he wouldn't hurt them. His gentle nature often had a calming effect on large throngs of people, keeping them well-behaved. She and Patty had been called to help with crowd control at one of the major jazz festivals of the year in West Australia, Corrigin Jazz and Blues Night. The last band had finished at midnight, and they'd managed to shoo the final stragglers out of the large fenced-off area just after one o'clock. Now they had to get themselves and their horses back to Perth.

'There were a couple of hotties there tonight, too. I thought it'd only be old folks. I'm glad I was wrong.' Charlize didn't bother to glance across the darkened cabin, but she could well imagine the lascivious look on Patty's face. 'There was one really cute guy patting VanDam. Maybe I should've asked for his phone number.'

'Patty, you were on duty.' Charlize was only half incredulous. She was used to Patty's antics by now.

'Yeah, yeah. I think VanDam is going to help me meet my future husband one day.' Charlize just snorted. VanDam wasn't nearly as sweet-tempered as Xeon. He was a large, black Waler, sturdy and bomb-proof. He was solid as a rock when it came to controlling unruly crowds, but he could be a bit of a grumpy old man, and always remained a little aloof from the noise and bustle, as if he were above all that silly human nonsense.

A set of headlights appeared over a low rise a long way ahead of them.

'Wow, he's going a little fast.' Patty's eyes fixed on the car coming toward them.

'Yeah, especially in this rain,' agreed Charlize. Fast and a little crazy. The car swerved across the road before it returned to its own side again.

'You should maybe—'

'I am,' Charlize replied as she pushed the brakes lightly to slow the car down. Just in case. The Land Cruiser with the float behind it was heavy and required a large stopping distance. She was trained to handle any emergency. This guy was possibly drunk, and he definitely shouldn't be on the road.

The other car careened around a last bend, then came down the straight toward them and she was almost blinded by the high-beam. She slowed the car even further. Then the other car started to veer onto their side of the road. Charlize pulled the Land Cruiser as far over to her side as she could get without dropping the wheel in the gravel at the edge.

'Move over, you fucker,' Patty screamed. But he kept coming until he was fully in their lane. Charlize had no choice, she had to go off the edge of the bitumen. The left wheel bit into the wet gravel and threatened to wrench the steering wheel from her hands, but she was ready for it and compensated, bracing her hands until her knuckles went white.

But the other car didn't stop there, it still veered toward them. The only way for her to avoid a head-on collision was to go completely off the road. The grass was thick and brown at the edge of the verge, slick with rain.

'Charlie, look out,' Patty screamed again just as the deep ditch appeared beyond the grass. The left-side wheels both dropped into the ditch and the car started to slide, the wheels spinning on the gravel, the float pulling them further sideways. Until with a sickening screech, the car and float flipped onto their sides and nosedived into the ditch. Gravel spewed up in front of the windscreen, and the world shattered around her.

'Charli, you okay?' A warm hand touched her shoulder and Charlize jumped.

'Sorry, I was miles away,' she replied as she turned quickly away from Patty to put the cup on the table with a clang, images still clinging to her mind.

'You've gone pale, are you sure you're okay?' Patty's face was creased with concern.

'I'm fine,' she said, putting more energy into her voice than she actually felt. 'I just…you know…sometimes, I still remember, like it was only yesterday.'

'Oh, Hon.' Patty's arms wrapped around Charlize and she held her friend in a fierce embrace. It was so like Patty. So warm and caring and spontaneous. Charlize hadn't had much human contact in the past eighteen months, and Patty's embrace was good. The warmth of her friend's arms around her shoulders loosened something that'd wound ever tighter in her chest. 'Me too,' Patty continued. 'But the psych said they would get better. The dreams. The bad thoughts. Slowly. But they will.' Patty tipped her head up and searched Charlize's eyes. 'We will be whole again one day. The both of us.' There was such fierce determination in Patty's tone, Charlize dare not argue with her. Not out loud, anyway. Her police-appointed therapist had said something similar, but Charlize hadn't seen a proper shrink since she'd been in Europe. She preferred to cope on her own.

They sat at the kitchen table and chatted for another half an hour about their day. Patty gently ribbed Charlize about her date with Jean-Luc, *again*, while Charlize denied it'd ever been a date. Patty could no longer contain the huge yawns that threatened to split her face.

'I've got to go to bed, Hon. So we can get up early to drive to Marseille.' Patty was flying home tomorrow. Which saddened Charlize. But there was a flicker of relief there as well. They said goodnight to each other on the stairs and Charlize climbed into bed with a sigh, then lay staring at the ceiling for a long, long time. She wasn't scared to go to sleep. Not exactly. But the dreams more than likely lurked there, waiting. Eventually, her eyes closed, and she drifted off.

Charlize opened her eyes a crack and surveyed her surroundings, tried to remember where she was. What'd just happened? Her head felt grey and vague, as if filled with the buzzing noise of a radio out of tune. It was dim, but not completely dark. A light came from outside. A headlight maybe? It cast crazy shadows on the tall brown grass crowding in on her from all sides. That's when it came to her. She was in the cabin of the Land Cruiser. But for some reason the car was on its side, and she hung at an awkward angle, her seatbelt the only thing that kept her from tumbling sideways.

The night was filled with sounds. Terrible sounds. Nightmarish sounds. Twisted metal creaked and groaned around her as the broken car and horse float settled into the mud. There was the hiss of steam escaping, and the patter of liquid splattering on the ground. Then she heard Patty give a moan. Not a low-pitched, quiet sound, but a high warbling snarl. Oh shit. Patty! She wanted to shout. Ask her if she was okay, but no words would form. Her tongue was stuck to the roof of her mouth.

Then Patty's pain dimmed to irrelevance. Her moaning was nothing compared to the screams of the horses. Guttural sounds that wrenched at her heart and mind. The car rocked with the movements of the two horses as they grunted and struggled to free themselves from the ruined float. Hooves smashed into wood, and she could hear loud, irregular thumps. They would've been tipped on their sides when the float had overturned, Xeon probably on top of VanDam. One of the horses squealed over and over and over again, terror and pain echoed in every gasp. She had to go to the animals, do something to ease their fear.

'Charli,' Patty shouted through gritted teeth. 'Charli, can you hear me?'

'Patty. Fuck. Fuck. Yes, I'm here.' She had to yell to be heard over the top of the screaming horses. Patty was curled into the foetal position on the bottom of the cab below her.

'Can you move?' asked Patty.

'I don't know. Can you?'

'No, there's something wrong with my hip. You'll have to see if you can get out.' Holy fuck. How was she going to get out of here? She'd have to break her side window. There was a small hammer, kept secured next to her seat for such an emergency.

'Cover your eyes, Patty, I've got to break the window.'

When she smacked the hammer into the window, small cubes of glass rained down on her. She was panting heavily now, the cool night air welcome on her sweat-soaked face. A light mist drifted down through the broken square of window. At least the heavy, pounding rain seemed to have eased up.

Next, she had to undo her seatbelt. Reaching her right arm through what was left of the steering wheel, she contorted her body, scrunching so she could reach down to her waist. That's when the pain seared through her abdomen.

'Argh,' she grunted, gritting her teeth against the pain.

'What?' Fear blossomed in Patty's voice.

'Nothing. I'm just a little caught up. Don't worry, I'll get us out of here.' After she jiggled the buckle a few times, it finally released, and she jolted sideways, gravity dragging her downwards. The movement sent shards of fire and ice slicing through her belly, and she only just managed to hang onto the wheel, to stop herself from crashing down on top of Patty. She squeezed her eyes shut and hung on, willing the pain to subside. After a few seconds, the knives cutting her insides to ribbons receded to a more manageable level, and she exhaled, readying herself for the ordeal of clambering out of the window above her.

Five minutes later, she stood in the long, wet grass, bent over nearly double, using the bonnet of the car to support herself. It must be an internal injury, perhaps the steering wheel had hit her in the stomach during the crash? She wanted to vomit, but she wasn't sure if it was from the pain or the shock. Tingles of panic, like a trail of ants, crawled down her spine. The baby! Oh God, the baby. Please, please, please, don't let her lose the baby.

Her mind shied away from the terror of those thoughts. She needed to focus. To get Patty and the horses out, call for help. The only way she was going to make sure the baby was okay was to get to a hospital. Once she had her breath back, she dialled 0-0-0 and conveyed their predicament in short, rational sentences. Help was on the way.

As she tried to straighten up, more mind-numbing pain slashed through her, so Charlize shuffled around the front of the car, bent over like an old woman. What was that smell? It smelt like... Oh Jesus; it was petrol. That's the sound she'd heard in the cab as liquid splashed on the ground. Petrol leaking from the tank. Not the rain, after all. She needed to get Patty out, fast. And the horses too.

Shuffling around in the dark, she must have looked like some kind of zombie come to life. In the beam of the headlights, she finally found what she needed, a broken piece of the metal bull-bar. Calling out to Patty to cover her face again, Charlize used the metal bar like a baseball bat and swung it at the windscreen. Every movement sent another fiery pain through her abdomen, sweat was now running freely down her back and between her breasts.

The window was broken, but she had to stop for uncounted seconds, bent over and gasping, just to get her breath back and quell the nausea and pain. The light mist of rain still drifted down and it seeped through her hair into her scalp, her police uniform turning a darker shade of blue in the damp.

'Patty, I'm going to drag you out through the front. Can you help me at all?'

'I don't think I can move, Charli. Can we wait until the ambulance gets here?'

'No, you have to get out, Pat.'

'I can't,' Patty wailed like a small child.

'You have to, there's petrol leaking everywhere.'

'Oh. Shit!'

'Can you move your feet, and your hands?' Charlize asked, trying to rein in her impatience, kneeling down in the gravel and mud, peering into the dim cabin.

'Yes, that's all fine. No spinal or neck injuries, as far as I can tell,' she finally replied. 'I'm going to kill that fucker when we get out of here,' Patty continued in a low growl. 'Why the fuck didn't he have the decency to stop and help us?' Charlize didn't bother to answer that question.

'Okay, we're still going to take it slow and careful.' Charlize braced her knees in the dirt and leaned forward through the broken window.

Suddenly Charlize stopped what she was doing and straightened up. There was something wrong. But what? The horses still struggled to get out, still emitted the occasional terrified scream. The rest of the world outside their bubble of light and smashed vehicle remained quiet and dark. Then it came to her on a waft of the night air.

Smoke.

She could smell smoke.

'Shit, Patty, we gotta get you out now.' Charlize bent in and started to haul on Patty's arms, ignoring her screams of pain, which turned to pleas to just leave her there, she didn't care if she died, just please stop hurting her. The smell of smoke got stronger.

Then flames licked up over the edge of the upturned car. Xeon. She had to get Xeon out. She couldn't let her horse die, not in some fiery inferno. Xeon was her life, her best friend. As much of a partner as Patty was. It took every ounce of determination she had not to rush around to the back of the float and open the door, to answer his squeals of fear and rescue him. But she couldn't leave Patty.

'Jesus Christ.' Her expletive was punctuated by a grunt of pain as she made one final haul and Patty slithered out of the smashed car cabin, to lie on her back in the mud at Charlize's feet. Patty was now hysterical with pain and would be no help. There was no way she'd be able to get Patty up onto her shoulder in a fireman's lift, so she did the only thing she could, she took her by the forearms and dragged her on her back, slowly but surely toward the road, away from the smoking ruin of the car.

'Please stop, Charli, please,' sobbed Patty, beyond hysterical now. They were about a hundred meters down the road, on the verge on the other side. Charlize would've liked to have taken Patty further away, but her friend's screaming, along with the tearing pain in her guts, gave her no choice but to stop there. They should be far enough away if the car did explode.

Charlize rolled Patty onto her uninjured side, as gently as she could, into the recovery position. The small grass fire had spread slowly but surely, lighting the car and float up in ghostly orange hues. Tall tongues of flame danced hungrily into the air.

Charlize took one step and then another toward the burning wreck. Every step made her want to stop and sob with pain. There was a flare and a bang, and then the fire grew exponentially in size. As fast as her legs would take her, she shuffled forward, toward the back of the damaged float. Xeon and VanDam still struggled inside, reacting to the smell of smoke. The double doors to the float remained closed, but the door on the left-hand side was buckled and bent, leaving a gap Charlize could peer through into the interior. Xeon must have heard or sensed her outside, because he suddenly started neighing, a wild sound, asking her to help him.

'I'm coming, boy,' she soothed, while desperately looking around for a piece of metal or wood she could use to lever open the door.

There was an almighty explosion. A whoosh of air blew her backwards off her feet and heat and flames rose like an orange supernova into the sky.

Screams filled her ears. Screams louder than anything she'd ever heard before. The sound tore at her throat and lungs so she could no longer breathe, but she kept screaming. Darkness engulfed her, she felt trapped, suffocated, unable to move. Her legs were burning, entangled in something…

'Charli. Wake up. Charli?' A voice sounded in her ear.

'Wha…' Charlize opened her eyes, but it took a few seconds to realise where she was.

'Charli, you were dreaming. Are you awake now? It was just a dream.' It was Patty. Turning her head, she found her friend's face hovering next to hers as she leaned over the bed. Everything was indistinct in the dim light of the bedroom, but she could make out her eyes wide with distress, her brows drawn together in a deep frown.

'Sorry,' Charlize said, struggling to sit up. 'I didn't mean to wake you.'

'It's not a problem, Hon. I was worried about you. You were screaming loud enough to wake the neighbours three doors up.' Patty let out a gush of relieved air now that Charlize was okay and went to sit on the end of her bed. Her heart rate was still skittering along at a thousand miles an hour, and she took a few deep breaths to calm herself. This had been a bad one. It'd seemed so real. It always seemed so real.

'It must be my influence,' said Patty with a smile in her voice. They both knew there was a kernel of truth in her statement. Patty visiting had brought all those raw memories crashing back to the surface. 'But when my dreams are bad, having Mike around helps a lot,' Patty confided. 'He makes me feel safer somehow.'

'That's good, Pat.' Charlize replied. 'I'm glad he's good for you.' Oh, how Charlize envied Patty the comfort that only a lover could give. She didn't begrudge her friend the fact she'd found someone. But her heart contracted at the thought she might never find her own. The lump in her throat tightened its grip, and she decided to change the mood. It did no good to dwell on these things, it only made her even more despondent and bitter.

So she plastered a false grin on her face and said, 'I bet that's not the only thing Mike's good at though, hey?'

'Charlize!' Patty leaned in and squeezed her kneecap in solidarity. 'How right you are. He is *very* good in bed.' Now it was Charlize's turn to act flabbergasted at her friend's intimate revelation.

They sat chatting for the next few minutes, Charlize content to let Patty prattle on about how great Mike was, as if she hadn't already heard most of his virtues being extolled already. While Patty's happy chatter filled the room, it slowly drove away the last vestiges of the dream, so that the flames no longer burned into Charlize's retinas and her leg no longer screamed in agony.

'You wanna try going back to sleep now?' Patty asked at last.

'Yeah, I think I'll give it a go. What about you?'

'Of course. When have you ever known me to turn down an opportunity to sleep?' Patty said with a laugh. 'Besides, I'll need some more sleep to get me through that horror flight tomorrow.'

'Are you sure you don't want to stay any longer, Pat? Five days isn't long, especially after you've flown all the way over here.'

'Nah, I've done what I came here to do. Make sure

you're okay and tell you my news. And now I have to get back and plan a bloody wedding. Do you know how much hard work they are?'

'Okay, I'll get you up around eight o'clock, then we can drive into Marseille.' Charlize deftly changed the subject, not able to face the whole wedding saga thing at this ungodly hour of the morning. Once Patty got started on that topic, she was like a runaway steam train. 'That'll give us enough time to have a bit of a look around and perhaps do some shopping before you get on your flight in the evening.'

'Sounds great. Those little boutique shops you told me about with all those wonderful dresses sound amazing. See you at eight then.' She bounced off the bed, came around and gave Charlize a quick hug, and then padded off to her own bedroom.

'Night, Patty,' Charlize called after her friend. She lay back down, but sleep was a long way away. She started thinking about how nice it'd be to have a man to wrap his strong arms around her, cocoon her into his chest and soothe her back to sleep with the sound of his strong heartbeat beneath her cheek. If only she had a man like Patty's. A pair of enticing golden-coppery eyes appeared on the canvas of her mind. Made all the more exceptional when paired with mocha coloured skin and a dark goatee beard.

CHAPTER EIGHT

While relatively small, Marseille's airport was still a bustling, busy, chaotic place. And Jean-Luc was fast becoming infuriated with it. Because he couldn't find her.

Pushing his way through a crowd of Japanese tourists, who'd stopped in the middle of the thoroughfare so they could all gather around a piece of luggage to open it and pull clothes out haphazardly, he let out an oath. He needed to find her. She was here somewhere.

Jean-Luc's stomach had been a twisted mess of knots for the past two days. Ever since he'd seen Enzo driving up the road toward Uzes in the dead of night. Running a hand over his face, he could feel the stubble emerging from two days of not shaving. He knew he looked worse for wear. He'd hardly slept in those two days, and now he was on edge and irritable. The urge to break into a run was great, but he fought it as he cast his gaze around the crowded main terminal, using his height to full advantage to spot her.

There. A flash of golden curls. It must be Charlize, headed toward gate number four. Lengthening his stride as much as the swirling mass of people and luggage would allow, he headed in her direction.

Relief poured through him like a warm breeze. It *was* her. And there was Patty's diminutive form standing next to her. Vincent wouldn't try something in broad daylight with thousands of people around. He'd found her just in time. If she'd made it back to the carpark, where there were fewer witnesses and easier escape routes, Vincent's gang would've snatched her.

There were six of them prowling the perimeters of the airport. Six of Vincent's men. Enzo was there, as well as Fabio—which Jean-Luc now knew was the name of the other guy who'd been in Uzes at the fateful meeting-gone-wrong. Jean-Luc had spotted them, looking out of place with their unsmiling glares and stiff, predatory stances. Only those two knew what Jean-Luc looked like, but they'd probably passed on his description by now. He'd just have to take his chances. He'd bought a cap sporting a motive of Marseille and some dark glasses from a souvenir shop out the front in a bad attempt at a rudimentary disguise. Then he'd managed to snatch up a suitcase that'd been sitting in a row with ten or so others, with only one teenager left to guard them, who was more interested in his mobile phone than watching bags. There was no way to change the colour of his skin, but with the huge multicultural crowd milling around the airport, he wouldn't stand out.

Pickard hadn't been pleased when he'd called yesterday with the news. Not one bit. Jean-Luc remembered with a grim smile having to hold the phone away from his ear at Pickard's vociferous disapproval. His main concern was the time Jean-Luc spent protecting Charlize, was time lost on the real mission. It chafed at Jean-Luc as well. He might be losing precious ground. But in the end, Pickard agreed they couldn't consciously let a civilian be put in jeopardy. His boss had tried damn hard to persuade Jean-Luc to take the meeting with the new partner he'd lined up for him, but Jean-Luc had fended off that suggestion. Both of them knew it was too late for anyone else to join in Jean-Luc's little game of cat and mouse. Not now. Not at this stage of the game.

Pickard wouldn't allow Patrice and Nico to be dragged away from their surveillance of one of the mansions attached to the businessman, Franco Pirajno. So as backup for Jean-Luc, he'd sent another man, Paul Donally, pulled from another anti-smuggling unit, pursuing a less urgent op, to help him out.

He stopped next to a large pillar. Close enough to see Charlize and Patty clearly, but partially hidden by the column. Let Patty leave first, board her plane, and return home. That'd remove at least one risk factor from the equation. He'd grab Charlize on her way back out of the terminal. Now he had her in his sights and knew she was safe, he allowed himself a couple of deep breaths. Pulling the cap lower on his forehead, he cast a shrewd gaze around the airport.

It'd been a hell of a few days. From the second he'd turned his motorbike around to chase the sleek black car back up the hill, his instincts had been humming, telling him something was off. He'd followed the car until it pulled up in the carpark in the middle of Uzes; the one with the alleyway running behind Charlize's house. The prickles running up his spine had become more like a march of ants. He'd switched the motorbike's headlight off and quickly parked it down a side street. Then he'd run back to the carpark, just in time to see two shadows slide around the corner into the alley. Approaching the mouth of the alley, he hadn't gone in. That would've been suicide. Standing at the corner, he peered around the edge. The two shadows stopped just outside the pool of light cast by the single, weak lamplight in the alley. Jean-Luc slowed his breathing as quickly as he could. He needed to hear what they were saying.

'That's the one,' he heard Enzo say in a stage whisper. 'The bitch in that villa there.' A silhouette of a raised arm pointing made Jean-Luc freeze. He was pointing to Charlize's back wall. *Merde*. How in hell did they find out?

'Right.' The other man answered in perfect, fluent French. Vincent's right-hand man, Enzo, was Italian, and spoke French well enough, but with a bastardised Italian accent. The other guy was obviously a French national, but it was too dark for Jean-Luc to see his face. 'I'll keep an eye on her then. Until you let me know.'

Know what? What was Vincent planning? To abduct Charlize? To force her to tell them what she knew about him?

'Keep your phone handy. I'll call when I have orders. And Fabio, keep your mind on the job.' The last had been said in a low growl, obviously meant as a warning.

'*Oui*, chief,' Fabio agreed blithely. Then Jean-Luc heard footsteps coming back toward the carpark and he'd retreated to find a better hiding spot. From which he'd watched Enzo drive away in the black car, leaving Fabio standing like a solemn black statue at the end of the car park.

Jean-Luc spent the rest of the night following Fabio

around like a wraith, to make sure he wasn't about to abduct Charlize straight from her villa. Once he caught a good look at his face, he confirmed Fabio was indeed the other man at the meeting in Uzes with Franco.

Surprisingly, Fabio knew his stuff. Jean-Luc made sure to be extra careful, so the guy didn't realise he was also being surveyed. But apart from walking around to find the front door to Charlize's villa—probably making sure the place was closed up for the night, and Charlize wasn't going anywhere—Fabio did little else. For the rest of the night, he found a few tables and chairs left outside a closed café at the end of Charlize's alleyway and settled in.

While the big man waited, Jean-Luc took the opportunity to call Pickard. He'd woken him up—it was now the small hours of the morning—to debrief him and ask for help. That's when Pickard had done all the yelling. But afterwards he'd said he'd try and find out what Vincent knew about Charlize and how he'd found her.

The following day, Jean-Luc followed Fabio, who followed Charlize and Patty as they meandered around the town, shopping in the little tourist shops and buying gelato. Twice. Patty obviously really liked the French ice-cream. He never got close enough to see their faces as he tailed them, but he could see the way Patty's hands would fly up to highlight some animated conversation, and the way Charlize would hunch her shoulders slightly, bending down to catch her friend's words. Then Charlize's face would be in profile, showing the slight curve of her nose where it tilted outwards at the tip, and even from this distance he could trace the plump outline of her lips as she parted them and her tongue darted out to lick her gelato. He didn't know why, but it was becoming tremendously important that he protect his woman. He hardly knew her, yet every time he caught sight of her, something stirred deep inside him. A terrible desire to safeguard her.

Jean-Luc didn't know who'd been more surprised, himself or Fabio, when, after a morning wandering around the town, the girls then came out of Charlize's villa with towels and swimming gear and headed for her little car. Jean-Luc had to scramble madly to make it to his motorbike in time, and just caught the little red Citroen as it rumbled down the hill out of town. The girls spent the afternoon at the Pont du Gard, doing the tourist thing, swimming and enjoying the sunshine. It had just about run him ragged, trying to stay out of their sight as well as avoiding Fabio. A dangerous dance that had left him hot, tired and irritable. Especially after no sleep the previous night, and not a lot to eat.

After a meal at a restaurant back in Uzes, the girls finally headed home late in the evening, and Fabio planted himself at an outdoor table in front of a pub, ordering a meal of steak frites and a red wine. Tired as he was, Jean-Luc's mouth salivated as he watched the man devour the meal from his hiding place atop the flat roof-top of a dress shop across the street.

Pickard phoned him, telling him he'd intercepted some of Vincent's men's chatter from their various phones he'd managed to bug. He didn't have a lot of intel, but whatever was going on wasn't going to happen in Uzes. It was probably too risky. She might be missed if she was snatched from her villa, especially with Patty as a witness. Pickard said Fabio might be recalled to Marseille. He also said he was sending down a replacement for Jean-Luc, someone who could guard Charlize and Patty, leaving

Jean-Luc free to return to his real job. Jean-Luc was dubious and told Pickard he could send whomever he wanted, but he wasn't leaving until he was sure he knew what Fabio was up to. Just because they were backing off now, didn't mean they weren't still going to try and grab her at some other stage. Pickard just grunted and told him the new guy would be in Uzes around midnight.

'We need to get her into protection,' Jean-Luc said, before Pickard could hang up on him.

'Yeah, yeah, I'm onto that as well,' Pickard answered gruffly. 'Give me a day or two, though.'

Fabio sat at his table for another four hours until well after midnight. Jean-Luc was fighting a losing battle with his eyelids, which seemed determined to close of their own will. Finally, Fabio was forced to move, getting up from his table when the restaurant closed and headed back toward the alley behind Charlize's villa. Jean-Luc's cramped muscles wouldn't respond as quickly as he would've liked, and it took him a while to get down off the roof and follow Fabio. Was this it? He tensed, ready for whatever was to come, reaching around to feel the reassuring weight of his gun.

But the man didn't stop at Charlize's back wall. He kept strolling toward the carpark, and then amazingly, sauntered over to a waiting black sedan. Tension oozed out of Jean-Luc's muscles as the car drove away.

Just as Pickard had said, Fabio had been called off, sent to Marseille to await further orders. Jean-Luc spent the next hour or so on the phone, but he finally discovered Patty Levine was booked on a flight to Sydney the following evening. Leaving from Marseille. It all started to fall into place then. It'd be much easier for them to snatch

Charlize away from Uzes in the relative anonymity of the large crowds in Marseille. Or on the road home. It'd be dead easy for them to hijack her car on one of those quiet country roads between here and Marseille. How the hell had Vincent's team found out about Patty's travel plans? Pickard needed to investigate that one further.

Then he met with the replacement Pickard sent to guard Charlize. Paul was a squat, broad man, reminiscent of a large toad. But that squat body was all hard muscle and Jean-Luc was satisfied the man could take care of himself and anyone else who might bother Charlize. Paul was a man of few words, and as Jean-Luc gave him all the details of what'd transpired so far, he only gave monosyllabic answers in response.

Jean-Luc finally went off to catch a few hours' sleep, back in his hotel room. When he'd woken again this morning, he made numerous phone calls, trying to find out from his boss what he thought Vincent might be planning. Paul tailed Charlize and Patty as they drove to Marseille in her battered old Citroen hatchback, while Jean-Luc followed further back in a rented car. They'd let Patty leave to catch her plane and then pick Charlize up.

Now Paul was stationed outside the airport, under the overpass leading to the carpark, ready to back Jean-Luc up if need be.

The first boarding call for Patty's flight came over the loudspeaker. Patty looked anxiously at Charlize and started to gather her hand luggage, obviously eager to get into the boarding lounge and onto the plane. The two women embraced, Charlize fighting back tears, Patty openly weeping. While he was able to keep a professional distance from the scene in front of him, the women's strong bond was obvious. They'd been partners back in the police force. And he knew from reading Charlize's file she'd been involved in a car crash while working for the police. He assumed that's where the scars on her legs came from. But the details were sketchy. Classified. Bloody cops and their confidentiality. Pickard still hadn't been able to find out the exact details, and not for want of trying, either. With no real contacts in Australia, his boss kept hitting a series of brick walls when it came to digging deeper into Charlize's life. One thing was obvious, Patty had been involved in the accident as well. Which leant him added insight into the parting, added gravitas to their connection. They were two women with an interesting past together, a noteworthy story to tell.

At last Patty wiped her eyes, picked up her carry-on bag and joined the queue of people straggling toward the door that led to security and beyond. She gave one more teary wave farewell and disappeared round the corner. Charlize had her back to him, but Jean-Luc saw her shoulders slump and she brought a tissue up to her face. Was she crying? Had she waited until Patty disappeared before letting the tears fall? His heart stuttered in his chest, surprised to find he didn't like to see her in pain. He'd give her a few minutes to recover her equilibrium, knowing she wouldn't appreciate him turning up and seeing her like this. She wasn't going anywhere, not in this state, but he readied himself for the moment when he could go and get her.

Charlize was wearing a thin cotton summer dress, with shoe-string straps and a pattern of large purple flowers. Pale strips of skin showed on her shoulders, where the sun hadn't had a chance to tan it golden brown. The hem draped to the ground, hiding those long legs of hers, covering the scars. It was very becoming for her tall frame, showing off the slender curve of her neck and the pale creaminess of her bare shoulders. It was so sheer he could see the outline of the bra she wore underneath, could just make out the swirls of lacy material of her underwear. A sudden desire had him wanting to take her somewhere quiet and peel back the straps of the dress, to reveal the white strip of lace beneath... *Merde. Get your head back in the game, Munulo.* Jesus, he'd never allowed the allure of a beautiful woman to break his concentration while on the job before. He'd need to keep a much tighter rein on his libido.

The crowd farewelling loved ones at the gate started to thin, and Charlize seemed at last to come to her senses. Standing taller, her chin came up. It was time to move.

Removing his sunglasses as he approached, he said in a low voice, 'Charlize.' He grasped her elbow. She flinched in alarm and stared at him wide-eyed.

'What the... Louis? What the hell are you doing here?'

'You need to come with me, Charlize,' he said again, keeping his voice low, gaze casting about for Vincent's men.

'Like hell I do,' she said, rearing backwards, away from his touch.

CLASSIC FRENCH STEAK FRITES

INGREDIENTS
4 x 300g Sirloin steaks, about 3cm thick
Good quality salt flakes
Freshly cracked black pepper
4 large Yukon Gold or yellow potatoes
4 cups Oil for frying
1 tbsp Good quality salt flakes

Bearnaise Sauce
3 free-range egg yolks
50ml White wine vinegar
400ml Clarified butter, melted and still warm
Juice of ¼ lemon
½ tbsp Fresh French tarragon, finely chopped
Salt and pepper to taste.

DIRECTIONS
Make Béarnaise sauce. Keep warm while you prepare the rest.
To Make the Béarnaise Sauce:
Put egg yolks in a bowl over a pan of simmering water.
Add vinegar and whisk until yolks are pale and fluffy.
Remove from the heat.
Slowly add the butter in a gentle stream, whisking continuously until consistency thickens.
Add the lemon juice, tarragon and season to taste. Put aside and cook the steaks and frites.
Wash potatoes but keep the skin on for maximum flavour. Cut into 1.5cm thick chips.
Heat oil in a deep-fryer to 160C. Drop in the chips and fry for seven minutes.
Remove chips from the oil and cool down.
Just before you're ready to serve, heat oil to 180C and fry chips again for two minutes or until crisp and golden.
Season with salt flakes and serve.
While the chips are cooking, pre-heat a heavy pan to a medium heat.

Fry steak for four minutes each side and rest for four minutes.
(Medium steak)
Season steaks well with salt and cracked pepper.
Serve with a green side salad.

Steak frites is a long-time French favourite and a staple meal at most restaurants. This meal is best enjoyed served with a glass of good French red wine on the back verandah of your family home.

CHAPTER NINE

'Let go of me.' Wrenching her arm free, she took a few steps away, her mind unable to comprehend what was going on.

She'd just said farewell to her best friend, her heart raw and stripped to the bone. Her chest was still tight with more unshed tears, and all she wanted to do was get to her car and let the flood loose in private. The only thing stopping the sobs from erupting now was her teeth clenched together in a rigid line of pain. Her mind wasn't capable of grasping what Louis was doing here.

The last person on earth she'd expected to see here was him. Why was he saying she had to come with him? His words were only half-understood by her foggy brain, as it raced to flip over from grief to understanding.

'What the fuck are you talking about?' Anger was the strongest emotion she could dredge up at this particular moment, so she ran with it. 'Start talking sense right now, or I'm leaving,' she ground out, taking another step away from him as he continued to try and take her by the elbow.

'For Christ's sake, keep your voice down.' His eyes

darkened with barely controlled frustration. 'Will you come over here, so I can explain what's going on.' He indicated toward a large pillar tucked away in a corner of the departure gate. Letting her take the lead, he swung his gaze around, as if searching for something. Or someone. His intensity was starting to worry her, and she found her gaze roaming over the crowd as well. Looking for what or whom, she had no idea.

'You need to come with me, Charlize,' he said as soon as they were behind the relative cover of the pillar.

'You've already said that.' She crossed her arms over her chest and gave him her best glare. 'But I'm not going anywhere with you. I'm going back to my car and then I'm going home to my villa.' She needed to get back to the safety of her familiar bed, to the soothing shade of her garden. To get over the melancholy Patty's departure left behind, like a crushing weight on her chest. To shore up the walls around her heart that were in dire peril of crumbling right now. And God knew what might happen if those walls did actually come down. All that grief, and sorrow and guilt she stored up inside, it might all come pouring out, turning her back into the emotional invalid she'd been before she arrived in Europe. And that just couldn't be allowed to happen.

'Remember when I said if anything became *problematic* then you should contact me straight away?' She could tell he was having trouble keeping his irritation under control, his body tense as a string on a bow. She nodded at her recollection of his phrase. 'Well, things have suddenly become *problematic*.' Pausing to let his words sink in, his hazel eyes bored into hers. 'There are six men here looking for you.'

'Oh.' Her heart rate skipped up. 'What do they want from me?'

'We're not really sure yet?' His words didn't contain the complete truth, she could tell he was hedging.

'What aren't you telling me, Louis?'

He let out an exasperated breath. 'Look, can we discuss the details later? At the moment, we just need to get you out of here. We both need to get out of here.' A little of his urgency broke through the haze that surrounded her mind, but the stubborn streak in her wasn't ready to submit. She didn't want to go with him. She wanted to be allowed to drive back to Uzes in her antiquated Citroen and lock herself in her villa, away from the rest of the world. 'Just so you know, Louis isn't my real name. It's Jean-Luc. I'm telling you that as a token of my good faith. Charlize, you have to believe me. You're in grave danger.'

She raised her eyebrows at his admission. Jesus, she'd been right. He had been lying to her. Big time.

'I don't care what your name is, I'm not going with you. You promised me everything would be alright, that I shouldn't be worried. You were the one who landed in my garden. You got me into this. It's your problem. You sort it out. I don't want a bar of it.' She sounded like a sulky teenager, but she no longer cared.

His dark eyebrows shot up in dismay. He looked decidedly scruffier than last time she'd seen him. Dark stubble covered his jaw, his clothes rumpled and perhaps even slept in. Definitely not the suave, gorgeous man she'd had dinner with the other night. Still gorgeous, she admitted, but now weighed down with worry and what looked like a severe lack of sleep. For the first time, she noticed he was wearing a tourist cap, pulled down low over his forehead and dragging a suitcase behind him. A disguise? Was he really that concerned?

'Look, I'm sorry I had to lie to you. But denying this situation isn't suddenly going to make it go away,' he said. Suddenly, the self-doubt kicked in and Charlize didn't know what to say. The only thing that made sense to her at the moment was being able to escape back to her little villa. Why should she believe him? She didn't know this man, not really. He'd already admitted he'd told untruths. What else was false about him? He could be trying to abduct her himself. Perhaps he was a serial killer, and he kidnapped women using this farce of a scenario all the time.

'I'm not denying it. I just want a bit more proof before I go gallivanting off with a practical stranger. Especially one who's been lying to me about something as simple as his name.' She shot him her best challenging stare. He took hold of both her shoulders in his hands, forcing her to look up into his handsome face.

'Let me go—' She started to struggle.

'Your life's not the only one on the line here, you know.' His quiet words finally had the effect he'd been looking for. She stilled in his arms. Shit. She was putting him in danger. He was putting himself in danger to try and help her. The old instinct, the one she'd relied on back when she'd been a cop, told her he was telling the truth. A groan escaped her lips.

'Oh God.' She sagged a little in his grasp. This couldn't be happening. Reality set up a tremor in her hands, which quickly ran up her arms and into the rest of her body. He must've felt it, because his hard eyes softened slightly.

'Don't worry, just do what I say, okay?' She nodded

mutely. Then he started speaking in urgent French and she wondered what'd gotten into him. It wasn't until she deciphered the words, *outside* and *carpark* that she realised he wasn't talking to her but to a man called Paul, obviously though some kind of coms set.

'I have a man waiting for us outside,' he said, reverting to English. 'We're going to take the side entrance, stay away from the main carpark entrance, where they'll be expecting you to come out.'

'How do they know…' She didn't need to finish her sentence. Of course, they knew where she'd parked her car.

Grabbing her hand, Louis… No wait, it was Jean-Luc now, proceeded to lead her with slow purpose toward the left-hand side of the terminal. His hand was warm, his long fingers smooth against her own, and she had to drag her focus away from the soft chafe of his palm against hers to concentrate on where they were going. She tried to keep her limp as understated as possible, not wanting to draw any more attention than necessary. Walls of glass glittered in the bright lights of the terminal, even the ceiling was made from square panes of glass. The reflections of people floating past on their way to find a lost relative or to board a flight made it look as if there were many more people than there actually were. Without conscious thought, her mind started running scenarios. First of all, they'd have to get down off the concourse that led to the departure gates. Which meant getting on one of the escalators. Wouldn't that expose them to the view of anyone below? She was about to say something to Louis when he gave an abrupt tug on her hand and they turned toward the back of the concourse.

Elevators. Of course. He led her into a waiting one, and pushed their way to the back, so they were hidden by the crowds filing in behind them. Charlize's heart was beating like a frightened rabbit, and she wondered if Jean-Luc could feel the hammering all the way through her hand. She still hadn't seen anyone who looked like they might be hired killers scouting the hallways. She'd just have to trust Jean-Luc knew what he was doing.

Then the elevator doors opened, and they flowed out with the rest of the people spilling through the doors. Charlize was lost now, never having taken the lifts in this airport before. Her breath was coming in short bursts, despite her attempts to control it, and she kept checking behind, to look for...quite what she didn't know. Men in black suits?. But that was just a classic stereotype from all those cops and robber movies on TV. As an ex-police officer, she knew better. Criminals looked just like everyone else. Which made her heart rate kick up even more. They could be watching her right now. It might be that man off to the left who was staring at her. She kept hold of Jean-Luc's hand, gripping so hard her knuckles turned white.

Her flip-flops made a quiet slapping sound against the tan-coloured tiles of the floor. Two men, both dressed in jeans and dark jackets, stood over near the farthest wall, well away from the worst of the milling crowd, surreptitiously craning their necks. Was that some of them? Jean-Luc led them left, so they ducked behind a row of large terracotta pots holding round bulbs of topiary shrubs. Every now and then, the hem of her long skirt caught in the back of her flip-flop and she stumbled, but Jean-Luc's hand always held her steady. She wasn't dressed for an escape mission. If she'd known, she would've worn pants and much more sensible shoes. But she was going to have to make do. Whenever the dress tightened around her calves, her scarred leg wrenched in pain. She hoped they wouldn't have to run for it.

All of a sudden Jean-Luc was pushing open a door with the words Emergency Exit in green neon above it. They emerged out onto a sidewalk, her eyes taking a while to adjust to the dim evening light after the brightly lit interior of the airport. The sun was just going down, meaning it must be around ten o'clock. A road ran parallel to the sidewalk, with the zebra stripes of a pedestrian crossing just in front of them, leading off into a small badly lit carpark. The door clanged shut behind them with a loud bang, and she flinched, ducking her head. Shit. For a split second, she'd thought someone was shooting at them. She was so on edge everything seemed to be moving at double speed right now.

There was no sign of anyone following them. So far, so good. Licking her lips, she found she was suddenly incredibly thirsty. There were a few people walking up and down the pavement, but this area was deserted compared to the main entrance. As she looked back, she could see the airport control tower, its round facade hovering high over the rest of the squat building. Jean-Luc talked low and fast into his coms set again and pulled her across the pedestrian crossing. How could he be so calm? Once upon a time, she'd been just as calm and controlled. But now her body jerked at every sound and every movement, and she couldn't stop the shaking in her hands. She'd lost that edge long ago. And it was never coming back.

Even though Jean-Luc had convinced her of the absolute seriousness of her situation, a little voice was still nagging at her, telling her to pull away from him, to let him escape on his own. Leave her alone, she wasn't worth the fuss. There couldn't possibly be a gang of thugs after her. She was insignificant. Not worth their time or effort. She didn't know anything, anyway. The sound of rushing blood still filled her ears, and she couldn't seem to quell her pounding heart. The words became more insistent. She wasn't worth the fuss; it kept repeating. Jean-Luc should just leave her. It was the voice of despair. The same despair that'd filled her after the crash. That voice had become a shadow of a whisper over the past six months or so, but obviously it hadn't gone completely. Charlize wanted to screw her eyes shut and disappear, let a black hole open up beneath her and swallow her up. She couldn't be here, she wasn't good at this kind of thing anymore.

She was just about to open her mouth to say something when Jean-Luc said, 'Paul's coming to meet us.' He nodded his head in the direction of the front of the airport, where a stocky man appeared in the distance. But as they watched, Paul stopped in his tracks, glancing back over his shoulder. Then he reached around behind his back, his hand reappearing, holding a black shape. A gun.

'Someone's following him,' Jean-Luc hissed. 'Quick, we need to get to the car.' He tugged her hand hard and nearly caused her to overbalance as they broke into a slow jog. She groaned out loud, but had little choice other than to follow him. Her flip-flops kept catching on her dress and every few feet she tripped and nearly landed on her knees. 'Charlize, what's wrong?' He glanced behind and saw the problem immediately. 'Get rid of them!' he yelled.

'What?'

'Lose the shoes, they're slowing you down.' As if on autopilot she did as he told her and ran barefoot, hoping to hell she didn't step on any broken glass or other nasty things found in airport carparks.

They made it to the first line of cars and Jean-Luc ducked down behind them, still moving, but bent over to stay out of sight.

'I'm hoping with all these people around, they won't resort to shooting. It'll draw too much attention.'

He *hoped* they wouldn't start shooting. Great! That's all she needed. She kept her breath for the exertion of jogging along half-bent over, so she didn't bother to answer. At least the action of moving seemed to have quieted the nagging voice of despair in her head. Jean-Luc knew what he was doing. He'd keep her safe. She might not be good at this sort of thing anymore, but he'd help her out of here.

She trusted him.

Really? Where had that thought suddenly come from? She hardly knew him. How could she trust him already?

'*Merde*,' Jean-Luc said quietly. 'Two of them are out the front, heading this way. Paul's going to try and distract them.'

Not what she wanted to hear. She wasn't sure if he required an answer, so she just said, 'Okay.' He came to a stop at the end of a row of cars and raised his head slightly, peering through the side window, back the way they'd come.

'Fuck,' he hissed. 'Another two just came out the side door.' Charlize chanced a quick glance up and saw that two men—the ones she'd spotted in jeans and dark jackets earlier—had indeed emerged from the emergency exit and were casting their gazes around the area. It looked so much like a stereotypical scene from some B-grade spy movie that Charlize almost laughed out loud. They had to be kidding, didn't they? These men looked like they belonged in some Italian Mafia film. This wasn't really happening. It was a dream, after all.

But as she looked at the men, a puzzling foreboding started to clench her gut into knots. Not a pulling sensation, more like a pushing sensation. The pushing sensation wanted her to move away. Away from those men near the door. Was it her clairsentience? If it was, it'd never happened before. She'd been faced with many criminals, felons, people who'd meant her harm, before. But her gift had never warned her like this. What was going on? This wasn't the ability to feel someone else's pain. This was a dark, savage sensation in her stomach, as if her entire insides were being covered with a thick, black sludge. A sludge made of fear and other immoral things.

'Keep coming,' Jean-Luc urged into her ear, 'I don't think they've seen us yet.' Shaking her head to free it of her strange thoughts, she couldn't get out of there quick enough as she followed the tug of his hand, keeping as low as she could, which wasn't easy for someone with her height. She kept worrying that her head was visible as they slunk along the row of cars.

'Could you have parked any further away?' she said in a stage whisper. He didn't answer, just shot her a patronising glance. At the end of the next row, Jean-Luc took another look. The dreadful need to keep going was still pushing at her insides, but it was waning the further away from the men they got. Perhaps it was just that she'd never been in such personal, immediate danger before.

Maybe that's why she'd never felt this way.

'They're coming this way,' he said, tone matter of fact now. 'We're going to have to run for it. Follow my lead and don't let go of my hand. Okay?' He stared straight into her eyes as he said this, demanding her unbroken promise that she'd do as he told her. She nodded, her heart beating so fast now it felt like it was lodged in her throat and not in her chest anymore. Yes, she was terrified. But there was something else as well. That voice of uncertainty had all but disappeared as they'd dodged and weaved through the cars. Replaced by adrenaline buzzing through her body, giving her a heightened awareness, a feeling of…strength. Her body remembered this feeling, and instinct started to kick in, the same as it had the night Jean-Luc appeared in her garden.

'We need to get to that car over there.' Jean-Luc pointed at a dark blue sedan about four rows away, parked on its own, well away from all the other cars. For an easy getaway. That's why he'd parked so far away.

'I can't run fast, Jean-Luc,' she said quietly.

'What?' He turned his head to stare at her, and then realisation dawned in his eyes. He'd seen the scars, and her limp, even if he'd never commented on them. She'd be a handicap to him.

'It's alright, I won't leave you behind. Just go as fast as you can,' he said, a gentler tone returning to his voice. *You might*, said that nagging voice, returning to snipe at her.

Popping his head up for a second, he said, 'Get ready.' She waited, tensing her muscles, free hand resting on the bumper of the car they were hiding behind, ready to push herself up and forward when he gave the word.

'Run.' He pulled on her hand and they surged upwards

together and ran for the car.

As soon as they took off, raised voices sounded behind them, but she didn't look, just kept her concentration on running as best she could. *Run and don't fall.* Every step pulled at the scars on her left leg, making it protest at the unusual activity. The bitumen was harsh beneath her bare feet, and now and then she'd land on a piece of gravel, which sent piercing shards of pain up her legs. The car loomed closer. But she wasn't going to make it. It was too much for her, fatigue and lactic acid were making her legs heavy. She began to stumble at each step.

'Slow down, Jean-Luc,' she panted, 'or I'll fall over and you'll never get me up in time.' She was tempted to tell him just to leave her if that happened, but she knew what his answer would be, so she saved her breath. He slowed, casting an anxious glance back over his shoulder at her. The car was only twenty or so meters away now. They could make it.

Suddenly, her gut clenched so hard she doubled over. 'Duck,' she yelled, wrenching Jean-Luc toward her and nearly hitting the pavement at the same time.

There was a low thudding sound, and something whizzed past her shoulder.

'Fuck,' Jean-Luc growled. They were shooting at them. The breath froze in her throat. Something had made her duck at just the right second. Her gift? Had it just saved her? Jean-Luc started to weave around as he ran, to give the mafia men less of a target to shoot at. The extra exertion ratcheted up the pain in her leg so it was almost uncontrollable, and she started to grunt with pain at every step. But she didn't stop running.

Again, that sudden seizure in her chest and she swerved

into Jean-Luc to knock him out of the way. Another bullet zoomed past them, this one a little further away. It seemed the two men chasing them couldn't run and shoot at the same time.

Then the solid metallic form of the car was in front of them, and Jean-Luc wrenched open the door and manhandled her into the passenger seat. He was around the car and in the driver's side before she could even straighten herself to a sitting position. Her breath came in huge, unstoppable gulps. The ping of another bullet embedding itself in the car's rear bumper sounded loud in her head. Then the car roared to life and Jean-Luc had it jumping forward like an unleashed racehorse.

'Put on your seatbelt and hold on,' he yelled. Fumbling for the belt buckle, she soon knew why he'd told her to do that. The toll booth loomed in front of them, but he wasn't going to stop to pay a parking fee. He kept his foot planted on the accelerator and they smashed through the wooden beam. Charlize ducked reflectively as bits of wood and plastic flew over the car's windscreen. They skidded around a corner, expertly dodging the slower moving traffic and went up onto a flyover and merged with traffic on a highway.

'Are they following us?' she managed to pant, still trying to control her breathing.

'I don't think so.' His gaze flicked between the road ahead and the rear-vision mirror. Then something occurred to her.

'Jesus, what about Paul? Is he alright?'

'He managed to draw those others into the underground railway. He got away.' She tried to read meaning into his words, into what he hadn't said. Was that guilt showing in the tight knit of his brows and the curl of his lip?

'Is he alright?' she repeated.

'He did his job, Charlize.' Shifting his intense gaze from the road to her face, he said, 'You don't need to worry about him right now. He got away, and they didn't catch us, that's all that matters.' Shit. Now she owed another man for saving her; a stranger at that.

Leaning back in the seat, she watched the cars pass by on either side as Jean-Luc sped down the highway, weaving in and out of the traffic. Whether she liked it or not, her life was in his hands, at least for the time being.

CHAPTER TEN

The adrenaline-high slowly drained from his limbs, leaving him on edge and shaking. Not that he let it show. He took a quick glance across at Charlize to ascertain how she was coping. Not very well if her vacant stare was anything to go by. Freaked out might be a better way of putting it. Which surprised him. Wasn't she an ex-cop? Hadn't she been trained to handle these kinds of situations? There'd been flashes of a cool, calm, in-control Charlize during their desperate get-away, but there'd also been a few moments when he thought she might seriously lose it; when he'd entertained the idea of throwing her over his shoulder like a sack of potatoes. He'd had to bite down hard on his tongue more than once to stop himself from yelling at her. This woman was all kinds of conundrums rolled into one.

She'd frustrated the hell out of him today. But the naked fear and the shadowy doubt that lurked in her eyes as she seemed to fight some kind of internal demon had done strange things to his insides. Had made him want to reach out and protect her. To hold her so she didn't get lost in that swirling maelstrom of emotions evident in her gaze.

But now wasn't the time or place to try and understand the depth of Charlize's emotional issues. Perhaps when they were safe, he'd get her to talk. Now he had other things on his mind.

He'd lost contact with Paul, the coms going out of range as soon as he hit the freeway. *Merde.* He hoped Paul had made it onto that train. Jean-Luc had only met the man twice, but he seemed to be a solid, dependable, likeable guy, and there was no way Jean-Luc wanted to be in charge of a mission where someone got injured... Or killed. It didn't sit well with him.

'Where are we going?' Her voice was small, as if coming from faraway. But at least she was functioning enough to ask a coherent question.

'I've got somewhere lined up on the outskirts of town. We'll go there and then I'll contact my superior to find out how things stand.'

'You knew they were coming for me?' Her voice grew stronger, the focus coming back into her eyes. Good, she was slowly pulling herself out of her panic-induced paralysis.

'We only found out this morning, and even then, the details were sketchy,' he replied. 'I'll tell you everything when we get to the hotel, okay?'

'Yep.' After a second's thought, she asked, 'We're going to a hotel?'

'I've used it before. I know it's safe, and I trust the owners.'

'Right.' There was a hint of challenge in her tone, but he ignored it. He wanted to say more, wanted to tell her how sorry he was, he'd gotten her mixed up in this mess, sorry that her life had just been turned upside down. But he kept his mouth shut. All that mattered was she was alive. And so was he. The rest would have to wait.

'What about my car?' she asked, as if the thought had just occurred to her.

'I'll make sure you retrieve it after all this is over.'

'That's going to be one hell of a parking bill.' Her lips twitched, and he was glad there was finally some humour creeping back into her voice.

* * *

When she'd first scrambled into the car, Charlize had been on autopilot, clasping her hands tightly in her lap to conceal their shaking as she allowed Jean-Luc to take charge of the situation. Once they made it up onto the freeway and were speeding away from the airport, reality started to sink in. She didn't want to be here. This couldn't be happening. Please, just let it be a dream. Closing her eyes, she willed it all to be just a figment of her imagination. Wished that she was sitting back in her own car, driving along the tiny back roads toward Uzes. Not speeding down a motorway with Jean-Luc at the wheel. She clasped her hands even tighter and fought the urge to open the door and jump out of the moving car. It was a totally irrational fear, but the car seemed to be closing in on her, the air inside thick and unbreathable. Xeon's screams echoed in her head. Patty's piercing cries pounded silently against the inside of her skull.

Ragged breaths filled her lungs, and she dug her fingernails into her palms as she willed the terrible images away. She could do this. She'd faced worse than this and survived. The psychologist she'd seen right after the accident had warned her she'd need to find an outlet for all these pent-up emotions, need to drain them away, otherwise they'd fester inside her head and get worse, not better. The woman had also told her not to fight her fear, but to try and travel through it, like a tourist visiting a foreign city. Acknowledge it, but not let it take over. Get on with her real life. As if that were possible. As if she could *float* through that overwhelming panic. Charlize gave a low snort. That woman had known nothing of how Charlize felt. How the fear affected her, froze the air in her lungs, constricted her throat as if big, unseen hands were wrapped tightly around her neck. Paralysed her.

The psych also told her the panic attacks were perhaps a symptom of an acute stress disorder and if she wasn't careful and didn't get treatment, it may get worse before it got better. Might even turn into PTSD. She wanted to refer Charlize to another psychologist who specialised in trauma, who'd give her a definitive diagnosis and then help with her recovery. But by that stage, Charlize had already started to ignore her advice, determined she didn't have PTSD. Eventually, she'd stopped going to see her altogether. And then she'd left Australia.

Her breath slowly returned to normal, the terrible tightness in her chest started to subside and the crushing nausea in her stomach retreated. Finally, she found the strength to ask Jean-Luc where they were going. Jean-Luc. She liked that name. As soon as he'd told her, it felt right. Well, as soon as she'd gotten over her boiling rage at his double-crossing, lying arse, that was. It suited him much more than Louis, rolled off her tongue in a smooth fashion. Talking made her feel better, so she kept asking him more inane questions and found her equilibrium returning as she listened to his answers, his confident voice soothing her. And, funnily enough, having him sitting next to her, his strong, capable hands on the steering wheel, also helped stabilise her. It wasn't something she wanted to analyse, but his presence was a calming influence, as if he were a buffer between reality and the voices trying to take over her mind.

He guided the car expertly through the encroaching night and she was drawn again to the smooth brown skin on his forearms. Fine dark hairs covered his arm like a layer of down; defined muscles running from wrist to elbow.

Before she knew it, they turned off the highway and wound down a back road. The houses became sparser, the countryside now impinging on the city. Then Jean-Luc pulled into a driveway and Charlize could just make out a quaint little row of cottages from the glow of the streetlights. There was a larger house situated right at the end. He took a dirt track around to the back of the cottages, effectively putting the car out of sight of the main road. Jean-Luc stopped behind the cottage nearest the main house and shut off the engine.

'Stay here. I'll get the key.' He locked the car as he got out.

She did as she was told, listening to all the various ticks and hums of the car as it cooled. Patty would be winging her way back home by now. The plane probably somewhere over the Mediterranean. It seemed like forever since she'd left Patty at the airport, but it'd been less than two hours. A lifetime.

A tap on the window made her jump. It was Jean-Luc, dangling a key. She got out and followed him inside the cottage. It was much more spacious than she expected.

There was a small kitchenette and a sitting room, with a cosy couch and a television.

'I need to report to my boss, then we can have a chat. Okay?' He pulled a mobile phone out of his back pocket.

'Sure, go ahead. I'm not going anywhere.' Charlize poked her head into each of the other three doorways as Jean-Luc strode toward the front window, punching numbers on his phone. There were two bedrooms, thank God, and a small bathroom. All very well-designed and quite pretty. If she wasn't on the run from a mob of madmen trying to abduct her for God knew what end, she might enjoy this little home-away-from-home.

Wandering back toward the kitchenette, she glanced around the bench-tops. The hosts had provided some tea and coffee bags. Opening the fridge, she found a small carton of milk as well. Bliss. She'd be able to make a cup of tea.

Finding a small kettle, she put it on to boil, and decided that Jean-Luc was probably a coffee drinker.

It was hard not to overhear what Jean-Luc was saying on the phone, the cottage wasn't very big. He gave short, to the point answers. 'Yes, there were six of them. It was Enzo and Fabio, didn't recognise the others. No, I'm pretty sure we weren't followed. Nope, I was hoping you'd be able to fill me in on Paul's whereabouts.' Then his voice got quiet, and she had to strain to hear what he said next. 'No, she's not happy about it. And neither am I.' There was a long silence as he obviously listened to instructions, and then he said, 'Right. Make it sooner, rather than later, will you?' And he hung up the phone.

He turned toward her and for a second there was worry evident in his caramel eyes, fatigue in the slump of his shoulders. The vulnerable side of Jean-Luc bared for her to see. Just for a second, then it was gone, and he was all business again. A tight smile replaced those unguarded emotions as he took the two steps to the couch, sat down and opened a computer bag he'd slung on the table as they'd entered.

That quick insight into the humane, softer side of Jean-Luc made Charlize go weak at the knees. Almost the same as when she'd first heard his honeyed French accent. She was reminded of their dinner date; it seemed like eons ago now. How he'd laughed with her, flirted, and she allowed herself to feel attraction to a man for the first time in… Forever.

She lifted the cup of tea to her lips and let the steaming liquid heat her tongue. An immediate sense of well-being spread through her body. She knew it was silly, but there was nothing better than a hot cup of tea to bring her back down to earth. To centre her, make her feel somehow safer. She'd picked up the habit from her grandmother. Her dad's mother had always welcomed them to her farmhouse when she was a little girl, with freshly backed scones and copious cups of tea. Charlize hadn't thought about it much back then, just knew she loved the homely feeling of warmth and inclusion every time she sat down at her grandmother's table. Thinking about it now, it must've been her grandmother's English influence. Bringing the tradition of tea-drinking with her when she'd emigrated to Australia all those years ago. Charlize sent up a silent thank you to her departed grandmother for passing on her love of the wonderful beverage.

She found herself staring at Jean-Luc. He patted the couch next to him and said, 'Come sit down. I'll tell you what I know so far. And you can tell me anything else you think might be helpful.'

After she grabbed his cup of coffee, she made her hesitant way over to the sitting area. The couch was only a two-seater, if she sat down, she'd be in close—really close—proximity to him. But there were no other options if she wanted to see his computer screen. So she sat.

He looked up in surprise when she put the mug down in front of him.

'I put milk in, I wasn't sure how you take it.'

'Milk's good, thanks,' he replied and lifted the coffee to his lips. 'I needed that.' He gave her a grateful grin. 'I hope you don't mind, but I've ordered the *plat de jour* from the host. I'm starving.'

'I could eat,' she admitted with an answering grin. She and Patty had a late lunch while they'd been shopping in Marseille, but now her stomach rumbled at the mention of food. 'Isn't it a little late for them to serve us dinner, though?'

'Probably. But they don't mind doing it for...particular guests.' He gave one of those typical French shrugs Charlize was becoming familiar with. 'Tonight's menu is one of their specialities, cheese souffle and beef stroganoff.' Her mouth started to water at his words. Cheese souffle—as long as it was done well—was fast becoming one of her favourite French dishes. All that creamy, melting, gooey cheese in a light and airy concoction. What was there not to love? And beef stroganoff, with its rich, buttery sauce, over succulent meat, would do more than nicely to top off the entrée. Bugger the calories. 'The host's wife, Marian, will bring it to our cottage soon.'

'I'll look forward to that,' she said with a smack of her lips.

He laughed at her obvious delight and then sobered abruptly. 'Before she gets here, I need to tell you some things. The truth about what I do, about why you've been targeted.'

'So the stuff you told me before, who you worked for and why you were in my garden? That's not the truth?'

'Not totally, no.' Why was she not surprised? A burning anger replaced the hunger in her belly. Leaning back against the couch, she crossed her arms over her chest and glared at him.

* * *

He shouldn't have expected any other reaction, really. She was pissed, and probably with good cause. If only she didn't look so bloody appealing in that summer dress, like she'd just stepped off the beach, then he might be able to take her seriously. *Concentrate.* She probably thought he was the biggest arsehole in the world right now, and here he was, perpetuating her opinion of him by thinking with his dick. Not good. He swung his gaze away from her face and stared at his computer screen instead. Just long enough so he could recover his composure. Not long enough for her to think he was avoiding her gaze. He took a deep breath. Pickard wanted him to tell her only enough of the truth as was completely necessary. Need to know, and all that bullshit. For some reason, he felt like he owed her more, but he'd keep to the script. For now, anyway.

'What I told you about being a security guard was a cover story.'

'Really?' Her tone dripped innuendo, but her stare was blank and totally unreadable. 'Just like your name?'

'*Oui*. I actually work for the… Well, it's complicated. I'm employed by an arm of the gendarme, called GIGN, but I've been seconded across to another unit set up by the UN, to target people smuggling.'

'What does GIGN mean?' Succinct and to the point. Wanting all the facts. A good trait for a cop. But her face was still unreadable.

'*Groupe d'intervention de la Gendarmerie Nationale*. It's a specialist unit. I worked in the counter-terrorism section over there.' She digested this information and a slight frown creased the skin between her brows.

'So, how do you combine counter-terrorism and people smuggling? Sorry, I don't see the link.' She uncrossed her arms and leaned forward on the couch, which he took as a good sign. At least she was interested in what he was saying. Still pissed off, but interested. 'Much less the link to me,' she added.

'I'll get to that,' he said, knowing how confusing this might sound to an outsider. 'People smuggling is a very lucrative business for those who care to dabble. But terrorism is even more lucrative. Terrorists are well-funded, they'll pay exorbitant sums, as long as you can supply them with what they want.'

'What's that? Guns, explosives, child soldiers?'

'Nope, a way into countries like France. An untraceable pathway, so they can slide under the radar and then wreak their havoc before anyone even knows they're here.'

'The terrorists pay the people smugglers to bring them in?'

'Yes, exactly.' She caught on quick. 'They hide them in the throng of humanity, make it look like they're just one more of the many illegal immigrants seeking asylum here in France. But the twist is, some big players have gotten involved. They've changed the rules. And the immigrants have started landing directly on our shores, making it even harder to detect them.'

'Why? Where do refugees normally land?' The creases between her eyes that'd warned him she was angry were disappearing, replaced with a thoughtfully raised eyebrow.

'Most immigrants come to shore in Italy. They have very… Let's just say lax laws there. And then the people trickle across the border into France. But at least we had a chance of catching them when they were crossing our border. Now, we have no idea they're even in the country until—'

'Something goes boom?' she finished for him. A little inelegant, but essentially correct. Jean-Luc quelled an urge to smile. 'Okay, now I know about people smugglers and terrorists. But I still don't see how this all relates to me.' He could always count on her to drive straight to the heart of the matter.

'We've been targeting one of these big players we think is involved in terrorist smuggling. He's rich and very dangerous. He believes he's above the law. The day I jumped over your wall, I was running surveillance on a meeting being held by some of his henchmen and a new player, someone we think might own a property where they could potentially land their boats. And they spotted me.'

'Ah,' she said. Her face closed over again at the mention of her garden. He ploughed on with his story.

'I dived over your wall, not expecting anyone to be in the garden. I never dreamed I'd be putting a civilian in danger.' Her eyebrows lifted at that comment. But it didn't look like she believed him. *Merde.* He really wanted—no, needed—her to believe him. 'After the smugglers had gone, and I hightailed it out of there, I assumed that was the end of it.'

'Except it wasn't,' she replied, mouth tight and pursed.

'No, it wasn't,' he agreed. 'My people at HQ are still working on it, but we think these men somehow tapped into the CCTV camera system. They got a mug shot of me from the cameras and started showing it around the town, asking if anyone had seen me. Offering a reward.'

'I'm assuming that's not easy to do? Tap into the CCTV?'

'No, they would have to have some bloody good…no make that a genius hacker to get into the CCTV security to view the feeds. As good as, if not better than, anyone in our bureau.'

'Okay, so they know what you look like. But why do they want me?'

'When I came back to Uzes, I thought I was being careful.' He ran a hand over his cropped head. This was harder to admit than he thought. 'I made sure I stayed away from all the camera's made sure I wasn't being followed, hadn't been spotted.'

'But?'

'Do you remember the waitress from the restaurant? On the night we had dinner together?'

She nodded, but the perceptive light in her eyes told him she was already starting to understand the waitress' overly familiar banter. She'd been trying to get information out of them.

'Well, it seems she might've sold me out. Sold us out.

She'd seen the photo the hired thugs were showing around and decided to cash in on the reward.'

'And I went and gave her all the information she needed.' Charlize hung her head as the realisation hit her. 'Jesus, I even told her where I lived. How stupid could I be?'

'You weren't to know.' Jean-Luc's voice was louder than he'd intended. 'Even I didn't know. None of this is your fault. Do you understand?'

'So it's your fault then?' She gave an unamused laugh and raised a hand to stop his apology. 'Alright, you know how they found me. What about the why? Why do they want me? Do they think I'm involved?'

'That one's a little harder to answer. Perhaps they think you're part of our operation. Or that you know details about our mission, might be able to dish the dirt on me. So, they want to…' How did he put this, so he didn't upset her? *Merde*, it was way too late for that. Her eyes blazed as she leaned alarmingly toward him.

'Kidnap and torture me and then dump my body when they find out I know nothing?' Her voice was deceptively quiet. 'Holy fuck, Jean-Luc, what have you gotten me into?'

He watched the knuckles of her hands go white around her cup and the colour drain from her face at the realisation of exactly how much danger she was actually in. Then the fight seemed to leave her body, and she slumped on the couch, her gaze directed inwards as her thoughts took her away to a place he couldn't follow. Exactly the same way she'd done earlier, in the car. Fighting internal demons he couldn't see. He wanted to reach over and lay a hand on her knee, but was unsure how she'd construe the gesture. Instead, he watched the emotions flicker across her face. Her mouth formed into a straight, bitter line, her teeth biting at her bottom lip as she hugged her arms around her body. He became mesmerised by that mouth, those lips. Even when she was desperately unhappy, he still found her mouth so damn attractive. Found himself wishing he could lean over and kiss those lips, ever so gently.

'So why the whole crap story about you working as a security guard and the false name? Why didn't you just tell me the truth when you took me to dinner?' His focus snapped back to the room and what she'd just said.

'Because you weren't in danger then. We thought you'd be safe, that Vin...that the thugs didn't know anything.' He'd almost said Vincent's name aloud. Charlize already knew more than was good for her. Jean-Luc and Pickard had come to an understanding as to just how much he was allowed to tell her, so she'd believe how serious this all was.

'But then why... Oh, you were checking up on me, weren't you? To make sure I hadn't been...how do you say it, compromised.' Her voice hardened as reality sank in, her beautiful sage eyes freezing with the knowledge that he'd doubted her. He hadn't been there for her safety alone, after all.

A band of iron closed around his chest and squeezed tight as the sense of betrayal showed on her face. He'd just been doing his job, hadn't meant to hurt her. If only he'd chosen some other wall to climb over. Pickard had said he should think of her as just collateral damage. The logical side of Jean-Luc agreed with Pickard. So then why was his heart having such a hard time with the concept?

'I'm sorry, Charlize.' It sounded trite, but was the only thing he could come up with, and at least it was sincere. He *was* terribly sorry he'd involved her. Now he was going to do everything in his power to get her out of this situation with minimal damage.

She glanced up at him, piercing him with those green eyes, and he waited to be flayed alive by her words. Because he deserved nothing less. Anger, regret, determination, frustration, sadness, all of those emotions alternated on her face. Then the emotional meter wavered and seemed to stay stuck on sadness. To his horror, her eyes filled with tears. Then her chest heaved and a great sob broke through. Oh, *Merde.*

'I can't...' She couldn't finish her sentence as another loud sob racked her willowy shoulders. Instinct had him gather her into his arms before he realised he'd even moved. She turned into him, her face pushed into the curve of his shoulder. Trembling hands curled into the fabric of his t-shirt. The skin of her upper back was soft beneath his fingers. The heat of her body, the weight of her head pushed against his neck, was doing strange things to his insides. Even though she was nearly as tall as him, right now she felt incredibly small and defenceless in his arms. Afraid that she'd startle and pull away from him if he so much as moved a muscle, he almost stopped breathing.

It was a peculiar feeling, to be needed by someone. By a woman. Not something he'd been used to over the past five years.

Shudders ran through her body as she sucked in large gulps of air, her tears forming a large wet patch on his shirt. She was trying to master her crying; the little he'd learned about Charlize so far warned him that she was probably horrified to be crying on the shoulder of a stranger. Well, perhaps not a complete stranger. They had shared dinner. And now he thought about it, even though they'd only met three times, all of those occasions had been intense. Enlightening for him on so many levels.

He'd discovered she was a very attractive woman. And his heart, which he'd previously thought encased in concrete, could still be swayed by this particular woman. He was becoming sucked into her life, into the enigma that was Charlize. Her moods were ethereal and unpredictable, but that endeared her to him more, not less. The fact that she was so vulnerable—as was evident in her crying fit right now—and then in a heartbeat she somehow managed to throw up a camouflage around that damaged section of her heart to become a strong, independent woman again, at least on the outside, tugged at emotional strings he'd thought long broken.

He had wanted to kiss her before. Not that he'd ever take advantage of a distraught woman, but the image of crushing her mouth beneath his own was an intriguing one.

Her quiet shudders were less violent now, and he knew she was going to withdraw from him any second. He shuttered off that part of his soul which'd been touched by Charlize's distress. His feelings for her would do neither of them any good. There was only one way to help her, and that was to make sure she was safe. To stop Vincent once and for all.

His phone rang, vibrating on the small table next to the couch. Charlize jumped at the sound and pulled away quickly.

'Get out of there. Now!' a voice demanded on the other end of the phone. It was Pickard, and he sounded as rattled as Jean-Luc had ever heard him.

'What's happened?' Jean-Luc demanded.

'They're coming. I'm not sure how. They must've got her phone number somehow and tracked her. You need to move. Now.'

'Right, boss.' In one fluid movement, he was off the couch. He rammed his computer into its case and grabbed Charlize by the hand. 'Sorry, we've got to go. They've found out where we are.'

'What? Why?' It was taking her too long to process the information, her eyes were still glazed with tears, her mind still fogged by her misery. He needed her to move.

'Where's your phone?' he demanded, pulling her up with him.

'In my handbag, on the bench.' She pointed toward the kitchen, understanding starting to flare in her eyes. When she finally produced the phone from inside her bag, he immediately cracked it over the edge of the bench top and then threw it in the sink, turning on the water full blast.

'Jesus, did they—' She never finished her sentence. The air was shattered by the sound of squealing tyres as cars sped into the driveway.

CHEESE SOUFFLE

INGREDIENTS
Melted butter to grease
2 tbsp Dried breadcrumbs, to coat
2 ½ tbsp Butter
2 ½ tbsp Plain flour
250 ml (1 cup) Milk
50 g Vintage cheddar, finely grated
50 g Gruyère, finely grated
50 g Parmesan, finely grated
2 tsp Dijon mustard
½ tsp Cayenne pepper
2 tbsp Chopped chives
2 tbsp Chopped flat leaf parsley
Salt and freshly ground black pepper, to taste
4 eggs, at room temperature, separated

DIRECTIONS
Preheat oven to 190°C. Brush four individual 250 ml (1 cup) ramekins or soufflé dishes with butter and then sprinkle with the breadcrumbs, turning to coat the dishes well. Place on an oven tray and set aside.

Combine the cheddar, Gruyère, Parmesan and set 2 tablespoons of this mixture aside for sprinkling the tops of the soufflés.

Melt the butter in a medium saucepan over a medium heat until foaming. Add the flour and stir with a whisk for about 1 minute until the mixture is bubbling and leaves the sides of the pan.

Remove the pan from the heat and gradually add half the milk, stirring constantly with the whisk until smooth. Gradually add the remaining milk, stirring until smooth. Return the pan to a medium heat, and stir constantly with the whisk until the sauce thickens and starts to simmer. Reduce the heat to low and simmer, stirring frequently, for 3 minutes.

Transfer the sauce immediately to a heatproof bowl and stir in the cheddar, Gruyère and Parmesan mixture, Dijon mustard, cayenne, chives and parsley. Season well with salt and pepper. Add the egg yolks and stir until well combined.

Whisk the egg whites with a pinch of salt until firm peaks form.

Add about a quarter of the whisked egg whites to the cheese sauce and use a large metal spoon or spatula to fold together until just combined to loosen the mixture. Fold in the remaining egg whites until just combined.

Divide the mixture evenly among the prepared dishes. Sprinkle with the reserved cheese mixture. Bake in preheated oven for 20 minutes or until the soufflés are well risen and cooked through (they should still wobble slightly when the dishes are tapped and an inserted skewer should come out clean but slightly moist). Serve immediately.

Best enjoyed on a cold winter's afternoon in front of a roaring fire with a glass of chilled chardonnay. Preferably not while there are men with guns chasing you.

CHAPTER ELEVEN

He pushed her between the shoulder blades, directing her down the tiny corridor toward the back entrance. She ran, Jean-Luc right behind her. Holy Jesus, they'd run a trace on her phone. Who were these people? What else were they capable of?

Working as a cop back in Perth, she'd sometimes come across criminal gangs or crime bosses, even members of the notorious Comancheros bikie gang, but none of them had been this vicious or this well-organised. Perth criminals seemed small-town, dabbling in petty crime compared to this. Respect for Jean-Luc and his team grew.

She burst through the back door and ran across the gravel parking bay. Remembered too late that she was still barefoot and nearly fell as the sharp stones bit into the soles of her feet. But Jean-Luc caught her by the arm just in time, half-carrying her toward the car.

'Get in.' For the second time that night, she scrambled into the rental car as Jean-Luc started it and reversed quickly. 'We only got out of there because I killed the signal from your phone. So now they're going to have to search each cottage. They must not have seen the road around the back here, otherwise we wouldn't have made it past the back door.' Perhaps the gang wasn't quite as well organised as she'd thought. The gang's mistake had given them the precious seconds they needed to escape. 'But there's only one way out of here,' Jean-Luc continued. 'Which means we'll have to go past them to get out the front driveway. So keep your head down until I tell you it's safe.' Charlize was amazed at how calm he sounded. She did as she was told, ducked down and curled up as small as she could go in the passenger seat and then hung tight on as he swerved around the bend in the dirt track and revved the car onto the main driveway.

'Watch out!' he yelled as bursts of gunfire boomed all around them. Jean-Luc swung the steering wheel wildly, keeping his head as low as possible while still managing to peer over the dashboard. The front wheel of the car hit something, but they kept going. At least three bullets thumped into the metal sides of the car, and she closed her eyes and prayed. To whom she had no idea, but it helped to stop her from screaming out loud. Then the car straightened out, stopped its crazy fish-tailing race, and she knew they must be on the bitumen road again. The gunfire receded into the dark.

'You can sit up now.' His voice floated to her through the protection of her arms covering her head.

'Holy fuck,' she said, slowly unfurling herself. The blood was still pounding in her ears and she was breathing hard enough to have just run a marathon.

'Are you okay? Were you hit?' Worry made his voice deep and demanding.

'No. I'm fine,' she replied after a quick self-assessment.

'You?'

'I'm good.' His reply was curt. It'd been an automatic question, one she'd asked her police teammates more than a few times over the years. Her relief at his reply was purely logistical—who was going to drive if he'd been injured? It had absolutely nothing to do with the way her heart suddenly felt tight and heavy at the idea of Jean-Luc being hurt. Or killed.

His eyes kept flicking to the rear-vision mirror.

'I think we got away.' He barely took his eyes from the mirror as he spoke, shoulders tense and hunched, knuckles white on the steering wheel, casting one quick, concerned glance her way before returning to the perusal of the road behind them. 'Their orders were probably to take us alive. Get in and get out, quick. Their boss will be furious they drew that much attention to themselves. The gendarme will be swarming all over that place in no time.'

'Are you sure?' She cast a couple of panicky glances out the back window. But it seemed he was right. The streets were quiet, no headlights followed them. Jean-Luc still pushed the rental car hard, he made the tyres squeal around corners as he darted down side streets, staying off the main road, until Charlize was well and truly lost. She took another look out the back window. Nope, those thugs would never catch them now. Her heartbeat finally returned to a semblance of normal as she turned to face the front.

Jean-Luc slowed slightly, and his grip slackened a little on the steering wheel. He gave her another surreptitious glance. She watched the outer suburban houses flash by, most windows dark now. People would be tucked up in bed at this late hour, sleeping.

Her mind was still whirling with all that'd just happened, but funnily enough, it didn't seem to want to go down that dark and twisty path it had earlier tonight. Which was probably why Jean-Luc kept looking at her as if she might turn into a crazy woman any second. He was waiting for another one of her panic attacks. Wondering if she was about to become a babbling fool again. Taking a few deep breaths, she gave a tentative probe into the shadowy recess of her mind. There was apprehension, trepidation and definitely fear, but that was fading fast along with the distance put between them and the gunmen. Nothing to indicate she was about to spiral downwards into the pit of despair and lose her shit. No flashbacks to the accident, no skewed sense of time, no chest pain or internal organs that felt like they were made of concrete.

Why? What was the difference between being shot at just then and what'd happened back at the airport. Nothing, as far as she could tell. What difference had a few hours made? Was she becoming acclimatised to danger again? The old Charlize making a show, perhaps. Some of that cop no-nonsense proficiency finding its way out from behind the wall where it'd been hiding. She'd heard of muscle memory before, when your muscles remembered how to do things, like ride a bike, without any conscious thought on your part. Maybe this was something like that, but instead of muscle memory, it was more like psychological memory. Her subliminal mind remembered to stay strong in the face of danger, as long as she didn't let her conscious thoughts carry her away. In other words, as long as she didn't think too hard about it, she might be fine.

'Sorry, that was pretty intense,' Jean-Luc said, interrupting her musings.

'Intense.' Her voice took on a high pitch. 'I used to be a police officer back in Australia, and I've never been involved in a shoot-out like that before.' The words were out of her mouth before she could stop them. Damn, she hadn't meant to reveal that.

He must've noticed the look on her face, because he said, 'I read your file, Charlize. I know all about you.'

'You what? I've got a file?' What the hell was he talking about? She stared at him, blinking rapidly, not able to fully comprehend what he'd just said.

'Don't go getting all huffy.' He smiled as she shot him a glare. 'You're a person of interest in our investigation. Of course you've got a file.' He said it in such a matter-of-fact way, but she still had to force the rising bile back down her throat. Of course, he knew everything about her. Why wouldn't he? It was part of his job. She would've done exactly the same thing if the shoe had been on the other foot.

'I'm not huffy,' she replied in a prickly tone. Just because she knew it was logical and part of protocol didn't make it any less invasive. If the truth be told, she was angry because it was another secret he'd kept from her. She wanted to straighten her pursed lips, but they stayed determinedly defiant. Okay, she was huffy. He'd just have to deal with it.

'So you knew all about me, even back when we had dinner that other night?' He had the grace to look sheepish, but didn't reply.

'Bastard.' She couldn't help herself, the word came out with explosive vehemence. To his credit he kept his mouth shut, and she could see by the glow of the intermittent street lights a hint of guilt in the clench of his jaw. And he bloody well should feel guilty. How dare he sit there at that table, looking as smug as the cat who'd got the cream, flirting with her, and lying through his teeth at the same time? Arsehole.

'Arsehole.' It helped to say it out loud. But didn't bring as much satisfaction as she'd hoped. Again, he didn't say anything, just kept driving on through the dark.

Disappointment swelled in her stomach. She'd thought better of him. *Stupid*. She was so stupid. She should've guessed he had ulterior motives when he'd asked her to dinner. Instinct told her not to take him at face value, but she'd given him the benefit of the doubt and now she found out just how bloody gullible she was. It didn't help that the logical part of her brain knew he was only doing his job. And why the hell did she care, anyway? She wasn't ever going to see him again after this was all over. Now she'd been handed the perfect reason to never *want* to see him again. God, she was so stupid.

Silence descended over the car as she sat and stewed in her thoughts, and he concentrated on driving.

'Where are we going now?' she growled, eventually. She just wanted out of this damn car. Away from his lying arse.

'Not sure yet. My superior was supposed to call us back with details, but that plan's all gone to shit. I've got an apartment in Nice. We might have to go there until I can figure something else out. I'll take the back roads though, make it harder to trace us.'

'Great, so we're just going to drive all over bloody France, with God knows how many madmen tailing us and hope that it's all going to be okay?' Her disappointment and disillusionment—in herself as much as in him—found an outlet by turning into full-blown anger.

'Still huffy then?' She could've sworn he was smirking at her in the dark.

The bloody nerve of the man. Her hand itched to reach out and smack that supercilious smirk off his face. Instead, she leant back in the seat and closed her eyes, shutting out the dark countryside now speeding past. Shutting out the gorgeous lying bastard sitting mere centimetres away from her.

Her mind rolled back over tonight's events. She couldn't believe she'd cried all over him. How humiliating. At least his phone had rung and saved her from having to look him in the eye afterwards. But it'd been nice to be encased in those strong arms, even if it was for just a few moments. Charlize was used to dealing with stuff on her own, had been doing so for over a year and a half now. But she couldn't deny how pleasant it'd been to be in the arms of a handsome man. And he was definitely tantalising, she could vouch for that after her close-up with him. His chest, which had cushioned her cheek, had been rock hard, she could feel the defined muscles beneath her face. There was a tattoo on his left bicep, too. She could only make out the bottom half of as it peeked from beneath the sleeve of his t-shirt, but it looked to be of a large elephant. The black ink against his chocolate skin had been sexy as hell. Charlize had always been fond of a tattoo or two, as long as it was done with class and style. She only had one tattoo, a small love heart on the inside of her left wrist. To honour her lost baby. The thought sobered her, and she opened her eyes, just in time to hear Jean-Luc swear. Loudly.

'What's the matter?'

'Not sure,' he grunted through gritted teeth. He seemed to be straining to hold on to the steering wheel. 'A stray bullet may've damaged something.'

'Well, pull over then.'

'Not sure I can, the wheel won't turn.'

'Jesus Christ,' she exclaimed, just as a set of headlights came around the bend toward them.

* * *

'I've lost control of the car,' he said as calmly as possible. The steering wheel wouldn't respond. Instead, it was trying to wrench out of his hands, send them careening off the road into the nearest tree. Even using all his strength, he knew he was fighting a losing battle. A few miles back, a shudder had started, and the wheel began to tremble beneath his hands. At first, he'd thought that whatever they'd hit on their mad dash out of the driveway might've put the wheels out of alignment. But this was a lot more than that.

'Stop the car,' Charlize wailed.

'I'm trying,' he bit back between gritted teeth. But whenever he touched the brake, the car pulled more to the right. He'd taken his foot off the accelerator, but he didn't dare remove one hand from the steering wheel to change down a gear. He silently cursed his decision to take the narrow back roads. If they'd been on one of the main highways, he would've had a lot more stopping room. Perhaps Charlize could operate the gear stick for him, if he told her when to do it.

'Charlize, could you—'

'Oh my God, that car's going to hit us,' Charlize said in a strangled moan. She was staring straight ahead out of the window at an oncoming car, enthralled by the bright headlights. That's when he saw the sharp bend up ahead. He'd managed to slow some of the car's hurtling speed by taking his foot off the accelerator, but nowhere near enough to make it around that tight bend. 'No, it's not,' he grunted, knowing the car wasn't the problem. 'But you need to brace yourself for this corner, it's going to be dicey.'

'Oh, no. Oh, no. Oh, no, Patty,' she said in the same strangled moan. The other car flashed past them and was swallowed by the dark night, leaving them alone again on the deserted road. The rental car was going about half the speed now from the time he'd first noticed the problem, but he'd been really pushing it before, so that wasn't saying much.

Still using all his strength to fight the steering wheel, he made the decision to use the brakes. It might send them hurtling off the road, but hopefully slow them down enough to save them from certain death if they hit something at this breakneck speed.

'Hang on,' he shouted and tramped on the brake, hard. The car started to skew to the right, the front wheel dropped into the dirt at the edge. Charlize gave a blood-curdling scream. He hurled the weight of his whole body against the wheel but it was no good, whatever part had been damaged by the bullet in the steering rack must've now completely snapped under this last onslaught and the steering wheel was as useless as a child's stuffed toy in his hands. So he kept his foot hard on the brake, leaning over to pull on the handbrake as well. Charlize's screams punctuated the sound of the loose gravel hitting the car.

The car started to skid wildly, the back end swinging

around in a 180 turn, and then they were flying backwards off the edge of the road and down an embankment. Tall grass and thick underbrush flew past the windows, crashing against the body of the car. *Oh merciful God, please don't let the car roll.* He used the steering wheel to brace himself, waiting for an impact, for them to hit a tree, or a rock, something.

Then they did hit something and came to a bone crunching halt. Everything went dark, the headlights smashed to smithereens. All the airbags deployed at once, pummelling him in the face and on the side. Pain speared through his left arm and hip as the metal door was crushed against him.

The car finally came to rest. An eerie silence descended, filled with the cracks of splintered trees and the hiss of escaping fluids from the smashed engine. That's when he realised Charlize had stopped screaming.

'Charlize,' he croaked. Then cleared his throat and tried again. 'Talk to me. Are you okay?'

It was deathly quiet beside him. He reached up with a shaking hand, found the interior light, and switched it on. A weak yellow light filtered down from above.

She was curled up in the foetal position on the seat next to him, her eyes open wide and staring, her mouth frozen into a soundless scream.

Was she dead? *Merde.* 'Charlize,' he said, panic starting to clutch at his throat.

She blinked, but didn't move. Jesus. She was alive. Catatonic, but alive. He clenched both hands around the useless steering wheel and dragged in a few much-needed breaths. Fuck, if she had died... It wasn't worth dissecting that thought right now. But the way his insides contracted like live eels were swarming around inside warned him her death would mean a lot more to him than it rightly should.

He needed to get them out of here. Twisting around, he found the door handle and pulled it. The door opened a crack, but then stopped. Leaning his entire weight against it, ignoring the pain shooting through his ribs, he managed to force it half-way open before it stuck for good. There was just enough space for him to slither out through the gap.

On hands and knees, he crawled away from the car and stood up, taking a few painful, wobbly steps and took an assessment of all his injuries. Using his undamaged hand, he quickly patted down his left arm and leg. No wet patches, which meant he wasn't bleeding, or at least not badly. Probably just bruised. Lots and lots of bruises if the pain was anything to go by. Gingerly, he felt around his lower leg where there was a shooting pain every time he moved. There was a tear in his jeans, and through it he could feel a ragged, oozing gash. He gritted his teeth and prodded a little more deeply. It was a long tear, but not deep. A doctor might advise stitches, but with no doctor in sight, he'd have to leave the non-life-threatening injury until later.

He straightened up slowly and looked up the embankment. They were now a good fifty or sixty meters from the edge of the road. The car swam in a pool of dim light cast by the interior lamp, only just bright enough for him to make out the dark shapes of many thin tree trunks surrounding the car. Saplings. They'd landed in a stand of saplings. Which was good. It might've even saved their lives. The young trees had broken on impact, acting more like a safety net. If they'd hit an impermeable, immovable object, say like the huge old oak tree only a few meters to their right, there might've been a completely different outcome. Someone was looking after them tonight.

Wading thought the thigh-deep grass, he went around to the passenger side of the car and tried the door. It protested, but swung open without too much force. That was good. It meant this side of the car hadn't sustained too much damage. Which hopefully meant Charlize was okay. Physically, at least.

Leaning in, he hovered over the woman crouched in the seat, unsure how to proceed. She was still staring straight ahead, still catatonic. He'd never had to deal with someone in this state before. What did you do? Yell at them to shock them awake, or treat them gently so as not to cause more anguish? He was no psychiatrist, but even he could see her reaction was way over the top. It probably had something to do with that accident, the one that'd been the cause of the scars on her leg. Her file had only stated the bare facts about the crash, and there was nothing about how she'd recovered afterwards. But right now, Jean-Luc had a sudden flash of insight that told him she hadn't coped all that well.

'Charlize,' he said in a quiet voice, taking her shoulder in a gentle grip. 'Can you hear me?' She groaned and blinked, but otherwise didn't move. 'Charlize,' he said, louder this time. He shook her shoulder. 'We have to get out of here.' This time she started, like a rabbit who just found herself in front of a hungry fox, eyes going wide and wild.

'It's okay,' he soothed. 'You're alright. I'm alright. We're both safe.' At last, she turned her gaze toward him. Her eyes swum with tears, but the focus slowly started to return. 'That's right, good girl,' he crooned again.

'I...' Her face was a deathly pale oval in the yellow light. 'Are you sure?' Her voice was thin and quavery, making his stomach clench with a need to pick her up and just take her out of here. Away from this dark embankment and the fear oozing from her pores.

'Are we really safe?' Her voice was so low it was almost a whisper.

'Yes, we're both safe. Come on, let me help you out of there.' He took her hand and pulled gently. At first she resisted, but then slowly started to unwind herself, to uncurl those long legs and reach for his other hand. Still so tentative and fearful, she reminded him of a frightened child. Finally, when both feet were on the ground, she stood up and glanced around, wide-eyed, in the darkness.

'Where are we? What happened?' She wouldn't let go of his hand. Clung to it as if it were her only lifeline to sanity.

'The car must've been damaged by a bullet. We skidded off the road. It's just up there.' He pointed up the embankment. While she turned her head to look back at the road, he took the opportunity to give her a quick once over. No obvious wounds. At least not that he could see in this dim light. She might still have internal injuries, though. There was a small gash above her left eye and blood dripped onto her shoulder. But apart from that, her face was free of other cuts or contusions.

'Can you turn around for me?'

'What? Why?' Her voice was still vague.

'I just need to have a look at you,' he murmured. It took him a few seconds to untangle her fingers from his, but then, surprisingly, she did as she was told. He ran an expert eye over her shoulders, down her back, over her backside and down both legs as she did a slow 360 turn. The long dress covered most of her from head to toe, but there were no obvious blood stains. She was still bare-foot, however. *Merde*, she wasn't going to get far with no shoes.

'Can you tell me if you're hurt anywhere?' he prompted. She was still staring about in an offhand way.

'What?' She turned and blinked at him. Then she reached up to her head and winced as she found the cut.

'I think I hit my head.' Good, she seemed to be coming around, shaking off whatever had held her enthralled. Making more sense. 'And my hip is sore too.' Her voice got stronger with every word. She placed a hand over the spot where her hipbone jutted out. 'But I think it's just a bruise.'

'Does it hurt anywhere else?' he commanded, the drill sergeant in him making an appearance as he started to work on practicalities. As long as she was coming good, then they needed to get moving. They needed to get as far away from this crash site as possible. In case Vincent's thugs were somehow miraculously still following them. 'Any pain in the stomach, or in the lower back?' Which might indicate any internal injuries.

'No. I'm fine.'

He let out a quiet sigh of relief. She seemed physically fit enough to travel on foot. To where he had no idea, all he knew was they needed to keep moving. Keep one step ahead of Vincent and his gang. Charlize crossed her arms over her chest and rubbed her hands up and down her bare arms. She started to shiver; the shudders becoming more obvious with each passing second.

'Wait here.' He opened the rear car door and pulled out

a duffle bag. His overnight bag. There was an old hoodie and a spare pair of joggers in there somewhere.

'Here, put this on,' he said as he helped her gently ease each arm into the jumper and then he zipped it up at the front, like she was a kindergarten kid who needed help to put on her clothes. And she let him. She was definitely in shock. He needed to keep her warm/ Even though it was summer, the night air was becoming chilly.

'Thanks.' The folds of his overly large hoodie swallowed her up. He couldn't help it, she looked so lost. His arms went around her and he held her against his chest for a few quick, tight seconds.

'I'm going to get you out of this,' he said thickly. She stiffened in his embrace momentarily, then her arms snaked around his waist and she clung to him. Needing his comfort. Accepting his support. He didn't know much about mental illness or trauma or stress disorders. But she obviously had a whole lot of something going on. Normally he'd pity someone in her situation, pity them and then move on. But for some reason, he was starting to admire her. She'd just relived one of the most terrifying moments of her life, and yes, she'd completely lost her shit, but now she was pulling herself back together, piece by ragged piece, almost in front of his eyes. It was a huge effort, and words weren't enough to describe how much he wanted to applaud her for her courage.

'I know,' she said, words muffled. 'I don't blame you for any of this.' Her voice broke the spell and, much as he hated to do it, he straightened his arms and slowly pushed her away from him.

'We've got to get away from here.' She just nodded in acknowledgement. 'These are all I've got, but you can't walk around in the wilderness with no shoes on,' he continued, as he dangled the size ten Nikes in front of her face. They were way too big for her, but anything was better than spearing her foot with a broken bottle or any of the other innumerable hazards out there.

While she sat down on a log to put the shoes on, he went back and dug out a long-sleeved shirt for himself from the duffle, noting the cool air on his bare arms. He may as well keep himself warm and ward off any symptoms of shock. It wouldn't do for him to succumb. Even a seasoned agent like himself wasn't immune to the after-effects of a dangerous car crash.

'What are we going to do now?' The shoes made it look like she had clown's feet, they were so big. Her cool facade was slowly returning, replacing the naked fear and hysteria. The extreme vulnerability was gone now, covered with a blanket of—if not calm, then at the least poised—professional efficiency.

'We're going to find some place to hunker down and I'm going to get Pickard to send someone to come and get us.'

'Right.' She stood up and stomped her feet once or twice, to get the feel of the over-large shoes. 'Let's get going then.' She straightened her spine and took a few steps toward the dark forest beyond the dim light. Yep, the steely purpose was returning to Charlize's face. Jean-Luc almost hummed with relief as they stumbled off through the black night.

CHAPTER TWELVE

'Do you have any idea where we are?' Charlize tried to keep the irritation out of her voice, but the longer she trudged along in the dark—in his shoes that were three sizes too big for her, chafing her heels and raising blisters on her toes—the more frustrated she became.

'Yep, there's a house a little way over the next rise. That's where we're heading.'

'Thank God,' she muttered under her breath. He kept looking at his phone, probably using Google maps or some other system to find his way in the dark. Every time he stopped to consult it, his face was lit with an unearthly glow. She could make out his strong jawline, chiselled cheekbones and high forehead. Even in the light from a bloody phone he was good-looking, goddamnit. How could any man look this good after being shot at, involved in a car accident, and then walking for miles through the wilderness in the small hours of the morning?

She went back to tagging along behind him in silence. They were following a dirt track, so at least she didn't have to stumble along through the undergrowth like they'd done when they first left the car. She'd kept tripping when the long grass tangled in her long skirt, until Jean-Luc had taken her by the hand, supporting her over the rough terrain.

She'd clung to his hand, using it as a lifeline. But also enjoying the buzz she got from his skin on hers. There was no denying the chemistry, the physical reaction she had to him. It was there every time she looked at him, or accidentally brushed against him. Was it mutual? She'd been certain there'd been a moment back in the cottage when he'd wanted to kiss her. He'd been staring at her mouth like a starving man. And even though she knew she looked a mess, nose red and dripping like a tap, eyes swollen from crying, tear tracks running down her cheeks, hair all over the place, she felt his need, his desire for her. And her own desire flared in answer.

Now they were walking along a relatively smooth surface, he'd dropped her hand so he could check his phone. Which was fine, she was a big girl, more than capable of walking on her own two feet. The only problem with being left alone with her thoughts, though, was the flashbacks from the crash, which started to come back to her fuzzy mind. And she didn't like what she saw. Most of the crash was hazy, vague memories of bright headlights and her screaming. Lots of screaming. Then...nothing, until she was standing next to the car and Jean-Luc was wrapping her in his hoodie. But she had a nasty suspicion there was more to the lost bit of time than she liked to admit.

Had she done something stupid, embarrassed herself? She couldn't remember. All she knew for sure was Jean-Luc was acting very solicitously toward her, treating her as if she might break at his touch. And it worried her. Had she had another panic attack? If only she could recall the entire crash. This fact, more than anything else, kept her quiet as she worried at her memories like a loose tooth, trying to piece together the few bits and pieces she could remember.

'There's the house,' Jean-Luc said, his voice loud in the dark, making her jump. She couldn't see much. The moon wasn't up yet, leaving only starlight to light their way, which didn't penetrate very far beneath the forest canopy. She could just make out the horizon, the dark shapes of the rolling hills in the distance, silhouetted against the backdrop of the indigo sky. In beneath the shadowy forms of the trees lining the dirt road, a squat, square shape appeared.

'There should be some kind of barn or large shed over to the left, we'll go in there.'

'Is anybody home?' Jean-Luc hadn't been forthcoming with much information on where they were headed. A few options had run through her still-scattered brain, like a safe-house—though that was probably too much to ask out here in the middle of nowhere—or a farmer who was sympathetic to the cause, perhaps. Anywhere would be better than tramping through the forest in the middle of the night.

'No, Pickard assured me this house and its shed have been derelict for some time.'

'Oh, okay.' Not a scenario she'd considered. But she could see why it might be better if no one else knew where they were. Less people she'd have to trust with her safety. And she was having a lot of trouble deciding who to trust at the moment. Hell, she still wasn't sure she trusted Jean-

Luc.

'Why don't we go into the house if it's empty, then?' Charlize stopped and stared at the dark shape of his back.

'It's safer not to.' He turned around to face her. 'Even Pickard's information isn't always foolproof.' Fair enough. If someone did suddenly come home, they were less likely to find them if they hunkered down in the shed. But she didn't like the uncertainty. She mulled that thought over as she followed Jean-Luc down a slight incline and then around a small track to the left of the house until a large square building loomed out of the dark.

Jean-Luc had made a few desperate phone calls straight after the crash, while she'd still been pulling on his shoes. She'd overheard enough to get the gist of what he communicated to Pickard. Jean-Luc had said grimly at least the thugs would never find them now, which, while probably true, still left her flabbergasted. How could Jean-Luc possibly think barely surviving a car crash, then walking around in the middle of nowhere—in the middle of the night—was a positive thing? Here she was, putting all her trust in a man she hardly knew, letting him lead her to supposed safety while all her instincts were screaming at her that this was plain crazy. She was tired beyond belief, scared out of her wits, she hurt all over and just wanted to curl up in her own bed in her own little villa and sleep for a week. Block out all the runaway emotions that circled her brain like a pack of howling wolves and just pretend none of this had happened. She'd managed to force all those frenzied impressions, the fear that blocked her throat and made it impossible to breathe, back into the box where they lived in her mind. For now. But it wouldn't take much to bring them tumbling back out again.

Besides all this, Charlize also had a suspicion Jean-Luc might've been injured in the crash, but he resolutely refused to admit it, or even let her take a look. Under normal circumstances, she would've demanded he stop until she'd checked him out. But these weren't normal circumstances.

Using the torch on his phone, he quickly located the door. He fiddled around with the latch until there was the squeak of hinges and then took her hand and led her inside.

'Give me a minute,' he said, dropping her hand so he could use the torch to do a quick reconnaissance. It'd might once have been a machinery shed. There was an old tractor huddled in the far corner and piles of discarded tools, bits of tin, rolls of wire, and engine parts scattered all over the large room. Off to the right was a large wooden workbench, running the length of one wall. And in the corner closest to them was a tatty old couch and a small table. Had the farmer used this space to escape his nagging wife, at one time or another?

'Over here.' He led the way toward the couch. It was dirty, covered in layers of dust and what might've been dead insects. But soft and dry. And better than blundering around in the dark for hours on end. She pulled the cushions off the couch and banged them against the bench, dislodging the worst of the dust, while Jean-Luc rummaged around under the bench. Using her bare hand, she tried to brush the rest of the remaining dust and muck off the back and armrests. Jean-Luc emerged from beneath the bench, carrying a handful of old rags and blankets. He shook them out, and the dust swirled up in clouds and made them both sneeze. He draped them as best he could across the couch and beckoned for her to sit down. Before her backside even hit the seat, she had reached to untie the shoelaces on those godforsaken shoes and kicked them off, releasing a sigh of ecstasy as she did so.

'That feels so much better,' she said, rubbing her sore heel.

'Sorry,' he apologised. 'They were all I had.'

'You don't need to apologise for the shoes,' she retorted. Her feet were protesting at their ill-treatment, but the shoes had done the job, her feet had remained mostly intact on their two-hour hike. As long as she didn't need to wear them ever again, of course. Then she might have a few choice words to say.

Jean-Luc produced two candles, along with a box of matches.

'Found these under the bench as well. Not sure if the matches work.' She took them from him and pulled one out, muttered a small prayer, and struck it down the side of the box. It fizzed into life. Hallelujah. One of the candles flared, and she dribbled wax onto the small tabletop, using it to fix it to the table. It threw out a weak, but very welcome light. Almost homely.

She had to laugh at herself then. When had a disgusting, filthy couch in a broken down shed in the middle of the wilderness become homely? She'd come a long way indeed from this morning, when she'd left the safety of her villa in Uzes. No, it was probably more like yesterday morning now. Dawn couldn't be too far off.

Jean-Luc went to sit next to her, and she saw him grimace in pain as he lowered himself down. It was a mere flicker of his mouth before he had control again, but it was enough.

'Give me the torch,' she demanded. His chocolate eyes found hers, widened in surprise. She expected him to resist her request, but he slowly gave her his phone.

'I need to make sure you're not mortally wounded,' she said as she took it from his outstretched hand. His gaze stayed fixed on hers as he seemed to weigh up her command, deciding whether to let her look under his shirt. Eventually, she had to flick her gaze away from his and pretend an interest in the phone instead. Try to hide the heat that rose in her cheeks from his prolonged gaze.

'Okay,' he agreed finally. Charlize narrowed her eyes at the weary note in his voice. 'But only if you'll let me do the same for you.' That caught her by surprise. But she knew she wasn't badly injured, so she nodded in agreement. He, on the other hand, if he was able to jump her garden wall —twice—and then escape on foot without letting a gunshot wound to the side slow him down, God knew what kind of injuries he was hiding from her now.

She scooted closer to him on the couch. His dark eyes watched her approach.

'Lift your shirt for me.' She used her best teacher's tone while aiming the torch at his torso. His fingers grasped the bottom of his shirt, but instead of just lifting the corner to reveal his left-hand side, the whole shirt came over his head, revealing his naked torso. Mere inches from her face.

She blinked once.

It was a glorious torso. As good as her imagination had conjured. No, better. Much better. Chiselled abs, hardened pec muscles, broad shoulders, tapering to a wonderful lean waist. Jesus Christ. He was beautiful. There was no other word to describe him. Physical perfection wrapped in silky brown skin.

Sucking a breath in over her teeth, she mentally kicked herself into gear, knowing he was watching her staring at him. Raising the torch higher, she trained it onto his ribs, where she could see bruises starting to flourish in all their dark, sinister colours. Blue, grey, purple. His whole side was the colour of some macabre, dark horror movie. She moved in closer to make sure there were no odd bumps or lumps that shouldn't be there. Then, to try and distract herself from just how close her face was to his chest—she could feel the heat emanating off his body—she asked the first question that popped into her head.

'How long do you think we'll have to stay here?'

'Pickard's sending a man to get us as soon as he can.' His voice, so deep and close to her ear, had a strange effect on her stomach. *Concentrate*. That meant at least a few more hours spent here. In this shed. With him. She shone the torch lower as she checked out more light bruising, which flowed over his ribs, leading to another dark bruise, purple and swollen just above his hip. Then she saw something that made her catch her breath. The half-healed gunshot wound. She could see where the bullet had entered the muscle just above the hipbone, ripping off a large slice of flesh as it passed through and out the other side.

'Jesus, doesn't that hurt?' The words were out of her mouth before she could stop them.

'*Pah*, not really. Not as much as when it first happened,' he said with a nonchalant shrug. That was no kind of answer. Bloody men, why did they have to be so bloody macho all the time? She'd never understood whether they were actually masking the pain to make themselves look tough, or if they really didn't feel as much pain in the first place—were able to focus their energy away from the physical discomfort somehow.

Taking a closer look, she could see the stitches were still in place. They seemed to be holding, and the wound was clean and healing well.

'Can I check for broken ribs?' she asked, her voice brusque with having to mask her thoughts on idiotic men who risked their lives and pretended they weren't in pain. For what? Glory? The greater good? Preserving humanity?

He nodded, his gaze following her every move. She wished he'd look somewhere other than at her, it was making her hot and bothered. And getting hotter by the second. With tentative fingers, she felt around the large, dark blue bruise on his third rib. As her fingers touched his side, he sucked in a quick breath, but managed to hold completely still for her exploration. She tried to be as gentle as possible as she probed with her fingertips.

'All good,' she said at last. 'Is that it, or do you have some other hidden gaping wounds you're not showing me?' She tried to keep the sarcasm out of her voice, but the corner of his mouth quirked up and he kept that unsettling gaze trained on her. That bloody precisely honed agent's gaze of his, calculating, interpreting, divining her secrets. The silence stretched between them and she was suddenly acutely aware of just how close she was sitting to him, their knees touching. Sending shards of heat up her thigh.

'Well?' she prompted abruptly.

'I've got a scratch on my leg,' he replied and bent down to pull up the bottom of his jeans. She let out a breath as his eyes left her. But then he bent to roll up his jeans and reveal the injury. The movement brought his left shoulder to within an inch or so of her face. She froze. Still as a statue. All that bare, brown skin within touching distance. Tasting distance. If she leant forward just a bit, her lips would land on his upper arm. What would it feel like to trail her lips over those strong shoulders, down his back? He was so close she caught a hint of his cologne, almost dwindled to nothing now after all these hours of walking, but still enough to tantalise her nostrils. Spicy, like cinnamon, mixed with the salty tang of sweat, which wasn't unpleasant, almost raw and macho.

'Do you want to take a look?' She gave a guilty flinch at his muffled voice.

'Sure. Sorry.' Holding the torch much like a talisman between them, she leaned over to have a look at his calf. There was indeed a large wound, around four or five inches long, caked in dried blood running down the expanse of his calf muscle. But while it looked sore, it wasn't deep and certainly not life-threatening. He seemed to have come to the same conclusion as he sat up again.

'Not as bad as I thought,' he said with a raised eyebrow.

'It could probably do with a wash, if we could find some water.' Her teacher's voice was back again, but she'd use any technique to fill the gap, so she didn't have to sit there and stare at his naked chest. Jean-Luc produced an empty plastic water bottle. They'd rescued it from the back seat of the car after the crash, but had drunk all the water already.

'I'll go and find some water in a minute. But now it's your turn.'

'My turn for what?' The question came out more like a squeak.

'I need to make sure your injuries aren't bad either.' Oh damn, no. It was bad enough having all that broad expanse of muscles and chest flexing only centimetres away from her. For him to actually touch her would be a really, really bad idea. She was already way too aware of him. Of his physicality. Of his maleness.

'I'm fine, really,' she said in her most convincing tone, while surreptitiously backing away from him on the couch.

'You promised,' he growled.

Oh, shit.

'Well, at least put your bloody shirt on then.' The words came out more severe than she'd intended, and it caused a smirk to form on those tempting lips, but he did as he was told. Perhaps now her breathing would return to normal with all that skin safely covered up again.

'Give me the torch,' he demanded, then proceeded to shine it on her forehead, nearly blinding her. She squeezed her eyes shut. 'It's a deep gash, but small. It just bled a lot, made it look worse than it really is. It could probably do with some stitches.' Then she felt his touch on her face, a gentle fingertip on her temple, tracing the line of her eyebrow. What was he doing? Her eyes flew open, only to be confronted with his face, suspended so close to hers. Her breath stopped dead in her chest.

'Any other injuries?'

'Ah…' Oh sweet Jesus. No coherent thoughts would come. 'I… ah… I bumped my hip. But it's just bruised, not bad at all.' There was no way she was lifting her dress to let him look at her bruises. No way in hell.

'Are you sure?' His chocolate eyes narrowed in uncertainty, and she could tell he was going to ask to take a look.

'Very sure.' She enunciated each word, making it clear that was the end of that conversation.

'Alright,' he said slowly. 'I'll go and see if I can find us some water.' He got up off the couch, but still he hesitated. 'Will you be okay here on your own for a few minutes?'

'Of course.' A few minutes to catch her breath was just what she needed. This man was as dangerous as she'd once surmised. Dangerous to her sense of stability, her heart, her hard-fought for security. Dangerous because if he'd touched her again, he'd have tipped her over that edge, the one where she let desire get the better of her. The last thing she needed—or wanted—in her life right now was a man. Especially this man.

CHAPTER THIRTEEN

'Then what?' Charlize asked, fixing him with that bottle-green gaze. She was dabbing at the cut on his leg with a piece of material she'd ripped from the bottom of her dress, dampened with water from the bottle. It stung like hell, but he wasn't going to let on. He'd managed to find a tap that worked around the back of the deserted house and filled their empty plastic bottle.

He'd dashed out of the shed fifteen minutes earlier, as if the devil himself was on his tail. Needed to get out into the fresh air. Away from *her* for a few minutes. *Merde.* He'd nearly kissed her. Again. Her lips had been so close, so inviting. But that would've been just plain stupid, for so many reasons and on so many levels. So he'd gone outside to try and restore his equilibrium.

He was a man who always took what he wanted when it came to women. And sex. He enjoyed women, enjoyed the feel of them, enjoyed having sex with them. But ever since Fleur, since the divorce, he'd also enjoyed quick, easy, no-tie relationships.

The thought of no-tie relationships brought an image of

Galina to his mind. She'd be more than a little pissed if she found out about Charlize. Or more to the point, about his confusing feelings for Charlize. But he and Galina weren't exclusive, and he'd never led her to believe he was going to make a commitment anytime in the future, either. Besides, he knew Galina saw other men when it suited her; knew that he alone wasn't enough to satiate her appetites. They only got together whenever he was in Nice, which was infrequent at the best of times, and definitely not long enough to form a lasting relationship.

'Then what?' she repeated.

'Then we get you into a safe house, and I get on with stopping this fucker,' he replied, only half-concentrating.

'What?' The high-pitched tone of Charlize's voice cut through his musings and it took him a few seconds to remember what he'd said. 'I'm *not* going into a safe house.' She stopped dabbing at the cut on his leg and glared at him. 'I will not be left to rot in some dingy backwater house forever, being guarded by a bunch of imbeciles, while you gallivant around in the real world chasing bad guys.' The vehemence behind her words shocked him, took him by surprise. They'd been having an adult, friendly conversation. But now she was looking at him like he'd just sprouted horns and was breathing fire.

'That's not what a safe house is like, and it wouldn't be for very—'

'Don't you sit there and lie to me, Jean-Luc. I worked in the police force, I've seen what happens to people put into police custody.' Her eyes flashed dark emerald in the candlelight and if the old cliche were ever true, he swore she was shooting daggers at him. He opened his mouth to tell her it was for her own safety and she'd got it all

Suzanne Cass

wrong, but she got in first.

'People can spend months, no, years, in safe houses. Left with no compensation or consideration, waiting for a trial or an arrest that might never come. That's no way to live a life. I don't care if I'm in danger, I won't be caged like some domesticated animal.' She sat up very straight to stare down her nose at him.

'How else am I supposed to protect you, Charlize?' He was stunned by her outburst.

'I don't need protection,' she blurted, flinging down the rag. She stood up and turned to glare down at him, hands on hips. 'I want to help you hunt this gang. To make sure they're put away once and for all. I was a cop once, I've got skills.'

What was she thinking? There was no way he was going to let her—a civilian—continue to take part in this mission for any longer than absolutely necessary. And certainly not one who was on Vincent's hit list. Apart from all her problems coping with certain situations. She read the incredulous look on his face correctly, because with a quick intake of breath, she changed tack with her conversation.

'Okay then, just let me go back to Uzes, I can look after myself there.'

He grunted in disgust. 'You can't be serious. You've seen how dangerous these guys are. I'm sorry, but you know I can't let you just go home.' He looked up at her from his spot on the couch. Her mussed hair stood out around her head in spikey tufts, there was still dried blood on her face and mud smeared on her clothes. She was a wreck. But that same fierce determination he'd first seen back in her garden was back. She stood like a boxer, ready to take him on in a fight. What was he supposed to do

186

with this impossible woman?

'Take me with you, or send me home. Those are your only two options. I'm not going into a safe house.' She shot him a challenging glare, eyes still blazing. A glimpse of the Charlize she'd once been, the fearless police officer, not willing to back down for anyone. Strong, sexy and demanding. Something twisted in his gut when he looked at her now. She was beautiful when she was fired up like this. But Pickard would never allow it. Retired cop or not.

He couldn't find the words to answer her.

'Alright, give me a gun. I know how to use one, I can protect myself. Then you can go off and do your macho, gung-ho, save the world thing, without having to worry about poor little me.'

'Charlize,' he sighed, exasperated and suddenly very weary. What had happened to the pleasant, open aura that'd surrounded them mere minutes ago? He'd swear the temperature had dropped several degrees, as Charlize turned into a spitting, hissing hell-cat and he found his anger rising to meet hers. He'd never expected her to fight him on this one, it should've been a foregone conclusion. She'd been in the force, for Christ's sake, she knew how these things worked. There was only one way he could get his head back in the game and onto catching Vincent and his gang, and that was if he knew she was safe, out of Vincent's reach.

'You know I won't give you a gun. And besides, do you really think that's such a good idea, given your—' He was going to say mental state, but pulled up short. The words he hadn't uttered hung in the air between them. Her alluring mouth twisted into a sneer and she narrowed those dark green eyes to slits.

'My what?' she snarled. Uh oh. He might've just given her the excuse she was looking for. He gave another sigh, this one heavier and louder than the last, and swiped a hand across his brow. *Merde.* He was tired. He didn't want to do this now.

'My what?' she said again, much louder this time.

Lowering his jeans back over his wounded leg—she obviously wasn't going to finish fixing it up—he stood up and took a step toward her, but she backed away.

'Look, Charlize, I don't really know what happened to you in Australia. You were involved in a car crash, that's all your file said. But it's obvious it affected you, that it was horrendous beyond words. I can't imagine what you've been through, but—'

'Shut up. You don't know anything about me. You don't know what happened,' she growled, her jaw rigid with anger, fists clenched into tight balls at her sides. 'I'm fine. I just have…panic attacks sometimes. But I'm fine.'

Really? She thought she was fine? He'd known her for less than a week, but it was patently obvious that she was nowhere near *fine*. He took another step closer, not really sure why, perhaps meaning to reach out, to touch her, to take away some of that pain and anger so clearly evident in her eyes.

'Just let me go, Jean-Luc. You go and do what you need to do, and just leave me here,' she ground out between gritted teeth. 'I can disappear into the countryside and you won't have to worry about me ever again. I'll survive. I'm good at surviving.' She was trying vainly to keep the pathetic, bitter tone out of her voice, but he heard her suffering clearly. Hell would freeze over before he let her do that. She must know that. He'd never leave her to the mercies of Vincent's men. But the beseeching look on her face told him otherwise. She was actually entertaining the idea that if he just turned her loose, she would be *fine*, as she liked to put it. Much as he hated to do it, it might be time for some home truths. He straightened his shoulders, his spine going rigid one vertebra at a time, steeling him against the unpleasant task. He didn't want to hurt her, but if it was the only way to get through, then…

'It's more than just panic attacks, Charlize. You can stop pretending now. I know your secret.' Her face blanched white as he spoke, but he kept going. 'My God, you were catatonic after the crash. You were buried so deep in your dreaded memories that you went to a place no one else could follow. I was scared you wouldn't come back. Scared I wouldn't be able to get through to you. Scared you might stay that way forever.' He didn't add he'd also been horrified because he'd been partly to blame for her terrible mental state, by embroiling her in this whole thing in the first place. The crash had obviously re-ignited all those memories she was trying so hard to suppress. But it hadn't been just the crash. She'd been shot at—twice—today, as well as involved in two car chases. It was his fault she was encountering the types of situations that triggered her memories. If he hadn't chosen her garden to jump into, she'd still be safe and well back in the cocoon of her villa. He needed to get her out of here, so that someone—a professional—could help her deal with all this anxiety.

He sure as hell couldn't help her, he was the least qualified person when it came to this kind of thing. The only way he'd been able to cope with the death of his son was to bury the memory deep. Refuse to accept his son's death meant anything at all to him. Lose himself in his work, keep so busy he never had time to reflect on his life. Never let images of Fleur or Leo interfere with his daily routine. His supervisor back then had tried to get him to see a counsellor, but Jean-Luc had resolutely ignored him, just kept turning up for work and doing his job until the supervisor had stopped making suggestions.

'What do you mean, catatonic?' Charlize asked, her voice was still low and dangerous, but at least she wasn't screaming at him now.

'I mean exactly that. You were non-responsive, staring at nothing, curled in the foetal position. Like your body was just an empty husk, as if your soul had departed or something.'

'Oh God.' Her hands flew to her face, eyes going large with dismay. He thought her face had gone white before, but now it was positively translucent. The pads of her fingers, where they rested on her cheeks, were causing purple indents in her pale skin. She really hadn't realised how pitiful she'd been? *Merde*, had he been wrong to tell her? Would the mere mention of it send her spiralling back down to that dark undertow again?

'I thought I just blacked out because of the accident,' she muttered, almost as if talking to herself. But her eyes were riveted on him. 'You sure I wasn't just unconscious? I got a bump to the head, maybe that had something to do with it?'

He considered her question for a second, then shook his head. She hadn't been unconscious, he'd seen enough people in that state during his line of work to know what to look for. He remembered her screams just before he'd lost control of the car. They had been hysterical, maniacal, the sound of sheer nightmares, of complete loss of hope, loss of all sensibility. Nope, her blank staring had been much, much worse than a mere loss of consciousness. Finally, her eyes left his and flickered around the room, as if looking for something familiar to land on. Her hands, still clasped to her face, started to tremble.

'I thought I was getting better,' she said in a small, broken voice.

'Come and sit back down,' he entreated, pointing at the couch, reaching out but stopping short of actually touching her. She might still turn on him like a wounded animal if she felt threatened. She shook her head and turned her back on him, limping toward the old workbench.

'I can't go back to Perth now.' He almost didn't catch her words as she mumbled into the dark.

'Why not?' He wasn't sure if it was the right question to ask.

'Because people will see.'

'See what?' he prompted.

'See, I'm not the same anymore.' That left him wondering what kind of person she'd once been. He'd seen her mercurial moods at work firsthand, almost as if she were two separate people. Every now and then she showed flashes of a vibrant, determined, strong woman, but more often than not, that person seemed to be overshadowed by a hesitant, worried, faded soul.

'I can't face them knowing they expect me to be who I used to be when, clearly, I'm not. I can never be that person again.'

'Family are forgiving, Charlize, they'll welcome you back no matter what.' Well, at least he hoped that was true and not just a bloody platitude, but he needed to say something to comfort her. Families could be complicated at the best of times, and he knew nothing at all about her family. Hell, his family was the most complicated of all. But in the end they usually loved you no matter what, accepted your failings, no matter what. He wished she'd turn around so he could see her face.

'I don't know how to go back there and not be a cop. And not have Xeon. People depended on me and I let them down. I let Patty down. At least here I can be whoever I need to be. There're no expectations from strangers.'

He grunted in reply. He had some inkling of how that felt. At least he hadn't run away to another country to hide from his grief when his son had died. But he had become a different person, a little piece of him lost forever. And he'd become obsessed with his job to cover up that gaping hole in his life. So could he really blame her for running away, too? For not wanting to seek help, even though her panic attacks—as she liked to call them—had become debilitating? Denial. Everybody went through it at some stage of their life. Denial had been his friend and companion for these past five years, so who was he to cast stones?

'I lost someone too, Charlize. I know how hard it is,' he said softly. She lifted her chin at this revelation, but didn't turn around. 'Perhaps rather than fighting the fact that you're a different person, it might be easier to embrace it.' She gave no answer, just kept staring at the dark wooden wall behind the bench.

'Who was Xeon?' he asked quietly. There was a loud intake of breath from her and then she swivelled slightly so she could peer at him over her shoulder. Even though he couldn't see them in the dim light of the barn, he knew those green eyes would be watching him, gauging, deciding whether to answer him.

He was surprised when she started to speak. 'Xeon and VanDam were our police horses. Mine and Patty's. They died in the crash. I couldn't save them.' Her shoulders hunched over at this admission, the shadows seeming to encroach in on her. There was pure agony in her voice, and it made him want to stride over and take her in his arms. Soothe away the hurt. But he kept right on standing there. Those horses had obviously been special to her. He wouldn't pretend to understand how losing a horse could be causing her so much grief, but he'd heard stories of how people were so attached to their animals it was as if a family member had died.

'So, Patty was there too?'

'Yes, I managed to drag her out before the car exploded, but I nearly killed her in the process. She had to have a whole hip replacement, spent months in rehab.' *Merde*, so the car had exploded, and it sounded like those poor damn horses had been trapped inside. Burned alive. It was enough to give anyone nightmares.

'But Patty's still alive. And going on what I saw of her outside your house, she's pretty darn healthy too,' he said.

'I guess.'

'And do you think she's happy that she's alive?'

Charlize considered this question, finally turning all the way around and leaning back against the bench. His over-large hoodie hung off her thin shoulders, and now he could see the thin, silvery tracks of her tears running down her cheeks. 'Yes. She just told me she's getting married and going to have a baby.'

'Sounds like she's more than just happy then.' In the flickering candlelight, her hair was golden orange. Her face was drawn, but he could see a glimmer of hope spark in her eyes at his comment.

'She's marrying the physio who treated her after the accident.' He made a noise of acceptance. Now there was irony for you. Patty would never have met the guy if it hadn't been for the accident, but he didn't put the thought into words, he knew Charlize wouldn't want to hear that right now.

'So it's not all bad then?'

She gave a careful shrug. He went back over to the couch, easing the ache from his cut leg as he sat down.

Patting the cushion next to him, he said, 'Come here, it's been a long night.' Her eyes flicked toward the couch, but she eventually straightened up and walked over, then sat tentatively beside him.

'Sorry. I seem to be spending an awful lot of time either crying on your shoulder or acting like a complete idiot.' She wouldn't look at him, instead preferring to play with a loose thread on the frayed edge of the couch.

'It's not a problem, Charlize,' he replied, meaning it. Her eyes were now dry and clear, more lucid and logical. Their argument from before about Charlize going into a safe house seemed to be forgotten for now. And that was the way he was going to leave it.

'I know firsthand how traumatising that kind of thing can be. So if you need to talk to someone…' Who was he kidding? He was as mixed up as she was, but she seemed to accept his utterance. He took the chance and laid his hand very gently on her knee. She didn't pull away, as if she was too caught up with her own internal musings to notice.

'It's just that tonight, when you started to lose control on the road and that other car came toward us, well it reminded me of the other crash, and then all I could hear was Xeon screaming. Patty screaming, over and over in my head.'

Merde. He wished there was something he could do, something he could say to take those terrifying images away. Or not to have caused them in the first place. But apart from owning a time machine, there was no way to do that. Moving by instinct, he drew closer and draped his other arm around her shoulders. As if she noticed his contact for the first time, she tensed. But instead of withdrawing, she leaned into his shoulder, allowing him to support her.

'Did you see a psychiatrist after the accident?' He was probably treading on thin ice again, but if the Australian police force were anything like the French police, it would've been compulsory for her to see a shrink afterwards.

'Yeah, but I stopped seeing her. I came here, to France instead…to learn to cook,' she finished a little lamely.

The kind of trauma she'd experienced was serious stuff. He'd worked with one guy for a few months who'd been diagnosed with PTSD after a drug bust gone wrong, where two innocent children were caught in the crossfire. For the most part, the other guy had seemed fine. But every now and then, he'd just disappear from work for days, or sometimes even weeks, on end. Jean-Luc had also heard stories, rumours, of other people being changed beyond recognition by what they'd seen or experienced in the line of duty. Was Charlize one of those people? Would she ever be the same again?

'You keep telling me what a great cook you are, but I still haven't had the pleasure of tasting your food.' He gave her a quick wink. His attempt at lightening the mood seemed to work, as she actually raised a small smile in response.

'I solemnly promise I will cook you my best ever meal as soon as we get somewhere with a decent kitchen.'

He decided to keep the lighthearted banter going. 'Your best meal ever, huh? Exactly what would that entail? I need to know. I'd hate to be disappointed.' Her smile got larger, but her eyes wouldn't meet his.

'What's you favourite?'

'Fish meuneire,' he said without hesitation and his mouth started to water at the thought of the delicate poached fish with a butter and herb sauce.

'I do a great fish meuneire.' She finally looked up and met his gaze. God, her eyes were intense in the candlelight. They sparkled like flints of jade and amber mixed together. Staring into her eyes, he suddenly found himself trapped, being drawn in.

That's when he realised he was actually closer than he'd first thought. The act of draping his arm around her shoulder as a support, a show of solidarity, a form of sympathy, meant their bodies were touching in all kinds of places. Right thigh pressed up against hers, her shoulder pressed into the crook of his underarm, his other hand resting on her knee.

A surge of longing speared through him as the awareness of her warmth, her soft curves held against him, brought him up with a jolt. She became motionless in his arms, perhaps sensing his change in mood.

The candlelight softened the planes of her face and the tip of her tongue darted out to wet her bottom lip. Her gaze flicked quickly down to his mouth and back. It was this unconscious act that made him realise she was just as drawn as he was, just as ensnared by the attraction pulsing between them.

Earlier, in the cottage, he hadn't kissed her, even though he'd wanted to with a yearning more powerful than he'd felt in a long, long time. It wouldn't have been right to take advantage of her while she was vulnerable and desperate in his arms. But now... *Merde*, he wanted to taste her. What would be the harm? Especially when she wanted it as much as he did. Was she still vulnerable? Was he taking advantage of her? The answer was probably yes, but his strength of will to fight this thing was fading fast. Stolen by a surge of heat through his veins. A desire to know once and for all if those lips were as soft as his imagination told him they'd be. Would they mould to his, press against his, telling him she wanted more?

He leant in, but stopped a few centimetres away from her mouth, poised to make his intentions clear. Would she pull away from him? She didn't. Instead, her breath gusted out over her lips and she leaned in toward him until finally their lips met.

She tasted...miraculous. All he'd wanted was for this to be a gentle kiss, an exploration of her mouth, to satiate his curiosity, then he would break away. But as soon as skin touched skin, flames burst to life and ran through him, heating him like a forge burned deep in his belly. His fingers pushed into her hair, drawing her head toward him and his mouth demanded she open her lips to him. For a second, the depth of his desire alarmed him. Would it scare her away? But Charlize responded to him with the same urgent need and that fear was swept away on a tide of wanting.

Her tongue darted into his mouth, discovering, while one hand found its way beneath the hem of his shirt, her warm fingers traveling over the taught skin of his stomach, and up, following the line of hairs leading to his navel. God, he wanted her fingers to roam downwards, to where the bulge in his pants was becoming uncomfortable.

He needed to feel her whole body pressed up against his, so he pushed her down, never letting go of her lips, until she lay on the couch with her head on the armrest. His body hovered over hers. With one knee, he nudged her legs apart and settled between them with a groan of pleasure. Then he slowly lowered his chest over hers, letting his hips press into the divot of her belly, letting his erection grind against her stomach. It was easy to ignore the pain from the bruises on his ribcage when the feel of her breasts jutting into him sent coils of lust through his veins, lighting an ache deep in his groin. He wanted her. He could take her right here.

She reacted by plunging her hands beneath the waistband of his jeans to smooth over the skin at the top of his buttocks. As if it were possible, she grabbed his hips and tried to pull him closer still, making small grinding movements of her own against him. The friction made him so hard he thought he might burst out of his jeans.

Breaking away from her mouth, he dipped his head and let his lips taste her slender neck, grazed down her collarbone. Her skin was soft, warm, a little musky, and all Charlize.

She made an indecipherable sound at his touch and her

fingernails dug into his back. Their legs twined together as they both hung near the edge of the couch. The thick cumbersome hoodie was in his way and he reached up and unzipped it, letting it drop open to expose both of her creamy shoulders and tempting collarbone. He made a low, guttural sound. All that soft skin. He wanted to be able to touch her, feel all of her beneath his fingers. With his free hand, he traced the side curve of her breast beneath the dress. She gave a small groan. Tugging the top of her dress down as far as the straps would allow, he revealed a strapless, flimsy scrap of lace that passed as a bra. Now he could see her nipples peeking through the lace, dark pink and erect, and he desperately wanted to take them in his mouth. More. He needed to see more, to touch more.

He was just entertaining the idea of ripping the top of her dress open with his teeth when his phone buzzed in his back pocket.

No.

No. Not now. He closed his eyes and gritted his teeth, his hand wrapped tightly around Charlize's ribcage. She twisted beneath him, wondering why he'd suddenly stopped his exploration.

It had to be Pickard. *Merde.*

He dipped his head and took her mouth in his, savouring her for three more long, glorious seconds, then opened his eyes and lifted his head, staring down into her jade eyes.

'Sorry.' With that, he pushed up on his biceps and levered himself off the couch. She'd never know just how truly sorry he was.

FISH MEUNEIRE

INGREDIENTS
4 Pieces skinless sole fillets
(other white fish works well, but is not as good as sole)
Salt and freshly ground black pepper
¼ cup Milk
¼ cup Plain flour
¼ cup Vegetable oil
4 tbsp Unsalted butter
2 tbsp Snipped fresh parsley, chives, or chervil
2 tbsp Fresh lemon juice

DIRECTIONS
Season both sides of the fish fillets with salt and pepper. Pour the milk into one shallow bowl and place the flour in another. Dip a fillet in the milk, letting the excess drip off. Place the fillet in the flour to lightly coat, shaking off the excess. Repeat with the remaining fillets.

Using a pan that's large enough to accommodate the fillets in one layer, heat the vegetable oil over medium-high heat. Add fillets and cook, turning once, until fish is golden- brown on both sides and flakes easily. Transfer fish to four serving plates and keep warm. Drain off any fat from the pan and add the butter and cook it over medium heat until nut-brown and frothy. Remove the pan from the heat.

Scatter the herbs over the fish fillets, sprinkle with lemon juice, and pour the browned butter on top.

This delightful, subtle meal is best served with a young sancerre white wine while enjoying a rendezvous with your lover.

CHAPTER FOURTEEN

Dawn stole over the horizon. Shadows were pushed aside by the light, revealing the shapes of trees and bushes and even the dirt track through the open door of the shed.

Charlize sat on the dusty old couch, arms wrapped around her chest, staring out into the early morning. She couldn't see Jean-Luc, but she knew he was out there, somewhere close by, waiting for their ride to appear.

She'd decided to wait in here. Making a show of needing to fix herself up, she straightened her dress and the hoodie and ran her fingers through her hair. He'd left her to her adjustments and gone outside. He probably needed this time alone as much as she did. To gather his thoughts.

Holy shit, what'd they just done? She'd let her libido take over her brain, that's what just happened.

But, oh God, the way he kissed her. It felt like nothing she'd ever known existed before. Not with Shaun, not with any other man had she felt this...combustible in anyone else's arms.

He drove away all logical thought, all fears and self-doubts. All she'd felt was him, the sharp planes of him pressed into her, his lips demanding more and more of her. And her body had given it to him willingly. The way he'd just laid her down on the couch, no questions asked, taking what he knew was his.

Her arms tightened further around her ribcage and she began to pace. She was disgusted with herself. Yes, he was the most gorgeous man she'd ever met. But did she have no shame? Memories skittered through her brain, of his deep brown eyes fixed on hers as he leaned in to take her lips. The way his goatee rasped her chin, but not in an unpleasant way. How she'd run her hands all over that wonderful mocha skin on his back, tracing the vertebrae of his spine, dipping down below the waistband of his jeans to find the muscular mounds of his buttocks. The way his erection had jutted into her belly, irrepressible and needy. Was the size of that bulge to do more with the denim of his jeans, or was it all him? *Charlize Brewer*. She couldn't believe her mind had wandered to that particular topic.

She needed to stop thinking about what it would be like to make love with Jean-Luc and start to concentrate on getting her life back on track. He wanted her out of the way so he could get on with his job. He thought he could do that if he holed her up in some safe house. But there was no way in hell she was going there. He'd have to knock her out, bind and gag her before she allowed that. Anger at the thought he'd do this to her simmered beneath her skin again. Her pacing quickened as she strode around the dim shed. How dare he think he could control her life?

In a funny way, she understood his predicament, could sympathise with him. Almost. He felt responsible for her plight, as if she were his burden, his liability. It was obvious in the conciliatory way he treated her. Because he felt accountable, he needed to know she was being looked after before he could go back to his job. She understood that. But she didn't have to like it. And a part of her understood she'd only slow him down if she stuck around. She didn't like to admit it, but despite her tough words, could she really be any help to Jean-Luc or his team in stopping this gang?

She was a cop. An ex-cop. She knew how to stay out of sight, keep her head down. And she was more than capable of protecting herself if the need arose. Sure, her panic attacks were a worry right now. She'd thought she had them under control because she hadn't had one in months. But they were being triggered by the countless dangerous situations over the past few days. By Jean-Luc and his bloody-mindedness. Hell, anyone who'd just been shot at twice and involved in high-adrenaline car chases would be freaking out by now, let alone barely surviving a car crash. Once she got free of him and away from his high-risk world, she'd be fine again. Would be able to gain control over her mind and body once more. Go back to Uzes and continue her healing.

She had a plan. When this Pickard arrived, she'd go along, meek as a church mouse, pretending Jean-Luc had persuaded her she'd be better off in their care. Then, as soon as an opportunity presented itself, she'd be out of there, give Jean-Luc the slip. She was even prepared to wait until they had her ensconced in the safe house to alleviate all their fears. The guards in these places were often not too bright, they paid more attention to stopping people entering the house, not considering that some might also want to break out.

The idea of jumping on a plane, going back to Western Australia, had been building ever since Jean-Luc had uttered the words safe house. Those thugs would never guess where she'd gone, and why would they bother following her to Australia, anyway? She would've removed herself from their territory, removed herself as a threat, as a source of information to them. Jean-Luc was right, she'd never be able to outrun them if she stayed in France. They'd track her down in days, hours even. She wasn't stupid enough to think she could stay hidden from them here, on their home turf. But back home. That was a different matter. All she had to do was get there.

The idea of going home still caused her to break out in a cold sweat. But it was becoming preferable to a life cooped up here in France. It was the excuse she needed to finally get her butt on a plane and head home. For Patty's wedding, or at least that's what she'd tell everyone.

'Charlize.' Jean-Luc's measured voice floated to her from just outside the door, warning her that an arrival was imminent. She'd been so preoccupied with her thoughts she hadn't heard anyone approaching, but now she could hear the low drone of a car engine. She squared her shoulders. It was time to put on her best impassive face, shore up all her thoughts of escape and freedom behind a mask of normality and walk out through the door. Time to go and meet Jean-Luc's boss.

Jean-Luc stood outside, half-hidden by a large, scraggly lavender bush, a remnant of the surrounding garden gone wild. He was side-on to her as he watched a trail of dust rise up through the trees, broadcasting the car's arrival. She studied his profile. His dark brows were lowered in concentration and in the growing light of day, she could make out the lines of worry etched around the corners of his eyes. His mocha skin glowed golden in the early morning light, and her fingers itched to run over those chiselled cheekbones, take his face in her hands and kiss those full lips one last time.

A pang of guilt threaded its way up her spine. Jean-Luc would be furious when she escaped. And if she'd learned anything at all about him after the last twenty-four hours, he'd probably freak out, be desperate to find her, to make sure she was okay. That overprotective streak of his would drive him crazy. But he'd get over it pretty quickly. Besides, he had much bigger fish to fry. She pushed the guilt aside and replaced it with determination. The small bout of remorse she might feel at disobeying Jean-Luc wouldn't be enough to stop her from leaving.

The sound of an engine got closer and Jean-Luc stepped out from beside the lavender to signal to the dark blue vehicle as it appeared down the driveway. Except there wasn't just one car, but two, winding their way down the dirt road.

'What's going on?' she asked loudly.

'They're doing a car-drop. Pickard will hop in the second car with the other driver, leaving the first one for us. The less we're seen with anyone else, the better.' It made an odd kind of sense. She stood at the side of the shed and waited. A tall, well-built man got out of the first car and strode over to meet Jean-Luc in the open space between the house and shed. It must be Pickard. Even though he looked to be around mid-fifties, with regulation cropped grey hair, he had an aura of someone used to being in control. He glared at Jean-Luc from behind square glasses and they had an animated, but very quiet, conversation. The second car remained idling mutely, the tint on the windows so dark she couldn't make out the driver's features.

They stopped speaking and Pickard swept an all-knowing glance her way, the meaning of which she couldn't decipher, then got back into the waiting car, which disappeared in a cloud of dust back up the road.

Jean-Luc walked toward her, brow furrowed. What had Pickard said to him? He kept his face blank, but she detected a tightness around his eyes, the cords of his neck more prominent. But she didn't really care what Pickard had to say, or what he thought. He was immaterial to her bigger picture.

Jean-Luc, on the other hand, well, she had to keep him onside, for a little while longer at least.

'Everything okay?'

'*Oui.*' He passed a hand over his eyes and she suddenly saw how tired he was. It reminded her how she'd been constantly on the go for nearly as long as he had.

'Let's get going.' His tone stopped just short of an order.

'Do you want me to drive?' He looked up in surprise. 'How long since you had any decent sleep?' she asked. He stopped, seemed to consider her question, then dismissed it with a wave of his hand.

'*Pah*, I'll sleep when we get to the...house. Hop in,' he said as he indicated the passenger side of the blue sedan. 'There should be some food and drink in the back seat for us. Can you get that organised?'

She nodded, but climbed a little too eagerly into the passenger seat and turned around. There was a basket on the back seat, filled with baguettes and cheese and cold meats. Heaven. She was starving, not having eaten since...

lunch time yesterday, if she remembered correctly. She and Patty had stopped at a wonderful little cafe on the boulevard near the port of Marseille, in a break between their boutique shopping expeditions. It was hard to believe that Patty had only flown out last night. It felt like she'd been on the run from these madmen for weeks, not just hours. And of course, they'd been cheated of their meal at the cottages last night, when the thugs had turned up and started shooting. Charlize sighed at the loss of the wonderful cheese soufflé she'd been so looking forward to.

While Jean-Luc drove up the dirt track, Charlize concentrated on crafting the perfect breakfast baguette for them both. There was even a thermos of coffee to share.

'Wow, your boss is thoughtful,' she said through a huge mouthful of bread and cheese.

'Yeah, thoughtful,' he repeated. But the tone of his voice gave her the distinct impression he was anything but.

'How long until we get to Nice?' she asked. He shot her an indecipherable glance.

'We're not going to Nice.'

'Oh.' The baguette stalled halfway to her mouth. 'Why not?'

'Pickard's probably just being over-cautious, but he thinks the safe house might've been compromised. So we're going…somewhere else for a day or so until he can clear things up.' Charlize's stomach clenched. Her plan rested on going to Nice. She knew her way around Nice, knew the airport there.

'Where?'

He threw her another of those indecipherable glances, although this time she thought there may have been a hint of embarrassment in those dark eyes of his.

'Sault.' Her mind ticked over for a few seconds, registering what he'd said.

'Isn't that where you're from?' she exclaimed as it hit her why the name was familiar.

'Yes, it is,' he replied darkly.

* * *

Jean-Luc gripped the steering wheel much tighter than was absolutely necessary. The potholed road was so familiar, every curve and bump, hill and tree he passed painted inexorably on his mind's canvas. How many times had he walked this dusty road as a child? Memories scratched at the doorway in his mind, wanting to be let in. Memories of scorching hot days spent bent over, packing bushels and bushels of lavender into the distillery. Of him and his two brothers hiding underneath the tractor in the dirt, giggling because they knew their father was looking for them. Of arguing with his mother, screaming at her that lavender was her dream, not his.

It was still early morning. They'd left the farmhouse where they'd sheltered at first light, and it was only a two-hour drive up to Sault. When the car had run off the road, they'd been around thirty kilometres out of Marseille, near the little commune town of Gemenos. He'd been bone-tired this morning, but the food and hot coffee had been a miraculous cure, enough to get him through the two-hour drive. He'd need to rest soon, or he'd start making mistakes. And mistakes could be fatal.

They'd made one stop in Cavaillion, a town large enough to boast an Orange Cell Phone shop, where he'd bought Charlize a cheap mobile to replace the one she'd had to leave back at the Hotel cottages. 'It's vital we are able to stay in touch,' he'd told her. And that was true. But he didn't tell her the part where he would be able to keep track of her with that phone. Pickard would put a trace on it as soon as soon as Jean-Luc gave him the number. Not that he didn't trust her. But you could never be too careful. She was probably smart enough to figure it out, but she didn't say anything, just tucked the phone away in her bag. As long as she kept it on her, that was all that mattered.

Now Charlize stared around her, eyes wide, excitement evident in the blush on her cheeks. At first, when he'd told her they were going to Sault, she'd scowled at him and said she wanted to go to Nice. But now they were close, she'd started exclaiming at the miles and miles of lavender fields unfolding before them. She even admitted she always wanted to visit a working lavender farm, it was one of her dreams. If only she knew how much hard work, sweat, blood and tears went into running this farm.

The farmhouse appeared for a moment as they crested a rise and then disappeared when they dipped down into a small hollow.

'Oh, it's gorgeous,' Charlize declared.

'Yep,' he replied, still caught up in his own thoughts.

Harvest season was just about to begin, the busiest time of the year. And here he was, going to drop in after not seeing his parents for over two years. With a civilian in tow, both of them in need of a place to hide. His father would welcome him home with open arms. His mother? Well, she would give him that disappointed frown, but she'd cover it up with her trademark smile and no one would be the wiser. And Herve? Jean-Luc wasn't sure how that was going to go. Herve had always been the prickly brother.

By the time they pulled into the courtyard, Charlize was practically bouncing in her seat. He hid a smile at her girlish antics. If only he could feel this excited about coming home again. Jean-Luc took in the gaggle of old buildings, formed in a rough U-shape around the main courtyard. It was so typical of farmhouses in this district, called a mas by the locals, built to withstand the constant ravages of the Mistral—the regional wind that often blew non-stop for days on end. His family had added to the buildings over the years, so there was a hotch-potch of different ages and styles. But the main house was original, built by hand using local stone back in the early sixteen hundreds. Jean-Luc was still amazed every time he thought about the age of this building. It'd seen so many generations of humans come and go, and still stood, unperturbed by the small minutiae of the beings who called this place home for a time. The old stone fountain still stood in the middle of the yard, water trickling from the lip of the roman inspired stone urn, the faint outlines of lovers entwined together on the surface of the urn all but obliterated by the green slime gathered over hundreds of years. Tall pencil pines towered like arrow points around the edge of the courtyard and a large age-burdened olive tree shaded the middle of the yard, its twisted branches forming a living roof, cathedral-like, over the yard.

He stepped out of the car and drew in a deep breath. That unforgettable aroma of lavender filled the air, the pervading smell charged through his lungs and jolted his memories.

Charlize popped out from the other side of the car and her head swivelled from side to side as she took in her surroundings.

As Jean-Luc's gaze slid around the familiar sights, his father, Jaiyan, stepped out from the side door of the main building. He held a half-eaten baguette in his hand. Jean-Luc knew his father would've already done a few hours' work and had come back in for a late breakfast.

Jaiyan stared at him, mouth slack, eyes wide, baguette forgotten.

'My son?' His voice was quiet, but the words rebounded around the yard like he'd struck a gong. 'Jean-Luc.' This time his voice was louder, and he took long-legged strides across the dusty ground toward the car. 'Helene,' he yelled back over his shoulder. 'Helene, Jean-Luc is home.'

His father embraced him in a bear-hug that almost lifted Jean-Luc off his feet, slapping him on the back so hard it hurt. Jean-Luc laughed at his father's exuberance. Jaiyan grabbed him by the shoulders and held him at arm's length to get a better look at him. Jean-Luc's fingers dug into the side of his father's shoulders as a surge of warmth and affection washed through him.

'Hey, Dad,' Jean-Luc was suddenly awkward under his father's piercing gaze. But he let him look his fill. He deserved that much after Jean-Luc's long absence. Then, remembering Charlize still standing at the open passenger door, he turned to introduce her. But before he could open his mouth, a high-pitched voice sounded across the yard.

'Jean-Luc? Is that really you?' His mother ran across the yard, surprising him with her frantic pace and nearly knocked him over when she swirled into his embrace.

'My boy. My boy. So good to see you.' Was that a tear in the corner of his mother's eye? Surely not. He hadn't been expecting quite this level of excitement when he'd decided to come home, but he accepted it with as much dignity as he could muster, realising that perhaps he had missed them nearly as much as they seemed to have missed him. His mother smelled strongly of lavender, she must've been in the fields already too, checking on the oil content of the flowers, trying to pick the exact time to start the harvest.

She didn't look a day older than the last time he'd seen her. Neither of them did. This was unsurprising for his father, his ebony dark skin never showed any wrinkles. But his mother, her pearly white complexion, was at the mercy of the sun's rays. It didn't matter how much she hid under her floppy straw hat, the sun still touched her skin.

He held her close for seconds on end, letting her take her time, offering her the comfort she needed from the embrace.

Gently, he broke away, keeping hold of her hand, and gestured toward Charlize, trying not to feel the slight embarrassed buzz at the fact she'd just witnessed a highly private moment. Not too many people knew about his family. Actually, apart from Pickard—and Fleur, of course —no one really knew about his family. It was safer that way.

'This is Charlize. She doesn't speak much French, so English if you don't mind.'

'Nice to meet you, Mademoiselle.' His father walked around the car and extended a hand to Charlize. When she shook his hand, Jean-Luc was hit by the incongruity of how small and white her hand looked, engulfed in his large, ebony one.

'This is my father, Jaiyan. And my mother, Helene.' He introduced them all. Then addressed his mother, who was still holding tight to his hand. 'We're going to be staying with you for a day or two, if that's okay?' One night, he hoped it would only be one night. Pickard should have the problem sorted by then. Two nights at the most.

'*Bein, bien,*' Helene said, also going around the car and taking Charlize by the hand. 'Welcome. Of course you are both welcome.' Please don't let her say what he knew she was thinking. That look in his mother's eye could only spell trouble. 'Come, come inside, I'll get you some coffee and breakfast.' She took Charlize by the arm, as if they were old friends, and guided her toward the side door through to the kitchen.

Almost as an afterthought, she called back to Jean-Luc, 'Shall I make up one…or two bedrooms?' Her wide smile fixed on Charlize as they walked.

Merde.

'Two rooms,' he ground out between clenched teeth, trying to catch Charlize's eye and give her an apologetic glance, but she never looked back at him. Damn. Bloody double damn. He knew this had been a bad idea as soon as Pickard suggested it. But his boss had been hopping mad about the whole way this operation had been handled. A debacle he'd called it. And there wasn't much room for negotiation when Pickard was that livid.

Jean-Luc walked alongside his father as they followed the women inside. His father laid one of his large hands on Jean-Luc's shoulder and said, 'It's really good to see you. I'm glad you came, whatever the reason.' His gaze slid to Charlize, obvious curiosity there. His parents only knew the vaguest details about what he did for a living. They knew he was a gendarme, but they certainly didn't know the intricacies of the undercover work he did, and nor did they know just how much jeopardy he put himself in on a regular basis. He'd have to tread carefully with the story he told his parents. He'd already primed Charlize on the car trip, of what to say and what to withhold. But he knew his mother, she would try and winkle every bit of information she possibly could out of Charlize. She'd see her as a soft target, knowing from past experience that Jean-Luc wouldn't reveal anything but the barest basics.

The kitchen was just as he remembered. Cool, grey flagstone floor, scuffed and worn by hundreds of years of footsteps. It looked like his mother may have given the rustic wooden cupboards a new coat of paint in his absence, a pale cream colour to complement the stone walls. A vintage steel stove his grandmother had installed filled the space where the old fireplace used to be, the walls at the back still scorched black from centuries of fires. His mother said the stove gave her cooking an authentic taste that was often missing from today's French meals, and she refused to have it updated. Which meant his poor father had to chop and carry wood to the kitchen every single day.

It was the old wooden table sitting in the middle of the large kitchen that drew him forward, evoking more memories. How many meals they'd eaten here, sitting down as a family and devouring his mother's delicious cooking. Charlize was already seated at the huge table and he drew out a chair to sit next to her. Jaiyan took a chair opposite. She looked small, lost, out of place at the large table. He had to resist the urge to take her hand in his, assure her she'd be safe here.

'Are you okay?' he asked softly.

'Yes, just tired.'

'We'll have breakfast and then I'll find us somewhere to

take a rest,' he said, holding her gaze for longer than was necessary, making sure she was indeed okay. It was asking a lot of her, first dragging her away from her quiet life in Uzes and now throwing her into the middle of his family dramas. But her green eyes were clear and open, and she cast him a quick, cheeky grin. Perhaps she might even be enjoying herself.

He knew their exchange wasn't lost on his parents, and he purposefully didn't look at his mother, but he did say, 'Do you have any of your special tea, Maman? I think Charlize would prefer that.' He glanced at her and she nodded.

'*Oui, oui,*' his mother replied.

It was cool in here, out of the heat of the summer day, which was already building outside. His mother bustled about, then placed two steaming mugs in front of them and another in front of Jaiyan.

'Thank you.' Charlize smiled at his mother. Helene would be intrigued, desperate to ask questions. Why were they here? Who was this woman? Were they a couple or not? But she held her tongue. He felt a wave of affection for her obvious self-restraint.

'Oh, this tea is amazing,' Charlize said after taking a few sips. 'It's like heaven in a cup. What do you put in it?'

Helene stood up straight from where she'd been carving baguettes at the bench and tapped the side of her nose. 'Ah, it's a family secret.' Then she laughed and said, 'But I can tell you. It's lavender. We mix a bit of fresh lavender in with the black tea leaves.'

'It's just amazing,' Charlize said again, letting her nose hover over the streaming cup to draw in the smell. 'You could sell this, you know.' His mother gave one of her wide-mouthed smiles and Jean-Luc knew that Charlize had just been accepted, no questions asked. Without knowing it, she'd found a certain way to her mother's heart. Compliment her lavender and you were a shoo-in.

'So, Jean-Luc, tell us why...' his father trailed off and Jean-Luc looked up.

Herve walked into the kitchen and Jean-Luc went completely still.

'Maman, what's—' Herve stopped when he spotted Jean-Luc sitting at the table, his eyes narrowing. In the silence, Jean-Luc stood up and walked over, offering his hand. No use in starting off on the wrong foot. The last thing he wanted was a scene in front of Charlize. He could be the bigger man. This time.

To his surprise, Herve took his hand and shook it. With what could've almost been called warmth.

'Jean-Luc. What are you doing here?' There was only the tiniest hint of defensiveness in his tone.

'I'm only here for a day or two,' Jean-Luc placated. 'Let me introduce my guest, Charlize.'

For the next few minutes, they shuffled around the kitchen in an odd, awkward dance, stilted small-talk filling the silences as Jean-Luc answered Herve's questions. Charlize threw him more than one concerned glance, but kept her smile bright as she watched his family drama unfold. It was all made a little easier when the kitchen was suddenly flooded by bright tinkling children's voices, as Herve's three kids came charging in to see who the new arrivals were. Jean-Luc bent down on one knee to meet each of his nieces and nephew in turn. Totty was the oldest, nearly eight now, she informed him. Then there was Villete, who stood quiet and shy next to her older sister, in awe of Jean-Luc. Of course she wouldn't remember him, it'd been two years since she last saw him. A lifetime in a six-year-old's world. The youngest was Beau, a tow-haired boy with plump cheeks and legs that never stopped moving. He ran around the kitchen squawking like a chicken, only stopping long enough to offer Jean-Luc a cheeky smile before he was off again. Until Celine also stepped into the kitchen, enticed by all the noise and commotion. Herve's wife was as beautiful as he remembered. Serene and unruffled, she glided up to Jean-Luc and gave him the traditional French kiss, thrice on the cheeks, then knelt down and reprimanded Beau, telling him that chickens weren't allowed in the kitchen.

If Celine was just as intrigued by Charlize's presence, it never showed on her smooth face. She tucked a stray stand of brown hair behind her ear, sat down next to Charlize at the table to introduce herself and they were soon chatting as if they'd known each other all of their lives.

Then a brightly clad figure shuffled in and Jean-Luc's heart lurched.

Grand-Mere Uduru was staring at him, her bird-like eyes boring into him.

'Grand-Mere.' He went over and took her hand gently. 'It's so good to see you.' She was possibly the one person in his life he truly revered. His grandmother on his father's side. She was the whole reason his father was here today, the whole reason Jean-Luc himself existed. An extraordinary person. To have made that dangerous journey by boat into a new country as a refugee. Her resolve and determination were his inspiration.

'You're home at last,' she said, her voice rasping with

age as she studied him with those perceptive black eyes of hers. She patted his hand and said, 'My boy.' So much more was left unsaid in those two words. He realised just how much he'd missed her. How much he missed his whole family.

'Who is this blonde girl you bring?' She nodded in Charlize's direction. Grand-Mere spoke only French, never needing to learn English, so Jean-Luc motioned Charlize over and introduced her, translating her words of welcome. Grand-Mere took one of Charlize's hands in both of hers, patting the back of it with her papery fingers. Even while they spoke, her gaze missed nothing, and he knew she was taking in the grime that covered both of them from head to toe, the spots of blood still evident on Charlize's dress and the dark circles beneath her eyes.

'Come sit down, Grand-Mere.' He took her by the elbow and led her to a large winged chair in the corner of the kitchen. Her chair. The place she always sat. For as long as he could remember. She folded gently down into the chair, arranging her layers of bright material so it tucked around her legs and feet. Grand-Mere always wore the traditional *thawb* dress of Sudan, a long colourful swathe of material wrapped around and around her body. Today she had a white sheer scarf wrapped loosely around her head as well, the colour underscoring just how black her skin was. Like a wrinkled piece of liquorice.

Charlize went to follow them to the corner of the room, but was called back to her place at the table when Herve asked her a question. She shot Jean-Luc a quick, curious glance. This must be all a bit confusing to her, but she seemed to take it all in her stride, conversing easily with Herve as she pulled Villete onto her lap so the little girl was included in the talk around the table.

Ignoring the others' conversation, Grand-Mere said quietly, 'Let me look at you.' She drew his face down to her level until he was bent over nearly double and stared into his eyes. He let her stare, knowing it'd do him no good to pull away until she'd found whatever it was she was looking for. Finally, she patted his cheek and let him stand up.

A gap-toothed smile erupted on her face. 'Ah, I'm happy for you, my boy.' Her words were low, meant only for him to hear. Not that he had a clue what she was talking about. There wasn't anything for her to be happy about, he was on the run from a deadly gang of killers with a high possibility they might now know his identity. And to top it all off, he had a civilian in tow, who was bringing him nothing but trouble. But for some reason, he was glad no one else heard her whispered words.

His eyes drifted of their own accord over to where Charlize sat. The morning light streamed in through the open window, turning her short hair to spun gold.

CHAPTER FIFTEEN

Charlize stretched and yawned. Sunlight played around the edges of the heavy curtains drawn across the window. What time was it? The sheets lay cool against her skin, the bed soft and comfy, hugging her like a long-lost relative. She cast her eyes around the large bedroom. Helene had called this the *visitors' room*, but it was more like a suite fit for a queen. The bed was so big she could roll over twice in it without falling out. The large room was filled with furniture made of some kind of pale blonde wood, and there were wonderful original watercolours on the walls. It was just so… French.

This house was huge, rambling and old. And she loved it. Drawn to the aura, the age of the place, so many hidden memories, the feel of the rustic wood beneath her fingers. Every nook, every corner told a story. A light tap at the door broke her train of thought. Was that what'd woken her?

'Come in,' she said, pushing herself up to sitting in the large bed. Jean-Luc poked his head around the wooden door. She pulled the sheet up a bit higher. She'd forgotten she was sleeping in only her bra and undies.

'*Bonjour*, sleeping beauty.' His bronze eyes sparkled with mirth. He placed a tray beside her bed before going over and opening the curtains. Sunlight streamed in.

'Whoa.' She shaded her eyes with her hand. 'How long have I been asleep?'

'Four hours.'

'So much for that cat-nap,' she laughed. 'I won't sleep a wink tonight.' She examined the contents of her tray. A cup of what smelled like more lavender tea, and some biscuits that could have been shortbread. Homemade. Of course.

'That's why I woke you,' he admitted. 'And also because my mother is going out into the fields and wants to know if you're keen to come along.' He came back and sat unselfconsciously on the edge of her bed. Only a few feet away from her. Her hands gripped the sheets tighter. Did he realise she was practically naked under here? Heat rose up her neck as he looked at her, an expectant smile playing over those sexy lips. Lips she'd been kissing only this morning. More than kissing. More like having her wicked way with them. The blush rose higher up her cheeks. Why did her bloody traitorous body have to react to his presence like this?

'So. Are you interested?'

'What? Oh, yes, definitely,' she countered. 'I'll just get dressed and be straight out.'

'Okay.' He didn't move from the edge of the bed, however, and a slow smile suffused his face. Oh yes, he definitely knew what she had on underneath the sheet. Or rather, what she didn't have on. She found her most indignant look and plastered it on her face.

'You'll have to leave for me to be able to do that.'

'Mmm hmm.' That slow smile turned into something much more smouldering and dangerous. One of his eyebrows quirked up and she could almost feel his fingers on the exposed skin of her neck and shoulders as his eyes roamed over her. The room grew hot under his gaze. Would she let him touch her if he leaned over? Let him run his tongue down her collarbone like he'd done this morning? Suddenly, he drew in a sharp breath and stood up, breaking the spell.

'I've brought you some spare clothes to put on.' He indicated a pile of folded clothes on a chair by the door. 'Some of my mother's stuff. It should fit you, she's tall like you. Your dress isn't suitable for traipsing all over the farm.'

'Thanks,' she said as he finally opened the bedroom door and disappeared. A whoosh of air escaped through her lips as the door closed and she fell back onto the pillows. She'd have to stop being so damned obvious in the way she reacted to him. They lived two completely different lives. She was planning on fleeing back to Australia the first chance she got. A strong attraction to a man *did not* mean she had to act on it. If only her body understood that.

Fifteen minutes later she strode down a dirt track behind the farmhouse, trying hard to keep up with Helene. Jean-Luc followed behind her. Herve's two oldest girls, Totty and Villete, ran ahead of their grandmother, hair streaming behind them as they laughed and yelled snatches of French phrases too quick for her to catch. Beau was having his afternoon nap, so he couldn't come, she'd been informed by an earnest Totty in halting English before they left the kitchen.

'Slow down, Maman,' Jean-Luc called out. 'The lavender isn't going anywhere.' Charlize threw him a grateful glance over her shoulder. If Helene had noticed her limp, she hadn't commented. No one had seen the scars on her leg, they'd been covered by her long dress when she arrived. And now she was wearing a pair of long beige linen pants, with a pair of robust sandals that Jean-Luc must've dug out of his mother's wardrobe. He'd also given her a white t-shirt that rode up to her midriff, so she had to keep tugging at it self-consciously, and a straw hat to keep off the sun. Jean-Luc insisted she wear it, and she'd been oddly touched by his concern over her pale skin. Especially when he came over and gently placed it on her head, his broad shoulders so close she'd had to quickly avert her eyes before she was caught staring. She felt a little awkward wearing Helene's clothes and had said as much when she'd come down to the kitchen. But Helene had waved away her discomfort.

Charlize liked Helene. She liked her no-nonsense, pragmatic attitude. It was obvious Helene ran this farm, made all the difficult decisions. Jean-Luc told her the farm belonged to his mother's family; she'd inherited it when her parents became too old to work it anymore. Her father had inherited it from his family before him, his grandfather before that, and his great-grandfather before that. The way he said it, with such pride in his voice, had made her skin tingle. What would it be like to have such a tradition, a family connection running through the land? It might be nice to feel so rooted to one place, to know you really belonged there.

Her family farm only went back three generations. Her

father had worked there all his life, side by side with her grandfather, then he'd taken over when her grandfather could no longer cope with the workload of running a canola farm full-time. In Australia, this was considered an achievement, having a farm passed down through even two generations. Agriculture—in Western Australia at least—had only been around for less than a couple hundred years. Compared to France, the country hadn't yet become steeped in history. And soon—perhaps sooner than she might've once thought possible—Letta and her husband Ben would take over from her dad. Charlize didn't begrudge Letta, her own passion had always been to join the mounted police corps. Something she dreamed of ever since she could remember, from the time she'd first held a toy horse in her hand, and then when her father had first sat her gently on the back of old Lucy, the palomino mare. Actually, she was glad the obsession with farming ran through Letta's veins. Didn't begrudge the fact she might be her father's favourite. She couldn't really blame him, if a child was prepared to take over your legacy, to take up the yoke and sweat tears and blood to keep the farm going, then why wouldn't he have a preference for Letta? In a way, it took the pressure off Charlize's shoulders.

Did Jaiyan have a favourite? Probably Herve, if she were to guess, but he hadn't shown any obvious preference while she'd been around. She liked Jaiyan, but she was still trying to figure out the relationships between Jaiyan and Helene. He deferred to her decisions, but he also seemed to have a core of steel running through him. A quiet strength that complemented Helene's boisterous dominance. Perhaps that's where Jean-Luc got his own self-assuredness, his own inner strength.

Shaking her mind free of thoughts of Jean-Luc's family, she let her gaze drink in the view before her. Patchwork fields of purple stretched as far as the eye could see. It was as if she'd been deposited right in the middle of a picture postcard. Neat row after neat row of lavender ran away like the grooves and humps on a piece of corrugated iron. And the smell. Nothing could really come close. The heat of the afternoon sun drew out the oil, so that she was completely engulfed in the sweet, floral, slightly grassy smell of lavender.

Running her fingers lightly over the row of flowers as she followed Helene and the disappearing laughter of the girls through the paddock, she compared these fields with her father's farm back near Perth. Canola was bright yellow when it was in flower, filling paddocks to the end of the horizon with the buttery, happy colour as the flowers dipped and swayed in the breeze. It made her a little nostalgic for her own family farm. Funnily enough canola was mainly used to produce oil as well, but a cooking oil rather than for perfumes.

She could see the lavender in the next field was a different colour, a much darker purple. 'How many types of lavender do you grow here?' she asked.

'Three,' Helene and Jean-Luc answered in unison. Charlize gave a quick laugh and Jean-Luc indicated his mother should continue.

'This pale lavender right here is actually called lavandin, because it's a hybrid, a cross between lavender and a wild variety called aspic. It's our main income earner and probably takes up eighty percent of the farm. We use it because it's the most prolific type. We harvest it with the big machines you can see parked in the shed over there.' Helene waved her hand back in the direction they'd just come. 'Maybe if you stay long enough, you might even get to see how we harvest it.' She cast a meaningful look back at her son, which Jean-Luc ignored. Charlize felt an odd polarity of emotions hit her chest. A part of her realised she'd love to stay and get involved in the harvest, submerge herself in the farm's easy rhythms, discover the differences between growing lavender and canola. But the pragmatic part of her was appalled at the thought of staying even one more day. She needed to get away from Jean-Luc's family, away from his farm, so she could get back to the business of reality and hatching her plan to return to Australia.

'The lavandin can be used to make perfumes, but is more often used for essential oils or its medicinal properties,' Helene continued as if she hadn't silently reprimanded her son. 'Then we have a much older variety, that dark one you can see over in the next field, with the two tufts coming off the top of the flowers, like rabbit's ears. It's a Spanish lavender.' Upon closer inspection, the purple flowers did indeed have two large petals extending from the top that looked a lot like tiny Bugs Bunnies.

'That one is special. It's hand-picked and distilled in a much smaller distillery. It's a favourite of the Molinard Perfumer in Grasse, because it has slight sage undertones that give it a quite different floral signature to normal lavender.' Charlize raised her eyebrows, looking suitably impressed, and nodded at Helene to continue. 'And the third one is an English lavender, picked for...how you say, Jean-Luc?'

'We keep the flowers whole. Then they're dried and

used in culinary dishes. It has a much sweeter smell and a light flavour.' She glanced back at him and nodded her understanding.

'Like in the lavender tea I had this morning.'

'Exactly.' He stopped and picked a flower, beckoning her over to him. The purple flower lay against the brown of his palm. He started to tell her how the different varieties of lavender produced different amounts and qualities of oil, and had different percentages of camphor, which was the main medicinal ingredient. She watched his lips move, only half-hearing what he said as she took the opportunity to study him.

His tall, lean figure was outlined against the blue Provencal sky, his chiselled features prominent, but made somehow more endearing by the warm honey colour of the afternoon sun. His cream linen shirt lay open at his neck, revealing a few dark curling hairs that disappeared down the bony plate of his chest. His strong hands holding the purple flower drew her gaze and she remembered how gentle they'd been stroking her face this morning. She remembered the hunger in his copper-brown eyes. Eyes that now sparkled with humour and enthusiasm.

When they'd first arrived at the farm, she'd thought Jean-Luc looked a little incongruous, out of place. She couldn't see how he fitted in, couldn't imagine what his life might've been like growing up here. But now, after he'd changed from his *secret spy uniform*—black jeans, snug fitting black t-shirt and dark glasses perched permanently on his head—into a pair of cargo shorts and a loose fitting linen button-up shirt and sandals, it was if years of worry and strain had been stripped away from him. The tough, no-nonsense, loyal gendarme had been transformed into—

if not quite a country bumpkin—a man who was much more at ease, unpretentious, not afraid to get dirt under his fingernails. She was seeing a side of him she would've never thought possible. And it intrigued her.

Without a doubt, there was no way she could've fallen for the serious, dangerous, hard-hitting cop side of Jean-Luc. Yes, there was something terribly sexy about a reckless, driven man who lived constantly on the edge of danger, but that kind of lifestyle would never have suited her. Not now anyway, not after the accident. She freely admitted she was too much of a homebody now. She liked her safe, uncomplicated life. But this other Jean-Luc, the one who had a caring family with roots that ran deep, who knew what it was like to live on the land and who obviously cared about his family in return. This was a different man altogether.

He stopped talking. Finished telling her about the lavender, he was now staring at her expectantly. She'd missed his question completely. She uttered a noncommittal 'uh huh,' and turned to hurry after Helene, who was still striding down the rows of lavender. They were heading up an incline, and Charlize could see a lone tree at the top of the hill, the girls' smaller figures already near the peak, almost lost in the heat haze rising from the fields.

It took a few minutes of walking, her breath becoming more and more laboured before they finally made it up and stopped under a very large, very old olive tree. She was glad she'd kept up her daily walks, kept her fitness up and her leg moving. Otherwise, she might not have made it up the hill. As it was, her leg was aching by the time they got to the top and she surreptitiously eased the weight off it when she thought no-one was watching.

Totty and Villete had collapsed in the shade of the giant tree. Having seen the view many times, they focussed instead on something kept secret in the palm of Totty's hand. Quiet giggles erupted from their huddle, breaking the silence sporadically.

'Our farm,' said Helene, unable to keep the pride from her voice. The hill gave a wonderful panoramic view of the whole area. Fields of lavender ran away down the hill, flowing like waves of purple water over the sloping ground. She could make out the roof of the farmhouse and the knife-points of the pine trees in the courtyard in the small valley below. A series of low rolling green hills ran off the edge of the horizon.

Jean-Luc stepped forward and grabbed her elbow, turning her a few degrees to the left and leaning in close so he could point out a jumble of tan square walls and a squat spire embedded into the side of a large sierra of rock.

'That's Sault,' he said. Her elbow burned where his fingers held it. Even through the linen of her shirt. She mumbled an interested kind of sound and then took a few steps away from him, around the other side of the olive tree, hoping to distract herself.

'Is all this down here yours as well?' she asked, pointing to the fields on the other side of the hill.

'Yes, we have one of the largest farms in the area,' he acknowledged. Charlize didn't know what to say. While this was probably considered large for a farm in France, her own family farm would dwarf it, probably three or four times the size. But she kept that to herself.

'It's beautiful.' Her compliment was heartfelt, and Jean-

Luc returned her smile.

'I used to come up here a lot when I was a kid. When I was Totty's age.' His eyes focussed away on the horizon as memories took him. 'Sometimes the sky was so blue, it made the clouds look almost transparent. Like they were made of glass.' There was a terrible longing in his face, bared for a second only before it was gone again.

'The land of glass clouds and lavender,' she said softly, touching his arm. It felt like iron beneath her touch. This man was such an enigma. On the one hand, indomitable and dangerous, a man who shouldn't care about anything or anyone. Then there was the side of him that dreamed about glass clouds.

Jean-Luc sobered, seeming to come back from far away, and the slight smile on his lips faded.

'Come on, let's get back.' He turned without waiting to see if she followed and headed down the slope.

She needed to find out more of his story. Why had he left a lucrative family farm—one he obviously loved—to become a gendarme in the French police force? Was it perhaps something to do with his older brother, Herve? It seemed there wasn't much love lost between those two. She stared after his retreating back.

'Ta ta, always in such a hurry, this one,' said Helene, but there was affection in her tone. 'Come girls, help me pick some flowers on the way back, and we can check the oil content when we get home. Perhaps it is time to start the harvest, *oui*?' With that she surged down the hill, Totty close on her heels and Villete scurrying to keep up. Charlize hurried to follow her indomitable figure before it was swallowed up by the lavender.

She could feel Jean-Luc's presence ahead of her, a

beacon calling her forward.

LAVENDER TEA

Is a refreshing, calming hot drink that's extremely easy to make. Just use any loose black tea leaves you have and add either a pinch of dried lavender, or 3 fresh lavender flowers and brew normally in a teapot for 3 minutes. Add milk and sugar to your taste.

FRENCH SHORTBREAD COOKIES

INGREDIENTS
10 tbsp Salted butter, softened
½ cup Sugar
1 Egg
2 cups Plain flour

DIRECTIONS
It's best to use a (hand) mixer for this recipe. In a bowl, beat together butter and sugar until pale and fluffy on medium speed. Add the egg and beat until smooth. Add flour and mix on low speed until just combined. Transfer dough to a work surface and form into a ball. Wrap the dough in plastic and refrigerate for 1 hour. Heat your oven to 180ºC. On a lightly floured surface, use a rolling pin to roll dough out to 0.5 cm thickness and, using a round cookie cutter, cut out rounds and transfer to paper-lined baking sheets. Bake until cookies are set but not browned, for around 8–10 minutes. Cool before serving.
Serve sprinkled with sugar and dried lavender.

Best enjoyed while sitting, tucked up in bed on a sleepy Sunday afternoon.

CHAPTER SIXTEEN

Firelight flickered over the walls and cast eerie shadows into the corners. Jean-Luc sat on the floor with his back resting against the couch, staring at the flames. Charlize sat on the couch at the other end and chatted to his mother. They didn't often light the fire in summer, but his mother had insisted tonight. Probably wanted to show off the wonderful cavernous living room to its best potential. He took another sip of his rather large glass of cognac and only half-listened as the two women talked companionably. It was his second for the night, and it brought on a mellow glow deep in his belly.

He'd only allowed himself a second glass because he knew they were safe here, knew he could sleep through the night unmolested by Vincent and his gang. This was the one place they'd never find him. Pickard had assured him again this morning at the car-drop that his alias was watertight. Even if Enzo had managed to commit his face to memory and been able to get his computer geek to hack into the police system, Jean-Luc's real life, his real family had long ago been buried deep. Replaced with a fictitious life and backed up by legitimate paperwork to make it seem completely authentic to anyone who wanted to dig into his life.

Herve and Celine and the kids had sat with them for a while after dinner, then left, saying they needed to put the children to bed. Remarkably, Herve had been almost civil toward Jean-Luc. Perhaps it had been the presence of the women, Charlize and Celine, who talked quietly, heads together, about the best way to roast a chicken so that it stayed moist. Whatever it was, Jean-Luc enjoyed the best conversation he'd had with his older brother in many, many years.

A small part of him envied Herve. The fact he knew so adamantly he was leading the life he was meant to lead. Helping his parents with the farm, married to a wife he loved, and who loved him unreservedly back, raising a family of his own, instilling in them the tradition and honour of being lavender farmers in Provence. Jean-Luc would never say this out loud, but his brother was starting to look more and more like their father. At nearly six feet four, Herve was the same height as Jaiyan, but he was also developing that same stoop, as if being up so high was tiring, and he wanted to come down to everyone else's level. They both had the same jaw, square and set in that familiar, determined way. Ready to take on the whole world if necessary.

His mother raised her voice, breaking into his musing. 'It's getting late.' She stood up and cast him an incalculable gaze. 'Well, it is for us country people,' she amended. It was just past nine pm, but his parents had always gone to bed early, it came with the territory when you worked on a farm; they got up before sunrise most days. His father had excused himself and was tinkering around in his study down the hall, probably doing the accounts, or replying to emails. But Jean-Luc knew Jaiyan wouldn't be far behind his wife.

'Oh, okay then.' There was faint surprise in the rise of Charlize's eyebrows. 'Thank you again for letting us stay here. We really appreciate it.' Then his mother did something surprising and out of character. She leaned down and gave Charlize a quick hug.

'And we love having you here'. She turned quickly, but stopped just before she stepped through the door.

'Fabien is coming out tomorrow. You will still be here then, won't you, Jean-Luc?' The obvious note of rebuff was there for him to hear, stamping her disappointment at his flying visit firmly in his head.

'Yes, Maman, we'll still be here, at least until tomorrow evening,' he placated. She left with a swish of her skirts.

His little brother was coming to see him. A spark of affection flared as he thought of Fabien. The two of them were so much more alike than he and Herve would ever be. So much closer. It'd be good to catch up with him.

'I forgot what a different lifestyle it is when you work on a farm,' Charlize said. 'But it's all coming back to me. The early mornings, the long hours, full of dust and hard work.' She gave a self-deprecating grimace, her fingers running up and down the stem of her wineglass. 'And here I was feeling nostalgic for my family farm.' That's right, she was a country girl too. He'd almost forgotten. 'Now I've remembered, I'm not so sure I want to go home.' That warm smile was back on her face, competing with the flames of the fire for the heat it started in his belly.

'What do you grow on your farm?'

'Canola.'

'Ah yes, I think I've seen photos of that. Enormous fields of yellow flowers, is that right?'

'Yes,' she laughed, then swirled the wine around in her glass and took a sip, watching him over the rim as she did so. 'But it's just as dusty and dry and back-breaking work as your lavender farm. So perhaps we're not as different as we think, you and I.' Jade eyes regarded him as she took another long, slow sip of the ruby red liquid. Jade eyes inviting him? It was hard to tell with the firelight casting shadows that altered the planes of her face.

'Perhaps not,' he agreed. 'I talked to Pickard again just after dinner. There's been no more movement from the cartel. It seems they lost our trail, even before we crashed off the road. We're completely safe here.' The cognac burned his throat as he took another large swig. He hadn't realised it before, but now he was here, he knew he needed this night. Needed time to reconnect with his family, no matter how short. Needed time to let go for just a few hours. He'd been holding on so tight for so many days and months. Hell, even years. It was nice to just be, for one night at least.

'That's good.' Charlize levered herself off the end of the couch and came to sit next to him on the floor rug. The air shifted as she drew close, leaving a buzz, like static electricity running over his skin. Did she know what she did to him, how she affected him?

'Tell me if I'm stepping over the line here, but something's been bugging me all day and I just have to ask.' He inclined his head for her to continue, the flesh on his cheeks tightening, unsure exactly what she was going to ask.

'You obviously love it here. And this farm is your birthright. So why did you become a cop?' He had to hand it to her, she was the queen of asking the direct questions. And she'd also been extremely perceptive, seen through his tough veneer, straight through to the question that still haunted him. Why hadn't he stayed? There was a place here for him if he wanted it.

'Is it because of Herve?' she asked when he didn't answer after many drawn out seconds. 'It seemed like there was some...rivalry there?'

'What? No, that's not it at all.' Their shoulders bumped gently together as he turned toward her. 'Herve and I only fell out after I decided to leave the farm. He thinks my place is here, as do my parents.' It was complicated. More complicated than he could explain. She couldn't possibly understand, she wasn't French. He put his glass down carefully on the floor and rubbed a finger over his temple. What would Herve do if he did suddenly announce he was coming back to work on the farm, that he was going to give up being a gendarme? Herve hadn't wanted him to leave, but would he want him to come back?

'Sorry,' she said, 'You don't have to answer that.' Warm fingers landed on his thigh, just above his knee. Comforting. Apologetic. Long fingers so sensuous and sublime.

'I was young and eager back then.' Not quite sure why he was telling her, the words started to tumble out of him. 'I was only eighteen when I joined the local gendarme. They sent me away for specialist training almost immediately. I guess I probably rebelled against the idea that I was expected to spend my life working on the farm. I even came to detest the smell of lavender in my nostrils.'

Her hand stayed warm and heavy on his leg. It became his only focus, the rest of the room fading around him, there was only the feel of her palm resting on his leg.

'I can relate to that,' she replied. 'I don't dislike my family farm, but I did see a very different path to the one my parents wanted me to take. In the end, they were very supportive of me becoming a mounted police woman. Well, my mum was at least.' Her gaze was locked onto the flames of the fire and her voice became low and indistinct as her memory turned inwards. 'And they have Letta and Ben to help them out, so they don't really need me, anyway.' She lifted her hand from his leg to run it through her hair, an unconscious gesture, but one he was starting to realise meant her mind was elsewhere. 'Letta's my younger sister,' she added quickly and caught her lower lip in between her teeth. 'She's tough and strong and loves the farm.'

'So I have Herve and you have Letta,' he replied with a wry grin.

She laughed out loud and flashed her straight, white teeth at him. 'I guess you're right. We both have the excuse we need not to go back to the farm.'

'I'm also allergic to bees,' he said, 'So being around lavender is an actual health hazard for me.'

'Really?' The turn of her head so she could stare at him made her hair shimmer and bounce in the firelight.

'Yep, really.' He wanted her to put her hand back on his leg. To come closer and lean her shoulder up against his.

'But why choose the gendarme?' Apparently, she wasn't finished with her probing questions. He wasn't even sure he could answer that one himself.

'It's hard to explain…' He wanted to say *to a white*

woman, but decided that wasn't going to win him any brownie points. 'When my brothers and I were growing up, we were always aware that, while our family was respected because of mum's pedigree, the colour of our skin made us more of a target for people's stupid comments.'

'Ah ha,' she replied slowly.

'So, I guess when I was young and full of rage and resentment, I wanted to go out and right some wrongs, rattle some people's cages, you know. To show society that not all people with African backgrounds are a pestilence.' He shifted a little on the rug, turned so he could see Charlize's eyes as he spoke, to gauge her reaction. For some reason it suddenly become important to him what she thought of him. And of his reasons. She pursed her lips, totally concentrating on what he was saying, glass of wine forgotten in her hand. The words seemed to come of their own accord then, pouring out of his mouth without any conscious thought.

'I also wanted to help those poor souls who're still making the journey.' He made a motion with one of his hands, indicating rolling waves.

'I know from my father's story what a harrowing and dangerous journey it was for him, and I want to make it easier for those who're still trying to attain a better life. But there is a right way and a wrong way to do it, and I want to help them do it the right way. People are desperate and they'll do whatever it takes to escape persecution and famine. Those people smugglers are a blight on humanity. Charging astronomical fees to people who are already so poor and ravaged by war or lack of food and who blatantly can't afford it. But if they do finally make it to

Europe, they find the conditions in the refugee camps are just as bad, if not worse, than what they've just left.' His voice got slowly louder as he spoke, so now it echoed around the room. It always made him so mad, thinking of Vincent and how he didn't give a shit about anything but money.

'I don't even pretend to know the intricacies of illegal immigration,' Charlize replied softly. 'But you obviously feel very strongly about it, and your passion, your determination are surprising. And admirable.' This time, her hand landed on his bare forearm, a token of her empathy. But this time there was no fabric to keep skin from touching skin. Her palm rested soft and warm near his elbow. His mind whirled back to early this morning, back in the farm shed. When he'd tasted the dip below her collarbone. When she'd responded to his touch with easy surrender. The beginnings of an erection stirred beneath his jean zipper. *Merde*. He needed to think about something else, anything else.

'It must be a hard life you've chosen? To be away from your family. Lonely even?' She cocked an eyebrow at him and then casually removed her hand. Did she know what she'd just done to him?

'Are you married?' Again, her question caught him off guard as he tried to rein in his rampant libido. Funnily, he'd thought about asking her the very same thing that night he'd taken her on a date in Uzes. At the last second, he'd decided against it. But now? The fact that he was desperate to kiss her right now meant he probably owed her the truth.

He sucked in a breath and pressed his backbone against the couch, wiping his face clean of any emotion.

'I was married once. We had a son, but he died. The doctor told us it was SIDS. You know, that thing where they just stop breathing when they're asleep.' A sharp pain scissored its way through his chest as he uttered the words, no matter how unvarnished he tried to make them sound. The same way it always did when he thought about Leo.

'Jesus, Jean-Luc.' Her breath expelled as a sharp exclamation. 'I'm sorry. I didn't mean to...' She never finished her sentence, her hand returned, grip tight on his arm. There was probably a lot she hadn't meant to bring up, would never have guessed in a million years before she'd asked that question. He raised a smile, and laid his hand on top of hers.

'You couldn't have known, so don't judge yourself. It was five years ago.'

'Time doesn't always heal all wounds,' she said in a small voice. He just shrugged in acceptance. He couldn't change the past. Yes, it hurt when he thought about his son, but that's why he buried it deep down, immersed himself in work, didn't talk about it. To anyone. Not even his mother. Had he been right to unburden his soul to Charlize? It might've just been a rash moment of lust that drove him to tell her. After all, if you had a woman's sympathy, they were much more easily swayed when it came to getting them into bed. If they felt you'd really *connected* with them. Disturbingly, he knew it was more than that. It was more than pure lust driving him tonight, it was the way she'd looked at him after his father had hugged him so tight when they arrived. As if she honoured his father's devotion, admired the fact he loved his son unconditionally. And it was the way he'd wanted to reach out and touch her hair, feel it slip like silk beneath his fingertips, as the sun's rays made it gleam golden this afternoon on top of the hill.

'What about you?' Would she tell him the truth? And would he even know the truth if he heard it?

Her nostrils flared. But she must've known it was coming, how could she not? A look of determination settled over her face.

'I had a fiancé back in Australia. I was also pregnant.' She looked away from him, as if unable to meet his gaze. 'But after I lost our baby in the crash, we kind of drifted apart.'

Now it was his turn to curse inwardly. He was such an idiot sometimes. No wonder she'd been freaked out by the accident yesterday. She'd lost so much more than just a horse in that fire. Understanding made him go weak.

'Charlize,' he said, reaching up and cupping her cheek with his hand. 'I'm so sorry.'

'I know.' She smiled, but her eyes shone with unshed tears. 'Look at us, we're both a complete mess.' He ran a thumb lightly of over her cheekbone, luxuriating in the lustrous feel of her skin.

She stilled beneath his touch. Jean-Luc was vaguely aware of the crackle of the flames, of the quiet music playing in the background, but that all faded out of existence, and it became just the two of them. Him and Charlize. He ran his thumb lower, tracing the line of her chin, and then up, drifting over her lips, feeling the texture of them beneath his finger. She was extremely beautiful, with that soft English rose complexion, cheeks pink with wine and firelight. Green eyes focussed on him. He'd never noticed before, but a darker ring ran around the outside of each iris, as if to contain the beautiful ocean green colour. Her pupils dilated under his touch. Carefully, he put his glass aside, on the floor behind the couch.

Her lips parted slightly, her breath pulsing over his thumb as she breathed in and out. A shot of heat went through his gut, straight to his groin. Her hot breath against his skin sent spikes of desire pulsing through his veins. The erection he'd managed to control earlier made a speedy reappearance. A hint of the outline of her breasts, nipples pressing against the fabric of her shirt, showed in the firelight.

His thumb stopped its slow exploration. They shouldn't be doing this. He shouldn't be doing this. He was here to protect her. That was all. She was a job to him, nothing more. Once this was over, they'd go their separate ways and never see each other again.

And yet.

The attraction he felt, the chemistry between them, was the strongest he'd ever known in his life. It wouldn't be ignored. Like she was a dangerous, illicit drug calling to him. A white woman. With a black man. His ex-wife, Fleur, had been from a well-to-do family, her father a rich businessman who owned several sports stores around the country. Fleur's mother was a beautiful woman who'd been dragged from obscurity in an African slum in Dadaab into the high life of a modelling career. Fleur had inherited her mother's beauty and her fragility along with the colour of her skin.

Every woman he'd dated, both before and after Fleur, had dark skin. Except Galina, with her Russian heritage and porcelain white skin. But in truth, Galina had pursued him, had aggressively hunted him down, using her sexuality as bait, and he'd been only too happy to surrender in the end. She was a tiger in bed, after all. He could appreciate a good-looking woman, no matter what her skin colour or race.

Apart from Galina, had he stuck to his own colour on purpose, or had it been a subconscious thing? His mother was white and his father black and he'd seen how much ridicule they'd had to endure. Had he made an instinctive decision not to emulate his parents? And if he had, what the hell was he doing now?

Charlize moved beneath his hand, uncomfortable with his sudden stillness. He stared into her face and her breathing hitched as her eyes flickered down to his lips and back up. He'd been doing his damndest all day to deny that he wanted her. Shutting down his body's reaction to her presence. When she'd stood next to him at the top of the hill this afternoon, pressing against his side as he showed her Sault, when he'd sat on her bed today, knowing she was practically naked under that sheet—it'd taken a will of iron to walk out of her room then. Even tonight at dinner, when some of the sauce from his mother's chicken dinner had dribbled down her chin. He'd watched her lick it off with her tongue. It was an unconscious move, not meant to be in the least bit sensuous, but he'd had to drop his napkin in his lap quickly to hide the sudden growing bulge at his own parent's kitchen table, what's more.

As he watched, she licked her lips, and that was his undoing. The last shred of his restraint disappeared. Sliding his hand around to the nape of her neck, he brought her lips to his, crushing them against his mouth.

She didn't resist, almost as if she'd been waiting for him to make a decision, and now she let him press her to him, snaking her own hand around his shoulders, urging him closer still. Their tongues entwined, and she was a heady mixture of red wine and honey and...lavender. The lavender was a surprise, but in an odd way, it was somehow right. The smell of lavender had always been associated with such complicated memories for him, but now perhaps it might also mean something wonderful.

The urgency he'd felt back in the machinery shed in the small hours of this morning came flooding back. *Merde*, he wanted this woman. Wanted to be inside her, feel her surrounding him. Tomorrow be damned.

He took her by the hand and pulled her up to standing, while keeping his mouth glued to hers. For a few seconds, he allowed his hands to roam over her body, down her long, slender back. Then he grabbed the tight mounds of her buttocks and lifted her against his body, so her breasts pushed into his chest. Jesus Mary, Mother of God, she felt so good. Long legs pressed up against his thighs, he hardly had to dip his head to reach her lips as her fingers tangled together at the nape of his neck, urging him closer, urging him to kiss her harder, deeper. A moan sounded deep in her throat as he massaged her buttocks and she ground her pelvis against his until he could feel her hip bones jutting into his stomach.

He broke away from her mouth and gasped, 'Come with me.'

She followed without a word.

* * *

Jean-Luc's hand burned like a brand in her palm. She followed him down the hall, not letting herself think.

She'd been overthinking everything for the past two years. Tonight, she was going to *feel*. This man was utterly gorgeous, and she wanted him more than she'd wanted anyone before. He was so damn sexy, the way his bronze eyes fixed on her, flooded with desire and yearning. The way his fingers traced her jawbone so softly had sent shudders like a shock wave through her belly. His taut chest beneath her fingers, heart pounding just as fast as hers.

Where were they going? They needed to get there soon, or she'd start tearing his clothes off right here and now, parents be damned. Being in his family home made it seem like she was a teenager again, sneaking around, hands clasped tight in a mixture of adolescent lust and apprehension. Please don't let Helene appear in the corridor right now. They finally arrived at the door to her bedroom.

Without a word, he led her inside, closed the door, then backed her up against it, trapping her hands in his and pressing her against the cool wood. The room was dark, lit only by the soft light of a new moon coming through the open window. But it was more than enough for her to see him. His mouth found hers again and devoured her like a starving animal. She felt hot, so hot she was melting. Too many clothes in the way, restricting her need to touch him. They needed to get their clothes off, she needed to see him naked.

Dragging her mouth away from his, she lay her head back against the wood and said, 'As good as you look in this shirt, I'd rather see it off you.' He let go of her hands and her fingers fumbled with the buttons, but the slippery little things wouldn't do her bidding. So she went to lift the hem instead, to rip it up over his head in one quick movement.

'Let me,' he said, voice ragged, and undid the buttons one by one. Then she remembered. Of course, his injuries from the car crash, that terrible bruising. She'd been about to do all sorts of damage by trying to drag the shirt over his head.

'I'm sorr—' A finger on her lips stopped her mid-breath, and he shook his head.

'Don't you dare apologise. I'm fine, don't worry about it.' Button by button, he slowly revealed a little more of that wondrous chest. His shirt dropped to the floor.

'Jesus,' she said on an exhaled breath. Then she swallowed hard as she took in the male body before her. He really was model-perfect. Defined abs flexed beneath her fingers as she trailed them downwards. A scattering of black curls covered the smooth, hard muscles of his chest, swirled together in the middle like a small whirlpool, then dived toward his navel. A fine trail of hairs dipped further south to disappear beneath the darker fabric of the shorts that hugged his lean hips. The bruising was almost invisible in the glow of moonlight. If he was going to ignore his injuries, then who was she to argue?

His nimble hands found her own buttons and her shirt soon joined his in the puddle on the floor. He trailed a hand over the top of her bra, between her breasts, over her belly and down to rest on the waistband of her linen pants. She watched his fingers through half-closed eyes. The contrast between his dark skin against the paleness of her belly made her start. She'd almost forgotten they were a different colour.

'You are so...' He didn't finish his sentence, leaving her

wondering, *so what*? So incredibly beautiful? So white? So scarred? So much trouble?

'I've never wanted any other woman quite as much as I want you right now.' Okay, she could live with that. That was definitely a compliment.

He dipped his fingers into the top of her pants and, with one swift movement, pulled her trousers down to her ankles and she kicked them the rest of the way off. Her heart started to pound so fast it almost took her breath away as she stood there in only her underwear, letting his gaze rake over her. Her nipples peaked as he stared and sent a tingle straight to the smouldering fire between her legs. Charlize reached around behind and unsnapped her bra, then slipped each shoulder out of the straps and let it slither the rest of the way down her body.

He stood and studied her, his hunger for her clearly evident in his eyes now. Moonlight was her friend tonight. Shedding enough light for them both to see contours, shapes, silhouettes, but not enough for him—she hoped—to see the details of the scars running down her leg. She waited, suddenly unsure, hoping this wasn't all just a dream. Then, in one quick movement, he'd unbuttoned his shorts and stripped down, underwear and all. Completely naked, skin back-lit by the filtered moonlight, the physical evidence of his desire for her all too obvious now. The slow burn between her legs became a throbbing need. This was surreal, knowing this gorgeous man wanted her as much as she wanted him.

But she had no time to second guess herself as he came back to her, pulled her up in his arms and crushed his mouth against hers. He lifted her up until her feet left the ground and she had no choice but to wrap her legs around his waist; her back hard up against the wooden door. Even through the cotton fabric of her underwear, she felt his erection, urgent and solid. Her body arched into his. The pounding of his chest as it slammed up against hers drove her almost wild as her own heart echoed the beat. His mouth trailed down her jaw to her throat, left scorch marks beneath the lobe of her ear, his teeth nipping lightly at the curve of her collarbone. The sweet, sharp pain sent the blood surging through her veins. She ground her hips again, a low moan escaping her.

All thoughts fled except for one that kept pulsing in her mind. There was him, only him, and she couldn't get enough of him. She needed him inside her.

One tiny, coherent thought did manage to break through.

'Condom,' she managed to get out through her constricted throat.

'Wait,' he said, voice equally husky. He let her gently down onto her tiptoes and bent down, reaching for something on the ground. He picked up his shorts and surged upward again, something crinkling in his hand.

She wrapped her legs around his hips for a second time and he held her up with one arm while he fumbled with the package with the other. Then he was pushing aside her panties and thrusting into her and she nearly cried out with the ecstasy of it. Oh God, his parents would hear. She shoved her face into the crook of his neck, trying to muffle the sounds coming out of her mouth.

CHAPTER SEVENTEEN

'One night. One night is all that you can give us.' Helene's eyes crackled with anger. Jean-Luc knew the only solution when she got mad like this was to appease his mother. Otherwise, she had the potential to erupt like Mt Vesuvius. That temper of hers was world famous.

'I'm sorry, Maman,' he soothed. She did have a point. It was way past rude of him to just rock up on their doorstep without having seen them for nearly two years, and then leave again the next day. 'I promise I'll come back soon.'

'*Pah*, I've heard that before,' she grumbled. He took a chance and gathered her gently up in a hug. She'd either fight him off or submit to his apology. She submitted, grabbing him tight for a second around the waist and saying, 'I miss you, Jean-Luc.'

A lump formed at the back of his throat. Her frankness surprised him. His mother wasn't normally one for sentimentality.

'I know, Maman. This time I will be back. As soon as this job is over, I'll take some leave and come and stay. Okay?' He pulled away from his mother's fierce embrace so he could look into her eyes. She nodded and blinked back tears. Again with the tears. Was his mother mellowing as she got older?

'We'll you'd better keep that promise, Jean-Luc.' Her voice was once more under control as she pulled out of his arms and straightened her skirts.

'I will.' And this time, he knew he would. He had weeks' worth of leave owing to him. It was time. As soon as he knew Charlize was safe. Then he'd come back.

The sound of wheels scrunching on gravel came through the open window.

'Fabien, that must be Fabien,' she said, turning away and rushing out the kitchen side door. Jean-Luc smiled at his mother's antics. He was looking forward to seeing his little brother as much as she was.

He heard the kids rushing outside as well, to greet their uncle.

'Uncle Fabien, uncle Fabien,' the kids shouted as a battered red Peugeot pulled up in the courtyard. Then his little brother stepped out of the car, smiling.

Fabien had chosen a life away from the farm as well. But somehow Jean-Luc was the one who was constantly berated for his choice. That's what came of being the baby of the family, Fabien could get away with just about anything. He was an artist, a sculptor, with a gallery in Sault. And that's probably one of the reasons his family hadn't disowned him, because he was still only a twenty-minute drive away; he'd stayed in the home country. He wasn't quite a starving artist; he made enough money to live on, was becoming well known for his engaging sculptures made of local stone.

Waiting patiently until his mother and father and the

kids had finished greeting Fabien, he stepped forward and punched his brother in the arm.

'Hey, little bro. How's the art business?'

'Not bad,' his brother countered with his trademark wide grin. Fabien had always been able to get away with bloody murder with that grin. It turned their mother to melted butter every time. Then Fabien grabbed him in a manly version of a hug, where they bumped shoulders and slapped each other on the back repeatedly.

Seeing his little brother now it cemented in Jean-Luc's mind just how much he missed his family. It was way pastime he re-connected with them.

Then he saw Fabien's stare lock on something over his shoulder, his eyes widening with surprise, then appreciation. Without having to turn around, Jean-Luc knew Charlize had just walked out the door.

Fabien gave a low whistle.

'Mmm hmm, bro, you sure know how to pick 'em.'

'It's not what you think,' Jean-Luc replied, taken aback at the sudden surge of jealousy that prickled hot beneath his skin. There'd always been a friendly rivalry between himself and his brother when it came to girls. But this was no girl. And there was no way Fabien was going to get close to her. Not this time. 'She's work related,' he finished determinedly.

'Really?' Fabien ran a hand through his mop of black curls. Fabien was popular with the women, with that wonderful hair of his, that wide inviting smile and an artist's aura of vulnerability. *Merde*. Perhaps he wasn't as happy to see his little brother as he'd first thought.

Stepping back, he waited till Charlize came over to them. 'Charlize, meet my little brother, Fabien.'

'The pleasure is all mine,' Fabien replied, and Jean-Luc felt his blood pressure rise another notch when his dastardly little brother took Charlize by the hand and planted a kiss on the back of her knuckles, as if he were some kind of medieval knight. His brother gave a sidelong smirk, and even though Jean-Luc knew he'd done it just to rankle him, he still had to clench his fists tight at his sides to keep from smacking him. Through gritted teeth, he managed to smile back.

'Come, come,' his mother interrupted, clapping her hands as she started to herd them all like sheep back into the kitchen. 'We're going to have an early meal, so Jean-Luc and Charlize can get on the road. Back to Nice.' She cast him a sideways glance, and he knew he still wasn't really forgiven yet. He gave a quiet sigh.

The kids ran into the kitchen, laughing, and jumped up to sit at the large table his mother had laid out for their family meal. Jean-Luc made sure he took Charlize by the arm, guided her to the end of the table, and pulled out a chair for her. She gave him a curious glance, but didn't protest.

'Keeping her all to yourself down there,' his brother said good-naturedly from the middle of the table. He just smiled back at Fabien. Let him think what he liked.

His mother had excelled herself with this meal. After he'd told his parents earlier this morning, they'd be heading back to Nice tonight, she hadn't said a word, but had started to bang and crash pots and pans around. His father had raised his eyebrows and told him to *leave her to work it out in the kitchen*. She'd get over it in the end. He perused the laden table as he sat down. Two whole roast chickens, brown crispy skin oozing juices, sat in the centre of the table. Helene's signature dish sat next to them; tartiflette, a French version of the humble potato bake, but made with a whole large camembert, and it had Jean-Luc's stomach rumbling. There were other platters piled high as well, green beans with pancetta and pine nuts, pan fried broccoli with garlic, and whole baked fennel, one of his favourites.

Pickard had phoned this morning, giving the all clear for Charlize to be taken to the safe house in Nice. He assured Jean-Luc that none of their security had been breached, the safe house was indeed clean. He reported that Vincent's gang had been making discreet but feverish enquiries, calling in all their favours to try and find Jean-Luc and Charlize. But it seemed they'd lost the trail. 'That car crash may have been a godsend in disguise,' Pickard had said dourly. It was decided they'd drive back to Nice after nightfall—no use taking any more risks than was completely necessary—and he could drop Charlize off at the safe house. Then they were going to double their efforts to catch Vincent in the act of smuggling once and for all. It felt good to be on the move again. To be doing something proactive. He needed to get this op finished. Too many things had gone wrong as it was, and he was suddenly more tired than he'd ever remembered being. Vincent needed to be stopped. But now his directive was skewed. He was doing this as much for Charlize's sake as he was to stop terrorists from entering the country.

Ever since he'd told Charlize they were going to the safe house in Nice, a sour look had settled on her face. The look was the complete opposite of the one he remembered on her face last night. Last night her features had been soft, inviting, hot with desire. They'd been so lost in the depths of their passion, they hadn't even made it to the bed. He'd taken her right there, up against the door. Then later on they'd made love the more conventional way, under the sheets. On her large bed. But their lovemaking had been just as full of urgent need and desperate wanting.

Just thinking about what they'd done last night made him hard. He slid the napkin further up his lap. *Merde*. He was at the family dinner table, for God's sake. He made a determined effort to put last night out of his mind. For now. But he could feel the heat emanating from Charlize where she sat beside him. He didn't even need to look around, he could *feel* she was there.

Fabien put his elbows on the table and leaned toward her, asking if she'd been to the township of Sault yet, and if she wanted to come and see his gallery. She pursed those beautiful rosebud lips while she contemplated her answer. Golden curls cascaded around her face, catching the sunlight streaming in the window and framed her high cheekbones, falling over her forehead in a way that made him want to brush the hair away from her eyes. She'd borrowed more of Maman's clothes today, as she only had the dress she'd fled Vincent's men to wear until he could take her shopping. This time it was a long, flowing dress made of soft knitted fabric in a wonderful royal blue, which draped off her shoulders in a very enticing manner.

The line of the dress was sheer and body-hugging, and he suddenly wondered what kind of underwear she had on beneath the dress. He'd forgotten to give her spare underwear. Perhaps she had nothing at all.

Stop it.

These thoughts would do him no good at all. And definitely wasn't helping him keep control of his libido.

His eye caught on the bright flash of material at the other end of the table. Grand-Mere sat next to his father, small and almost swallowed by the enormous table in front of her. Quiet. Insubstantial almost. But he knew better. She was the heart of this family, the load-stone that tied it together. It was her serenity, her deep belief her family would succeed, that coloured everything the Munulo family did and said, even if they never realised it. The true epitome of the word matriarch. Her gaze zeroed in on Jean-Luc, deep and thoughtful. There hadn't been many chances for Jean-Luc to talk to Grand-Mere alone in the past twenty-four hours. He needed to find the time before he left.

A dark, crooked finger beckoned to him over the top of the chicken carcass. He rose and walked around the table and hunkered down on his knees next to her chair. A gnarled hand landed on top of his head, almost as if she were giving him a blessing.

'Jean-Luc, my boy.' Her voice was low and intense as she spoke in French to him.

'Yes, Grand-Mere. Sorry I haven't had more time to spend with you on this visit. How are you doing?'

'Ta, ta, I'm always the same.' She looked at him with those wise, dark eyes the colour of a deep tar pit. 'But you, my boy, how are you doing?'

He was about to say, *I'm fine*. Utter platitudes and wave away his problems, but he knew she'd see straight through all that.

'I've been better,' he confided.

'I know. I see it in you. So does your mother.'

He shot Helene a guilty look, but her back was turned as she engaged in a very loud conversation with Fabien on the other side of the table.

'She worries about you. But that is a mother's job. I don't worry about you.' He smiled at that.

'Why not, Grand-Mere?' he asked gently.

'Because I know the lavender will call you back.' A flash of surprise whipped through him, almost sending him tumbling backwards. He grabbed the back of her chair for support. What exactly did she mean by that?

'Jean-Luc.' His mother's voice sounded from further down the table. 'Where are you?'

He stood up. 'Here, Maman.'

'Come over here and explain to Fabien exactly why he can't use me as the inspiration for his next sculpture. It would be most undignified,' she said, waving her arms around animatedly. His mother was a little tipsy. Jean-Luc smiled affectionately.

'I'll come back and finish our conversation later,' he promised Grand-Mere.

'Ta, ta,' she said and waved him away with one of her bony hands.

* * *

Charlize sucked her fingers one by one with relish. That was the best roast chicken she'd ever tasted. She was definitely asking for the recipe. It looked like Helene had made a stuffing of bay leaves, rosemary, thyme, and, of course, lavender. And the tartiflette. She needed the recipe for that as well. She could still taste the remnants of the rich camembert on her lips. Sitting back in her chair, she patted her overfull stomach and sighed, watching the antics of the three kids as they teased each other while Fabien joked with them. He was just a big kid himself. The youngest sibling often never grew up, remained the baby of the family.

Helene and Jaiyan watched on with unconcealed pride from their places at the other end of the table. Celine shot her a satisfied grin before she went back to cutting up a piece of chicken for Beau. Charlize was starting to really like Celine. She'd known the woman for less than twenty-four hours, but her sense of humour, mixed with her down-to-earth practicality and kindness, was engaging. Herve, she wasn't so sure about. He was good-looking, all three brothers had inherited that trait, and he'd definitely taken on Jaiyan's height—he was the tallest of the three, but his looks were tempered with a dourness, a sense of responsibility that seemed to weigh on him more heavily than it did on the other two. He'd probably grow on her, given time. As long as he could get over whatever his problem was with Jean-Luc. And now she'd met Fabien as well. The joker of the family, it was hard not to be drawn to his personality. She'd love to have had the opportunity to see his gallery in Sault.

Late evening sunlight streamed in through the windows, touching everything with its warm orange rays. This kitchen was so beautiful. What she wouldn't give to be able to cook in a kitchen like this one. To live here. Everything, from the old steel stove that needed to be stoked with firewood every few hours, to the rough wooden mantelpiece above the fireplace that held a collection of old blue and white plates, spoke to her. Plates lay jumbled in the sink, waiting to be washed, the remnants of a delicious meal lay scattered on the huge table in front of her. Joyful voices filled the room, the sound piling all the way up to the high ceilings and catching in the exposed rafters. The sound of life and laughter.

Suddenly, it hit her. She was happy. Sitting here, surrounded by Jean-Luc's family, felt so right. Then she had another realisation. She and Helene were the only two white people at the table. She'd become so enmeshed in Jean-Luc's family she no longer saw the colour delineation. Which was a good thing.

Jean-Luc bumped her elbow and turned to apologise with a grin, his teeth white against his brown skin. A surge of…something, coursed through her gut at his smile. It was warm and gooey, like caramel, mixed with a fluttery thing, as if there were live crickets jumping around inside her chest.

Oh Jesus.

No.

No. She wasn't falling for this man. She couldn't be. It wasn't allowed. Their eyes locked for interminable seconds and then he winked at her and everything they'd done last night in her room came flooding back.

In the cold light of day, she could ask herself what the hell she'd thought she was doing last night. But in reality, she knew there was no way she could've resisted him. Everything about him drew her in. And the sex last night had been amazing, mind-blowing, earth shattering. All of those horrible clichés and more. He was as good a lover as she'd imagined. Better even. And perhaps because of that, she'd found herself responding to him with equal fervour. Doing things she'd never dreamed she would. They'd made love three times last night. The first time was so hurried they hadn't even made it to the bed and he'd taken her up against the bedroom door. The memory of his taking control, the way he'd captured her hands and held her enslaved to his attentions, still made her shiver with delight.

But today was a new day, and it was time she forgot about their little interlude. They were about to leave, to drive to Nice. And then he was going to deposit her in some horrible safe house and take his leave of her. She hated him for that. Hated him for the fact he could ignore everything that'd just happened here and, as if flicking a switch, go back to the predator he was. Go back to hunting this smuggler guy and leave her to moulder in the backstreets of Nice. Bile rose in her throat at the thought, but she kept her eyes downcast in case he saw the change in her face. She'd need to keep acting as if nothing was wrong. As if she'd accepted her fate.

But she hadn't. She was going ahead with her plan. The only problem was, her passport was back in her villa in Uzes. She'd have to go back and retrieve it if she hoped to leave the country. Surely those gunmen wouldn't still be keeping her house under surveillance. After all, what person in their right mind would go back to the one place they'd know to look for her? She should be able to sneak in and out of her villa, unseen.

'Have you packed yet?' Jean-Luc leaned in and whispered in her ear. She painted on her brightest smile and nodded. What did she have to pack, really? Only the dress she'd arrived in. Helene was kindly lending her some clothes. She'd make sure they were returned as soon as possible. There was no point in being indebted to his family any more than she absolutely had to. The dress Helene loaned her for tonight was simple, comfortable, and stunning. It made her feel desirable, beautiful. She'd have to see if she could find a similar one when she got back home. Her heart constricted at the thought she'd never get to be part of this wonderful family ever again. The happy spark that'd flared in her chest only moments earlier died. Replaced by cold reality.

Dark, beetle-like eyes appraised her from down the other end of the table. Grand-Mere's gaze bored into her and Charlize had to fight the urge not to squirm. The jury was still out where Jean-Luc's grandmother was concerned. Jean-Luc obviously revered her, and she gained a lot of Charlize's respect for that. But it was as if the old woman could see right through her well-built defences, right down to the very core of her soul. And Charlize didn't like it. Not one little bit. What did the old woman see there?

Then the wrinkled lips puckered upwards in a small smile, meant only for Charlize to see. She couldn't help but smile back. Perhaps she liked what she saw, after all? For some reason, what the old woman thought of her truly mattered to Charlize, even though every part of her being wanted to deny it.

Bloody hell, she really was getting way too involved with Jean-Luc's family. The sooner they left the farmhouse, the better.

TARTIFLETTE

INGREDIENTS
1kg Potatoes, peeled
500g Camembert cheese
2 Medium onions peeled and chopped
200g Streaky bacon cubed
5tablespoons Creme fraiche
400ml Dry white wine
Salt and Pepper

DIRECTIONS
Grease an oven-proof dish. Boil the potatoes until just tender. Let them cool and them cut into thick slices. Fry up the bacon and onions together until the bacon is crispy and the onions are tender. Mix the crème frache and wine together and season with salt and pepper, remembering the bacon will be quite salty. Layer half the potatoes over the base of your dish, then cover with half the bacon and onion mixture and pour over half of the wine and crème frache mix. Repeat for a second layer. Cut your large camembert in half and lay over the top of the whole dish. Put in the oven at around 200°C for 45 minutes, or until it is brown and bubbling.

This is the best comfort food you could ever wish for. The most decadent, most fattening, most remind-you-of-mum's-home-cooked-meals dish ever. Best eaten in the family kitchen, surrounded by those you love. Don't forget the crusty baguette to mop up all the wonderful juices.

CHAPTER EIGHTEEN

Jean-Luc looked like he wanted to punch the wall. Dark brows drew over equally dark eyes and the corners of his mouth turned down in irritation. If she hadn't known better, she might have gone as far as to say he looked daunting.

'Charlize, please. You know this is the only option.'

She wasn't going to give him the satisfaction. Keeping her face impassive, she said, 'I'll see you later, Jean-Luc.' With that, she turned in the hallway and went back into the bedroom, quietly closing the door behind her.

She heard soft footsteps follow her to the door and stop outside, but it didn't open. His voice came through the wood.

'I'll be back in a few days. Hopefully, we'll have a solution by then. We'll talk some more, okay?' She didn't answer and eventually the footsteps disappeared down the hallway again. She slumped against the door, squeezing her eyes shut. That'd been so much harder than she was expecting. Saying goodbye to Jean-Luc. He thought she was pissed off, but he was assuming she'd get over it. There was no way he could predict she wouldn't be here when he got back. Then it'd be his turn to be pissed off. No, he'd be much madder than that, he'd be gutted, livid, and desperate to find her.

Jean-Luc had introduced her to her two *prison guards* when they'd first entered the house. Alfonse and Edgard. They'd both shaken her hand and given her a professional nod, making it obvious how this relationship was going to play out right from the start. They were here to do a job. And that was fine with her. The less friendly these guys were, the less nosey, made it all the easier for her to make her escape. They were both big guys, one with an impressive beard, way too powerful for her to ever think of taking on by herself. But that was all right, there was more than one way to skin a cat. If she wanted to get out of here, she'd have to use her ingenuity. Perhaps even throw a little guile into the mix as well. Most guys were never completely immune to a woman's charms. No matter how professional they seemed on the surface.

Jean-Luc must've headed back to the main living area, probably to have one last chat with the guards before he left. The villa they'd turned into this safe-house was nice enough. With comfortable modern furniture throughout and a well-equipped kitchen, it'd do well enough for any length of stay. Bland and unrecognisable from the outside in a street full of similar villas. The only difference was what this one contained on the inside. High-tech security in the form of cameras, perimeter alarms, and bulletproof glass on all the windows. It was meant to keep people out, but it'd also work equally well as a jail, to keep people in. Specifically, to keep her in.

She made her way over to the bed and flopped down

with one arm thrown over her eyes, recalling the past few hours.

She'd pretended to be asleep for most of the trip back to Nice. Avoiding conversation. She didn't want to talk to Jean-Luc. She was afraid if she did, her resolve would waver. He might see through her disguise, see that she was more than just cross at being put into the safe house, at being left behind like some recalcitrant child. She'd told him once, when they'd first gotten into the car, that she didn't want to go. But he'd just stared straight ahead at the road. The tough-guy persona unquestionably back in place. If only they hadn't gone to his family farm, she'd never have seen that soft underbelly of his. If only they hadn't made love last night. He would've been so much easier to resist. To leave.

So she'd laid her head back on the seat and closed her eyes. But closing her eyes hadn't banished the swirling emotions in her head. She was so confused. After the night they'd spent together, she'd thought... Well, she wasn't sure what she thought. But she knew there was a connection that went deeper than just pure lust. It went right to her core.

But he was acting as if nothing had happened. And if that's the way he wanted to play it, then she could play the game equally well.

As they came into the outskirts of Nice, she'd *woken up* and asked him to stop at the nearest large department store. He'd argued against it, saying all the henchmen were still on the lookout for her, she was back in mortal danger now. But she'd given him one of her best death-stares and declared that if he was going to coop her up for days and weeks on end, not allowed out to buy the bare necessities then he owed her an hour to get some more clothes and toiletries. He'd relented by giving her half an hour.

She'd rushed around the store, grabbing things at random, while he waited impatiently at the main door for her, then climbed back into the front passenger seat of the car, avoiding his gaze.

She levered herself off the bed, went over to the backpack she'd bought earlier, and tipped all the contents out onto the bed. There were clothes, shoes, a toothbrush, soap, shampoo and underwear. But she pushed all those aside, looking for one item in particular. She'd been sure Jean-Luc would ask to check her bag when she came out of the store, but he hadn't. More fool him. It was right at the bottom. A mobile phone. And a new SIM card. Her ticket out of here.

As she examined the phone, a random thought occurred to her. She'd never got the chance to cook that meal for Jean-Luc she'd promised him way back on the night in the shed. And now she never would.

* * *

The motorbike flashed through the dark streets, going way too fast. Jean-Luc crouched over the handlebars, pushing his bike to its limits, winding his way through Nice's outer suburbs, taking corners like he was competing in the Grand Prix. He should slow down. He could kill himself. Or someone else. But the streets were empty; it was three fifteen in the morning and everyone was in bed. And he had to get there. To see for himself.

Alfonse had phoned him just over three hours ago, to tell him Charlize was missing. 'How the hell could she be missing?' he'd yelled down the phone. He couldn't come up with enough expletives to describe how he'd felt at that particular moment.

Nearly there now, only a few more corners, and he finally pulled into the street where the safe house sat. He slowed the motorbike and tried to compose himself as he rolled into the driveway and punched in the code to make the garage door go up. Once the bike was safely ensconced away from prying eyes, he took a few deep, calming breaths. He'd promised himself he wasn't going to punch Alfonse, but, *Merde*, his fingers itched to fold into a fist. How stupid could they be!

The internal doorway from the villa to the garage opened and a large shape loomed out of the shadows. It was Edgard, by the shape of his bearded outline. Alfonse, the coward, was probably hiding inside.

'Edgard,' Jean-Luc said in a gruff voice as he brushed past him through the doorway.

'Jean-Luc,' the other man returned coolly. The guards were probably both feeling a little foolish, letting a woman slip past their defences. But it'd been Alfonse on duty when Charlize had disappeared. He was the man Jean-Luc wanted to talk to. Edgard was sleeping. The guards took it in turns, six-hour shifts. One sleeping or eating—still close enough if they should be needed—while one kept watch. But that procedure hadn't worked well tonight.

Sure enough, Alfonse was pacing to and fro in the living room as Jean-Luc entered.

'Tell me what happened,' Jean-Luc barked, dispensing with all niceties. He'd told them to keep an eye on Charlize, that she was a reluctant witness who didn't comprehend exactly how much danger she was in. But even Jean-Luc hadn't truly entertained the idea that she would actually escape. What in hell had she been thinking? He ran a hand over his short-cropped hair and took a seat as he waited for Alfonse to tell him the story. It was safer if he was sitting, he wouldn't be quite as likely to punch the man from down here. Edgard came in and took a seat in the corner of the room, leaning forward, elbows on his knees.

'She tricked me,' Alfonse admitted with a wry smile. Was that admiration in his voice?

'I warned you she was smart,' Jean-Luc growled.

'I know,' he confessed. 'I should've guessed what was going on. But at the time, I was more worried about not drawing undue attention to the house.'

'What do you mean?' asked Jean-Luc, trying, and failing, to keep his irritation under control.

'There was a pizza guy banging the door down. Making a hell of a noise. I had to go and answer the door before he woke up half the neighbourhood.' At this, Edgard let out a quiet snort.

'Shut up, Ed,' Alfonse said, rounding on him. 'You would've done exactly the same thing.' Edgard raised his hands in the air in surrender and folded himself back into his chair.

'Then what happened?' asked Jean-Luc, wanting to get the story back on track.

'Of course, I checked everything outside before I opened the door. I followed procedure, Jean-Luc. But the little pizza delivery guy was going crazy, yelling that he'd been searching for the place for hours, and his boss would kill him and the pizzas were gonna be cold. He wanted me to go over and help him get them out of the car, said there were too many for him to handle on his own.'

'What?' said Jean-Luc, confused. 'How many pizzas were there?'

'At least twenty from what I can gather,' Alfonse said with another of those wry grins. 'It's against protocol to leave the house, so of course I refused to go and help him. But that's when he started to go mental and said he was just gonna dump them all on the doorstep to rot, he didn't care.'

'So you went over to the car,' Jean-Luc surmised.

'Yeah,' Alfonse agreed sheepishly. 'I know it's against protocol,' he repeated again. 'But the guy was making such a racket, he was calling all kinds of attention to the house. I saw a light go on in one of the villas across the road. So I made the decision to duck out and help him. I double—no triple checked the area first. Surely that was better than compromising the safe-house's anonymity?'

Jean-Luc was too dumbfounded to even bother with an answer to that question. 'Why didn't Edgard wake up with all that noise?'

'I'm a heavy sleeper.' Edgard gave a tight shrug. 'What can I say? It's a problem, I know. I'm working on it.'

'That's not good enough,' Jean-Luc growled. 'Why didn't you go and wake him up?' Alfonse shrugged and continued to look sheepish.

'What if that'd been a trap? What if it'd been one of Vincent's men?' Jean-Luc was only keeping his temper under control by the slimmest of threads right now. It wouldn't take much for him to get up and walk over there and smash his hand into—Calm, he needed to stay calm. Punching the idiot in the face wouldn't help him get Charlize back.

'I only had my back turned to the door for thirty

seconds. A minute at the most. I paid the guy off and got rid of him.'

'So she slipped out the open door while you were paying for pizza?'

'That's what the cameras show,' said Edgard, joining the discussion. 'We can see her sneak out of her bedroom and through the door before Alfonse was more than half-way to the delivery guy's car.'

'Fucking idiots.' Jean-Luc couldn't control himself. He said it quietly, but he knew both men heard him.

'She must've got an extra phone from somewhere,' Edgard continued, as if he hadn't just been called a fucking idiot. 'It wasn't her phone she used. We would've known immediately if she'd dialled the pizza place from her phone.' Jean-Luc's blood ran cold. She'd only had her new phone for two days, the one he'd bought her near Sault, and he'd made damn sure they had a trace on that phone. She shouldn't have been able to do anything without them knowing. Unless she'd turned the phone off. He hadn't told her that he could track her via her phone. But being an ex-cop, she'd more than likely figured that one out by herself.

How in hell had she managed to get another phone? There was only one time she'd had the opportunity, when they'd stopped on their way into Nice the other night, so she could buy clothes. Smart girl.

If she had used her phone, an alarm would've sounded on the guards' own phones, telling them it was in use. Then they would've been able to tap into whatever conversation she was having.

'I don't know how she managed to get the guy so riled up, but she must've said something unpleasant to him, because he wasn't about to just up and leave. He wanted to stay and rant and rave at me. It took quite a hefty bribe before he eventually decided to hightail it out of there.' Alfonse raised his eyebrows in mock disgust at the guy's perseverance. Jean-Luc couldn't help it. He had to hand it to Charlize. Her plan had been terribly simple. And terribly effective. Bloody woman.

'Did one of you go out after her when you discovered she was missing. Do you know which way she went?' he asked in clipped tones, already going through scenarios in his head of how the search would pan out.

'We didn't know she was missing for about half an hour.' Edgard took up the retelling, as Alfonse again looked chagrined.

'What the fuck? Why not?'

'Alfonse came and woke me, told me what happened, to fill me in. We didn't think it was a big deal. I only decided to check the security footage as a precaution to corroborate Alfonse's story. That's when we saw her escaping, on the footage.'

'So you didn't even bother to check her room after the pizza guy left?' Jean-Luc asked, unable to keep the incredulous jeer off his face. Alfonse just shook his head.

'*Merde.*' Jean-Luc clenched his fists so hard his knuckles cracked, but he swallowed down his furious urge to yell and scream at these two imbeciles, to show them just how badly they'd fucked up with his fists. It'd do him no good, even though it would make him feel better. So much better.

Alfonse's phone beeped. He glanced at it and said, 'Pickard's coming in.' Alfonse showed them a grainy video feed on his smart phone, displaying the keypad on the side of the house, with an angry-looking Pickard punching numbers in.

This early hour of the morning didn't sit well with Pickard and he stomped in, his normally neat, squared-away clothes looking rumpled and worn, face lined with fatigue and worry.

Without even acknowledging the two guards, he turned to face Jean-Luc, who stood up to greet his boss. 'I can't believe this happened tonight of all nights. Did you get what you needed?' he asked in clipped tones.

'Yes, I got what we needed,' Jean-Luc replied. He'd almost forgotten in his mad dash up the coast from Marseille to Nice what he'd been doing before he'd been interrupted.

'Thank Christ.' Pickard sagged down onto the nearest couch, dragging a hand across his forehead, knocking his glasses askew. Jean-Luc sat down opposite him.

'And is it what we thought?'

'Yes. Vincent is using the beach that belongs to Franco to land his illegal boats. I got it all on video,' replied Jean-Luc.

'Was Vincent there?' Pickard asked, fixing him with a direct stare.

'No, but I can identify at least two of his henchmen. Both Enzo and the other one, Fabio, were there.'

'Good. Good,' replied Pickard, expelling a loud breath. Jean-Luc's knee wouldn't stop bouncing up and down, as if it had a life of its own. A physical manifestation of the impatience thrumming through him. He needed to be out, looking for Charlize, making sure she was safe. Where would she have gone? That question had rolled around in his head the entire ride back from Marseille. Surely she wouldn't be stupid enough to try and go back to her villa? Surely even she understood that would be just plain suicide. But then, where else would she go? Would she try and stay in France, or perhaps duck out through Italy—the border wasn't that far away—or go to Paris and catch a ferry over to England? The different permutations had been driving him crazy.

She had talked about going back to Australia for her friend's wedding. Would she perhaps do that now? Hoping Vincent's gang wouldn't track her across the continent. She'd be wrong. His reach was long and unforgiving.

If only he'd listened to her when she'd said she didn't want to be here. If only he'd come up with some other plan to keep her safe. Bloody stubborn woman.

Jean-Luc started pacing, unable to sit still any longer.

'Right, what's the plan? We need to get onto Charlize's trail as soon as possible, she's already got a three-hour head start on us.'

'You're not going after her,' said Pickard. Jean-Luc stopped in his tracks.

'What? What do you mean?'

'I mean, you've wasted enough man hours on this woman already.'

'No.' Jean-Luc stood in front of Pickard, not quite believing what he was hearing.

'Yes, Jean-Luc. I've made my decision. This woman has caused more than enough trouble already.' Pickard was using his totalitarian voice, glaring at Jean-Luc from over the rim of his glasses.

Jean-Luc stood directly in front of Pickard, almost toe to toe. 'What if they find her and kill her?' He was almost shouting now. 'Will you be able to live with yourself when you have her death on your conscience?'

'You've done all you can for her, Munulo. That's the end of it. I want you back in the office for debriefing with the rest of the team by oh-nine hundred today. This op is too important to sacrifice you any longer. The next twenty-four hours are going to be crucial to catching Vincent. He'll be moving those illegals soon, and we need to know where he's taking them.'

Jean-Luc stepped away from Pickard, shaking his head as if he could block out his boss' words.

Pickard dropped his voice and said, 'I'm not sure what you've got going on with this woman, but she's become a liability to the operation, Munulo. You have to let her go.' He laid a hand on Jean-Luc's shoulder, which he shook off with a grunt.

'Don't touch me, Pickard,' he ground out between gritted teeth. 'I can't believe you'd be such a cold-hearted bastard as to leave a civilian to the mercy of Vincent and his men.' It was none of Pickard's business, what'd gone on between Charlize and himself. Besides, he wanted to help her because it was the right thing to do, not because he had feelings for her. He was a professional, he could keep his private emotions and his work-related needs completely separate. She needed their help, that was all.

'I'm not a complete bastard, Jean-Luc. I'm assigning Gabriel and one of his men to look for her. You know, the sniper on secondment who was supposed to be your partner. The one you'd never agree to meet.' His sneer made Jean-Luc ball his hands into fists. He'd never been so close to hitting his supervisor in all the years he'd worked for him. 'Charlize has met your family, Jean-Luc, she's a liability. To you and to this team. I will find her, don't worry about that.' And there was the crux of the matter in Pickard's mind. The fact she was a liability to the op. Not because it was the right thing to do, to rescue a civilian from the clutches of Vincent's men. 'Whatever's going on in that head of yours, Jean-Luc, you need to sort it out. Soon. I'll see you in a few hours in the office.' Pickard fixed him with his steely blue gaze, but Jean-Luc refused to be cowed and stared truculently back.

Without another word, Pickard strode out of the room, but turned just before the doorway. 'You other two can report to my office at oh-eight hundred today.'

Jean-Luc caught both guards' grimace. Good, he thought nastily. It was the least they deserved for failing in their jobs. He didn't even care that Pickard was probably going to sack both men. It was their stupidity that'd lost him Charlize. Possibly forever.

He waited for Pickard to leave, pacing the floor the whole time, not even bothering to look at Edgard or Alfonse. As soon as the driveway was clear, he slammed his way out into the garage and kicked his bike to life. What was he going to do now? Vincent and his terrorist smuggling had to be stopped. Lives depended on it. Lots and lots of lives. There'd been increased chatter hinting at terrorist cells planning bombings in Paris. All they were waiting for were more recruits to join them. Perhaps the very recruits who'd just landed on that illegal boat tonight.

But he couldn't abandon Charlize to her fate. He just couldn't.

CHAPTER NINETEEN

There was no air. It felt like there was no air in here. Charlize sucked in huge lungfuls through her mouth and nose, but none made it into her depleted body. She gasped and gasped like a stranded fish. Lights danced before her eyes and she was light-headed and dizzy. She was going to pass out if she didn't stop hyperventilating.

Calm down. She couldn't afford to pass out. Who knew what might happen to her if she did. She needed to be awake and lucid when they finally hauled her out of this car trunk.

She should've listened to Jean-Luc. Why hadn't she listened to Jean-Luc? Because she was a stubborn, pig-headed, prideful woman who thought she knew better, that's why. Her chest hurt with the effort of trying to drag air into her lungs. She had to calm down. In through the nose, out through the mouth, wasn't that how it went? At least she remembered telling hysterical victims back when she was a cop that was how to do it. She took controlled streams of air into her nose, then expelled it slowly out through her mouth. In and out. In and out. Gradually it started to work. Her pulse rate went down bit by bit, and the roaring in her ears began to subside. There was enough air in here to keep her alive until they got to their destination. There was. She didn't really know if it was just some stupid myth that car trunks were airtight or not. And she didn't really want to find out.

The space was dark and cramped. Every now and then she saw a red glow from the brake lights, and knew to brace herself, as it meant they were going around a corner. But apart from the times the red glow lit up the space, it was pitch black. Her hands were tied behind her back and her feet roped together. Trussed up like a Christmas turkey, her grandmother would've said.

Vincent's men had caught her; snatched her off the street and shoved her into this trunk like she was nothing more than a piece of garbage littering the gutter. They'd been rough, and she'd have bruises on her knees and more on the side of her head where they'd shoved her ungently into the car. But they hadn't beaten her, which they so easily could've done. They were probably keeping that little pleasure for later.

Had she really been that transparent? That much of a foolish, predictable woman? She'd thought her plan of going to the Australian embassy had been foolproof. They would issue her with an emergency passport and she could be on a plane back to Australia, hopefully within twenty-four hours. If she'd told the people in the embassy she was in danger, they might've even offered her shelter while she waited for the passport to be processed. All she wanted to do was get home. That'd become her one and only objective now.

Wanting to preserve the little cash she had left and not

wanting to use her credit card—it'd act like a red flag for anyone who was tracking her—she'd decided to go on foot through the back streets of Nice. Without the luxury of being able to use the internet—one of the many disadvantages of being held captive in the safe house—it'd taken her a while to find out exactly where the embassy was. About ten minutes after she'd escaped the safe house, she'd taken a risk and stopped to ask a friendly receptionist at a little boutique hotel to look the address up for her on the internet. The young woman had been more than obliging, probably bored with no customers at this late hour of the evening.

Luckily she'd been closer than she could've hoped, the safe house was only three suburbs away from the embassy. It'd taken her another twenty minutes to find her way onto the right street. But that's where things had started to go wrong. Of course she'd been vigilant, aware she might be followed, on the lookout for anything out of the ordinary, sticking to the darkest shadows and fading back away from the light every time a car went past. At this time of night, just past midnight, these suburban streets were mainly deserted, so it was easy to see if anyone was trailing her. But really, the chances of the gang finding her out here were completely negligible. That thought had been her downfall.

She turned the corner onto the street where the embassy sat and started to congratulate herself. The large, formidable iron gates loomed like ghoulish monsters beneath the street lamps just outside the imposing embassy building. She was nearly there. Now all she needed was to get to the twenty-four-hour emergency intercom and convince someone to let her in. Her steps quickened.

A man stepped out of an alcove doorway, hidden by black-as-pitch shadows, and blocked her way. She drew in a sharp breath and turned on her heel to run. A car screeched around the corner and two men piled out of the car even before it came to a complete stop at the curb ten meters or so away from her. She changed the angle of her run and dashed across the road, running as fast as she could. But her bad leg had let her down. There was no way she was faster than three burly men. They caught her just as she reached the other side of the road. She screamed then, loud and guttural, and one of them had sworn loudly and clamped his hand over her mouth. Struggling like a demon, she defied them as long as she could. But one of them picked up her legs even though she kicked and kicked and the other grabbed her shoulders, keeping his hand firmly over her mouth, and she was caught, like a fly in a spider's web. They'd second-guessed her. Had been waiting for her to do exactly what she'd done. Fuck, she was such an idiot.

Tears cascaded out of the sides of her eyes, leaving hot, wet trails before they eventually dripped off her cheek. For minutes on end, she let them fall, allowed herself to dwell in self-loathing and misery. How could she have been such an idiot? All her years of police training, gone to shit. She should've fought them harder. She should've crept down that street, not waltzed down it like she hadn't a care in the world. More tears burned her eyes, and she was almost howling in despair. But eventually the tears stopped, and she drew in large, hiccupping breaths to steady herself. Crying wasn't going to get her out of this situation.

Think, Charlize, think. She needed to turn her phone on.

The one Jean-Luc had given her. It was tucked safely inside her bra, but how was she going to reach it? Jean-Luc would be tracking her phone. If she could turn it on, then he'd know where she was. And come and get her. Though, God only knew she didn't deserve to be rescued. Not after betraying him like that. Not after being such a selfish bitch, putting them all in danger. Thank God she'd been carrying that other burn phone she'd used to call the pizza guy as well. The thugs had found that one immediately and smashed it with glee on the pavement before shoving her into the trunk. But they hadn't suspected she had a second phone on her, hidden in her bra.

This was going to be the gymnastic feat of the year if she could pull this off. How the hell was she going to get the phone out of her bra and then near her hands so she could turn it on? In between the time when the car turned the corners—when she had to brace her feet and hands against the inside of the trunk to stop from being thrown around —she started thrusting her chest out, wriggling around on her side, squishing her boobs together as if she were some kind of crazed night club dancer.

It took a while, but eventually, the phone slipped out of her cleavage and onto the floor of the trunk. It then took another few minutes of cursing and swearing, and wriggling like a demented fool, until she finally worked the phone underneath her body so it came out behind her back, where her hands could grab hold of it. She nearly lost the phone once, when the car took a sharp corner and the phone slid across the floor until it hit the rear wall of the trunk. But thankfully, it rebounded again, almost straight back into her hands. It took another age for the numb fingers of her bound hands to hold the button down long enough so she heard the soft *ping* of the phone turning on. Hallelujah.

She'd turned it on, now it'd be transmitting her location. Hopefully. Could she call Jean-Luc? It turned out to be an impossible task. With her hands behind her back, there was no way she could see which buttons she was pushing. But she tried anyway, hoping that by some random chance she managed to get her phone to make a call. Someone, anyone, would do, if only she could get through.

The car turned another corner and slowed down, then went over a couple of bumps and came to a complete stop. Shit. Shit. There was no way she was going to get the phone back into her bra now. So she did the next best thing and shoved it down the back of her pants, into her underwear. That was going to be uncomfortable. But if she could just keep the phone on her for a little while longer, it might give Jean-Luc the time he needed to find her. At least she had jeans on, so the phone should stay hidden in her crotch.

That's when it hit her, the all-encompassing feeling of people in need. Not just one person, many, many people. She nearly retched at the strength of emotions pouring into her. The feeling was so powerful even somebody without her gift could surely perceive these emanations. The strongest emotion was desperation, but it was threaded through with equal parts of frustration and fear...and also hunger. Why would lots of people be here, hungry and desperate? The emotions bombarded her. She couldn't shut them off. Her brain was so fogged with the overwhelming influence of the flowing auras, she was practically senseless to everything else around her. This was the first time she hadn't been able to control her clairsentience. It scared her and she struggled uselessly against her bonds, trying to get free.

'Let me go. Let me go,' she yelled. 'I need to get away from here. I can't shut them out. I can't shut them out.' The last words were uttered in a near whimper.

Through the haze of her near-crazed mind, she made out the trunk being opened and then rough hands pulled her out. The man who manhandled her out of the car stood her on her feet. But the all-pervading emotions confusing her made it hard to know which way was up and which way was down, and the ground felt like it buckled beneath her feet. Combined with the rope around her ankles, she found herself toppling over, unable to stand. She let out a yell of surprise before she hit the ground, hard, only just managing to save her head from crashing into the pavement, but smashing her elbow and shoulder in the process. A grunt of pain and shock left her lips. But at least the pain cleared away some of the worst of the frenzied emotions in her mind and allowed her to think again.

'For fuck's sake, watch what you're doing!' one of the thugs yelled from the other side of the car. The man who'd dropped her just let out a raucous laugh, as if he found watching her topple over like a tenpin in a bowling alley was the funniest thing he'd seen all day.

'Why? He only said he wanted her alive. Didn't say nothing about what shape she needed to be in.' The laughing man could barely contain his mirth. She ignored him and did a quick body scan instead. No bones were broken, but she'd have some wonderful grazes and bruises to show off later. Then the man picked her up off the ground as if she were no more than a rag doll and slung her over his shoulder.

Now that she was off the ground, her clairsentience threatened to go haywire again. *Concentrate.* She needed to concentrate. Not let whatever, or whoever, was producing all these mind-blowing impressions take over again. Lifting her head, she chanced a quick glance around. There was one lonely spotlight doing its best to illuminate a large open space—possibly a car park—and a large building loomed out of the darkness next to them. A warehouse, perhaps? She could hear the muted hum of cars on a freeway, but that didn't really help. She was pretty sure they were nowhere near the coast, because she couldn't smell that distinctive tang of sea air. Which meant they were inland of Nice. This building had a dilapidated, unused look to it. And they'd been driving for over twenty minutes, which took them well outside the city limits of Nice. She shook her heard. The emanations of people in need grew stronger with each step they took toward the building and began to mask any more logical thought process she might've had. She had no idea how she was going to escape from here.

'Nothing for you to see,' came a voice out of the dark, and she felt a hard blow to the head, which left her reeling. After that she kept her head hanging down the man's back, but managed to take surreptitious sideways peeks when she could. Information, no matter how small or insignificant, could mean the difference between incarceration and escape. Life and death.

They went through a large door cut into the side of the building and one of the thugs flicked on a light switch, which allowed a sickly yellow light to filter down from above. Definitely a warehouse.

The desperation oozing out of the walls threatened to turn her mind to mush again. Charlize tried an old remedy a psych had given her a long time ago to dampen the tugging emotions, stop them from engulfing her, so she could concentrate on her surroundings a little better. She took a deep breath and acknowledged the feelings, let them flow through her like a fiery wave rolling over her, burning her synapses with the intensity. Slowly she encased the runaway emotions within four walls, herded them into a box she'd created in her mind. Then she pulled the walls closer and closer together, until she had a virtual box inside her head, containing all those straining emotions. The thoughts were still there, clamouring to be let out, but they were manageable, allowing the other junctions of her brain to start processing data, so she could once again focus on what was going on around her.

From the corner of her eye, Charlize made out large bits of machinery and odd pieces of boats scattered everywhere. There was even a whole hull poking out from underneath a tarp. But it was mainly bits and pieces, an empty hull here, a windscreen there, a mast from a sailing ship, even a couple of outboard engines. A scrap metal yard for boats, perhaps?

The man carrying her started to climb some stairs, and he grunted with every step beneath her weight. A large functional metal staircase wended its way up toward a second level in the warehouse. She let her head bob against his back, feigning complete surrender, as if she'd gone limp and pliable. She was anything but, however, eyes and ears open to every stimulus she could pick up, no matter how small.

At the top of the stairs, he continued down a long

gangway made from metal mesh; Charlize could see through the mesh to the floor a long way below. All three men trooped across this gangway single file. Then they all stopped, and she heard the thug in front fumble with what sounded like a large handful of keys. A loud creak announced a metal door opening in front of them. Once the door was open, the feelings became so strong again she could almost levitate along the invisible lines of sensation that were streaming into her. A gaggle of noise and human voices assaulted her ears, almost drowning out the mental commotion going on in her head.

'Shut up,' roared the man in front. The sound echoed around the room, and all the yelling stopped abruptly. Charlize was dumped unceremoniously on her backside onto the cold metal floor, her breath leaving her with a whooshing sound. She heard a loud crack as she hit the ground and pain shot up her tailbone. Shit, the phone. She'd landed on the phone.

'Don't any of you little bastards move, or I'll shoot ya. I'll shoot ya's all.' That must've been the man with the keys speaking. Charlize shook her head, trying to clear it from the pain of landing on the hard ground. Who was he talking to? It'd sounded like there were people in there; lots of people.

'Food. Please, we need food,' came a voice from the darkness behind her. She wanted to swivel her head and take a look, but daren't remove her gaze from the three thugs in front of her, one of whom had his gun out and pointed at something behind her.

Charlize sucked in a sharp breath. If she'd been able to cover her ears, she would have. This was definitely the source of all the human suffering. The walls of the box she'd created in her head threatened to collapse under the surging wave of raw emotions. She squeezed her eyes shut tight and pushed against those walls with all her might. And they held. She wasn't going to go completely crazy just yet. She opened her eyes again.

'Shut up, I told ya's,' the same man repeated. Then the three thugs started to back out of the door they'd just come through. Once he reached the safety of the doorway, the man swung his gun to point directly at her and for a second she held her breath, her heart skittered erratically in her chest.

'Mr Dellucci wants to speak to you. So make sure you don't go nowhere, will ya.' His loud laugh followed him out the door as he shut it behind him with a clang of finality.

It was the smell that hit her first. Dirty, unwashed humans, all crammed into an impossibly small space. There were whispers behind her that grew in intensity. But she almost didn't want to turn around, afraid of what she'd see.

The room was dark, lit only by the weak light from some kind of hurricane lamp, held aloft by a man coming toward her. The man was extremely tall and black as night. Charlize stared into the darkness beyond the lamp, catching glimpses of other faces that peered at her, eyes shining with the reflection of the light. All had coal-black skin. Lots and lots of faces. Perhaps hundreds of them. Men, women and children. She felt sick to her stomach. Nauseous from the auras of destitution and anguish pouring out of this tide of humanity. This is why her gift had gone haywire when they first arrived. So many people, all in desperate need.

Then it hit her. Refugees. These people must be the illegal immigrants Jean-Luc had been talking about. She'd found them. How ironic. She almost let loose a laugh. If only Jean-Luc knew where she was right now.

A memory of a small, scared face thumped into her conscious. All these people staring at her reminded her of the little boy she'd found back in Uzes. He'd been just as scared and desperate, but he'd also been terribly, terribly alone. Perhaps someone here knew him, or at the very least knew something about his family. She would ask, just as soon as she figured out where she was and what was going on.

She tore her stunned gaze away from the huddled group of people to take in her surroundings. They were in a large room, with a high ceiling that disappeared off into the gloom, but no windows as far as she could see. The walls looked to be made of folded steel, much like that of shipping containers, and most probably impenetrable. A prison hidden within an innocuous warehouse. The room was stuffy, humid and warm, even at this time of the night. She hated to think how hot this place might get during the middle of a summer's day in Nice.

Now she was imprisoned in here, with all these people her clairsentience started to fade, almost as if her subconscious knew there was no way she could help these people right now, unless she could help herself first.

'Could you please untie me,' she said to the approaching man. He nodded his head and bent down to free her arms. Shaking them out, she tried to get the blood flowing again.

'Thank you.' The man started to work on the ropes that bound her feet.

'You're welcome,' he said in heavily accented English. He must've been the man who'd pleaded for food with the thugs when they'd first entered.

While he finished with her ankles, she reached around into her pants and fished around for the phone. Pulling it out, she studied it in the weak lamplight. Smashed to smithereens. It was totally useless. The screen was black, glass cracked, and no amount of pushing or prodding brought it back to life. It was probably a small mercy the phone had been facing outwards, away from her backside, otherwise she might be pulling tiny pieces of broken glass out of her skin for the next few days. She wanted to hurl it against the wall in frustration. Had it been turned on long enough for Jean-Luc to locate her position?

Hang on. Hadn't Jean-Luc mentioned something about terrorists being smuggled in with the refugees? Wasn't that the whole point of his operation? Jesus Christ, was she now shut up in a makeshift prison with a bunch of crazy fanatics?

CHAPTER TWENTY

The motorbike idled beneath him as Jean-Luc sat at the crossroad, wondering which way to turn next. He'd been riding up and down random streets for the past hour hoping to find Charlize walking down one of them. This was no way to conduct a search, Jean-Luc knew that, but he couldn't gather his thoughts, couldn't seem to settle on a logical plan of attack. All he knew was she was missing, and he had to get her back. Pickard could go and get stuffed. He certainly wasn't going to be reporting to HQ at oh-nine hundred this morning. He checked his watch. It was only a few hours away.

He pulled his helmet off and ran a hand over his short hair. *Merde,* what was he going to do? Pickard had made it crystal clear Charlize was no longer his concern.

A part of him was screaming, *what the hell has gotten into you, Jean-Luc,* and he knew he was acting on a whim. Not at all like the hardened, totally in control, lethal agent he was so used to being. It was as if Charlize had somehow removed a piece of his soul when he wasn't looking and then walked out of the safe house with it. He'd never feel completely whole again until he had that piece of him back. Until he had Charlize back. Which was crazy. He'd known the woman less than two weeks, starting the day he'd jumped into her garden.

Granted, there was an overwhelming physical attraction between them, but he should be able to handle that, he was a mature adult. And yes, they had slept together, and yes, he couldn't get her body out of his head now; the way she'd responded so greedily to him.

Sex had been different with her. He was a man, he loved sex as much as the next man, and he certainly enjoyed it as often as possible. Galina had been his latest partner, and they had a most agreeable and satisfying sexual relationship. She was a beautiful woman with a stunning body. But she was no longer an option for him. There was no doubt in his mind he'd never go back to Galina now. Charlize had changed that. Nothing was the same.

Merde. He couldn't possibly be... No. He wasn't some soft-in-the-head pushover who'd fall for the first woman who came along. He was a man in charge of his own destiny. And that destiny definitely didn't involve falling in love with an Australian woman. A woman with her own demons, her own past to battle.

He'd created a safe life for himself, with no ties, no attachments, no commitments. It was the only way to live. He'd learned the hard way if you allowed love in, it ended up tearing your heart to shreds. He would never, ever get over the loss of his son. The loss of Fleur he might get over one day. Had she really been the love of his life? He wasn't so sure now. But he'd never get over the loss of his son. Leo would haunt him till the day he died. Which meant he was damaged goods, no use to anyone. It was easier to keep his emotions under tight rein, his heart locked behind a metaphorical concrete wall.

So why was he even contemplating letting Charlize into his life? It was a bad, bad idea.

His phone vibrated in his jacket pocket, shaking him out of his train of thought. Taking it out, he checked caller ID. He nearly put the phone back in his pocket unanswered, but something made him push the talk button.

'What do you want, Edgard?' He sounded rude and gruff, but was beyond caring right now.

'Just thought you might like to know we got a ping from Charlize's phone about ten minutes ago,' came Edgard's controlled voice down the phone.

'What? Did you have enough time to pinpoint its location?' A sudden surge of adrenaline hit him and he couldn't keep the anticipation out of his voice.

'She must've just turned it on, because we were getting nothing for hours and then, all of a sudden, both mine and Alfonse's screens lit up like Christmas trees. But the signal's stopped now,' continued Edgard, calm and matter of fact. Jean-Luc wanted to reach down the phone and grab the man by the throat and shake the information out of him.

'So? Did you get a location?' Jean-Luc repeated clearly, enunciating every word.

'Yes, we did. It's coming from an industrial area, just across the river from the stadium.' What in hell was she doing way over there? It was possible she could've walked there in the four hours she'd been missing, but it was a long walk, especially with her damaged leg. Why in hell would she want to go there? What could possibly be of any use to her in an industrial area? It didn't make much sense. And why had she suddenly turned her phone on, when she'd been smart enough to keep it off until now, if she didn't want to be found?

Unless she wanted to be found.

Unless she was sending him a signal.

Unless she was in trouble.

'Send me the address,' said Jean-Luc hurriedly.

'Already done,' replied Edgard, just as Jean-Luc's phone vibrated with an incoming message.

Jean-Luc hesitated. 'Thank you.' The man had in no way redeemed himself for letting her get away in the first place, but this info might be crucial to getting her back.

'You're welcome. Just so you know, I'll also pass this information on to Pickard. For the two men he's actually assigned to find her. Might be nice if you didn't mention to Pickard we had this chat,' said Edgard and rang off. Jean-Luc smiled grimly to himself. He could do that much of a favour for the man. Pickard was already going to come down on them like a ton of bricks for losing Charlize, he didn't need any more ammunition. And the guy had just done him a huge favour. He didn't need to let Jean-Luc know anything; was, in fact, going against Pickard's orders. A grim smile made its way on to his lips. Perhaps Edgard wasn't so bad after all.

Programming the address into the map app on his phone, he studied the location, using the satellite version to make out buildings, car parks, open spaces, and other landmarks. She might not even be there anymore, but he had to start somewhere. He'd never been to the area before, so he'd need to take it slow and careful.

He slammed the helmet back down over his head and spun the bike around in the empty crossroad and roared off through the night.

* * *

People crowded around her, blocking out the meagre light and making her slightly claustrophobic. Hands reached out and touched her, plucked at her clothing and stroked her hair as if they didn't believe she was real. She struggled to stand up, not wanting to be sitting on the floor amongst all these people. Thank God her clairsentience had settled down to a dull roar in her head now. At least she could think straight.

'Let me help you,' said the man with the lantern in his strong accent. She took hold of his overly large hand and he pulled her up to standing. 'Let her be,' he said, and started shooing some of the children away, opening up a small clearing around her. Many pairs of eyes still stared at her curiously, but at least they stopped touching her.

The tall man, the one Charlize was starting to think of as their leader, stood calmly next to her, like a rock in an ocean of human beings, still shooing back the odd child who couldn't help themselves. His dark eyes rested on her. Curious and assessing. Obviously wondering what she was doing here. A white woman thrown in amongst this multitude of blacks.

She met his gaze and gave a shrug. 'I have no idea what I'm doing here either,' she said. And that was the truth. She really didn't have any idea why they'd dump her here in the middle of their illegal haul of human cargo. But the implications weren't good. If they were willing to let her know all these people were here, then they didn't plan on letting her talk to anyone about where she'd been or what she'd seen. Dead, in other words. She would end up dead. A heavy weight settled deep in her stomach, making her feel slightly ill. Nope, she wasn't about to give in so soon. She still had plenty of skills and a whole lot of hope to use up yet. And Jean-Luc might be out there somewhere, too.

'You wouldn't happen to have any food?' he asked, his words halting, even though his eyes told her he already knew the answer.

'I'm so sorry.' She shook her head.

'They haven't given us any food for two days.' He lifted his chin toward the door to indicate the thugs who'd just disappeared. 'When we heard the door opening, we thought....' He trailed off, but she knew what he meant. 'At least we have plenty of water. They gave us a whole pallet-load of bottles.' That was a good sign. It meant they didn't want all these people dying. Not just yet, anyway.

'Why are you here?' The question had to be asked, even though she thought she probably knew the answer. Her sweeping gaze took in all the people, some huddled into the corners sleeping, but most still massed around her.

'They said they will release us in small groups, so we don't raise too much suspicion,' he replied with a vague wave of his hand. 'And they have done that very slowly. Mohammed and Amani were the first to be let out. Then Omari and his family. And Sumin and her two children went just yesterday.' He didn't need to say anything about the fact they were illegally here, or that they'd arrived by boat, there was a tacit understanding in his blunt gaze. 'But they haven't released anybody else in over a week now.'

Could the little boy in Uzes have been one of the children they'd let go? She had to ask, it might be her only chance.

'Can you tell me the age of the children from the two

families?' He gave her a curious look.

But he answered her in his calm voice. 'Omari's children were only babies, one was six months old, and the other was only two.'

Jesus, so young. They'd made that terrible journey with two young, vulnerable kids. Her skin began to crawl at the mere idea of it, and surprising tears pricked the corner of her eyes. But neither was her boy from Uzes, he was definitely older than that. The man didn't seem to notice her discomfort.

'Sumin's two children were both teenagers. Perhaps thirteen and fifteen, maybe?' His voice took on an uncertain tone, but it was enough for her to know that these couldn't be her boy either; they were much too old. And what about the two men who were released first? Were they some of the terrorists Jean-Luc was looking for?

'Thank you. Do you know where we are?' she asked, suddenly changing the topic. There were more urgent things to think about right now. The boy from Uzes and some phantom terrorists could wait.

He shook his head. 'No, they brought us in at night, straight from the beach, in covered trucks. I don't even know what town we're in.'

'You're near the town of Nice,' she told him, her shoulders drooping. 'I was hoping you might know where in Nice we were.' Damn, that was no help. She licked her lips and suddenly realised how dry her throat had become.

'Would you be able to spare one of those bottles of water?'

'Of course.' He dipped his head as if he were a most remiss host and went off to the back corner to retrieve one for her. When he returned, she thanked him and took great gulps of the liquid. She hadn't realised how thirsty a person got when they'd just been abducted. As she drank, she mentally catalogued how she was faring. Her body was covered in minor—and some major—bruises and abrasions, including the older ones from the day of the crash. And her leg was aching like a bitch from all the walking she'd done earlier. But for the most part, she was still in pretty good nick. Definitely up for an attempted escape mission. Because she wasn't going to just sit here and wait for those thugs to come back. She had to do something.

She eyed the man sitting by her side, calmly waiting for her to finish drinking. Then she remembered her manners.

'My name's Charlize,' she said, extending her hand. 'Nice to meet you.'

'I am Fumbe.' He engulfed her small hand in his.

'I'm assuming you've tried to get out of here?' She cast her gaze around the thick steel walls, her heart sinking at how impenetrable they looked.

'Of course,' he replied with a smile that showed off his white teeth in the darkness. 'We have all tried.' He waved a hand around at the crowd of people. How in hell did she think that she was going to find a way out of here when none of these people could? But it had to be tried. Her life depended on it. She was left in little doubt, if and when those thugs eventually came back, it'd be to take her away, and she wouldn't be coming back; not alive anyway.

'Would you mind if I had a look?' Perhaps her trained police eye might possibly see something they'd all missed? It was a slim hope, but something she had to cling to for her own sanity.

'Sure.' He got up and offered her a hand and she was struck by his soft-spoken courteousness. After all, he'd probably been through the trials and tribulations, the danger and uncertainty, here he was, able to show kindness and help a stranger. It brought a strange kind of lump to her throat.

'Thank you,' she said humbly.

The idea that there might still be more undercover terrorists hidden in here haunted the corners of her mind, but there was absolutely nothing she could do about that right now, so she put the thought out of her head.

Fumbe took her for a slow stroll around the outer perimeter of the room, holding the lantern aloft so she could see up into corners and peer for any gaps in the walls. They had to step over many sleeping bodies, and she kept her whispered questions and comments to a minimum, trying not to wake anyone.

Once they'd done a full circuit, she was certain the walls were impenetrable.

'What about the ceiling?'

'There is nothing,' he replied. 'No manholes, no trapdoors, no gaps or cracks anywhere. It is made of very thick steel, from what we can guess. They have chosen this place well.' Her spirits sagged. None of this sounded good.

'The floor?'

'Also steel,' he replied. 'There is only one way in or out of this prison, and that door over there is it,' he said, pointing to the door she'd come in.

'What about ventilation? Are there any grates or shafts?' There had to be some kind of ventilation in here, otherwise they'd all die of asphyxiation, with this many people all breathing the precious oxygen.

'Yes, there are around ten ventilation grates, up high, where the ceiling meets the wall. But they are long thin slits, too small for even a child to crawl into.' One more idea bit the dust and she was fast running out of any more.

'What about waste?' she asked. Surely they had to do something with all the waste these people produced. It'd be extremely unhygienic, not to mention disgustingly smelly, if it wasn't disposed of.

'There are two toilet cisterns over here.' He pointed to the corner they'd skirted around because it had tall wooden pallets stacked around it. 'We tried to make it a little private with the left-over pallets from the water and blankets they delivered to us.'

Okay, now she was officially out of ideas. What next? She didn't want to tell him about Jean-Luc. The possibility was slim to none that he'd come, and she didn't want to get all these people's hopes up for no reason.

'Do you mind if we sit down?' she asked, indicating a clear spot in the middle of the room. He inclined his head in agreement. Sharp spikes of pain shot up her leg now with every step. She was exhausted and deflated. Curling up into a little ball on the floor and going to sleep seemed awfully tempting right now. Charlize sat down with a sigh on the cool metal floor and eased her aching leg out in front of her.

'How long have you been locked up in here?'

'I've been here for nearly a month,' he replied. 'But new people arrive now and then. We had a new bunch come in two days ago. They brought us food then. We heard rumours they might be bringing in more people soon, but so far no one else has come.' The large man settled himself more comfortably on the ground, crossing his long legs in front of him.

'What happens when new people arrive?' she asked, a sudden flare of hope sparking in her chest.

'They file them in through the door, one by one, throw in some food and close the door again,' he replied. Perhaps there was some way they could come up with a plan. Rush the guards when they least expected it, while they were concentrating on the newcomers. How many of them had guns? Was it all three of them, or just the leader?

'Is it usually just the three guards, or are there different men every time?' She tapped her chin with her index finger, formulating different schemes even as she spoke.

'Usually the same three,' he said.

'And do you know if they all have guns?' This was a tricky question, because even if he said the other two didn't have a gun, how could he be perfectly sure?

'Only the head guy ever shows us his gun,' Fumbe answered. 'But I'm pretty sure I saw one of them with a holster under his jacket. I would say they all have guns.' Charlize's throat constricted at his words. He was right, of course. Escape sounded more and more impossible. She tried not to let her wretchedness show on her face. She was tired and hungry and not thinking straight. There had to be a way out of here, there just had to be. But right now, all she wanted to do was lie down and let the tears take over again. But she'd already cried enough tears in the trunk of the car. She slammed a fist into her other hand. Why was she behaving like some lily-livered, weak little girl? She'd been strong and determined and practical once. She could do it again. *It's not hopeless. It's not.* If she kept repeating those words over and over, maybe she'd start believing them. She would get out of here.

Thinking back to her trip up here on the broad shoulder of one of her captors, she tried to catalogue the rest of the warehouse in her head. The other thing they had against them was the fact the door could only be reached by crossing the gangway. It turned the place into a bottleneck. There was no way they could all scatter and hope some of them might escape in the ensuing panic. Every single one of them had to cross that walkway, making them sitting ducks for anyone below.

Hang on, how had her plans for escape just gone from getting herself out of here alive, to rescuing all these people as well? She couldn't possibly help free everyone here. But then she couldn't possibly leave them all here to their fate, either. A large sigh left her lips. She wasn't a cop anymore. These people weren't her responsibility. But just because she was no longer employed by the West Australian Police Force, didn't mean that strong protective streak wasn't still a guiding force in her life. Now she was encased in here, with these people, her gift had stopped turning her inside out. It'd done what it was supposed to do; lead her to people in need. Now her subconscious considered its job done and was waiting for her conscious self to do its part; rescue these people.

And what if some of these people she wanted to rescue were actually the terrorists Jean-Luc was trying so hard to stop? How was she supposed to know? Most probably, if there had been terrorists smuggled in, they'd be long gone by now. Like those two men Fumbe mentioned had been released first. Would Fumbe know? And if he did, would he tell her? Probably not. Shit, shit, shit.

FUL MEDAMES SUDANESE FAVA BEANS

INGREDIENTS
2 Cans fava beans
1 Large red onion, diced
2 Large ripe tomatoes, diced
2tsp Cumin
2 tsp Coriander
Salt and pepper
4 Boiled eggs, quartered
Feta cheese, crumbled
Sesame oil

DIRECTIONS
Pour beans and the liquid from the cans into a saucepan.
Smash beans lightly to crush them. Add the onion, tomato, cumin, coriander, salt and pepper and bring to the boil.
Cook for 10 to 15 minutes. Spoon into shallow serving bowls and drizzle with sesame oil, top with crumbled feta cheese and boiled eggs.

This is normally a protein rich meal served for breakfast with bread.

CHAPTER TWENTY-ONE

Jean-Luc checked his phone again. This was definitely the place he'd pinpointed on the map. But it was just a run-down, deserted warehouse as far as he could see.

He'd have to get closer to check it out. Leaving the motorbike parked a block away, he went on foot, creeping up the street, gliding through the ghostly shadows cast by the large buildings inhabiting the industrial area. At least his eyes had time to adjust to the darkness. With only the occasional street lamp positioned at intersections, the place was eerily murky, uninviting, and quiet.

What the hell would Charlize be doing here? He still had no firm idea. But unease was spreading thick and hot up his spine the closer he got.

The area was completely deserted. Jean-Luc wasn't surprised, it was four o'clock in the morning. The witching hour. When all sane people were fast asleep in their beds. Even Vincent's thugs. Well, at least that's what he hoped. But something told him otherwise. This place smelled of deceit. Like it had Vincent's taint all over it.

The road was wide and open in front of him, shopfronts

and warehouses made of brick and steel hunkered down on each side, like waiting behemoths. The place he was looking for was just up on the right, set back a little from the road and not lit by any security lights. Left in the dark on purpose. There was no signage, nothing to indicate what kind of industry was carried out here.

Jean-Luc did a slow reconnaissance, making his way around the front of the building—noting there was no entrance, only some high up windows—then around the side and finally into a large, empty carpark at the back.

At last, he found a door into the warehouse. The only entrance, by the looks of it. Jean-Luc wasn't happy about that scenario, he never liked to feel confined, he liked to know there was at least one other way out at any given moment.

Was Charlize in there? And if she was, why was she in there? The unease that'd been agitating at the back of his brain gained momentum. He'd learned to listen to his instincts. They'd been right more than once; saved his life more than once. This was crazy, him going in alone, with no backup. He hadn't let Pickard know where he was going. His boss would've put a stop to it if he'd found out. Which didn't leave Jean-Luc with many options. Gabriel, or whatever the hell his name was and his sidekick, might turn up at any moment. Or they might not appear for hours yet. What to do?

There was nothing else for it. He'd go in alone. If he found something that warranted backup, then he'd call Pickard. He reached for the door handle, beads of sweat breaking out on his brow. The comforting weight of his Sig Sauer sat heavy at the back of his jeans, and that thought alone calmed him. The knowledge he had a smaller Glock

26 hidden under his jeans in a leg holster also helped. Two guns were always better than one. For some reason, though, he was still jittery and unsure, which was abnormal for him. The only thing that could cause this level of uncertainty was the fact it was Charlize in there. He couldn't afford to get this wrong, or he might lose her. And he wouldn't be able to live with himself if that happened.

With his left hand, he tried the door. Locked. Of course. A simple thing like a locked door never stopped him before. It was an old door, but it had a brand-new lock system. The warning buzz grew louder in his head. Not too many locks were a match for him, and he soon had it open. Easing the door ajar, he waited. It didn't take his dark-adjusted eyes long to see the gloomy depths were devoid of any human forms. Hulking shadows and dark silhouettes loomed in the darkness, but nothing moved in there. It was all just lots of dusty piles of ancient machinery. A plain old warehouse, exactly what it'd looked from the outside.

Jean-Luc slipped through the crack in the door and let it close quietly behind him. Again, he let his eyes adjust to the dim light inside the building while he stood next to the wall for a minute to get his bearings. It was full of some kind of boating paraphernalia if he wasn't mistaken, but nothing to suggest any reason why Charlize would've come here.

A set of stairs in the far corner ran up to a second level. With no other lead, he headed toward them, careful not to make any noise as his shoes hit the metal rungs of the stairs. At the top, he stopped again. He stood on a small landing joined by a thin metal gangway. There was nothing else up here, just the gangway, which hugged the wall and led toward the other side of the warehouse. What was over there at the end of the gangway? He couldn't see that far in the gloom. There was nothing else for it, he either went over the gangway or went back down and gave this all up as a bad joke. His instincts screamed at him not to go across. If he were caught on this metal platform suspended in the air, he'd be a sitting duck.

With a deep breath, he stepped gingerly out onto the walkway. It was solid beneath his feet and didn't creak or groan under his weight. Quiet as a cat, he stalked across the metal path, until at last he could see a door etched into the wall at the far end.

A single door set into this huge wall that stretched the entire length of the left side of the warehouse. The warning bells were clanging loudly now inside his head. Was this an elaborate way to hinder access to this door, or was this just some really bad engineering done by a lazy builder three decades ago? This door had a brand-new handle and lock installed into it as well, and a large shiny bolt hefted into place at the top and bottom. All meant to be locked from the outside. To keep whatever—or whoever—imprisoned in the room beyond.

He took the Sig out of his jeans and kept it lowered as he leaned in to place an ear against the door. Nothing. He could hear nothing. Then there was a faint cough. A human sound. And the weak sound of a child crying. It sent chills racing down his spine. People. There were people in there. And at least one child. Was Charlize behind this door too?

It was going to be much harder to break open than the one downstairs. The easiest way would be just to shoot out the lock, but that wasn't an option if there were people on the other side. Or if he wanted to keep his presence unannounced.

He tucked the gun back into his jeans, took hold of the top bolt and slid it as slowly and silently as possible back across the door until it was free. Then he did the same for the bottom bolt. He pulled the lock pick set out of his pocket and knelt down in front of the door to get to work. The hairs on the back of his neck stood up, he was exposed here, his back toward any danger. But he forced his fingers to keep working, ears pricked for any sounds coming from the warehouse below, his fingers almost invisible in the dark. As he worked, there were a few more low coughs from behind the door, cementing in his head that many people were behind this door.

At last he felt the lock mechanism give beneath the probing of his pick and with a final twist of his fingers on the tiny tension wrench, there was a click and the door unlocked.

Retrieving his gun, he leaned into a crouch, pointed the gun at the door and, ever so slowly, edged it open.

The room was lit by one feeble lantern, but it was enough to see by. Lots of people were crammed in together, most lying on the floor, probably sleeping, some sitting in a small huddle over in a corner. And there, off to the left near the wall, was Charlize, scrambling to her feet next to a tall black man doing the same. She took the stance of someone preparing for a fight, rising up on the balls of her feet, fists clenched. A formidable scowl lined her forehead; a warrior princess ready for battle. He could see her clearly in the light of the lantern, blond hair aglow, green eyes flashing. His face was probably wreathed in darkness back here, out of the light from the lantern. The black man who towered over Charlize also clenched his fists. More faces turned toward him, laced with fear and confusion. Who were these people?

He took a chance and called out to her. 'Charlize, it's me.' Her face changed at the sound of his voice, the scowl lifted and her eyes lost their fierce suspicion, softening at the sight of him.

'Jean-Luc?' It was half question, half statement. Then she was running toward him, listing to one side because of her limp. But she didn't seem to care. He stood up just in time, as she threw herself into his arms, making him stagger back a step.

Other people were stirring now, woken by the commotion, they got up and rubbed sleep from their eyes. A murmur of voices, rising in volume as they took in what was happening. They began to point toward the door, their eyes widening at the sight. The tall man who'd been standing next to Charlize also made his way over at a much more sedate pace. But all of that only registered in some vague corner of Jean-Luc's mind. The rest of his brain was filled with Charlize. In his arms. Melting into him, her hands around his neck, her body warm and supple against his, her face buried in the lapel of his shirt. She was alive. And obviously very pleased to see him.

'You came,' she said, finally lifting her face to look at him. There was relief and a strange look of deliverance in her eyes. He wanted to kiss her, to crush his lips against hers and tell her with his body what he couldn't say in words; that he'd been terrified he'd find her dead. And that he wasn't sure he wanted to live without her. She felt so good in his arms. So alive. So real.

'We need to get out of here. Now.' Her voice brought him back to reality.

'Charlize, what the hell…' People started to jostle him as they moved past toward the door. A human tide with only one directive. To get out of this room as fast as possible.

'We need to get out of here,' she said again as she dropped her feet to the ground and pulled out of his arms.

What in hell was going on here? His mind raced to keep up with all the permutations. He didn't need to be told, these people were all illegal refugees, being held possibly against their will in this makeshift prison. Was this Vincent's stash of refugees?

The tall black man loomed over them suddenly. 'I assume this is a friend of yours?' he asked Charlize in a slow, unhurried way.

'Sorry. Yes. Fumbe, this is Jean-Luc. He's a gendarme, and he's here to help,' replied Charlize, inclining her head toward him.

'Nice to meet you,' said Fumbe, extending his hand and smiling in welcome. Jean-Luc nearly laughed with incredulity. The man greeted him as if he were the most gracious host in the world, and Jean-Luc's entrance into this hell-hole was an everyday occurrence.

He shook Fumbe's hand. It was good to know this man was on their side. Whatever their side was. He needed more intel about exactly what was going on here, and fast.

'Charlize, how did you get here?' he asked urgently. 'Was it the same men as before?' She nodded in reply, her eyes darting toward the growing crowd of people, who were now causing a bottle-neck at the door, all clamouring to get out.

As he stood, unsure, mind racing to calculate everything

he was seeing, his phone vibrated in his pocket. Instinct made him reach for it.

It was a message from Patrice. Jean-Luc read it quickly and then let out a loud curse.

'Jean-Luc, we have to go. Now,' Charlize urged, concern etched firmly into her brows. 'Please. You can check your phone later.'

'You have to stop these people from leaving,' he said in a harried voice. 'That message was from one of my team. It said the smuggler's men have just pulled up outside.'

'What?'

'Patrice just told me they've followed a truck load of illegals here. As well as a car holding Vincent Dellucci. He's the leader of this whole cartel.'

'Shit.' Her eyes grew wide with fear. 'They'll shoot these people if they see them trying to escape.' She turned to the big man beside her. 'Fumbe, you have to stop them.'

Then her eyes narrowed, and she took a step backwards. 'Hang on a second. This isn't some elaborate plan of yours to stop all these people leaving just so you can check if there are any terrorists mixed in with this bunch, is it?' Her hands came up to rest on her hips.

'What? No.' What in hell was she talking about? 'Here, take a look at the text for yourself.' Did she honestly think he'd worry about a minor detail like that right now?

She swatted his phone away. 'Sorry. Sorry to doubt you. It's just that I've spent the night with these people. They need our help, not our condemnation.'

'I get it,' he said. If there were any terrorists hidden in this swarm of humanity, he'd find them later. She was right, it was secondary to saving these people's lives. 'But we need to stop these people from leaving. This warehouse is like a death trap.' He was already moving toward the door, trying to stop the human tide, using his body to turn them away. But it was useless, they were completely single-minded in their desperation for freedom and they pushed and pulled him out of the way. At one stage he almost stumbled and fell, was nearly trampled underfoot. He moved to the side, helpless.

Then he heard a voice roar from the middle of the crowd. 'STOP.' The hubbub of excited voices died down and people slowed their mad dash. 'There are men with guns waiting outside to kill you. Do not leave,' the voice said again. It must be the man Charlize had called Fumbe.

The refugees stopped their forward rush and milled around in the doorway. Jean-Luc's phone vibrated with an incoming call. It was Patrice.

'Munulo. Where are you?'

'I'm in the bloody warehouse,' he barked into the phone. 'Don't ask how, just listen. There are at least one hundred refugees in here, being kept against their will. They're all trying to escape. How close is Vincent's team?'

'They're in the carpark,' Patrice replied, all cold efficiency, seemingly not fazed by the fact Jean-Luc had somehow materialised inside the very warehouse they were staking out. 'They've started to unload a new lot of refugees. You won't get out now. Vincent's men are right there.'

'*Merde.*' What were they going to do? This was already way beyond his control. Fumbe had stopped most of the people from leaving the room, but Jean-Luc could see through the doorway at least a dozen already making their way across the walkway, ignoring Fumbe's pleas to stop.

'Can you create some kind of diversion?' he asked

Patrice.

'It'll blow our cover,' Patrice replied, steady and calm.

'I think it's already too late for that. There are at least twelve people heading outside, they'll be massacred if they charge through that door straight into Vincent's men.'

'Fuck,' exclaimed Patrice. It was the first time Jean-Luc had heard him swear. 'We'll see what we can do. Get ready to move when I tell you to. I'll call for backup,' he said, before hanging up with a hurried click.

Jean-Luc strode back to where Charlize was still standing in the middle of the room. Her eyes cast around the room, reminding him of an animal trapped in a cage, willing to do just about anything to get out.

'I'm so sorry, Jean-Luc.' She grabbed his arm, her voice pleading. 'I did this. I made you come in here. And now you're going to be killed. We're all going to be killed.' Hysteria sounded in the hitching little breaths she took between each sentence.

'Oh God. Oh God. I'm so sorry.'

Merde, was she about to have one of her panic attacks? He needed the strong, confident Charlize right now. Not the one who doubted her every move.

'Charlize, look at me,' he commanded. 'I won't let you die. Okay?' He took her by the shoulders and gave her a gentle shake. 'And I'm kind of fond of my own skin, too,' he said softly. 'We'll get out of here, as long as we work together.' Finally, she looked up at him. A shaft of light from the lantern caught her sea-green eyes as they connected with his. Determination returned.

'Can you keep the rest of these people in here?' He connected with Fumbe's gaze over the top of Charlize's head. 'Let me through, I'll go down first.' Fumbe nodded back and Jean-Luc started to push through toward the door. Then he felt a hand on his shoulder and Charlize's voice in his ear.

'I'm coming with you,' she said. He opened his mouth to argue, when an almighty explosion rocked the warehouse.

* * *

The whole building shuddered like a dog shaking water from its coat, and waterfalls of dust cascaded down onto Charlize's head.

'Shit. What was that?' There was an audible tremble in her voice.

She needed to get a grip.

She'd be no help to Jean-Luc if she couldn't get a grip on this fear. Ever since he'd arrived like a white knight—or should that be black knight—in shining armour, she'd felt like a silly teenager. A foolish relief flooded through her veins at the sight of him, as if he were the answer to all her problems. But he was in just as much trouble as the rest of them now, and a part of her knew her reaction to his arrival, the way she'd thrown herself at him was not only pathetic, but immature. She was an ex-cop, she should be able to handle this situation blindfolded. He'd need her help to get them all out of here alive. But the doubt and the anxiety were still there, lurking like great beasts in the corners of her mind, unwilling to let her banish them completely. Voices told her she wasn't capable of doing this. Told her to leave it to the professionals, she wasn't up to the job any longer.

'That was the distraction,' Jean-Luc replied without looking back. 'Come on, let's go.' He'd been about to argue with her before the explosion. Whatever had changed his mind, she wasn't going to second guess him. She followed him through the gloom, holding on to the back of his shirt so she didn't lose him. Thank God for the kerosine lantern, still shedding its meagre light into the room.

'Give me your spare gun,' she said through gusting breaths. He carried a spare, but would he give it to her?

He stopped in front of her, but didn't turn around and she studied his broad shoulders, noticing the way the sinewy muscles of his back bunched, like a cat ready to pounce beneath the tight fabric of his shirt. Then he reached down and pulled a small Glock from a holster strapped to his calf, handing it back to her, flicking her a quick, assessing gaze at the same time.

'I assume you know how to use that?' She bit back a retort and just nodded in reply, acknowledging he'd just given her a large concession. When she'd asked him to give her a gun back in the shed, he'd refused. Laughed in her face. But now he handed it over with only a second's pause. Now wasn't the time to ask why he finally trusted her. His need probably outweighed his unease at handing her—a civilian—a loaded weapon. She tested the solid weight of the gun in her hand. Checked to see it was indeed loaded. The cold steel against her palm made her feel calmer and her breathing slowed down at last. In the gloom of the warehouse she could see the people who'd obeyed Fumbe's order huddling around the doorway, uncertain.

Fumbe cleared a pathway to the door for them.

'Wait here,' Jean-Luc said to Fumbe as he passed. 'It's the safest place for now. Try and barricade that door if you can. Don't let anyone in unless it's me or the police. Understand?' Fumbe nodded, black eyes flashing obsidian in the flare of the lantern.

Then they stepped through the doorway and it clicked closed behind them. The blood started to pound through her veins again, but she ignored the roaring in her ears and concentrated on the room spread out below them; the walkway in front of them. It was hard to see right down to floor level in the semi-darkness. When would it be dawn? She'd lost all track of time, but dawn must be close, surely. The sun's rays would be most welcome right now. But if this Vincent person was here unloading his next batch of refugees, there must still be a while until dawn. He wouldn't be stupid enough to do his business in the cold light of day. She shrugged off the thought and kept going. Whatever the next few minutes held for them, it'd be carried out under the shroud of darkness, so she'd just have to get used to the idea.

'Stay behind me,' Jean-Luc whispered as he crouched down, taking small, cat-like steps forward.

Holding the gun lightly in both hands, muzzle pointed down, she felt a familiarity enter her body. Her muscles remembered how to do this. How to press forward into the unknown, taking light easy steps, ready to swing the gun up to shoulder height at any given second. A tingle of awareness spread over her limbs and down her spine, chasing the fear away. For the moment. She became acutely aware of her surroundings, of the small shuffling sounds coming from below. The people who'd escaped the room behind and were now milling like frightened sheep near the doorway downstairs. None of Vincent's men had entered the building. Yet. Patrice's *distraction* seemed to be working for now. Vaguely, she could hear guns reporting in the distance, possibly further down the street from the warehouse. Was it Vincent's men shooting at the gendarme? Or the other way around? There was only one way to find out. They needed to get outside.

She kept half an eye on Jean-Luc's lithe form as he edged forward ahead of her, taking point, gun raised, shielding her with his body. He reminded her of a black panther stalking its prey. Now her eyes were becoming accustomed to the dark without the lantern, she could make out the walkway more clearly. They were nearly at the stairs leading down to the lower ground. She remembered these from when the thug had carried her up on his shoulder. She also remembered the half-completed boat hull almost directly below them, tucked beneath the rise of the stairs. It might make a good place to hide the refugees downstairs, at least get them out of the direct line of fire.

She touched Jean-Luc lightly on the shoulder and whispered her idea into his ear. He nodded his head in agreement and pointed down the stairs and to the left, indicating he would peel off that way to make sure no one was hiding in the back, while she herded the refugees away from the door and behind the relative safety of the boat.

The stairs were tricky to manoeuvre with her bad leg, while still keeping the gun held in both hands, but she managed it. No use putting Jean-Luc even more on edge by worrying him with inane problems like a malfunctioning leg that might let her down at any second. Nope, she'd keep that information to herself. Once she reached the bottom of the stairs, she called out softly to alert the others she was there. At first, they startled like scared rabbits, ready to run at the slightest provocation, but one of them soon recognised her and their panicked faces broke into nervous smiles of relief. Not sure how much English they understood, she mimed, using hand signals to show there were men with guns outside and to make it clear where she wanted them to go and hide. The sound of the gunfire had obviously frightened them and there was no need to warn them to keep quiet, they seemed to understand that part perfectly well. Moving in behind, herding like a sheepdog, she pushed them in behind the fibreglass hull lying on its side.

Once the last refugee was hidden, she peered around the edge of the boat, wondering where Jean-Luc had got to. What was their next plan of attack? Every now and then, a muffled shout came from outside and there was sporadic gunfire nearby. Then everything went quiet. It made her edgy and tense, not knowing what was going on outside.

A thought struck her. For the past few minutes—while she'd been focussed on her task of getting those people to safety, of protecting Jean-Luc's back, the metal of the gun warm against her fingers—the constant fear, the niggling self-doubt that always plagued her, had been absent. Pushed into a corner by the greater concerns of staying alive. Suddenly, she felt a ray of hope. A slim hope that perhaps she might be able to control this debilitating fear, which up until now had been controlling her. Perhaps, when this was all over, she might seek some help. It was time to unearth the old Charlize again. The one who wanted to grab life by the throat and live it to the fullest.

There was a slight movement beside her as one of the children fumbled around, wanting her mother to pick her up. Even the children were sensible enough not to speak, knowing without being told this was a highly dangerous situation.

These people had already been through so much. Her heart went out to them, wondering how they must feel about this new turn of events. Thinking they'd made it to a safe haven when they finally landed on the beach, only to have men with guns ordering them around and keeping them captive. Their future was still so uncertain. What would become of them, even if they made it out of this predicament alive? Would they be shipped off to one of the many camps around the country, left to live in cramped, filthy conditions, with no idea whether they'd be granted asylum, or just shipped back to their home country like cattle?

The image of dark eyes fixing her with bright intensity shimmered in front of her. The little boy lost from the car park back in Uzes. The naked fear and desperation that'd washed in waves over her, emanating from the boy, were still fresh in her mind. It seemed now he wasn't one of these refugees Vincent had smuggled across in his dirty boats. So where had he come from? Had the authorities who took him away managed to find his family—his mother or father?

The image of his small feet tucked up under skinny legs, his tattered clothes and hunger pinched face haunted her memory. Perhaps the only way to clear him from her conscience was to make sure he was finally reunited with his family. That way, she could lock the memory of him away safely in her mind, secure in the knowledge he was being cared for. But what if she found out he was alone in this world, after all? What if no one came forward to claim him? What would she do with that information?

A hand landed on her shoulder and she stifled a scream as she brought the gun up on instinct, aiming it directly at…

Jean-Luc. She exhaled and mentally kicked herself for letting her guard down and allowing him to sneak up on her.

'I'm going outside. You stay here and keep these people safe,' he whispered in her ear.

No way. She wasn't going to be told to stay behind like some well-trained poodle. 'I'm coming with you,' she whispered flatly. She couldn't see his expression in the dim light, but she hoped her voice conveyed enough of her determination that he understood she wasn't going to give in.

'I need you in here, Charli,' he said. The use of her nickname unbalanced her for a second. It was the first time he'd said it. 'You're these people's only line of defence if any of Vincent's thugs make it through that door. I'm trusting you to shoot them in the head if they make a move in this direction.'

Shit. He had a point. A very good one. And really, what help did she think she could give him outside, where she didn't know Vincent's men from Jean-Luc's team? She might shoot the wrong person by mistake.

She let out an indignant huff, just to let him know how unhappy she was about his decree, and replied, 'Fine, I'll stay here.'

Then Jean-Luc did something totally unexpected. He leaned in and kissed her on the lips. Just a quick, light peck, but it was enough to fire up all her nerve endings.

'Thank you,' he said, and then he was gone. There was a glow of a light from outside as he opened the door and then his dark form slipped outside. Nothing happened for seconds on end. Suddenly there was shooting close by, an automatic rifle. Another semi-automatic returned fire. Jean-Luc's gun? Perhaps. This not knowing was killing her.

Yelling. Men's voices yelling, shouting in French, *'aller sur le terrain, maintenant,'* over and over. Get on the ground. Now. Then everything went quiet again. Minutes ticked by.

The refugees behind her became restless, as if sensing that this siege—or whatever it was—was now nearly over.

Jean-Luc's voice rang out from the doorway. 'You can come out now. We got them all.' A gust of air left Charlize's lips from the breath she hadn't known she'd been holding.

She ushered her charges toward the door, but once outside was met by a scene of complete confusion. Africans were scattered all over the carpark, most still lying on the ground covering their heads, cowering from the nightmare of the shootout between the cops and Vincent's gang. Some were just starting to lift their heads and peer around them. Jean-Luc reassured some of them lying close by that it was all okay.

Many gendarmes in full battle gear—dark blue bulletproof vests, helmets, some with sub-machine guns strapped to their chests—also filed across the car park, threading through the crowd of refugees like dark avenging angels. There was a group of two or three gendarmes holding down a struggling assailant. Another group rounded up one more of Vincent's men, demanding he cooperate, or else.

At least two bodies lay unmoving on the ground. Dead.

Hopefully, they were the bad guys and none of Jean-Luc's team had been hit.

She averted her gaze from the bodies and located Jean-Luc, who was on the edge of the field of refugees, just starting to pick themselves up off the ground.

He gave her a quick, satisfied smile, and said, 'Could you let Fumbe know it's okay to come down now?' She nodded and went off to do his bidding, grateful to be given a job. Especially one that took her away from the nightmarish scene outside.

Fifteen minutes later, she was back outside and Fumbe and the last of the refugees were being counted and debriefed. She found a spot on the ground next to the neighbouring warehouse and sat down with a heavy sigh. It was heaven to get off her scarred leg, just for a few minutes. Jean-Luc hovered over her, watching her with that quick, measuring gaze of his.

When he was sure she was settled and comfy, he said gently, 'Wait here. I'm going back in to make sure no one else is left inside. The rest of the team will take care of the people out here. I won't be long.'

'I'm fine,' she replied. 'Go and do what you need to do. I'm not going anywhere.' That much was true. Her legs were leaden and lethargic, a symptom of coming down from that adrenaline high. She needed to sit here for a while, to get her composure back.

'It's over, Charlize.' He smiled, and her heart flipped at the sheer beauty of him. Kneeling down, he brought his face within inches of hers so he could stare into her eyes. 'You're free.' It was hard to believe, her mind still refused to accept the concept.

'Thanks to you,' she whispered.

'You did okay in there,' he replied, one eyebrow raised in an appreciative salute.

'Go on, get in there.' She waved him away, and he walked toward the warehouse. It was then she noticed the sky above had lightened ever so subtly, turning from ebony to iron grey. Finally, dawn was breaking. She smiled as she welcomed the start of a new day.

Jean-Luc's panther-like form opened the door to the warehouse and stepped inside, still cautious and careful, and she lost sight of him.

The cold concrete of the carpark seeped through the fabric of her jeans. She wriggled around, trying to ease the pain a little in her bad leg, and did a few exploratory stretches. Nope, stretches weren't going to help ease the pain tonight. She'd more than overdone it, with all the walking earlier tonight and the rough treatment from Vincent's thugs. The only thing that'd help her leg now was rest, and lots of it.

At least she'd be able to do that now. Now she was free of the danger Vincent presented. She was free to go back to her villa in Uzes. What about Jean-Luc? Would he come and visit her? The thought skittered through her brain, igniting all sorts of hopes and dreams, which she quickly put back in the box where they belonged. She'd have time to work things out later, and if Jean-Luc wanted to be part
—

Holy crap!

Agony shot through her leg, like a knife slicing through butter, making her grunt with pain.

What the hell—

Instinctively, she grabbed her thigh, clutched at it with all her might to stop this terrible sensation. If she hadn't known better, she'd have sworn she'd just been shot. She stared down at her leg, but could see nothing wrong with it. She expected to see blood leaking from a bullet hole in her thigh, but there was nothing. What in God's name was happening?

Then her head slammed back against the wall as a wave of sensations overwhelmed her. She squeezed her eyes shut and tried to block out the terrible awareness that something was wrong. Pain undulated through her, bright and strong and livid. Then anger rose up, dark and dangerous. But the edges of that black emotion were tinged with fear.

Need. Someone was in desperate need.

Jesus. Jean-Luc. Something had happened to Jean-Luc. She was suddenly terribly sure he was in mortal danger.

She gritted her teeth against the phantom pain as she stood up. The injury wasn't real, she just had to keep telling herself that. She could walk, it wasn't real.

Someone else must be inside the warehouse with Jean-Luc. But who? Jean-Luc had confirmed they'd caught every last one of Vincent's crew, including Vincent himself. Could they have missed one of the thugs? Or could it be a refugee, refusing to be caught, causing trouble?

She took a few uncertain paces forward and scanned the car park for signs of something… Exactly what she wasn't sure.

Police sirens wailed in the distance and there was the screech of tires as more squad cars pulled up out the front of the warehouse.

The refugees milled around in the car park, scared and confused. Afraid of the gendarmes, of what was going to happen to them now. The place was a confusing, cyclonic mass of humanity, shouting, pleading, crying, people going in all directions, police shouting orders. The din was so loud she knew no one would hear her if she shouted for help.

Her eyes sought out the back corner of the car park, the spot Jean-Luc had pointed out to her not long ago, where two gendarmes guarded the ring-leader of this smuggling gang, the man who'd made it his personal duty to try and kill her—Vincent Dellucci.

But he wasn't there. Last time she'd seen him, he was standing tall and arrogant, as if he wasn't actually cuffed to the doorframe of a police vehicle, glaring menacingly at the closest gendarme. She couldn't be sure, but she thought she could see an unmoving lump, half-hidden in the dim shadows of the recessed corner. One of the gendarmes? Where was the other one? Surely Vincent couldn't have escaped? A set of handcuffs dangled uselessly from the police car where Vincent had once stood. He was gone. Her eyes darted back toward the door into the warehouse.

'Over here,' she shouted. 'I need help.' But no one heard her. Surely Vincent must've known there was no way he was going to escape the tight police net. What else could he possibly do in there?

She reached around behind her and touched the small Glock tucked into the back of her pants. The cold steel reassured her, but her feet wouldn't take those first steps forward. What was wrong with her? Jean-Luc needed her help. She was armed and trained to handle these kinds of situations. Hadn't she just banished these demons for good? But it appeared they were back in abundance, like a hoard of giggling gremlins, voices in her head telling her she wasn't cut out for this job. Let someone else do it. She should stay here, where it was safe, where she never need to feel that fear again, to be hurt or afraid again. The pain was all too real in her leg.

But the voices were wrong. She would be hurt if something happened to Jean-Luc. Terribly, irrevocably hurt. If he were to die. Somehow, he'd wormed his way into her broken heart and lodged a piece of himself in there. Now she knew she'd never be whole again if he weren't in this world with her. If he was killed by Vincent, then a part of her would die too.

Her head was screaming at her to stay where she was. Her heart was screaming at her to go into the warehouse. Into danger. For Jean-Luc's sake.

Her heart won.

She limped toward the doorway and into the warehouse.

CHAPTER TWENTY-TWO

It was dark and relatively quiet in the dusty open space of the warehouse. Jean-Luc took a few seconds to breathe in the solitude after the madness of everything that'd just happened outside. Feeling around on the wall, he found the light switch and flicked on the faded yellow bulb, which swung from a string above his head. The melee was still going on outside, but it was muffled by the metal walls of the warehouse.

It was all over. And it'd all happened with comparable ease, too. One last sweep of the interior of the warehouse, just to make sure there were no illegals left hiding in here, and he could go and report to Pickard on a job well done. Then he could look forward to a glass of cognac or two. Or three. He had a bottle of the good stuff waiting at home and he deserved it after the past few days. Charlize seemed to like it, too. She'd definitely enjoyed the glass they'd shared after their pizza the other night.

His head was full of thoughts of Charlize laughing at his jokes outside the little restaurant in Uzes as he began to climb the stairs and he didn't bother about the noise his boots made on the metal. Patrice had confirmed they'd rounded up all of Vincent's thugs, so he needn't worry about being heard by anyone. The gun went back into the waistband of his pants.

As he clomped up the stairs, mind still crunching the numbers, trying to fathom exactly how many illegals Vincent had managed to smuggle into France—two hundred and thirty-three at last count—he thought he heard a noise downstairs. A quick glance over his shoulder confirmed there was nothing there, the yellow bulb still cast flickering shadows as it swung slowly on the string.

But there'd definitely been a noise, a quiet clang, as if someone had tried to shut the door with stealth, but misjudged the last few centimetres. The hair on the back of Jean-Luc's neck stood to attention. The beat of blood through his veins quickened. Turning on his heel, he backtracked down the stairs, quiet as a mouse this time. The gun came back out of his waistband, held loosely in one hand as he scanned the dark interior for anything amiss.

There was a muffled crack, and his leg buckled beneath him. He fell the last few steps to the ground and landed in a heap on the cold concrete, pain making a loud roar echo in his ears.

He'd been shot.

He shook his head to clear the red haze of pain away. He needed to get up, get back to his feet. But his body wouldn't respond, like he was made of jelly all of a sudden. *Merde*. His leg hurt like a bitch and he couldn't stop a loud groan from leaving his lips.

Who the fuck had shot him?

Then a black Italian leather shoe landed on the arm that

held his Sig, pinning it to the ground. The muzzle of a gun fitted with a silencer appeared in front of his eyes, aimed directly at his forehead.

'Don't move, pig,' a voice growled out of the darkness. He knew that voice. Had listened to it too many times on the surveillance tapes.

Vincent Dellucci.

'Drop the gun and get up.'

'I can't,' Jean-Luc gasped. 'You shot me in the leg, you fucking bastard.'

'I don't care. Get up, or I'll shoot you in the head as well,' Vincent replied, cool as a cucumber.

Jean-Luc let his fingers go limp and his gun fell with a clang onto the concrete. Vincent picked it up and tucked it into the front of his trousers.

Experience told Jean-Luc that Vincent would do exactly as he threatened—he was a nasty mother-fucker—so he started to pull himself slowly to his feet. Every second he could stay alive was terribly important now. Each minute he wheedled out of this man was precious. Jean-Luc knew he was a dead man, unless he could come up with something, quick.

'You won't get away,' Jean-Luc warned. 'This whole place is surrounded.' He glanced over at Dellucci, taking in his stocky figure, the expensive Italian suit not able to hide the man's bull neck. Thick and all muscle. Vincent grinned at Jean-Luc, a smug grin full of arrogant disdain. Waving the gun in Jean-Luc's face, he indicated for him to start walking toward one of the darkened corners of the warehouse. Where the hell had Vincent got a gun? It looked to be a Sig Sauer, a slightly older model than his own. Standard issue for all French police. Last time Jean-

Luc had seen him, he was standing between two very fierce gendarmes, weapon-less and cuffed. *Merde.*

'*Pah*. You pigs know nothing. Besides, I've got a hostage now.'

Jean-Luc hardly heard Dellucci's answer, as waves of pain washed over him with each tentative step he took. The bullet had gone in just above the knee, leaving a gaping hole in his jeans. There was blood, lots and lots of blood. But not enough for the bullet to have hit the femoral artery. He could still bleed to death, but not in the next few minutes, at least. And the fact he could put some weight on the leg—admittedly not a lot, but some—meant the bone was still intact. Small mercies, really.

'If I don't come out in the next few minutes, they're going to send men in to look for me,' he threatened. 'You'll be cornered. There's no way out of here.'

Which was technically true, but there was no guarantee anyone *would* miss him for at least fifteen minutes or so. More than enough time for Dellucci to kill him, or do whatever other sick thing he might have in mind. How had he got away from his guards?

'You're a slippery bastard, aren't you?' Jean-Luc punctuated his speech with grunts of pain. But he had to keep the man talking, keep him distracted. Appealing to the man's enormous ego, he said, 'I should've made sure I put more guards on you. Did you kill them?'

'No, I didn't kill the pig. I wanted to, but it might've attracted unwanted attention. Let's just say he won't be waking up for a long time, though.' Vincent's deep, menacing chuckle broke the darkness. Jean-Luc took another step, and more pain shot up his leg. Fuck, he was going to pass out. He took a deep breath and then another.

'So how did you get away?'

'You pigs, you all underestimate me.' Vincent made a disgusting sound and then spat on the ground behind Jean-Luc. 'One of your so-called guards got called away to subdue an angry reffo. And the other one, well, he was just plain sloppy. Let's just say I'm a whiz at picking locks.' Again, that intimidating chuckle filled the air.

Merde. Vincent was right, they had been sloppy. Vincent had been thoroughly searched for a concealed weapon, but it would've been easy to conceal something small enough to pick a lock with.

Jean-Luc opened his mouth to demand how he'd managed to wrestle away an armed gendarme's gun, when Dellucci said, 'Stop talking and walk.' For once, Jean-Luc did as he was told.

Jean-Luc knew the pain was altering his judgement, but where did Dellucci think he was going? The man was stupid, but even he wasn't stupid enough to think he could shoot his way out of here. The man was completely unworried about his current predicament, however. Which must mean he knew something Jean-Luc didn't.

He shuffled forward, grunting at every step and soon found himself in the darkened corner behind the old boat hull Charlize had hidden her group of illegals during the shootout.

'Stop right there,' Vincent's deep voice said from behind him. He stopped in front of a large wooden crate, parts from an outboard motor laid out on top. 'Push that crate as far to the left as it'll go.' Vincent's words sent a chill down Jean-Luc's spine. What was under that crate?

'I can't, my leg…'

'Just fucking move the crate,' Dellucci growled. So he

pushed, making a show of grunting and moaning at the strain on his leg. Which wasn't really that much of a show, as his leg hurt like hell. The crate was lighter than it looked and made a deep scraping sound as he dragged it across the dusty concrete.

Finally, he moved it far enough so he could see what lay beneath. A square door cut into the floor, with a handle cut out of the metal. An escape hatch. Of course, Dellucci would have an escape plan.

'Open it,' said Vincent, waving the gun in his direction. A greasy grin spread over his face as he eyeballed Jean-Luc. Self-satisfied bastard. His shoulder-length black hair was slicked back, giving him even more of a Mafia look and Jean-Luc was suddenly struck with a worrying thought. Had they seriously underestimated Dellucci? They'd pegged him as having loose connections with the Italian Mafia, but decided he was only interested in amassing obscene amounts of wealth for himself. Did he have more of a connection with the Mafia than they first supposed? Especially if he thought he could get away with something like this.

Jean-Luc leant down and grabbed the handle, the back of his neck crawling, waiting for the bullet in his back.

It didn't come.

With a gush of breath, Jean-Luc propped the trapdoor open and peered into a tunnel, black as a grave. He couldn't see a thing down there.

'Get in,' Dellucci said, impatient now.

'I'm not—'

The air left his body with a grunt as Dellucci shoved him in the back and he tumbled through the darkness.

* * *

What in hell did she think she was doing? She should back out right now and go find a helpful gendarme or two. But the invisible string pulling her forward, her clairsentience, wrenching her toward Jean-Luc, wouldn't let her turn back. He was in grave danger, and there wasn't time to go and find someone else to help. She was it for now.

The Glock shook a little in her hands and she stopped her stealthy creep into the warehouse to take a few deep breaths, steadying her aim.

The sensation of someone—Jean-Luc—in pain and need was getting stronger the further into the darkened corner she ventured. She wished she'd brought a torch, but the light would've given her away. So she struggled on in the dim, dusty space. A black shape loomed in front of her, square and made of wood—a crate of some kind—and then some sixth sense warned her to stop exactly where she was. Perhaps it was plain old animal instinct that made her not take that next step, but she was eternally grateful to whatever it was. Because when she stopped and looked down, letting her eyes adjust to the deeper darkness, she could just make out a large hole cut into the floor beneath her.

A trapdoor.

That hole definitely hadn't been there before. She was sure of it. A hidden bolt-hole Vincent must've devised for just such an occasion.

Crouching down onto her knees, she peered into the hole. There was a drop of around ten feet, and then a tunnel ran off in a northerly direction. From her lower vantage point, she could just make out a faint light issuing from the tunnel, as if someone had turned on a small torch away in the distance.

A low laugh echoed from somewhere in the depths of the gloom. The laugh contained no humour. Just cold malice. Then a sound like something solid hitting a punching bag, followed by grunts of pain, emitted from the tunnel. The sensations in her head, the colours of red and black and orange, went crazy with every grunt. Jesus, that bastard, Vincent, was beating Jean-Luc. Her blood boiled in her veins. How dare he.

She felt around the top of the hole. How was she going to get down?

Oh shit, a ladder. Her scarred leg wasn't good with ladders. But she had to get down there. The little insidious voices in her head started up again, telling her it was too hard, ladders were dangerous things, she didn't know how far the drop was if she fell. She needed to go and get a gendarme to do this. Shutting the voices down, she concentrated on the best way to descend the blasted ladder.

There was no way she was going to make it down while holding a gun in one hand, so she tucked it into her jeans and turned around, lowered herself onto the top rung and hung on like a limpet to the sides.

It was a slow and painful process as she took each rung one at a time. The last thing she wanted to do was fall and announce her presence. Or break her neck. But she managed, feeling terribly exposed as she did so. What if someone was waiting for her at the bottom? Every now and then she could hear more punches, or kicks, whatever they were, but the sound was getting fainter, as if they were moving further down the tunnel. But no voices. Whatever Vincent was doing to Jean-Luc, he was doing it with silent glee.

The pain was still in her leg, above her knee, a phantom pain. The pulling sensation telling her to hurry to his aid was getting stronger and stronger, almost overwhelming her. She needed to get it under control, otherwise she'd run down that tunnel like a screaming banshee and fling herself over Jean-Luc to protect him from whatever Vincent was doing. It was the logical part of her brain she needed right now, not her heart, which was howling at her to run after him.

Not that she was going to run anywhere, with her bad leg aching from the climb down the ladder and her good leg pulsing with phantom pain. She almost laughed at how absurd her situation was.

So, with only a slow walk at her disposal, she crept down the tunnel toward the flickering light. The passage was narrow, wide enough for her to walk down without scraping her shoulders on the side, but not much more. Trying to gauge her position underground, she worked out she was probably below the street right now. Perhaps this tunnel came out in one of the warehouses across the street. Ingenious really.

She wiped sweat from her brow so it wouldn't drip into her eyes and kept her gun aimed steadily in front of her. Slowly but surely, she caught up with the mirage-like glow. And now she could make out two people in front of her. Jean-Luc was in front, his black t-shirt and jeans and dark skin making him almost indiscernible from the dim walls. He was limping heavily and leaned against the wall for support.

The other man—Charlize assumed it was Vincent—walked along behind Jean-Luc, a weapon pointed at the back of his head. As she snuck closer, Jean-Luc's laboured breathing became louder in the quiet tunnel. He was in a lot of pain.

Suddenly, Vincent glanced over his shoulder.

Charlize flattened herself against the wall and froze, not even daring to breathe, expecting a bullet to come whizzing down the passage any second.

But Vincent just turned and kept walking. He must not have been able to see her in the darkness. Perhaps his eyes were night-blinded by the glow of the torch he was holding. She had an advantage, but how was she going to use it? She couldn't just shoot Vincent, the tunnel was too narrow and she couldn't take the chance of hitting Jean-Luc. After two years out of the force, her aim would be more than a little rusty. And what if she did try and shoot him but only managed to wing him instead of taking him down? The risk he might pull the trigger and kill Jean-Luc was enormous. Too many risks. Too many things to go wrong.

As she sifted through various plans of attack, all the while inching closer to the two men, the voices in her head muttered louder. Her subconscious ramped up and images of the fiery wreck assaulted her mind, Xeon's screams filled her head, halting her in her tracks. The gremlins were working overtime to stop her from breaking free of this debilitating fear.

No. You're not going to win this time. Go away. I'm going to help Jean-Luc, whether you like it or not. I don't have time for this shit anymore.

The voices and visions stopped as suddenly as they'd started. Her mind became crystal clear and her body thrummed with adrenaline-induced anticipation. As if shutting the door on some imaginary box inside her mind, she knew her decision to ignore her fears was a momentous one. She *could* do this. There was no other choice. Rescue Jean-Luc or die in the process.

'Get a move on, you piece of shit,' Vincent muttered. Then he struck Jean-Luc on the shoulder with the butt of his gun. 'If you keep slowing me down, I'm gonna kill you right here.'

From her spot around thirty metres behind them, she could see Jean-Luc hunch his shoulders in pain, as if expecting another blow. He took another ten or so stumbling steps forward, before again stopping to lean against the wall.

Charlize silently thanked Jean-Luc for his diversion and took the opportunity to quietly close the gap between them. If Vincent's focus remained fixed on Jean-Luc, she could sneak up close enough to hit him over the head with her gun. It was a simple plan—the good ones often were—but it relied on Vincent not taking another glance behind him in the next twenty or thirty seconds.

Closer and closer, she took advantage of the loud rasping of Jean-Luc's breathing, counted on it, covering any sound of her approach. Ten metres. Five meters. Gun raised. Only a few more steps.

Vincent stopped, perhaps on instinct, and turned around, gun raised.

Charlize didn't have any other option. She squeezed the trigger.

Two loud gunshots sounded almost simultaneously in the passage, nearly deafening her.

Vincent dropped like a bag of cement onto the cold dirt floor. A bullet hole through the centre of his forehead, eyes still open and staring. The torch rolled from his unmoving fingers, landing on the ground to cast eerie shadows on the walls.

'Fuck! What the fuck? Who's there?' Jean-Luc yelled as he pressed against the wall, unsure of what'd just happened.

'It's me, Jean-Luc.' She stepped around Vincent's inert body and went toward him, taking his weight under her shoulder and eased him to the ground. 'We're okay. I killed him. We're safe,' she said. 'Where are you hurt?' She was all businesslike now.

'My leg, he shot me. Jesus, Charli, what the hell... Are you okay?' Jean-Luc was shaking with shock and pain beneath her, but funnily enough, her hands were solid as a rock.

She was back. Charlize was back.

'I'm good, Jean-Luc. We're good.' She sat down next to him, helping him put pressure on the wound in his leg.

God, he felt so good, so alive and so true beside her. She listened to his voice as he told her in a rush what she already knew. It wasn't his words she was listening to, but the lovely, deep baritone in his voice. She loved that voice. She loved him.

COGNAC

Cognac is an aged brandy only made in the west of France. It's expensive, but when served in a large snifter over ice, is a smooth, interesting and delicious spirit.

CHEESEBOARD

Three beautiful cheeses, consisting of; *Pont L'Eveque*, an orange rind cheese with an ivory, oozy centre and a delicate flavour that is quite addictive; *Roquefort*, made from sheep's milk, this famous blue vein cheese is the king of cheeses, with a punchy, spicy, sweet flavour; *Tomme de Cherve Aydius*, made from goat's milk, this is a sweet aged cheese, fruity and smooth and Charlize's favourite swoon-worthy cheese.
Serve with sliced apples, grapes, walnuts and figs and tear off pieces of fresh, crusty baguette to eat with the cheese.

A combination of Jean-Luc's chosen spirit, cognac, pairs well with Charlize's ideal cheeses. This is best relished on a balcony in an apartment in Nice, overlooking the Mediterranean at sunset.

CHAPTER TWENTY-THREE

Charlize stood at the edge of the stairs and took in the view over the terracotta roof tops of Uzes. Eight months ago, when she'd first stood here, she'd marvelled at the wonder of the vista of the township spread below her and a feeling of belonging had descended over her as she soaked it all in. And now, that same feeling was still there, stronger than ever. This was where she needed to stay, at least for a while. In this wonderful country, with all of its culture and vibrant people and delectable food yet to be discovered, and cooked.

A sigh left her lips as she descended the stairs carefully into her walled garden. Placing her plate on the wrought-iron table, she pulled up a chair and sat down, smiling as the little brown mouse poked her nose out of the wall in greeting, whiskers twitching in anticipation of a crumb or two. She'd miss this place terribly. Bags almost packed, just awaiting a few odd pieces of clothing and some toiletries, she was nearly ready to catch her flight back to Australia the day after tomorrow. Which only left her one more day to spend exploring the wondrous Uzes markets.

She'd have to be up super early on Sunday to be at the Nice airport by nine am to catch her flight.

She couldn't wait to see her hometown again. There was nothing like the wide brown paddocks, the smell of the eucalyptus trees, sap thrumming through them on a smouldering hot day. The sheer openness of the never-ending blue sky fading to wispy clouds on the horizon. But she was coming back to France. This was where she needed to be right now.

As soon as she'd assured her family she really was fine, happy, safe, content, she'd return. It'd be hard, especially on her mother, but she'd make them understand. Somehow.

Still, she'd miss this wonderful villa in Uzes. It'd been her perfect safe-haven, her shelter from the storm for the past six months. But the lease was up and someone else was moving in in a few days' time. No matter, she'd find somewhere equally as enthralling when she came back. Perhaps in another town, there were still hundreds of places yet to be explored in Provence, each with their own slightly different take on food and culture.

Her focus went to her plate and her eyes devoured the offering she'd cooked up in her kitchen today. Her mouth watered as she picked up her knife and fork, and her stomach rumbled loudly. The old adage that a meal is eaten as much with the eyes as it is with the mouth was certainly correct. She'd really outdone herself with this one, even if she did say so herself. It'd taken her most of the afternoon to cook, but she knew it'd be worth the wait.

Roasted quail with a white wine jus and baby leeks, asparagus, fava beans and vine-ripened tomatoes.

She cut into the succulent quail breast and put it into her

mouth, letting the subtle flavour linger on her tongue. Oh God, it was to die for. Combining some leek and asparagus with the white wine jus, she popped the morsel into her mouth and swirled it around. She would never have learned to cook like this if she hadn't come to France. When she got home, she'd cook this meal for her parents and her sister, they would never have tasted anything like it in their lives before. A smile formed on her lips at the thought.

As she continued to eat, her thoughts wandered, and as usual, it settled on the one topic always lurking at the back of her mind.

Jean-Luc.

It'd been eight weeks since that day at the warehouse when Vincent had nearly killed them both. Eight long weeks, and she'd only talked to him over the phone, never in person.

In those weeks she'd missed him, ached for him to come to her. But as time had passed, and he hadn't materialised, her mind spiralled downwards into negative thoughts. They were just too different. He was a man committed to his job, a very dangerous job, with no time left over for romance, or women with scars on their legs. And scars in their minds. No matter how much she wanted him, this thing they had would just never work. She wasn't sure whether she'd ever get the chance to tell him exactly how she felt. And that left her feeling distracted and helpless.

Admittedly, he'd been a very busy man over those last eight weeks. First, there'd been his ten-day stay in hospital to recover from the gunshot wound. It wasn't too bad, as far as gunshot wounds went, or at least that's what Jean-Luc told her. It'd gone in just above the knee, nicked the edge of his femur and exited out the other side with minimal damage. No infection or any other complications that might hinder his healing. The doctor assured him he'd be back to catching the bad guys in a few months, but his knee may not ever be one-hundred percent again. Then, as soon as Jean-Luc was released from hospital, his boss, Pickard, had commandeered his every waking minute—in between rehab sessions—with reams of paperwork, aimed at cleaning up the mess he'd made.

Charlize thought back to the day she'd gone with him in the ambulance to the hospital and then waited through the hours he spent in surgery, so she could sit at his bedside and be there for him when he woke.

The first time he'd opened his eyes had made all they'd just been through together seem almost worth it. His gaze flittered around the room, searching, until copper eyes settled on her. He raised his arm and stretched it toward her, so she rose from her chair to take his hand in hers.

'Charli,' he rasped, voice still husky from the anaesthetic. Warm fingers tightened around hers. Compelling. Possessive.

'I'm here. Don't try to talk too much,' she soothed. His gaze was locked onto her, all kinds of emotions swirling in the depths, but she could see he was still groggy and unfocussed from the operation.

'I... I have... things I want to say. To you.' His eyelids drooped even as he fought to keep them open. Taking his hand in both of hers, she knelt beside his hospital bed.

'And I to you,' she replied. 'Soon. Soon we'll talk.' He didn't reply, his eyelids remained closed. He looked so untroubled, his stark black lashes laying on his coffee-coloured cheeks like a child sleeping.

Yes, there were things she wanted to say to him. But now wasn't the time. The doctor warned he'd drift in and out of conciseness to start with. She wasn't about to say something he might forget the next time he awoke. When they did finally have their conversation, she wanted him to be completely lucid. So he heard her loud and clear when she told him she was falling in love with him.

It was a decision she'd made back in the tunnel. That she wasn't going to run away from life anymore like a frightened child. She was going to grab it by the balls. In a manner of speaking.

With a gentle fingertip, she stroked the back of his hand and continued to watch him sleep.

Later he'd woken up properly, but when he'd reached for her this time, all sorts of alarms sounded, bringing a brigade of nurses into the room. Charlize was forced to stand back by the wall and watch as they checked his vitals and prodded and poked.

As if he'd been summoned by the alarm in the heart-rate monitor, Jean-Luc's boss also materialised. Pickard seemed genuinely concerned for Jean-Luc's welfare, but that was the only sign she ever got of his actual humanity. As soon as he understood Jean-Luc was out of any danger, Pickard had whisked her out of the room to *debrief her*. Jean-Luc had been most unhappy when he noticed Pickard lead her away, but there wasn't much he could do from his hospital bed, especially with three nurses fussing around him. While Pickard towed her away, she could still hear him trying to call them back all the way down the hospital corridor. Why had she let Pickard take her away like that? She still wasn't sure. And now she wished she hadn't been so compliant.

Mathieu Pickard was most accommodating and made sure she was comfortable, with a cup of tea in her hand and seated in a soft armchair before he started her debrief. But he was also stern and direct, never wavering from his target; which was to get the truth of the matter from her. She told him everything she could remember about her ordeal and her time with Jean-Luc. Three times. There was no reason for her to lie, after all. Neither she nor Jean-Luc had done anything wrong.

One thing she wanted to make damn sure of was the gendarme who was supposed to have been guarding Vincent and then left his post, was giving a stern talking to. At least on that point, Pickard agreed wholeheartedly with her, telling her the particular individual had been demoted to desk duty, perhaps permanently. The other gendarme who'd been knocked out by Vincent was also being dealt with. It seemed the French gendarmerie took their professions very seriously, and for an unarmed man to have overpowered him with such ease was a source of great chagrin and embarrassment. He would be going back to training school for a few months refreshment. Charlize didn't wish him ill, but if he'd done his job, she would never have had to go in and rescue Jean-Luc in the first place.

Once he was certain she was going to stick to her story, Pickard gave her a rare, implacable smile and made it very clear to Charlize just how much she'd be in the way if she tried to hang around—they still had a mission to mop up —and Jean-Luc needed peace and quiet in order to recuperate. Wouldn't she feel much safer and more comfortable if she went back to her villa in Uzes? Jean-Luc would be sure to contact her there directly.

Charlize opened and shut her mouth a few times, much like a stranded fish, but by the time she found the words, Pickard was on the phone to one of his underlings. He'd sent her home like a wayward child, without even letting her go back and say goodbye to Jean-Luc. Put her in a sleek, low-slung car with two agents to *escort* her, and never even looked at her as she was driven away.

True to his word, Jean-Luc had phoned her as soon as she got home, raging at her treatment by his boss, vowing he'd punch the man in the face as soon as he could get out of bed. But after he'd calmed down, he'd almost started to agree that perhaps it was for the best if she stay in Uzes, and promised he'd come and see her just as soon as he was released from hospital. She'd tried to phone him more than once while he was in the hospital, but there always seemed to be a procedure happening or a doctor speaking to him at that particular moment, and would she care to call back later. The hackles on the back of her neck rose up at her obvious snubbing, but what else could she do about it?

When he was released from hospital, he phoned her from Nice, where the GIGN rehab unit was situated. There was also the huge clean-up operation after the raid on the warehouse to work on. So many refugees to be sorted, all of Vincent's men to be charged. And Vincent Dellucci's business dealings, properties, all had to be gone through with a fine-tooth comb. Even though the man was dead, many of his associates and business partners were implicated in the smuggling ring. Charlize had finished that phone call confused and close to tears. Had she misread him all along? Had he changed his mind since she last saw him? If not, why hadn't he come to see her? She needed to tell him how she felt about him, but it was a conversation that had to be done face to face, not over the phone. It was all very frustrating.

Now Jean-Luc was in Paris. He'd phoned her a few days ago, stressed and anxious, telling her there was still months and months more work left to untangle this whole mess. They were still trying to ascertain whether there had actually been any terrorists included in the rag-tag bunch of refugees. It was time-consuming and frustrating work. He couldn't really discuss it with her, but he hinted that the GIGN had detained at least three men for *further questioning*. She could make of that what she would.

He was still the same Jean-Luc when she spoke to him. Still warm and funny; worried about her. They talked about their stay at his family's farm and how much she'd loved it there. The new dishes she learned to cook at Armand's cooking school. How well his leg was healing now, he was even able to walk without crutches. And still he kept promising he'd come and see her soon, very soon. She was left more confused than ever. Was he just uttering useless platitudes, or did he mean it?

And she was off to Australia for Patty's wedding in less than forty-eight hours.

At least that thought didn't scare her as much as it once had. If nothing else, her near-death experience had purged her of the fear of going home—of facing her family. There was nothing more precious than family, and she needed to treasure them, because who knew when life might change on a dime. For better or for worse. Take every moment she could with them and make the most of it.

It would've been nice to see Jean-Luc once more before she left. But she wasn't even sure if he'd heard her when she mentioned she was leaving soon. He was probably neck deep in back-to-back meetings with department heads on how to handle this crisis that'd just been averted. She wanted to feel sorry for him, tried to summon up some compassion for him working so hard, driving himself to the edge for the sake of his job and the ultimate safety of his country. He should be applauded for his willingness to do what needed to be done. But all she could feel was a sense of loss, and a rising anger that he'd forgotten all about her, even though the logical part of her brain knew they could never be together. It would never have worked. But she missed him so much. Her body hungered for his touch, and her soul thirsted for the sound of his voice.

Determined to push the rising tide of sadness away at the thought of what could've been with Jean-Luc, she took another bite. It'd do her no good. She would focus on the good, the positive things in her life from here on.

A rustle at the edge of the garden made her lift her head. It was coming from the back wall, where the alleyway ran behind.

As she stared, the shape of a man appeared over the top of the wall and dropped slowly into the gravel below, wincing and favouring one leg as he did so.

'Jean-Luc! What the—'

'*Bonjour, Mademoiselle.*' He took a deep bow and then limped toward her. He was here. Here in her garden. In the flesh. Her gaze roamed over his wonderful face, drinking in the way his light chocolate eyes stared at her, desire in their depths, and the way his lips curled up in the faintest hint of a smile. Then he really did smile, white teeth accenting his coffee skin. A stunning smile. His familiar face lost the lines of worry, and he looked lighter and more carefree than she ever remembered.

Up out of her chair and in his arms, she couldn't recollect exactly how she got there. He held her against his chest, the impressive solidity of it lay beneath her fingers.

'Charlize.' The way he said her name spoke of a mixture of longing and relief and adoration. It was as if he'd just poured a cup of gooey, warm molasses through her veins. Only now that he was here, the sleek wall of hard muscles in his back beneath her hands did she allow herself to acknowledge just how much his absence had hurt in the past weeks.

'*Mon Dieu*, I've missed you,' he whispered into her ear, brushing her earlobe with his lips as he spoke. The soft touch sent shafts of sensation spiralling through her stomach. 'I'm sorry it's been so long.' His lips went lower as he caressed her neck and collarbone. She closed her eyes and let the intoxicating awareness overwhelm her. His lips left her skin as he lifted his head and the spell was broken. Slowly, she pried her eyelids open, wishing he'd just keep on kissing her. He was staring at her, open longing in his gaze. A blond curl hung over her eye and he pushed it back from her face with long fingers, cupped her cheeks in his hands, locked her in with his stare. She stared back into those eyes, pools of liquid gold temptation. Shivers of anticipation raced through her body.

'*Ca va*, Charlize?'

Now was not the time for talking. Now was the time to slide beneath cool sheets with him, to feel his naked body against hers, have him inside her, deep inside her. Everything else could wait. They had lots to discuss, but it could all wait. Right now, she needed to be loved. Utterly and completely. Their eyes met. Held. Invitation was there in the lift of his lips. She stroked a finger down his temple, over his brown skin and goatee beard, let the short bristles tickle her fingertips.

He was the most exquisite man she'd ever met.

Did he know how good it felt to be touching him? Did he feel the same tremble in places deep inside; the same buzzing tingle that ran through her fingertips? This was much more than just a sexual connection. It was a cognisance that ran between them, a bond formed from their time together on the run. An unbreakable bond, as if they were destined to be together. Forever.

Whatever happened afterwards, at least tonight, would remain in her memory. Cherished. A prize to be kept safe in a place where wishes did come true.

'Come upstairs,' she said, surprised at the huskiness in her voice. She could've uttered some kind of platitude, like '*I missed you too,*' or '*it's so good to see you,*' or '*how is your leg?*' but those simplistic phrases didn't come close to telling him how she felt. The only way she could think was to show him. With her body. With her essence.

Without waiting for an answer, she took his hand, leading him up the back stairs, through the kitchen and up to the second floor. Her plate of quail and baby leeks left forgotten on the wrought-iron table. He came willingly, without another word. The soft squeak of his shoes on the wooden floor told her he was following. A slight hitch in his step betrayed his limp.

Before she could even close the bedroom door behind her, he'd driven her up against the wall, pinning her hands by her sides, his lips meshing with hers. The maleness of him pushed against the softness of her womanly curves;

they fitted together flawlessly. He was hard and oh so ready. Yes, she could safely say he felt the same craving, the same desperate need for her as she did for him.

She'd left her bedside lamp on, and it cast a soft glow around the room. He pulled his mouth away to look at her, his gaze full of sensual heat, full of memories from the other times they'd spent together. When they'd kissed. When they'd made love.

Up close, in the light from the lamp, she could see the lines of fatigue drawn on his face.

Her body heated with want, started to beat with a fizzing lust that wouldn't be tamed. The wild side of her had awoken. Again. He did this to her.

A groan vibrated through his chest, pulsing into her as she pushed her breasts up against him. Two-day-old stubble scraped her palm. Shirt. She had to get his shirt off. Pulling at the buttons until they popped, she almost ripped it from his torso.

With haste she undid his jeans, pushed at them impatiently until he finally helped her by kicking them all the way off. He was naked in front of her now. A picture of raw male beauty. Following the mounds and dents of his six-pack abs, she drank in the view of his silky brown skin. She leaned in and traced the jut of his hip bones with her palms. Saw the raw wound from where the bullet had pierced his leg, bent down and traced the line of it with her fingertips.

'Aren't we the pair now?' she said ironically.

'*Oui*, my beautiful mademoiselle, we are a pair.' She caught her breath at the double meaning of his words.

Now it was her turn, and she tore at her clothes, until she too was clad in nothing but her pale skin and her ache for him.

The scars on her leg were no more, forgotten in the heat and rush of desire.

Then he came for her, crushing her mouth to his lips, crushing her body against his chest. His erection pounded against her stomach and she backed toward the bed, feeling her way with her feet, not letting go of his mouth. She never wanted to let go of his mouth again. He tasted of musk and dark chocolate and pure male.

The backs of her legs hit the bed and then he lowered her down ever so slowly, as if she weighed nothing. She watched his biceps flex and mould as he brought himself down on top of her. The tip of his erection slid between her legs and the fierce burning hunger to have him inside her returned a hundred-fold.

This time she didn't even have to say it, he produced a condom from God knew where and had it on in seconds flat.

Slowly, ever so slowly, he entered her, until he was buried deep inside. It was good, felt so right. Then he started to thrust, sending shivers racking through her core. There was nothing else in this world; no one else in this world. Just him and her. She cried his name out into the night.

* * *

'I'm flying back to Australia in tomorrow.' Her words were quiet in the early morning light.

'I know, *ma cherie*,' he replied. 'You told me on the phone the other day.' He let the silky swirls of her hair fall between his fingers back onto the pillow. Curls the colour of whipped butter, he decided abstractly; the yellow colour dramatically highlighted against the chocolate of his skin. Soft sunlight from the rising sun drifted in the open window, throwing mottled shadows across the carpet and onto the bed where they lay together.

He could lie here all day. Just like this, with her by his side. It was so peaceful. That's it, he was at peace when he was with her. The burning need to save the world, to protect the innocent, was dampened to a level where he could ignore it, just for a while.

He shifted and draped one leg over her thigh, pulling her closer to his chest. The sheets were a tangled mess beneath them as they lay naked and twined together. Eyes shut, her head on the pillow, hair like a halo all around; she was a picture of wonderment to him. So beautiful, it was almost a physical pain.

'I wasn't sure if you'd remember,' she said in that same quiet tone.

He leaned up on one elbow so he could look down at her. 'You what?'

She opened those stunning bottle-green eyes and stared up at him. A rose blush crept up her cheeks. 'You sounded ultra busy... I wouldn't have blamed you if you didn't take it in,' she replied and he could see he'd flustered her. Of course he'd heard her, every word of it. His hands had gone clammy around the phone, and his heart had squeezed tight in his chest at the mere thought of her leaving France. Leaving him.

But he hadn't been sure then. Not completely and utterly sure. There'd still been a kernel of doubt. And because he'd been due in another of those bloody meetings five minutes ago, he hadn't allowed his mind to process what she'd said. So he hadn't responded to her revelation. Because he hadn't known what to say. Later, however, lying in his hotel room, unable to sleep, he'd made his decision. A life changing one.

There were things he needed to do once he made the decision, loose ends to be tied up and files to be handed over. But he'd finally broken away from Paris, away from Pickard and all that terrible life-sucking duty. He was done with duty.

'That's why I'm here, Charli,' he replied, smiling at her look of confusion, savouring the wanton surprise in her eyes. 'I want to come with you.' She opened her mouth and closed it again, either unable or unwilling to find words to answer him. 'If you'll let me, of course,' he finished hurriedly.

'If I'll let you?' she mimicked, still staring up at him, eyes going sea-green. They changed colour even as he watched, went darker, more lustrous with hints of amber, like a fiery emerald. 'Of course you can come,' she sputtered. 'I'd love for you to come. Really? Do you really want to come?' He laughed at her sudden childish enthusiasm. 'You know you'll have to meet my family?' This was said with such an air of warning, as if it might be the single most scary thing he'd ever do.

'Yes, of course. I'm looking forward to it. From what you've told me, your mother is a lot like mine, *oui*?'

'Yes. No. I mean... I don't know, I hadn't really thought about it.' She wriggled around in his grasp, her breast brushing the side of his chest as she tried to sit up. He hardened at the fleeting touch. *Merde.* They'd made love three times last night, and still he was as ready to go as a teenager after his first time with a woman. 'But... Jean-Luc, you're saying you'll come for a holiday with me?'

He tried to pull his focus back from her appetising

breasts and onto her lips and what she was asking.

'*Oui*, a holiday. If that's what you want.' Her eyelashes fluttered down over her cheeks as she lowered her gaze at his words, trying to hide her disappointment. He smiled and trapped her chin in his fingers, raising her head so she was looking directly back at him. 'But I plan on staying long after the holiday is over,' he said with a grin. Different emotions skittered over her face until understanding finally won out.

'You'd stay in Australia? For me?'

'*Oui.*'

'But what about your job? Your family? The terrorists?'

'I'm sure I could find police work in Australia.'

'I honestly don't know what to say, Jean-Luc.'

'Say yes,' he entreated.

'Of course I'm going to say yes, Jean-Luc. But are you sure? Really sure this is what you want?'

How did he make her understand? That night he'd lain awake after her declaration she was leaving France had been long and daunting. Some may say he'd had an epiphany. Others who were more cynical might just say he'd finally lost his edge. Perhaps it had something to do with the refugee bust as well. The fact that no matter how hard he tried, he couldn't seem to turn the tide of humanity who thought they'd be getting a better life by coming to France; refugee or terrorist. And with that realisation came another equally harsh one. In his bid to stop the terrorists from entering this country, he'd lost his own identity. But it was all just a cover. A cover for what he was really running from.

'I think perhaps I need to stop chasing ghosts.'

'Oh?'

'*Oui.*' He smiled at her. 'The ghost of my son.'

'Oh.'

'You helped me realise that.' Tiny frown lines marred her beautiful brow. 'I am in love with you, Charlize.'

'Oh!'

'Is that all you can say?' he laughed.

'No… I just—'

'It's okay, I was teasing. Let me finish before you answer.' Her face grew pink and serious all at the same time. 'I love all of you. I want to take your good with your bad. Your happy moods and you're sad ones. Your ups and your downs. I love them all equally. You wouldn't be the person you are without your scars. Both physical and mental.'

There, he'd said it. Admitted he loved her. Would she say the same? He waited for her answer.

Finally she said, 'You are an amazing man.' There were tears welling in her eyes. He really hoped they were happy tears, and she wasn't about to tell him he was a fool and she wasn't in love with him after all. He wasn't sure he could stand that. Charlize made him want things again. Want love. A life. A family. All the things normal people took for granted. And all the things he'd been denying himself for so long.

'Thank you, Jean-Luc. Thank you for offering me your heart, for being prepared to give up your life for me.' She took both his hands in hers, staring into his eyes. There was a blissful smile on her face, but he was still unsure. He'd fought long and hard with himself until he was finally able to put his heart on the line for her. He knew there was a possibility she might not feel the same way as him. Please, please let all his soul searching not be for nothing.

'But I do have a confession to make,' she continued. Uh oh, here it came. His shoulders tensed instinctively, his spine stiffening in anticipation of the news. Had he misjudged her? Would she reject him after all?

'I'm not going to stay in Australia.'

Her words threw him for a nano-second.

'No? Where are you going?'

'I'm coming back to France. To live here. And I have something else to tell you, I hope it doesn't scare you too much. But first of all...' She turned around and raised up on her knees so she was facing him. He couldn't help but be distracted by those wonderful curves all on display right in front of him. Her pale skin so luminous and soft and smooth, such a contrast to his darker skin.

'I love you, Jean-Luc. I think I've loved you from that very first moment you scared the shit out of me when you jumped over my wall.'

His heart ignited in his chest, like fireworks let off inside him. A unique feeling, one he'd only ever come across once before in his entire life. When he'd held his little son in his arms for the first time. He knew it meant unconditional love.

'That's good. Very good. *Bien*,' was all he could say, the words to express how he felt just wouldn't come. But she knew. She knew what he meant, because she tumbled into his arms, flinging herself on top of him, pinning him to the bed and bringing her face to hover mere centimetres from his own. Her beautiful eyes were alight and dancing.

'Yes, *bien*,' she repeated. Then her mouth covered his, and they kissed, long and deep, a phenomenal kiss. And it felt like his whole life was starting anew.

CHAPTER TWENTY-FOUR

'I need to tell you one last thing. Something you need to know. Something that'll affect us both.' Charlize finally found the strength to pull back from kissing Jean-Luc. His copper eyes followed hers, never leaving her face. Both his arms were wrapped tight around her waist, trapping her on top of him. As if he'd never let her go again. Well, there was actually a lot more she needed to tell him. About her clairsentience for one. The gift that allowed her to come to his rescue. She'd glossed over the question when he'd asked how she'd found him while they were in the ambulance. And he'd never broached the subject again. But he would accept it, she knew he would, because it was another integral part of her.

Because he loved her.

She could still barely believe he'd said the words. It was more than she could've hoped for.

And she loved him. More than life itself. But he needed to know what she intended to do. If they were to share any kind of life together, he deserved to know. After all, it may well be a deal-breaker. He had lost a child, after all. He may not be able to cope with what she was about to tell him. May not be ready to welcome another child back into his life.

'Nothing you can say will scare me now, *ma cherie*,' he said, his accent made thick with desire, his deep, gentle voice turning her insides molten.

But then she thought about what she had to say and a lump formed at the back of her throat and she steeled herself.

'I'm going to foster a child. A little Sudanese boy. The one I told you about. The one I found at the back of the shops here in Uzes.'

Now it was his turn to be rendered speechless. His hands stopped their slow caress along her back and he lay beneath her, completely still, eyes glued to her face.

'*Mon dieu*,' he finally breathed. But Charlize wasn't sure if it was just a shocked reaction or a horrified one. Or perhaps a mix of the two. His eyes glazed over, as if he was deep in some kind of internal dialogue.

Needing to fill the unbearable silence, she prattled on, saying, 'I've already filled out the paperwork. It took me ages to track him down. His name is Kariem. Both his parents are dead. They told me his story. His dying grandfather put him on the boat when he knew he wouldn't be able to care for him anymore, hoping he'd find a better life over here. That's one of the reasons I'm coming back to France. I'm applying for citizenship, so I can become his foster carer.' She stopped speaking when she ran out of words, wishing Jean-Luc would do something more than just stare at her. She was babbling now.

As soon as she'd made the decision to track down the

little boy, it'd felt fitting somehow. Good. As if she could right a wrong in the world, even out the balance just a little.

She'd learnt a lot about herself in the past few weeks and months. She'd learnt she didn't need to be a slave to her gut-freezing vulnerabilities anymore. Those voices which told her she was useless, the flaming guilt that'd locked her heart away in stone for so long, it was all slowly dissolving. Driven away when her desperate need to save Jean-Luc had finally overcome all her fears. She still had a long way to go before she truly became her old self once more—and she'd be the first to admit she needed help from a professional if she was to do this properly. Perhaps she'd never truly be able to banish Xeon's screams from her mind. But locking her true self and her heart away behind thick walls wasn't the answer. She needed to share her life again. With Jean-Luc if he'd let her. And with the child, Kariem. Please let him feel the same way about fostering a child. She didn't want to have to do this alone, not now she'd found him. Found them both.

But a part of her knew she could do it alone if she had to. Even though she desperately wanted to share this with Jean-Luc, if he couldn't cope, then she was strong enough to do it without him.

In the ensuing silence, Jean-Luc drew in a rasping breath and pulled himself upright, so he was sitting on the bed, facing her. He ran a hand over his cropped hair, closing his eyes momentarily. She sat cross-legged on the bed too, neither of them seeming to notice they were both completely naked, staring at each other.

'Charlize. You never fail to surprise me.'

'I'm sorry, I know I sprang this on you, but you needed

to know. Before you make a decision…' She didn't utter the words *to be with me*, but they both knew what she meant.

He blinked once and took her hands in his.

'Like I said before, *ma cherie*, you can't scare me away easily. I think what you are doing is a wonderful thing. Just give me a little time to get used to the idea, *oui*?' Jean-Luc leaned in, so his forehead touched hers. 'I love you, Charli. I want to spend the rest of my life with you. And Kariem, too.'

Taking one hand from his grasp, she lay it on his chest, fingers splayed, wanting to feel his heart beating, craving that connection.

'Thank you, Jean-Luc. You are my hero.'

'*Pah*.' He gave a very French shrug, and she loved him even more for his humility. Because he really was her hero. A man with decency and strength. Intense and tenacious. A dangerous man, but one who would never hurt her. Who'd overcome the loss of his baby son, but could still open himself back up to love. To love her.

He smiled at her, a radiant, glowing smile that outshone the sun. White teeth gleaming against his cocoa skin, eyes sparkling in the morning sunshine.

'Now you are staying in France, I have a suggestion.'

'I'm all ears,' she replied, pushing him back down onto the bed, snuggling into his chest, wanting to feel his warm skin along the length of her body.

'I've heard of an opening at a local gendarme office, out in the country.' The deep rumble of his voice echoed through his chest and into her ear.

'Oh. Okay.'

'In Sault.' She lifted her head from his chest and looked

up at him.

'Your home town?'

'*Oui*. What do you think, would Kariem like to live on a lavender farm?'

'Jean-Luc. You know that would be a dream come true.' Her heart lifted with hope. An image came to her, of all of them seated around the large table in the farmhouse, laughing, eating, loving together. Perhaps she might even learn some of Helene's secrets in the kitchen.

'You don't want to work for the GIGN anymore? Catch terrorists anymore?'

'I've done enough for my country. It's time I did something for my family now. And I'll still be a gendarme, only this way I'll be spending more time rounding up drunk farmers and sending them home to their wives, and less time being shot at by immoral bastards who are only driven by greed and malice.'

'What about Herve? How will he feel about us?' she asked.

'I'll talk to Herve. I think he might be happier than you realise to have us on the farm. Besides, I'll be working as a gendarme, so I shouldn't step on his toes too much. And my parents. Well, they'll be over the moon.' Charlize could well imagine the smile of sheer joy on Helene's face when her son came home for good. Yes, they would welcome him with open arms.

'Perhaps I'll have time to finally cook you that meal I always promised you.'

Jean-Luc placed his mouth over hers, and she kissed him with her heart and soul. Now she knew what it was to be courageous. To want to take a flying leap of faith and be able to land in the arms of one gorgeous man with skin the colour of warm chocolate. A part of her would always miss Australia, but she knew home was where the heart was. And her heart was here, with the man of her soul.

FRENCH ONION SOUP

INGREDIENTS
100 gm Butter, coarsely chopped
2 kg Onions, thinly sliced
1 litre Beef stock
4 Sprigs thyme
3 Stalks parsley
1 Fresh bay leaf
8 thick slices of baguette cut on diagonal, lightly toasted
250 gm coarsely grated Gruyère

DIRECTIONS
Melt butter in a large heavy-based saucepan over medium heat.
Add onions, cover and cook, stirring occasionally, for 20 minutes or until onions are soft.
Remove lid and cook for 1 hour or until soft and starting to caramelise.
Add stock, ½ a cup at a time, and simmer for 5 minutes or until stock has almost evaporated. Repeat three times more until 2 cups of stock have been added.
Add herbs with remaining stock and season to taste with sea salt and freshly ground black pepper. Bring to the boil, reduce heat and simmer, for 40 minutes or until thick.
Preheat oven to 200°C. Ladle soup into 1½ cup capacity oven-proof bowls and transfer to an oven tray. Scatter with half the cheese, top each with two toasted baguette slices and scatter with remaining cheese. Place in oven and cook for 5 minutes or until cheese melts.
Serve immediately.

DUCK a l'ORANGE

INGREDIENTS
¼ cup Granulated sugar
2 tbsp Water
2 tbsp Sherry vinegar

1½ cups Orange juice
2 tbsp Shallots, minced
1 ½ cups Chicken stock
4 Oranges, sections cut from membranes
2 Duck breast halves
Salt and pepper
¼ cup Cold unsalted butter
2 tbsp Orange zest

DIRECTIONS
To Make the Orange Sauce

Boil the sugar and water for several minutes until the syrup caramelises and turns a golden brown colour. Add the vinegar, juice, shallots and chicken stock and simmer until the sauce is reduced to a little less than a cup.

Cut the butter into small pieces and add them to the pan with 1 tablespoon of orange zest. Shake the pan over medium heat until the butter has melted and is incorporated into the sauce.

Stir in the orange sections.

Set the sauce aside and proceed with cooking the breasts.

Cooking the Duck Breasts

Slash through the fat on the breast with a sharp knife to create a crisscross pattern. Sprinkle both the meat side and the fat with salt and pepper.

Heat a pan over high heat. Sear the duck breasts quickly on both sides, then cook the duck for about 9 to 11 minutes on each side.

Remove the breasts from the pan and place them on a warm plate. Cover them with paper towels and leave to rest for 5 minutes.

Reheat the sauce. Spoon the sauce over duck. Garnish the plate with the remaining orange zest and serve immediately.

<u>CRÈME BRÛLÉE</u>

INGREDIENTS

2 ½ cups Cream
1 Vanilla bean, split

6 Egg yolks
½ cup Caster sugar
2 tbsp Brown sugar

DIRECTIONS

Preheat your oven to 150°C. Place six ⅔ cup capacity ovenproof dishes in a large roasting pan. Pour cream in a medium size saucepan. Use a small, sharp knife to scrape the seeds from the vanilla bean into the cream. Place over medium heat and bring to a simmer, but do not boil.

Meanwhile, use a whisk to whisk the egg yolks and caster sugar together in a medium bowl until well combined. Remove the cream from the heat and gradually whisk it into the egg-yolk mixture until well combined. Pour the mixture evenly among the prepared dishes. Add enough boiling water into the roasting pan to reach halfway up the sides of the dishes.

Bake in preheated oven for 25-30 minutes or until just set. Remove from oven and transfer the dishes onto an oven tray and set aside for 30 minutes to cool, then cover with plastic wrap and place in the fridge for at least 4 hours to chill.

Preheat a grill on high. Sprinkle the brûlées evenly with brown sugar. Cook under the grill for 1-2 minutes or until sugar bubbles and caramelises. Alternatively, you can use a brûlée gun to caramelise the sugar (which is much more fun).

Best enjoyed on a cool autumn evening in the hills of northern Provence, wrapped in a blanket, with the man of your dreams, sitting at a rustic table for two overlooking spreading fields of lavender.

Connect with the Author

I really hope you enjoyed reading Glass Clouds. For more action romance info, upcoming release dates, and access to free books join the exclusive Suzanne Cass reader club. As an added bonus, you'll get a copy of my FREE STORY.

Solar Flare

https://landing.mailerlite.com/webforms/landing/k9h2l6

Or you can stay in touch via my website
www.suzannecass.com

Facebook: www.facebook.com/suzannecassauthor/
Instagram: www.instagram.com/suzanne.cass/
Pintrest: www.pinterest.com.au/suzanne_cass/
Twitter: twitter.com/SusieCass1

Also by Suzanne Cass
NEW
Stormcloud Station Series
(A Stargazer Spinoff Series)
Small Town Romantic Suspense
Clear Skies
Starlit Skies
Crystal Skies

Stargazer Ranch Romance Series
Small Town Romantic Suspense
Combustion: Prequel Novella
Wildfire
Firelight
Snowbound: A Christmas Novella
Snowfall
Cloudburst

Island Bound Series
Mystery Romance (on an Island)
Books can be read as stand-alone
Bound by Truth
Bound by Silence
Bound by the Stars

Colors of the Earth Series
Small Town Romantic Suspense
Books can be read as stand-alone
Shadows in the Dust
Shadows in Deep Blue
Shadows of Red Earth

Romantic Suspense
Single Title
Island Redemption

Glass Clouds
Chasing Bullets

Love in the Mountains Novella Series
Small Town Short Romance
Novellas can be read as stand-alone
Rain on a Tin Roof
Lost and Found
Rescue his Heart

Please Leave a Review

The greatest gift you could ever give an author is to leave a review. You will be helping other people to discover this book and making a difference to me as an Independently Published Author. If you liked this book and want other people to read it to, please leave a review.

About the Author

Suzanne Cass is an Australian author who writes rural romance and romantic suspense abounding with passion and danger.

Her debut novel, Island Redemption, won the Romance Writers of Australia Emerald Award in 2016. Suzanne was also a finalist in the 2019 Romance Writers of Australia RUBY award.

She had always had a fascination with the tough resilience of people who live in our amazing red-dirt outback country. When not writing about the characters that inhabit her head, Suzanne can be found roaming the Perth beaches with her border collie, or encouraging from the sidelines as her two sons play sport.

Visit her website www.suzannecass.com or subscribe to her newsletter via: www.suzannecass.com/contact

Acknowledgements

This is my third published book and it was surprisingly straightforward to write. The wonderful vistas of Provence, France, inspired me so much that Charlize and Jean-Luc came to me as almost fully formed characters.

I am so very grateful to all the readers who have bought and enjoyed my books and who will continue (hopefully) to do so. Writing my books for you is what keeps me focussed and invigorated.

To all my sensational friends, who are forever supporting me in my writing efforts, reading my books, offering ideas and putting up with my (sometimes hard to understand) obsession for all things books and the written word.

A special thanks to Rachel, forever encouraging and helpful, keeping me inspired and on track. Our many Skype sessions have helped in so many ways, as well as making me laugh and see the lighter side of this writing life.

And to Jillian and Rose, for helping me to sharpen the focus of my story, iron out all those pesky little plot bugs and keep my grammar on the straight and narrow.

And to the amazing organisation, Romance Writers of Australia, whose volunteers give up their time for the love of books and writing. I've learned so much through my association with them over the past years.

And finally, as always, to Gary the one person who never questions my ability to create a story and live my dream.

www.ingramcontent.com/pod-product-compliance
Lightning Source LLC
Chambersburg PA
CBHW030345120726
47901CB00007B/1917